BLACK EVENING

ALSO BY DAVID MORRELL

*Limited edition. With illustrations. Donald M. Grant, Publisher, Hampton Falls, New Hampshire.

DAVID MORRELL

BLACK EVENING

WARNER BOOKS

A Time Warner Company

WARNER BOOKS EDITION

Copyright © 1999 by Morrell Enterprises, Inc.
All rights reserved. No part of this book may be reproduced in any form or by any electronic or mechanical means, including information storage and retrieval systems, without permission in writing from the publisher, except by a reviewer who may quote brief passages in a review.

The stories in this collection were originally published in the following places:
"The Dripping," *Ellery Queen's Mystery Magazine,* August 1972.

"The Partnership," *Alfred Hitchcock's Mystery Magazine,* May 1981.

"Black Evening," *Horrors,* ed. Charles L. Grant (Playboy Press, 1981).

Copyright information continued on page 440.

Cover design by Stanislaw Fernandes

Warner Books, Inc.
1271 Avenue of the Americas
New York, NY 10020

Visit our Web site at
www.twbookmark.com

 A Time Warner Company

Printed in the United States of America

First Printing: February 2000

10 9 8 7 6 5 4 3 2 1

To Philip Klass and William Tenn
once again

From the American heartland to the edge of Hell, David Morrell, the bestselling author of the classics *First Blood* and *The Brotherhood of the Rose*, presents a career-spanning examination into his own life . . . and the fears we all share. From his first published short fiction to his latest, award-winning stories, including:

"The Beautiful Uncut Hair of Graves"—Winner, Best Novella, Horror Writers of America Award: Both your parents die suddenly; now, going through their legal papers, you find adoption papers, dated on your birthday . . . *signed in a town that has been abandoned . . .*

"Orange Is for Anguish, Blue for Insanity"—Winner, Best Novella, Horror Writers of America Award: Beneath the placid, beautiful landscapes of a master's paintings lie hidden levels of pain, madness . . . *and unearthly horrors . . .*

"Dead Image"—Finalist, Best Novella, World Fantasy Award: You know, of course, that Hollywood movie stars think fame is more important than life itself . . . *but you don't know the half of it . . .*

"The Shrine"—Nominee, Best Novella, Horror Writers of America Award: Parents grieving the deaths of their children find a hidden place that offers lost hope . . . *or eternal madness . . .*

❖   ❖   ❖

"Everything [David Morrell] writes has a you-are-there quality, and that, coupled with his ability to propel characters through a scene, makes reading him like attending a private screening."

—*Washington Post Book World*

For anything, the most banal even, to become an adventure, you must (and this is enough) begin to recount it. A man is always a teller of tales, he lives surrounded by his stories and the stories of others, he sees everything that happens to him through them, and he tries to live his own life as if he were telling a story.

But he has to choose: live or tell.

—Jean-Paul Sartre
La Nausée

Contents

Foreword

REREADING THE STORIES IN THIS COLLECTION, I WASN'T
prepared for the flood of powerful memories they
evoked. I suddenly recalled the circumstances under
which each was written—where I was living, what I was
feeling, why I was motivated to compose each tale. Those
emotion-filled memories extend back more than thirty
years, and yet it seems like only last week that I was a
graduate student in American literature at Pennsylvania
State University.

The year was 1967. I was twenty-four, about to complete my master's degree, anticipating course work for
my Ph.D., but unable to ignore a compulsion that had
gripped me since high school: to be a fiction writer. Penn
State's English department had recently hired a noted
science-fiction writer, Philip Klass (whose pen name is
William Tenn), to teach composition. He was the first
professional writer I'd met, and with the innocent brazen-

ness of youth, I asked him for personal instruction. He answered politely that his schedule was already full to bursting and that if I wanted to be his student, I should sign on for a course. I explained that I felt I would benefit more from one-on-one discussions. He responded that certainly every student would benefit from that approach but that, unfortunately, there wasn't time. Sensing that I would persist, he told me that if I gave him a story each week, he might reconsider. For how many weeks? I asked. For as long as necessary, he replied.

Obviously, Klass was trying to discourage me. A story each week, in addition to my considerable course load, would be burdensome. The odds were, he clearly thought, that I would soon get tired and give up. After all, even if I *did* deliver a story a week (and for heaven knew how long), there still wasn't any guarantee that he would teach me. He had only promised to reconsider my request.

But my mother hadn't raised a quitter, and I kept at it. Finally, after having submitted a story a week for six weeks, I was heartened to receive a note in which Klass invited me to his office. This is it, I thought. My big chance. He'll tell me he liked my stories, and he'll arrange to have them published. To my dismay, the stories *weren't* satisfactory. He told me to stop bothering him.

"Your subject matter isn't special enough," Klass explained. "All successful writers have a distinctive, compelling approach, a particular worldview that makes them unique. Look inside yourself. Find out who you are, find out what you're most afraid of. That will be your subject for your life, or until your fear changes. But I don't mean fear of heights or water or fire," he continued. "Those are the superficial symptoms of much deeper fears. Your true fear is like a ferret darting within the tunnels of your psyche, desperate not to be discovered."

I did my best to nod wisely. "I think I understand."

"Good."

But I *didn't* understand. Confused, I went off and did exactly what Klass had warned me not to do: I wrote stories about fear of heights and water and fire. To my credit, this new batch of stories didn't fool me. I knew they lacked something, that they didn't have the spark of inspiration that separates ordinary stories from memorable ones. Nonetheless, I persisted. And persisted.

And suddenly felt something give way in me. My willpower finally snapped. After all, writing is an act of faith. And if you lose faith in yourself, if insecurity makes you realize just how unnatural it is to sit scribbling all alone, to sacrifice time with your wife and daughter, to give up your few moments of leisure, to gamble against the unlikely odds that you will be one of the very few (only about two hundred) fiction writers in the United States who are able to support themselves by writing . . . well, you run out of hope.

I found myself wishing I was somewhere else. Years before, there had been an iron mine outside State College, where Penn State is located. Known as the Barrens, it was a large open pit that had been abandoned after a dynamite blast released an underground lake. On occasion, I went there to hike, and now, discouraged with my writing efforts, I decided that a walk there would clear my head. It was a blazing August afternoon. The forest was dense and humid, drooping in the summer heat, closing in on me, and as I walked along the narrow trail, careful of snakes that might be in the underbrush, I heard a sound behind me—the snap of a branch. A squirrel leaping from tree to tree, I thought. I kept going, wiping the sweat from my brow, when I heard another branch snap and the crunch of what sounded like a footstep on dead leaves.

Someone else was in the forest, I realized. Someone else was out for a hike, looking for relaxation. So I continued along the narrow trail, and the next time I heard a branch snap and a footstep crunch on dead leaves, a cold spot surfaced between my shoulder blades. The primal reaction seized me without warning. It was inexplicable. I had an abrupt premonition that whoever was in the forest meant to harm me. This irrational apprehension grew in strength as I heard yet another snap, another crunch, something coming closer. No matter how hard I strained to peer behind me, I saw no movement in the forest.

I walked faster along the trail. To my relief, the sounds behind me stopped. I breathed easier, only to stop breathing altogether as I heard the approaching snap and crunch begin again, but this time in front of me. I froze, paralyzed for a moment, until adrenaline gave me motion. I backed up, then froze again as I heard someone behind me. I turned in a circle, on guard against every flank.

And blinked in surprise when I found a desk and a typewriter before me. The intense, vivid, visceral experience had been a daydream. I had so disappeared into my psyche that I had lost touch with my surroundings. Imagination had become more real than reality. Nothing like this had ever happened to me before. It made me remember what Klass had said: "Your true fear is like a ferret darting within the tunnels of your psyche, desperate not to be discovered."

But sometimes it might be possible to get close to it, I realized. The daydream had certainly scared me. What was it about? What would happen next? The urge to know the outcome made me realize how much my earlier stories had lacked forward motion, suspense, a fresh vision. I didn't know any fictional situation like the one I had just imagined. James Dickey's *Deliverance* would be published three years later. That 1970 novel about terror on a backwoods canoe trip amazed readers with its new approach to describing fear. But in 1967, before *Deliverance,* I felt on my own. By surrendering to my problem of how to be a fiction writer, I had, in Zen fashion, allowed my problem to solve itself.

Feeling vitalized, I immediately set to work to write a story about my experience so that I could find out what happened next. I called it "The Plinker," referring to a man who goes off one morning to do some target shooting (the slang term is *plinking*) and discovers that someone else is in the woods, someone interested in a different kind of target shooting. The story was written long before serial killers and stalkers became popular subjects of fiction, and when I showed it to Philip Klass, he must have sensed my excitement, because he read it much sooner than he had the others I had given him. He phoned and invited me to join him at a coffeehouse at 4:00 P.M., and thus began one of the most unique afternoons, evenings, and nights of my life.

First, Klass told me he was amazed that I had written a story so different from the others, one that had strongly engaged his attention. Then he asked if I'd been reading Geoffrey Household. I shook my head no. "Geoffrey who?" I asked. "The British suspense writer," Klass answered. Household's two most famous novels were *Rogue Male* (1939) and *Watcher in the Shadows* (1960), the former about a British big-game hunter who stalks Hitler on the eve of World War II. Later, when I read Household's work, I did recognize a kinship. Household's fiction is best when it deals with threats from unknown forces. The more frightened and vulnerable the heroes were, the more I identified with them. That ferret in my psyche again.

My ignorance about Geoffrey Household revealed another limitation, I hadn't read any suspense fiction or popular literature of any kind. As a teenager, I had been motivated to write because of my fascination with Stirling Silliphant's scripts for the 1960–1964 television show *Route 66*, in which two young men drove across the United States in a Corvette, searching for America and themselves. Silliphant combined action with ideas. But my desire to emulate him had led me more toward ideas than action. After years of studying literature in college, I had become so saturated with Hawthorne, Melville, Faulkner, and other classic authors that my fiction felt stale and imitative, literary in the worst sense of the word. But not anymore. I remembered the thrilling contemporary feel of *Route 66* and why I had wanted to be a writer in the first place. I resolved to read as many contemporary novels, *popular* novels, as I could, beginning with Household—because if I was going to write action stories with a difference, I realized that I'd better find out what the best action writers had already done so that I wouldn't repeat what they'd accomplished.

At the coffeehouse, Klass and I discussed these issues and were surprised to discover later that three hours had passed. I was due home for dinner, but Klass invited me to go to his apartment, meet his wife, and continue the discussion. After months of trying to get Klass's attention, I felt my heart leap at the invitation. Quickly I phoned my wife and explained the situation. Klass and I went to his apartment, where our discussion became deeper and more intense.

"The best fiction," Klass said, "comes from a writer's compulsion to communicate traumatic personal events. Often the writer so represses those events that he or she isn't aware of the source of the compulsion. But whether consciously done or not, this self-psychoanalysis makes a writer's work unique—because the psychological effects of trauma are unique to each person. You can tell the bad writers from the good writers because bad writers are motivated by money and ego, whereas good writers practice their craft for the insistent reason that they *must* be writers, that they have no choice, that something inside them—the ferret—gnaws at their imaginations and the festering pressure has to be released. Often daydreams are a signal of those pressures," Klass said. "They're spontaneous messages from the subconscious, subliminal hints about stories that want to be told."

What were my own festering pressures? My fiction would reveal them, Klass said, and it has. In retrospect, I'm amazed by the disguised revelations in what I've written: that my father died shortly after I was born, that he was killed in World War II, that I grew up with a morbid fear of war, that economic necessity forced my mother to put me in an orphanage for a time, that I could never be sure whether the woman who reclaimed me was the same person who had given me up, that I persistently felt the lack of a father figure, that my fear of violence eventually prompted me to confront my fear by joining a street gang. . . . I could go on, but it isn't wise to face traumas directly. Otherwise, I might lose the compulsion to write about them.

These were the sorts of things that Klass and I talked about in his apartment. Again, time sped by, and we were surprised to discover that it was now 10:00 P.M. Klass's engaging wife, Fruma, had participated in the discussion. Now she invited me to stay for a late dinner. Until midnight, the three of us ate pot roast and talked. Then we cleared the dishes, and Klass spread the pages of my story on the dining room table. He analyzed every sentence for me, explaining why this technique worked but that one didn't, showing me new ways to accomplish a scene, giving me pointers about dialogue, about structure, discussing pace, teaching me how to make description feel like action.

At last, he reached the final sentence on the final page, summed up his remarks, handed me the story, and said, "That's all. That's the limit of what I'm going to teach you." Through the window behind him, the night was turning gray. Birds began to sing. Dawn was approaching. Spellbound by Klass's wisdom, I had lost track of time. Now that the session was over, I was exhausted. But after thanking him and starting home, despite my fatigue, I felt buoyed by an excitement that seemed to lift me off the sidewalk. The memory is vivid to me: the night I became convinced that I would be a writer.

What happened to "The Plinker"? It was never published. The magazines to which I submitted it found it too graphic (although it wouldn't be today). I tried for a year. One magazine kept it so long, I had hopes, but one day the story was returned to me—wrinkled, dog-eared, coffee-stained—with a note informing me that the magazine was going out of business and someone had found my manuscript stuffed in a drawer. Undaunted, I eventually put the pages away, because my attention had become fixated on another story—a novel, actually. It was about a Special Forces Vietnam veteran who engages in a deadly duel with a small-town police chief, a Marine Corps veteran from Korea. The plot was about the generation gap, about the difference between Korea and Vietnam, about hawks and doves and mental programming. I called it *First Blood*. It was dedicated to Philip Klass and his pen name, William Tenn, "each in his own way," because the generous teacher and the gifted fiction writer, both the same person, had helped me. I sent the novel to Geoffrey Household. He wrote a kind letter back to me, telling me that the action was too strong.

"The Plinker" doesn't appear in this collection. As important as the story is to me, I find it unsatisfying now—the work of an apprentice. Some readers might even mistakenly conclude that it is derivative of *Deliverance* rather than a predecessor of it. Protective of it, I keep it to myself. But the stories that *are* included here, presented in order of composition, seem to me to have aged well. Tales of dark suspense, their approach is different from that of my international thrillers. You won't find spies and round-the-globe intrigue here. What you *will* find are the stark emotions behind that intrigue: fear and trembling. The ferret keeps scurrying in my psyche. Some of its tracks lie on these pages.

The Dripping

"*The Dripping*" *was my first published story and, as such, despite its horrifying content, has great sentimental value for me. I had started writing* First Blood *at Penn State in 1968, but graduate courses, student teaching, and my dissertation on John Barth slowed the novel's progress. It was slowed even more after I graduated and moved to Iowa City, where most of my time was filled with teaching, course preparation, student conferences, faculty meetings, and my other responsibilities as an assistant professor of American literature at the University of Iowa. I finally completed the novel in the summer of 1971. Instead of feeling exhausted, however, I was bursting with energy and immediately began the story you are about to read. It is one of the few that occurred to me, complete, in a dream. When I wakened, I rushed to a typewriter and wrote it in one sitting.*

THAT AUTUMN, WE LIVE IN A HOUSE IN THE COUNTRY, my mother's house, the house I was raised in. I have been to the village, struck even more by how nothing in it has changed, yet everything has, because I am older now, seeing it differently. I feel as though I am both here now and back then, at once with the mind of a boy and a man. It is so strange a doubling, so intense, so unsettling, that I am moved to work again, to try to paint it, studying the hardware store, the grain barrels in front, the twin square pillars holding up the drooping balcony onto which seared, wax-faced men and women from the old people's hotel above come to sit and rock and watch. They look like the same aging people I saw as a boy, the wood of the pillars and balcony as splintered.

Forgetful of the hours while I work, I do not begin the long walk home until late, at dusk. The day has been warm, but now in my shirt I am cold, and a half mile along I am caught in a sudden shower, forced to leave the gravel road for the shelter of a tree, its leaves already brown and yellow. The rain becomes a storm, streaking at me sideways, drenching me. I cinch the neck of my canvas bag to protect my painting and equipment and decide to run. My socks are spongy in my shoes, repulsive, when at last I reach the lane down to the house and barn.

The house and barn. They and my mother alone have changed, as if as one, warping, weathering, their joints twisted and strained, their gray so unlike the brightness I recall as a boy. The place is weakening her. She is in tune with it. She matches its decay. That is why we have come here to live. To revive. Once I thought I could convince her to move away. But of her sixty-five years, she has spent forty here, and she insists that she will spend the rest, what is left to her.

The rain falls stronger as I hurry past the side of the house, the light on in the kitchen, suppertime and I am late. The house is connected to the barn the way the small base of an *L* is connected to its stem. The entrance I have always used is directly at the joining, and when I enter, out of breath, my clothes cling to me cold and wet. The door to the barn is to my left, the door to the kitchen straight ahead. I hear the dripping in the basement, down the stairs to my right.

"Meg. Sorry I'm late," I call to my wife, setting down my water-beaded canvas sack, opening the kitchen door. There is no one. No settings on the table. Nothing on the stove. Only the yellow light from the sixty-watt bulb in the ceiling, the kind my mother prefers to the brightness of a one-hundred-watt. It reminds her of candlelight, she says.

"Meg," I call again, and still no one answers. They're asleep, I think. With dusk coming on, the dark clouds of the storm have lulled them, and they have lain down for a nap, expecting to wake before I return.

Still the dripping. Although the house is very old, the barn long disused, the roofs crumbling, I have not thought it all so ill-maintained, the storm so strong that water can be seeping past the cellar windows, trickling, pattering on the old stone floor. I switch on the light to the basement, descend the wooden stairs to the right, worn and squeaking, reach where the stairs turn to the left the rest of the way down to the floor, and see not water dripping, but milk. Milk everywhere. On the rafters, on the walls, dripping on the film of milk on the stones, gathering, speckled with dirt, in the channels between them. From side to side and everywhere.

Sarah, my child, has done this, I think. She has been fascinated by the big wooden dollhouse that my father made for me when I was young, its blue paint chipped and peeling now. She has pulled it from the far corner to the middle of the basement. There are games and toy soldiers and blocks that have been taken from the wicker storage chest and played with on the floor, all covered with milk, the dollhouse, the chest, the scattered toys, milk dripping on them from the rafters, milk trickling on them.

Why has she done this? I think. Where can she have gotten so much milk? What was in her mind to do this thing?

"Sarah," I call. "Meg." Angry now, I mount the stairs to the quiet kitchen. "Sarah," I shout. She will clean the mess and stay indoors the remainder of the week.

I cross the kitchen, turn through the sitting room, past the padded flower-patterned chairs and sofa that have faded since I knew them as a boy, past several of my paintings that my mother has hung on the wall, brightly colored old ones of pastures and woods from when I was in grade school, brown-shaded new ones of the town, tinted as if old photographs. Two stairs at a time up to the bedrooms, my wet shoes on the soft, worn carpet on the stairs, my hand streaking on the smooth, polished maple banister.

At the top, I swing down the hall. The door to Sarah's

room is open. It is dark in there. I switch on the light. She is not on the bed, nor has she been. The satin spread is unrumpled, the rain pelting in through the open window, the wind fresh and cool. I have a bad feeling then and go uneasily into our bedroom. It is dark as well, empty. My stomach has become hollow. Where are they? All in my mother's room?

No. As I stand at the open door to my mother's room, I see from the yellow light that I turned on in the hall that only she is in there, her small torso stretched across the bed.

"Mother," I say, intending to add, "Where are Meg and Sarah?" But I stop before I do. One of my mother's shoes is off, the other askew on her foot. There is mud on the shoes. There is blood on her cotton dress. It is torn, her brittle hair disrupted, blood on her face. Her bruised lips are swollen.

For several moments, I am silent with shock. "My God, Mother," I finally manage to say, and as if the words are a spring releasing me to action, I touch her to wake her. But I see that her eyes are open, staring toward the ceiling, unseeing although alive, and each breath is a sudden full gasp, then a slow exhalation.

"Mother, what has happened? Who did this to you? Where are Meg and Sarah?"

But she does not look at me, only toward the ceiling.

"For God sake, Mother, answer me! Look at me! What has happened?"

Nothing. Her eyes are sightless. Between gasps, she is like a statue.

* * *

What I think is hysterical. Disjointed, contradictory. I must find Meg and Sarah. They must be somewhere, beaten like my mother. Or worse. Find them. Where? But I cannot leave my mother. When she becomes alert again, she, too, will be hysterical, frightened, in great pain. How did she end up on the bed?

In her room, there is no sign of the struggle she must have put up against her attacker. It must have happened somewhere else. She crawled from there to here. Then I see the blood on the floor, the swath of blood down the hall from the stairs. Who did this? Where is he? Who would beat a gray, wrinkled arthritic old woman? Why in God's name would he do it? I imagine the pain of the arthritis as she struggled with him.

Perhaps he is still in the house, waiting for me.

To the hollow sickness in my stomach now comes fear, hot, pulsing, and I am frantic before I realize what I am doing, grabbing the spare cane that my mother always keeps by her bed, flicking on the light in her room, throwing open the closet door and striking in with the cane. Viciously, sounds coming from my throat, I flail the cane among faded dresses.

No one. Under the bed. No one. Behind the door. No one.

I search all the upstairs rooms that way, terrified, constantly checking behind me, clutching the cane and whacking into closets, under beds, behind doors with a force that would certainly crack a skull. No one.

"Meg! Sarah!"

No answer, not even an echo in this sound-absorbing house.

There is no attic, just an overhead entry to a crawl space under the eaves, and that has long been sealed. No sign of tampering. No one has gone up.

I rush down the stairs, seeing the trail of blood my mother has left on the carpet, imagining her pain as she crawled. I search the rooms downstairs with the same desperate thoroughness. In the front closet. Behind the sofa and chairs. Behind the drapes.

No one.

I lock the front door, lest he be outside in the storm, waiting to come in behind me. I remember to draw every blind, close every drape, lest he be out there peering at me. The rain pelts insistently against the windows.

I cry out again and again for Meg and Sarah. The police. My mother. A doctor. I grab for the old phone on the wall by the front stairs, fearful to listen to it, afraid he has cut the line outside. But it is droning. Droning. I ring for the police, working the handle at the side around and around and around.

They are coming, they say. A doctor with them. Stay where I am, they say. But I cannot. Meg and Sarah. I must find them. I know they are not in the basement, where the milk is dripping—all the basement is open to view. Except for my childhood things, we cleared out all the boxes and barrels and shelves of jars the Saturday before.

But under the stairs. I have forgotten about under the stairs, and now I race down and stand, dreading, in the milk, but there are only cobwebs there, already re-formed from Saturday, when we cleared them. I look up at the side door I first came through, and as if I am seeing through a telescope, I focus on the handle. It seems to fidget. I have a panicked vision of the intruder bursting through, and I charge up to lock it, and the door to the barn.

And then I think, If Meg and Sarah are not in the house, they are likely in the barn. But I cannot bring myself to unlock the barn door and go through. *He* must be there, as well. Not in the rain outside, but in the shelter of the barn, and there are no lights to turn on there.

And why the milk? Did he do it, and where did he get it? And why? Or did Sarah do it before? No, the milk is too fresh. It has been thrown there too recently. By him. But why? And who is he? A tramp? An escapee from some prison? Or asylum? No, the nearest institution is far away, at least a hundred miles. From the town then. Or a nearby farm.

I know my questions are a delaying tactic, to keep me from entering the barn. But I must. I take the flashlight from the kitchen drawer and unlock the door to the barn, forcing myself to go in quickly, cane ready, flashing my light. The stalls are still there, listing—and some of the equipment—churners, separators—dull and rusted, cobwebbed and dirty. The must of decaying wood and crumbled hay, the fresh wet smell of the rain gusting through cracks in the walls.

Flicking my light toward the corners, edging toward the stalls, hearing boards creak, I try to control my fright. I remember when I was a boy how the cattle waited in the stalls for my father to milk them, how the barn was once board-tight and solid, warm to be in, how there was no connecting door from the barn to the house because my father did not want my mother to smell the animals when she was cooking.

I scan my light along the walls, sweep it in arcs through the darkness before me as I draw nearer to the stalls, and in spite of myself, I recall that other autumn when the snow came early, deep drifts by morning and still storming thickly, how my father went out to the barn to do the milking and never returned for lunch, or supper. The phone lines were down, no way to get help, and my mother and I waited all night, unable to make our way through the storm, listening to the slowly dying wind. The next morning was clear and bright and blinding as we waded out, finding the cows in agony in their stalls from not having been milked and my father dead, frozen rock-solid in the snow in the middle of the next field, where he must have wandered when he lost his bearings in the storm.

There was a fox nosing at him under the snow, and my father's face was so mutilated that he had to be sealed in his coffin before he could lie in state. Days after, the snow was melted, gone, the barnyard a sea of mud, and it was autumn again and my mother had the connecting door put in. My father should have tied a rope from the house to his waist to guide him back in case he lost his way. Certainly he knew enough. But then he was like that, always in a rush. When I was ten.

Thus I think as I aim my flashlight toward the shadowy stalls, terrified of what I may find in any one of them, Meg and Sarah, or him, thinking of how my mother and I searched for my father and how I now search for my wife and child, trying to think of how it was once warm and pleasant in here, chatting with my father, helping him to milk, the sweet smell of new hay and grain, the different sweet smell of fresh droppings, something I always liked, although neither my father nor my mother could understand why. I know that if I do not think of these good times, I will surely go insane, dreading what I might find. I pray to God that they have not been killed.

What can he have done to them? To rape a five-year-old girl. Split her. The hemorrhaging alone can have killed her.

Then, even in the barn, I hear my mother cry out for me. The relief I feel to leave and go to her unnerves me. I do want to find Meg and Sarah, to try to save them. Yet I am eager to go. I think my mother will tell me what has happened, tell me where to find them. That is how I justify my leaving as I wave the light in circles around me, guarding my back, retreating through the door and locking it.

Upstairs, my mother sits stiffly on her bed. I want to make her answer my questions, to shake her, to force her to help, but I know that will only frighten her more, push her mind down to where I can never reach it.

"Mother," I say to her softly, touching her gently. "What has happened?" My impatience can barely be contained. "Who did this? Where are Meg and Sarah?"

She smiles at me, reassured by the safety of my presence. Still she cannot answer.

"Mother. Please," I say. "I know how bad it must have been. But you must try to help. I must know where they are so I can find them."

She says, "Dolls."

It chills me. "What dolls, Mother? Did a man come here with dolls? What did he want? You mean he looked like a doll? Wearing a mask like one?"

Too many questions. All she can do is blink.

"Please, Mother. You must try your best to tell me. Where are Meg and Sarah?"

"Dolls," she says.

As I first had the foreboding of disaster at the sight of Sarah's unrumpled satin bedspread, now I begin to understand, rejecting it, fighting it.

"Yes, Mother, the dolls," I say, refusing to admit what I suspect. "Please, Mother. Where are Meg and Sarah?"

"You are a grown boy now. You must stop playing as a child. Your father. Without him, you will have to be the man in the house. You must be brave."

"No, Mother." My chest aches.

"There will be a great deal of work now, more than any child should know. But we have no choice. You must accept that God has chosen to take him from us, that you are all the man I have to help me."

"No, Mother."

"Now you are a man and you must put away the things of a child."

Eyes streaming, I am barely able to straighten, leaning wearily against the doorjamb, tears rippling from my face down to my shirt, wetting it cold where it had just begun to dry. I wipe my eyes and see my mother reaching for me, smiling, and I recoil along the hall, then stumble down the stairs, down through the sitting room, the kitchen, down, down to the milk, splashing through it to the dollhouse, and in there, crammed and doubled, Sarah. And in the wicker chest, Meg. The toys not on the floor for Sarah to play with, but taken out so Meg could be put in. And both of them, their stomachs slashed open, stuffed with sawdust, their eyes rolled up like dolls' eyes.

The police are knocking at the side door, pounding, calling out who they are, but I am powerless to let them in. They crash through the door, their rubber raincoats dripping as they stare down at me.

"The milk," I say.

They do not understand. I wait, standing in the milk, listening to the rain pelting on the windows while they come to see what is in the dollhouse and in the wicker chest, while they go upstairs to my mother and then return so I can tell them again, "The milk." But they still do not understand.

"She killed them, of course," one man says. "But I don't see why the milk."

Only when they speak to the neighbors down the road and learn how she came to them, needing the cans of milk, insisting that she carry them herself to the car, the agony she was in as she carried them, only when they find the empty cans and the knife in a stall in the barn, can I say, "The milk. The blood. There was so much blood, you know. She needed to deny it, so she washed it away with milk, purified it, started the dairy again. You see, there was so much blood."

That autumn we live in a house in the country, my mother's house, the house I was raised in. I have been to the village, struck even more by how nothing in it has changed, yet everything has, because I am older now, seeing it differently. I feel as though I am both here now and back then, at once with the mind of a boy and a man.

The Partnership

*F*or the next ten years, I worked exclusively on book-length fiction. After finishing First Blood *in 1971, I wrote several different types of novels, including a pursuit novel,* Testament; *a non-supernatural horror novel,* The Totem; *and a historical western,* Last Reveille. *Simultaneously, I continued to commit myself to teaching. There wasn't time or energy for short fiction—when I did sit down to attempt a short story, I found the effort frustratingly difficult. My block finally broke in 1981 with "The Partnership." My inspiration for the story was a graduating senior who was worried about his job prospects. He did well, as it turned out, but I got to thinking about the lengths that some graduates might go to land a job.*

SURE, IT WAS COLD-BLOODED, BUT THERE DIDN'T SEEM another way. MacKenzie had spent months considering alternatives. He'd tried to buy his partner out, but Dolan had refused. Well, not exactly. Dolan's first response had been to laugh and say, "I wouldn't let you have the satisfaction." When MacKenzie kept insisting, Dolan's next response was, "Sure, I'll let you buy me out. All it takes is a million dollars." Dolan might as well have wanted *ten* million. MacKenzie couldn't raise a million, even half a million or a quarter, and he knew that Dolan knew that.

It was typical. MacKenzie couldn't say "Good morning" without Dolan disagreeing. If MacKenzie bought a car, Dolan bought a bigger, more expensive one, and just to rub the salt in, Dolan bragged about the deal he got. And if MacKenzie took his wife and children on vacation to Bermuda, Dolan told him that Bermuda wasn't anything compared to Mazatlán, where Dolan took his wife and kids.

The two men argued constantly. They favored different football teams. Their taste in food was wildly different (lamb chops versus corned beef). When MacKenzie took up golf, his partner was suddenly playing tennis, pointing out that golf was just a game, while tennis, in addition, was good exercise. But Dolan, even with his so-called exercise, was overweight. MacKenzie, on the other hand, was trim, but Dolan always made remarks about the hairpiece MacKenzie wore.

It was impossible. A Scotsman trying to do business with an Irishman, MacKenzie should have know their relationship would never work. But at the start, they'd been rival builders, each attempting to outbid the other for construction jobs and losing money in the process. So they'd formed a partnership. Together, they were more successful than they'd ever been independently. Still trying to outdo each other, one would think of ways to turn a greater profit, and the other would feel challenged to be twice as clever. They cut costs by mixing too much gravel with the concrete, by installing low-grade pipes and subspec insulation. They kept special books for the IRS.

MacKenzie-Dolan Enterprises. Oh, the two of them were enterprising all right. But they couldn't bear to talk to each other. They tried to solve that problem by dividing work so MacKenzie ran the office and Dolan went out troubleshooting. For a time, that did the trick. But, after all, they had to meet to make decisions. Although they saw each other less, they saved their tension up and aggravated each other more.

To make things worse, their wives became good friends. The women were constantly organizing barbecues and swimming parties. Both men didn't dare argue at these get-togethers. If they did, they heard about it later from their wives.

"I hate that guy. He bugs me at the office, and he makes me sick at parties."

"You just listen to me," MacKenzie's wife said. "Vickie Dolan's my friend, and I won't have your childish antics ruining that friendship. I'll be sleeping on the couch tonight."

So both men braced their shoulders, staring toward the distance or peering inside their highball glasses (Scotch whiskey opposed to Irish) while their wives exchanged new recipes.

What finally caused all the trouble was that Dolan started making threats. "I wonder what the government would do if someone let them know about your special way of keeping books?"

MacKenzie replied, "And what about the subspec plumbing and the extra gravel in the concrete? You're the one responsible for that."

"The judge would simply fine me," Dolan quickly answered. "Now the IRS, that's a different kettle. If the tax man knew you were keeping separate books, he'd lock you in a dungeon where I'd never have to see your ugly puss."

MacKenzie stared at Dolan and decided there wasn't another choice. He'd tried to do the right thing, but his partner wouldn't sell. His partner even planned to turn him in and take the business for himself. There wasn't any way around it. This was self-defense.

The man was waiting at the monkey cage. A tall, thin, friendly-looking fellow, he was young and blond. He wore a tailored light blue jogging suit. He was eating peanuts.

At the water fountain, leaning down to drink, MacKenzie glanced around. The zoo was crowded. Noon, a sunny weekday. People on their lunchbreaks sat on benches, munching sandwiches. Others strolled among the cages. There were children, mothers, old folks playing checkers. MacKenzie heard tinny music from an organ-grinder, muffled conversations, strident chattering and chirping. He was satisfied that no one was paying attention to him, so he wiped some water from his mouth and walked over to the monkey cage.

"Mr. Smith?" MacKenzie said.

The young man didn't bother turning. He just chewed another peanut, and MacKenzie feared that he was speaking to the wrong man. After all, the zoo was busy. There were other men in jogging suits. Besides, no matter what the newspapers said, it wasn't easy finding someone who would do this kind of work. MacKenzie had spent several evenings haunting low-life bars before he even got a lead. Once, someone had thought he was a cop and threatened to break both his legs. But hundred-dollar bills were good persuaders, and at last he'd had a conversation on a pay phone. He'd have done this job himself, but, after all, he needed an alibi, and what was more, he readily admitted, he didn't have the courage.

Now he'd made a mistake and approached the wrong man. Apparently, the man he was supposed to meet had decided that the meeting was a trap and so he wasn't going to show up. As MacKenzie moved to leave, the young blond fellow turned to him.

"Hey, just a second, Bob."

MacKenzie blinked. "Mr. Smith?"

"Just call me John." The young man's smile was brilliant. He held out the bag. "You want a peanut, Bob?"

"No, I don't think—"

"Go on and have a peanut." The young man gestured amiably with the bag.

MacKenzie took a peanut. As he ate, he didn't taste it.

"Sure, that's right. Relax and live a little. You don't mind if I call you Bob?"

"As long as we can get this settled. You're not what I expected."

The young man nodded in agreement. "You were counting on a guy in a tight suit with a scar on his face."

"Well, no, but—"

"And instead you got a young man who looks like he ought to be surfing. I know exactly what you mean. It's disappointing." He frowned sympathetically. "But nothing's what it seems today. Would you believe I was a business major? As hard as I tried, I couldn't get a job in management, so now I'm doing this."

"You mean you're not experienced?"

"Just take it easy, Bob. I didn't say that. I can handle my end. Don't you fret. You see these monkeys?"

"I don't . . . What does . . ."

"Take a look at them."

MacKenzie turned in puzzlement. He saw a monkey in a tree, masturbating.

"No, I don't mean that one, Bob. Just watch this."

When the young man threw some peanuts, all the monkeys scrambled, fighting for them.

"See, they're just like us. We're all scrambling for peanuts."

"Well, I'm sure that's very interesting, but—"

"All right, you're impatient. I'm just trying to be sociable. But no one takes the time." The young man sighed. "So what's your problem, Bob?"

"My partner."

"He's stealing from the kitty?"

"No."

"He's fooling with your wife, then?"

"No."

The young man nodded. "Bob, I understand."

"You do?"

"Of course. It's very simple. What I call the 'marriage syndrome.'"

"What?"

"It's like you're married to your partner, but you hate him, and he won't agree to get divorced."

"That's incredible."

"Excuse me?"

"You're right. You do understand."

The young man shrugged and threw a peanut toward the monkey who'd been masturbating. "Bob, I've seen it all. My specialty is human nature. So you don't care how I do it."

"Just as long as it's—"

"An accident. Precisely. You recall my price when we discussed this on the phone."

"Ten thousand dollars."

"Half now, and half later. Did you bring the money?"

"In my pocket."

"No, don't give it to me yet. Go over. Put the envelope in that waste container. A few seconds from now, I'll walk over and stuff this empty bag in. When I leave, I'll take the envelope."

"His name's Patrick Dolan."

"The particulars are with the money?"

"As you wanted."

"Then don't worry, Bob. I'll be in touch."

"Hey, wait a minute. Afterward, I don't have any guarantee that—"

"Blackmail? You're afraid I'll extort you? Bob, I really am surprised at you. That wouldn't be good business."

Dolan left the hardware store. The afternoon was glaringly hot. He wiped his brow. He squinted. There was someone in his pickup truck.

A young man eating corn chips. Blond, good-looking. In a jogging suit.

"Of all the—"

Dolan stalked across the parking lot. He reached the truck and yanked the door open.

"Hey, buddy, that's my truck you're—"

But the young man turned, his smile disarming. "Hi, Pat. You want some corn chips?"

Dolan's mouth hung open. Sweat trickled from his forehead. "What?"

"The way you're sweating, you need salt, Pat. Have some corn chips."

Dolan's jaw went rigid. "Out."

"Excuse me?"

"Out, before I throw you out."

The young man sighed with disappointment. Tugging down the zipper on his jogging coat, he showed the big revolver bulging from its shoulder holster.

Dolan felt something in his stomach drop. He blanched and stumbled backward, gaping. "What the—"

"Just relax now, Pat."

"Look, buddy, all I've got is twenty dollars."

"You don't understand yet. Climb on up here and we'll talk a little."

Dolan glanced around in panic. No one seemed to notice him. He wondered if he ought to run.

"Don't try to run, Pat."

And relieved of that decision, Dolan quickly climbed inside the truck. He ate the corn chips he was offered, but he couldn't taste the salt. His sweaty shirt was sticking to the truck seat. He kept squinting toward the bulging object underneath the jogging coat.

"Pat, here's the thing," the young man told him. "I'm supposed to kill you."

Dolan straightened so hard that he bumped his head against the roof. *"What?"*

"Your partner hired me. You're worth ten thousand dollars."

"If you think this is a joke—"

"I think it's business, Pat. He paid five thousand down. You want to see it?"

"But that's crazy!"

"Pat, I wish you hadn't said that."

Dolan flinched. The young man reached inside his jogging coat.

"No, wait a minute! Wait, I didn't mean that!"

"Pat, I only want to show you the note your partner gave me. Here. You'll recognize his writing."

Dolan glared at the note. "It's just my name and my address."

"And your description and your habits. See, he wants your death to seem an accident."

And Dolan finally accepted that this wasn't a joke. His chest heaved with sudden rage. His face went red.

"That dirty bastard! Why, he thinks he's so damn smart! He's always bitching at me!"

"Temper, Pat."

"He wears that crummy hairpiece, and he wants to buy me out, but I won't let him have the satisfaction!"

"Pat, I understand. It's like the two of you are married, and you want to make him suffer."

"You're damn right I want to make him suffer! I put up with him for twenty years! So now he figures he can have me killed and take the business for himself? That sneaky, rotten—"

"Bob, I'm afraid I've got bad news for you."

MacKenzie almost spilled his scotch. He turned. The young man stood beside him, eating popcorn at the bar.

"Don't tell me you botched the job!" MacKenzie's eyes went wide with horror. He glanced quickly all around, as if expecting he'd be arrested.

"Bob, I never got the chance to start." The young man picked at something in his teeth.

"My God, what happened?"

"Nearly broke a tooth. These kernels aren't all popped. I ought to sue—"

"I meant with Dolan!"

"Keep your voice down, Bob. I know you meant what happened with him. No one cares if someone breaks a tooth. They only care about themselves. A shame. Do you believe in competition?"

"What?"

"Do you support free enterprise, the thing that made this country great?"

MacKenzie felt his knees go weak. He clutched the bar. "I do," he muttered weakly.

"Then you'll sympathize with my position. When I went to see your partner—"

"Oh my God, you told him!"

"Bob, I couldn't simply kill him and not let him have a chance to make a bid. That wouldn't be American."

MacKenzie started trembling. "Bid? What kind of bid?"

"Don't get excited, Bob. We figured he could pay me not to kill him. But you'd just send someone else. So what we finally decided was that he'd pay me to come back and kill *you*. He offered double, ten grand now and ten when you were shoveled under."

"He can't do that!"

"But he did, Bob. Don't go simple on me now. You should have seen his face. I mean to tell you, he was angry."

"You accepted what I offered! You agreed to take my contract!"

"But a verbal contract isn't binding. Anyhow, you're in a seller's market. What I'm selling is worth more now."

"You're a crook!"

The young man's face looked pained. "I'm sorry you feel that way."

"No, wait. Don't leave. I didn't mean it."

"Bob, you hurt my feelings."

"I apologize. I don't know what I'm saying. Every time I think about that guy—"

"I understand, Bob. You're forgiven."

*   *   *

"Pat, you'll never guess what Bob did."

At the railing, Dolan shuddered. He was watching as the horses thundered toward the finish line. He turned. The young man stood beside him, chewing on a hot dog.

"You don't mean you told him."

"Pat, I had to. Fair is fair. He offered double our agreement. Twenty grand now, twenty later."

"And you've come to me to raise the price?"

"They're at the stretch!" the track announcer shouted.

"It's inflation, Pat. It's killing us." The young man wiped mustard from his lips.

"You think I'm stupid?" Dolan asked.

The young man frowned.

"That I'm a moron?" Dolan asked.

"Excuse me, Pat?"

"If I pay more, you'll go to him, and he'll pay more. Then you'll come back to me, and I'll pay more. Then . . . That's my limit! I'm not paying!"

"Fine with me, Pat. Nice to see you."

"Wait a minute!"

"Why? Is something wrong?"

"Of course there's something wrong! You're going to kill me!"

"Well, the choice is up to you."

"The winner is—" the track announcer shouted.

Horses rumbled by, their jockeys standing up to slow them. Dust drifted over the crowd.

"Damn it, yes, I'll pay you," Dolan muttered. "Do it this time. I can't sleep. I'm losing weight. I've got an ulcer."

"Pat, the race is over. Did you have a bet?"

"On number six to win."

"A nag, Pat. She came last. If you'd asked me, I'd have told you number three."

"You'll never guess what Pat did, Bob."

"You'll never guess what Bob did, Pat."

Dolan stopped beside MacKenzie, looked around and sighed, then sat on the park bench.

"So you figured you'd have him kill me," Dolan said.

MacKenzie's face was gaunt. "You weren't above the same temptation."

Dolan spread his hands. "Self-defense."

"But I should sit back while you sic the IRS on me?"

"That was just a joke."

"Some joke. It's costing me a fortune."

"Hey, it's costing me, as well."

"We've got a problem."

They nodded, feeding bread crumbs to the pigeons.

"I've been thinking," Dolan said. "The only answer I can see—"

"—is both of us will have to kill him."

"Only way."

"He'll bleed us dry."

"If we pay someone else to kill him, the new guy might try something cute, as well."

"We'll do it both together. That way, you can't point the blame at me."

"Vice versa."

"What's the matter? Don't you trust me?"

They glared at each other.

"Hi there, Bob. How's tricks, Pat?" The young man smiled behind MacKenzie's desk. He munched a taco, going through their records.

"What the hell is this now?"

"But he claimed that you expected him," the secretary said.

"Never mind. We'll deal with this."

"Just shut the door."

They stared at him.

"Hey, fellas, I've been going through your records. They're really a mess. This skimping on the concrete. And that subspec insulation. I don't know, guys. We've got lots of work ahead of us."

A drop of taco sauce fell on the records.

"*Us?*"

"Well, sure, we're partners now."

"We *are?*"

"I took the money you gave me. I invested it."

"In what?"

"Insurance. You remember how I said I was a business major? I've decided this sideline doesn't suit me. So I went to a specialist. The things a graduate's forced to do to get a job these days."

"A specialist?"

"A hit man. If the two of you decide to have me killed, you'll be killed, as well."

MacKenzie's chest felt stabbed. Dolan's ulcer burned.

"So we're partners. Here, I even had some cards made up."

He handed one across, a greasy taco stain along one edge. MACKENZIE-DOLAN-SMITH. And at the bottom: CONTRACTORS.

Black Evening

I *don't often use humor in my fiction. The story you just read is one of the exceptions. You'll come across a few other examples later. In contrast, this next story, "Black Evening," has no trace of humor whatsoever. Dark and disturbing, it is more in the tone of "The Dripping." Part of a series of stories about houses, it first appeared in a 1981 anthology entitled* Horrors, *edited by Charles L. Grant, and marks the beginning of a long association with Charlie. A skillful fiction writer, he also edited some of the most influential dark suspense anthologies of the seventies and eighties, including the much-praised* Shadows *series. Part of the reason I didn't write any short fiction from 1971 to 1981 is that I couldn't find a market for the type of stories I wanted to write. When I learned about Charlie's anthologies, I discovered I had a soul mate. Many of the stories in this collection appeared in publications that Charlie edited. Along with numerous other writers of dark suspense, I'm indebted to him.*

SO WE ALL WENT OUT THERE. I CAN SEE YOU'RE APPRE-hensive, as we all were, and so I'll tell you at the outset that you're right. The house was in the poorest section. It had been among the best homes in the twenties, I'd been told, but its shutters had long ago fallen; its porch was listing; its paint was chipped and peeling, gray at dusk, although I could guess that it had once been brilliant white. Three stories: gables, chimneys, dormer windows, balconies. Nobody could afford to build so large a home these days, and no doubt it had required someone rich to build it then. A mansion in its dotage. Sad, I thought, imagining the pride of those who had first owned it and their disappointment should they see what had happened to it. But they would all be dead now, so it didn't matter. All that mattered was the stench.

I say we all went out. I mean my deputy, the doctor, and myself. We stood beside the police car, staring at the dark, silent, decrepit mansion. We saw the neighbors on the porches of the other ill-kept, once-great houses, sil-houetted by the dying sunset. Then we held our breaths and started toward the picket gate, which fell off in my hand. We moved up toward the front steps. The sidewalk was weed-cracked, the yard overgrown. We felt the cool air, almost misty, as the sun dipped below the horizon, and in the dark, our flashlights glaring, we climbed the cracked, creaking steps that led to the porch. We had to work around some broken boards on the porch. We stared down at a pile of newspapers. Then we squinted through the stained-glass window, dusty and opaque, the darkness in there absolute. At last, I twisted at the grip that rang the bell. The tone was flat, without enthusiasm. No echo or reverberation followed.

No light came on. No weak footsteps shuffled near to let us in. I twisted at the bell again. We waited.

"Now what?" The deputy looked nervous.

"Give them time. They're old," I answered. "Or maybe they're not at home."

"Just one," the doctor told me.

"What?"

"There's only one. Her name is Agnes. She's eighty at least."

"Maybe she's sleeping."

"You don't think so. Otherwise, we wouldn't be here."

I twisted the bell again. I hadn't lived in town for long. After too many years in the city, I'd brought my family to what I'd hoped was a better place, and as the new police chief, I was hardly eager to antagonize the townsfolk by disturbing an old woman.

All the same, the stench was horrible. It made my stomach rise, my nostrils widen with disgust. The neighbors' phone calls had been so persistent that I couldn't ignore them.

"All right, let's go in."

I tried the knob. The door was locked. I pushed, and the door came open with a muted sound, as if the jamb were cardboard. No sharp crack, instead a rip, a tear, so soft, so effortless. The wood was rotten at my feet.

"Is anybody here?" I called.

No answer.

So we looked at one another, and we stepped inside. The hall was dusty, the odor more intense.

We flashed our lights. The living room, or what I guess had once been called the parlor, was beyond an oval entrance to our right. The room was filled with stacks of newspapers, from the floor to above my head. There was a makeshift corridor that we could walk through, but the newspapers towered on each side.

"This could be it," I told the doctor. "Papers, wet and musty. If they molded . . ."

"You don't think so."

We went through another oval doorway.

"Anybody home?"

I saw the grand piano, cobwebs glistening in my flashlight's glare. More newspapers towered around it.

"Hoarding. Some old folks . . ." The deputy's voice quavered. Abruptly he coughed, gagging from the stench.

"I guess we do it room by room," I told them.

So we went up to the attic, starting downward, trying for some order, some sane balance. Newspapers, 1929 and 1936, each room devoted to a decade, 1942 and 1958. We found a bedroom on the second floor, and it at least was normal, if by that is meant no clutter and no useless objects. But the bedroom was from the twenties, at least so I guessed. I have no eye for furniture. The canopy above the bed, the stained-glass fixtures, and the heavy hopsack covers on the chairs, these clearly were from another time.

The bed had not been slept in. We had tried the lights. They didn't work.

"She didn't pay her bill, I guess." The deputy coughed again.

The dust, the cobwebs, that pervasive cloying stench. We went with flashlights to the first floor, and the cellar is the place that you suspect you ought to check first, but you always wait until last.

We stood inside the pantry on the first floor in the back, the stench even worse there. I strained to muster control as I pulled the door. The smell was like a veil that struck us, wafting up. We went down slowly, board by creaking board.

You know I'm a trained observer. I've been taught to stop emotion, just to take in what I see. But that's difficult, especially when you're staring by the aid of flashlights, and you see only one object at a time, the horror mounting until you don't think you can bear it.

First, the woman's headless body on the floor, the stench like old potatoes that have turned to liquid in their jackets. Something has seeped from her. The urge to vomit is uncontrollable.

Then, for no reason you can understand, you scan up with your flashlight, and you see her head jammed in the noose, the white hair dangling, flesh now viscous on her cheeks, her open eyes dissolving toward you.

But that isn't it yet, not the final detail, for once more without a reason you can understand, as if you know that it will be there, you aim your flashlight toward a corner, toward a tiny table meant for dolls and set for tea, where tied to a toy chair, slumped, is another body, small and lonely, a young girl. You know this from the long hair and the bow and dress; you wouldn't know it from the face, which has been food for insects. And that isn't it yet, not the final detail, for the clothes she wears are not from our time, but, rather, from the old days, straw hat, button shoes, and yellowed crinoline, a moth-eaten satin party dress, as if she wore a costume or had been compelled to act a part she didn't like, the bow around her neck so tight, her blackened tongue is bulging out.

"My Christ," the deputy moans behind me, and the bile that spews up in my mouth is bitter, scalding.

"All right, help me understand this."

We are in my office downtown, its lights glaring painfully. Although the night outside is cold, filled with sudden autumn gusts, I have opened all the windows, turned the fan on, anything to clear the stench.

"She killed the child, then hanged herself—that much is obvious," I say. "But why? I'm new here. I don't understand this. What would make her do it?"

I hear the rattle of the fan.

The doctor clears his throat. "Agnes lived there since the house was new. She and her husband built it."

"But I thought that . . ."

"They had money then." The doctor goes on without pause. His voice is weak. "He was a banker. They were prosperous."

"The husband?"

"Andrew was his name. In 1928. The world was theirs. They had a child, a daughter who was three. She died that fall. Diphtheria. I know this from my father, who was the doctor in the case. He couldn't save the daughter, and he watched the parents ruined by their loss.

The husband left one day. The wife became a recluse. It's so easy now in retrospect to understand. You see, from time to time there have been children missing, usually in autumn, just as now. That girl we found, for instance. All the people who've been looking for her. You'll soon have to notify her parents. I don't envy you. My guess is that as Agnes aged, as she became more lonely and reclusive, she went crazy. She tried to find a substitute for what she'd lost. She kidnapped children, but of course she couldn't let them live to tell what she'd done. She killed them but believed that they were still alive, her own child."

"The way children play make-believe with dolls?" I ask.

"If that analogy helps you. This is sickness so bizarre, it threatens sanity to think about it. Where did she put the corpses of those other children? Maybe when they started rotting, she couldn't sustain her make-believe. Maybe this final time she understood what she'd become and hanged herself."

"It works," the deputy says, nauseated, his face still ashen. "It makes sense."

"That's the trouble," the doctor says. "A lunatic's always logical, but the logic's horribly twisted."

There were many things to do. I'd put off phoning for an ambulance. I'd wanted to understand before the scene became disturbed, a clue destroyed, but I knew I had to act now, make those calls, tell the parents. I reached for the phone, but it rang in anticipation.

"Yes?" I asked, and then I listened, and I realized how wrong we'd been.

I set down the phone and peered at them.

"It wasn't her. It wasn't Agnes."

"What?" The doctor and the deputy stared.

"It was Andrew," I told them as I rushed toward the door.

"He left in 1928," the doctor repeated.

"No, he *never* left."

They ran out with me toward the cruiser.

"He's still in there."

"But we searched the place," the deputy insisted.

"He was in there. We were just too dumb to see him."

We scrambled into the cruiser. I sped from the station's lot.

"But I don't understand," the doctor said.

I didn't have the will or time to argue. I skidded around corners, raced up side streets. At that once-great, now-dilapidated section of the town, I ran out, hurrying past the ruined gate, up the weed-choked sidewalk, past the porch holes, through the stained-glass door.

"I know you're in here, Andrew! Come out now! Don't make me look for you!"

The house was silent, grotesque, as I flashed my light and charged in toward the parlor.

"Damn it, Andrew! If you've harmed her, I swear I'll punish you, the way you punished all those children!"

In a frenzy, I yanked at the stacks of newspapers.

"Chief, you'd better get control," the deputy said.

But I kept pulling, yanking, and the one side of the room was no good. I swung toward the other.

"Help me!" I yelled to the deputy, the doctor.

And we found him, Andrew, in the music room, or

rather, in a room within a room, a room whose walls were stacks of newspapers. He was in there, almost eighty, brittle and yet strangely spry. He glared up at me, smelling old, like ancient papers, squirming to hide his secret, but I grabbed his shirt and yanked him to one side, and there she was, another young girl, dressed in clothing from the twenties, gagged and bound and staring, wide-eyed, fearful, for it had been Andrew who grabbed the children. He had never left. He'd only lost his mind. Agnes, to protect and preserve him, hid him. But each time he killed a child, her loyalty had weakened, until at last, faced with awful choices, she had hanged herself, unable to reveal him.

I'd guessed that he was there because that phone call had informed me of another missing child, a child who from fright was now white-haired, always would be, and if Agnes hadn't done it, who else but Andrew? Yes, that girl, an adult now, is white-haired. I can prove it, for that small child was my daughter, and she sometimes seems to know me when I visit her on weekends.

The Hidden Laughter

A *final story about a house, "The Hidden Laughter," was published the same year as "Black Evening": 1981. Ever since I attended modern-poetry courses in college, I've been haunted by T. S. Eliot's* Four Quartets—*in particular, the first section, "Burnt Norton," with its eerie, otherworldly tone, the sense it creates of falling through and out of time. When my family and I first arrived in Iowa City, we lived in a small, pleasant ranch house, which we eventually outgrew. But even after we moved to a larger house in a different section of town, we often drove back to the old neighborhood and paused to savor the memories associated with our six years in that house. It represented our postcollege youth. We associated it with the excitement and difficulty of getting started in the world. I got to wondering if, under the right circumstances, a house could be loved enough that a person might develop a mystical bond with it, to the exclu-*

sion of everything else. The house, which I continue to remember fondly, is described in this story.

THERE'S A LINE SOMEWHERE IN AN ELIOT POEM, "Burnt Norton," I think, about unheard music and leaves being full of children, hidden in excitement, laughing. I have sensed that music, almost seen those children, not in leaves, it turns out, but in a house where I used to live, except that all this was so long ago that now I think of "I" as "he" and how he turned to see her walking toward him.

She was looking very puzzled. "Something's funny at the house we sold," she told him. "All the neighbors say there are children inside laughing."

What was odd, of course, was that he'd locked it when they'd moved out, and besides, there were few children in that neighborhood, all of them accounted for. "I think I'd better look," she said. She had a key, you see, until the new owners came to take possession, just in case some trouble happened in the meantime, and she loved that house, the one that she'd been married in, so she was going back to take a final look. He didn't think she ought to, but he couldn't talk her out of it. Because he was working on some bookshelves, he just told her that he'd wait to hear about the laughter, which he knew would be imaginary. So she left, and that's the last he ever saw of her.

This happened in the morning. He postponed his lunch and waited for her. Finally he ate. He figured she was visiting some friends in the old neighborhood, and, after all, the kind of marriage that they had, they both were free and easy, so he didn't worry. Then the evening came, and it was time for supper. Still she didn't come, and now he did begin to worry. After he made a meal and fed his children, he began to phone, but no one at the old neighborhood had seen her. Not since lunch at least.

She'd checked the house, he was told, and, as he had expected, there was nothing. Then she'd visited some friends, again as he'd expected. After lunch, she'd gone back to the house, just to see it one last time, and people in the neighborhood had gone on with their business. But yes, wait a minute, yes, her car was still parked in the driveway down there, and she must be with some other friends. When he made more calls, however, he learned that no one else had seen her, and he worried even more. He thought that maybe she'd had some trouble with the car and left it. But she would have phoned him then. That much was certain. He got a sitter for the children and drove over.

The house was much the same as he'd left it. Oh, the grass was somewhat high, the shrubs in need of a little trimming, but except for that and dust on the outside windows, it looked as if they still lived there. As he stood at the curb and surveyed the place, he felt a yearning: for his youth, for the days when he and she were just beginning. Don't mistake. The place was not impressive. Oh, acceptable, but nothing more. A single-story ranch house with a lush maple tree on the right, a stunted plum tree on the left, and in the middle an overhang that formed a porch. What they used to call "low-income housing" when a house was something that ambitious, saving people could afford. A lot of things had changed since then, more money and more complications. That moment, as he stood there watching, brought back fond memories of early days and innocence.

He walked up toward the house, and of course the door was locked. That was exactly like her. She had felt so close to all the house had meant to her that she would never have left it unsecured. He had a key as well, though, and he turned it, going in. There was an echo off the bare walls and the floor. The cabinets that they'd built, the hardwood floors that they'd varnished, these brought back a sequence of quick images, the two of them starting their marriage.

He waited, and he listened. "Honey?" But he really didn't think there'd be an answer. He walked through the living room to the kitchen, looking for some sign that she had been there. But the kitchen was the way it should be, and he continued to the stairs down to the basement. Maybe she had fallen. When he took a breath and opened the door to look down, though, the concrete floor below was silent, and he almost didn't go down, but he knew he should be thorough. So he checked the basement, even looked behind the furnace and the washer and the dryer they had sold with the house. He glanced inside the crawl space. Then he went upstairs and checked the closets, the two bedrooms, the small bathroom, but he didn't see a sign of her, and now he didn't know what else to do. He almost went back to the front door before he thought of the attic, and for reasons he didn't understand, he felt a chill.

At first he just dismissed it. Then he thought that she would have had no reason to go up there, and he almost left the house. But he'd been determined to be thorough, and he knew that failing to check the attic would soon nag him, so he walked back to the hallway, moving toward the trapdoor. When he stretched, he barely touched the ring, but then he had it, and he pulled, and the fold-out steps came down to reach the floor. He waited just a moment longer. There was something like the *coo-coo-coo* of pigeons up there, one on top the other, faint and soft and gentle, and it sounded just enough like laughter that he guessed this maybe was what people had been hearing. Not exactly laughter, more like giggling. *Coo-coo-coo*. And then it stopped.

Of course. Some birds had somehow gotten into the attic, and they'd heard him, going silent. She had gone up there to look, and maybe she was hurt. He didn't think until later that the trapdoor would be open if she had. He knew only that he needed to look, and quickly, so he scrambled up, and there was nothing. Insulation, cobwebs, wiring. But no sign of her, no birds, no laughter, nothing. There was must all through the close, stale air, and he checked in the corners, sweating, and he still found no sign of her. He thought too late that he had climbed around up there without first looking for a disturbance in the dust. Now, with the smudge marks where he had knelt among the rafters, he could never tell if someone had preceded him. He listened for the cooing, looking for some explanation. When the sweat became too much for him, he eased back, leaving.

Outside, he was puzzled. He checked with the neighbors again. There'd been a man she talked to. Someone now remembered that. But everyone was certain that she'd been alone when she'd returned to the house. He walked back, looking. Then he asked if he could use a neighbor's phone. He called other friends. He called the hospital and, on an impulse, the police. No help, no sign of her, and since there was no evidence of something wrong, he learned that no policemen would be coming out. "Just give her time. She'll be back."

He left the neighbors, returning to the house. But this time when he studied it, the dusk now gray around it, he was conscious of a sound—no, something less than that, something on the other side of hearing, more a presence than a sound, coming from the house. He took a step. The thing subsided. A moment later, it rose again, closer, stronger. He could almost touch it, hear it. He continued toward the house. Music, unseen, unheard, faint and tinkling, merry, far away, yet close. When he reached the door, he recognized the *coo-coo-coo,* and yes, he did hear laughter, children's laughter, but he burst in, and the house was dark, and there was no one. The laughter stopped, although it hadn't really been there. It was all in his imagination.

He has heard it many times since then, however, and he comes back often just to stand and wait and let it happen, so much so that now he owns the place again. He lives there with his children, who don't remember her. The years have led them forward. Flashes now and then, but little recollection, and he asks them, but they do not hear the laughter.

And the answer? The police at first suspected that he killed her, but they found no body, and he managed to convince them of his innocence. He had seldom argued with her, had always seemed to like her. There was no other woman and no insurance as a motive. Still he often wonders. With this tendency of his to be both "I" and "he," in past and present, he could maybe have a double personality. He could have killed her, and as someone else, he never would have known about it, although he can't find a reason he would have.

All right, she was kidnapped. But there was never a ransom note, and his mind can't sustain the thought of what a kidnapper who left no note would do to her. Imagining his wife alone and trembling, he continues to hope that one day she'll come back to him. He even hopes, although this would normally be painful, that she left him, that the changes they'd been going through weren't half so good as when they first had started, that the man whom someone might have seen had been a secret friend who led her to a better life.

He wishes, and he grieves, and, in his constant emptiness, imagines that she actually is with him, all around him, that she never went away, but only back.

To where? he asks himself, and then answers, To her youth, her innocence.

His theory is fantastic, although consoling: that in every person's life there is a place that one can fall through, even by choice slip through, that she lives now with the laughter in a better time and space; and sometimes he can hear a woman in among the children's laughter, playing games perhaps or just enjoying, bringing home to him Eliot's poem again. What might have been. What has been. My words echo with the laughter.

The Typewriter

*F*our stories in ten years. I'm not prolific. Do authors who are prolific have a secret weapon, something that increases their output—a special typewriter, for example? The following story, a mix of darkness and humor, portrays the bleak side of author envy. It's longer than my previous stories and, with a few exceptions, establishes a trend—from this point on, you'll be reading mostly novellas. Many of the cultural references in this piece, Truman Capote and Johnny Carson, for example, are now out of date, but when I attempted to substitute current equivalents, the story didn't work. At first puzzled, I finally realized why Truman and Johnny had to stay. This story belongs in 1983, the year it was published. After all, if it were current, it would have to be about a word processor.

ERIC TINGLED AS IF HE'D TOUCHED A FAULTY LIGHT
switch or had stepped on a snake. His skin felt cold. He
shuddered.

He'd been looking for a kitchen chair. His old
one—and the adjective was accurate—in fact, his *only*
kitchen chair, had been destroyed the previous night,
crushed to splinters by a drunken, hefty poetess who'd
lost her balance and collapsed. In candor, *poetess* was
far too kind a word for her. Disgustingly commercial,
she'd insulted Eric's Greenwich Village party guests
with verses about cats and rain and harbor lights—"I
hear your sights. I see your sounds": a female Rod
McKuen. *Dreadful,* Eric had concluded, cringing with
embarrassment.

His literary parties set a standard, after all; he had
his reputation to protect. The Subway Press had just released his latest book of stories, *After Birth.* The title's
punning resonance had seemed pure genius to him.
Then, too, he wrote his monthly column for the *Village
Mind,* reviewing metafiction and postmodern surreal
prose. So when this excuse for a poetess had arrived
without an invitation to his party, Eric had almost told
her to leave. The editor from *Village Mind* had brought
her, though, and Eric sacrificed his standards for the sake
of tact and the continuation of his column. In the
strained, dry coughing that resulted from her reading,
Eric had majestically arisen from his tattered cushion on
the floor and salvaged the occasion by reciting his story
"Cat Scat." But when he later gaped at the wreckage of
his only kitchen chair, he realized how wrong he'd been
to go against his principles.

The junk shop was a block away, near NYU. *Junk* described it perfectly. Students bought their beds and tables from the wizened man who owned the place. But sometimes, lost among the junk, there were bargains, and more crucial, Eric didn't have much choice. In truth, his stories earned him next to nothing. He survived by selling T-shirts outside movie theaters and by handouts from his mother.

From the hot humid afternoon, Eric entered the junk shop.

"Something for you?" the wrinkled owner asked.

Sweating, Eric said aloofly, "Maybe. I'm just browsing."

"Suit yourself, friend." The old man sucked a half an inch of cigarette. His yellow fingernails needed clipping. He squinted at a racetrack form.

The room was long and narrow, cluttered with the leftovers of failure. Here, a shattered mirror on a bureau. There, a musty mattress. While the sunlight fought to reach the room's back reaches, Eric groped to find his way.

He touched a grimy coffee table with its legs splayed. It sat on a sofa split down the middle. Dirty foam bulged, disintegrating. Pungent odors flared his nostrils.

Kitchen tables. Even one stained kitchen sink. But Eric couldn't find a kitchen chair.

He braved the farthest corners of the maze. Tripping over a lamp cord, he fell hard against a water-stained dresser. As he rubbed his side and felt cobwebs tickling his brow, he faced a dusty pile of *Liberty, Collier's,* and *The Saturday Evening Post,* and saw a low, squat, bulky object almost hidden in the shadows. That was when he shuddered, as if he'd touched a spider's nest or heard a skeleton's rattle.

The thing was worse than ugly. It revolted him. All those knobs and ridges, curlicues and levers. What purpose could they serve? They were a grotesque demonstration of bad taste, as if its owner had decided that the basic model needed decoration and had welded all this extra metal onto it. A crazed machinist's imitation of kinetic art. Abysmal, Eric thought. The thing must weigh a hundred pounds. Who'd ever want to type on such a monster?

But his mind began associating. Baudelaire. *Les Fleurs du mal.* Oscar Wilde. Aubrey Beardsley. Yes, the *Yellow Book*!

He felt inspired. An ugly typewriter. He grinned despite the prickles on his skin. He savored what his friends would say about it. He'd tell them he'd decided to continue Baudelaire's tradition. He'd be decadent. He'd be outrageous. Evil stories from an evil typewriter. He might even start a trend.

"How much for this monstrosity?" Eric casually asked.

"Eh? What?" The junk man looked up from his *Racing Form.*

"This clunker here. This mutilated typewriter."

"Oh, that." The old man's skin was sallow. His hair looked like the cobwebs Eric stood among. "You mean that priceless, irreplaceable antique."

"No. I mean this contorted piece of garbage."

The old man considered him, then nodded grimly. "Forty bucks."

"Forty? But that's outrageous! Ten!"

"Forty. And it's not outrageous, pal. It's business. That fool thing's been on my hands for over twenty years. I never should've bought it, but it came with lots of good stuff, and the owners wouldn't split the package. Twenty years. Two bucks a year for taking space. I'm being generous. I ought to charge a hundred. Lord, I hate that thing."

"Then you ought to pay me to get it out of here."

"And I should go on welfare. But I don't. Forty. Just today. For you. A steal. Tomorrow it goes up to fifty."

Tall and good-looking, Eric was also extremely thin. An artist ought to look ascetic, he told himself, although the fact was, he didn't have much choice. His emaciation wasn't only for effect. It was also his penance, the result of starvation. Art paid little, he'd discovered. If you told the truth, you weren't rewarded. How could he expect the system to encourage deviant opinions?

His apartment was only a block away, but it seemed a mile. His thin body ached as he struggled to carry his purchase. Knobs jabbed his ribs. Levers poked his armpits. His knees bent. His wrists strained at their sockets. God Almighty, Eric thought, why did I buy this thing? It doesn't weigh a hundred pounds. It weighs a ton.

And ugly! Oh, good Lord, the thing was ugly! In the harsh, cruel glare of day, it looked even worse. If that junk man turned his lights on for a change, his customers could see what they were buying. What a fool I've been, he thought. I ought to go back and make him refund my money. But behind the old man's counter, there'd been a sign. The old man had jabbed a finger at it: ALL SALES FINAL.

Eric sweated up the bird-dung-covered steps to his apartment building. *Tenement* was more accurate. The cracked front door had a broken lock. Inside, plaster dangled from the ceiling; paint peeled from the walls. The floor bulged; the stairway sagged; the banister listed. A cabbage smell overwhelmed him; onions, and a more pervasive odor that reminded him of urine.

He trudged up the stairs. The old boards creaked and bent. He feared they'd snap from the weight he carried. Three flights. Four. Mount Everest was probably easier. A group of teenagers—rapists, car thieves, muggers, he suspected—snickered at him as they left an apartment. One of the old winos on the stairs widened his bloodshot eyes, as if he thought that what Eric carried was an alcoholic hallucination.

At last he lurched up to the seventh floor but nearly lost his balance and fell back. As he struggled down the hall, his legs wobbled. He groaned, not just from his burden but from what he saw.

A man was pounding angrily on Eric's door: the landlord, "Hard-Ass" Simmons, although the nickname wasn't apt because his rear looked like two massive globs of Jell-O quivering when he walked. He had a beer gut and a whisker-stubbled face. His lips looked like two worms.

As Eric stopped, he nearly lost his grip on the ugly

typewriter. He cringed and turned to go back down the stairs.

But Simmons pounded on the door again. Pivoting his beefy hips disgustedly, he saw his quarry in the hall. "So there you are." He aimed a finger, gunlike.

"Mr. Simmons. Nice to see you."

"Crap. Believe me, it's not mutual. I want to see your money."

Eric mouthed the word as if he didn't know what *money* meant.

"The rent," the landlord said. "What you forget to pay me every month. The dough. The cash. The bucks."

"But I already gave it to you."

Simmons glowered. "In the Stone Age. I don't run a charity. You owe me three months' rent."

"My mother's awfully sick. I had to give her money for the doctor's bills."

"Don't hand me that. The only time you see your mother is when you go crawling to her for a loan. If I was you, I'd find a way to make a living."

"Mr. Simmons, please, I'll get the money."

"When?"

"Two weeks. I only need two weeks. I've got some *Star Trek* T-shirts I can sell."

"You'd better, or you'll know what outer space is. It's the street. I'll sacrifice the three months' rent you owe me for the pleasure of kicking you out the door."

"I promise. I've got a paycheck coming for the column I write."

Simmons snorted. "Writer. That's a laugh. If you're so hot a writer, how come you're not rich? And what's that ugly thing you're holding? Jesus, I hate to look at it. You must've found it in the garbage."

"No, I bought it." Eric straightened, proud, indignant. At once the thing seemed twice as heavy, making him stoop. "I needed a new typewriter."

"You're dumber than I thought. You mean you bought that piece of junk instead of paying me the rent? I ought to kick you out of here right now. Two weeks. You'd better have the cash, or you'll be typing in the gutter."

Simmons waddled past. He lumbered down the creaky stairs. "A writer. What a joke. And I'm the King of England. Arthur Hailey. He's a writer. Harold Robbins. *He's* a writer. Judith Krantz and Sidney Sheldon. *You*, my friend, you're just a bum."

As Eric listened to the booming laughter gradually recede down the stairs, he chose between a clever answer and the need to set his typewriter down. His aching arms were more persuasive. Angry, he unlocked the door. Embarrassed, he stared at his purchase. Well, I can't just leave it in the hall, he thought. He nearly sprained his back to lift the thing. He staggered in and kicked the door shut. He surveyed his living room. The dingy furniture reminded him of the junk shop where he'd bought the stuff. What a mess I'm in, he told himself. He didn't know where he could get the rent. He doubted his mother would lend him more money. Last time, at her penthouse on Fifth Avenue, she'd been angry with him.

"Your impractical romantic image of the struggling, starving artist . . . Eric, how did I go wrong? I spoiled you. That must be it. I gave you everything. You're not a youngster now. You're thirty-five. You've got to be responsible. You've got to find a job."

"And be *exploited*?" Eric had replied, aghast. "Debased? The capitalistic system is *degenerate*."

She'd shaken her head and tisk-tisk-tisked in disappointment. "But that system is the source of what I lend you. If your father came back from that boardroom in the sky and saw how you've turned out, he'd drop dead from another heart attack. I've not been fair. My analyst says I'm restricting your development. The fledgling has to learn to fly, he says. I've got to force you from the nest. You'll get no further money."

Eric sighed now as he lugged the typewriter across the living room and set it on the chipped, discolored kitchen counter. He'd have set it on the table, but he knew the table would collapse from the weight. Even so, the counter groaned, and Eric held his breath. Only when the counter stopped protesting did he exhale.

He watched water dripping from the rusty kitchen tap. He glanced at the noisy kitchen clock, which, although he frequently reset it, was always a half hour fast. Subtracting from where the hands were on the clock, he guessed that the time was half past two. A little early for a drink, but I've got a good excuse, he told himself. A *lot* of good excuses. Cheap scotch from the previous night's party. He poured an ounce and swallowed it, gasping from the warmth that reached his complaining empty stomach.

Well, there's nothing here to eat, he told himself, then poured another drink. This albatross took all the money

I'd saved for food. He felt like kicking it, but since it wasn't on the floor, he slammed it with his hand instead. And nearly broke his fingers. Dancing around the room, clutching his hand, he winced and cursed. To calm himself, he poured more scotch.

Christ, my column's due tomorrow, and I haven't even started. If I don't meet my deadline, I'll lose the only steady job I've got.

Exasperated, Eric went into the living room, where his faithful old Olympia waited on its altarlike desk opposite the door, the first thing people saw when they came in. This morning, he'd tried to start the column, but, distracted by his broken kitchen chair, he hadn't been able to find the words. Indeed, distraction from his work was common with him.

Now again he faced the blank page staring up at him. Again his mind blocked, and no words came. He sweated more profusely, straining to think. Another drink would help. He went back to the kitchen for his glass. He lit a cigarette. No words. That's always been my problem. He gulped the scotch. Art was painful. If he didn't suffer, his work would have no value. Joyce had suffered. Kafka. Mann. The agony of greatness.

In the kitchen, Eric felt the scotch start to work on him. The light paled. The room appeared to tilt. His cheeks felt numb. He rubbed his awkward fingers through his thick blond neck-long hair.

He peered disgustedly at the thing on the kitchen counter. "You," he said. "I'll bet your keys don't even work." He grabbed a sheet of paper. "There." He turned the roller, and surprisingly it fed the paper smoothly.

"Well, at least you're not an absolute disaster." He drank more scotch, lit another cigarette.

His column didn't interest him. No matter how he tried, he couldn't think of any theories about modern fiction. The only thing on his mind was what would happen in two weeks when Simmons came to get the rent. "It isn't fair. The system's against me."

That inspired him. Yes. He'd write a story. He'd tell the world exactly what he thought about it. He already knew the title. Just four letters. And he typed them: *Scum.*

The keys moved more easily than he'd expected. Smoothly. Slickly. But as gratified as Eric felt, he was also puzzled—for the keys typed longer than was necessary.

His lips felt thick. His mind felt sluggish as he leaned down to see what kind of imprint the old ribbon had made. He blinked and leaned much closer. He'd typed *Scum,* but what he read was *Fletcher's Cove.*

Astonishment made him frown. Had he drunk so much he couldn't control his typing? Were his alcohol-awkward fingers hitting keys at random? No, for if he'd typed at random, he ought to be reading gibberish, and *Fletcher's Cove,* although the words weren't what he'd intended, certainly wasn't gibberish.

My mind, he told himself, it's playing tricks. I think I'm typing one thing, but unconsciously I'm typing something else. The scotch is confusing me.

To test his theory, Eric concentrated to uncloud his mind and make his fingers more alert. Taking care that he typed what he wanted, he hit several keys. The letters clattered onto the paper, taking the exact amount of time they should have. Something was wrong, though. As he frowned toward the page, he saw that what he'd meant to type (*a story*) had come out as something else (*a novel*).

Eric gaped. He knew he hadn't written that. Besides, he'd always written stories. He'd never tried—he didn't have the discipline—to write a novel. What the hell was going on? In frustration, he quickly typed *The quick brown fox jumped over the lazy dog.*

But this is what he read: *The town of Fletcher's Cove had managed to survive, as it had always managed to survive, the fierce Atlantic winter.*

That awful tingle again. Like ice. This is crazy, he thought. I've never heard of Fletcher's Cove, and that redundant clause, it's horrible. It's decoration, gingerbread.

Appalled, he struck the keys repeatedly, at frenzied random, hoping to read nonsense, praying he hadn't lost his mind.

Instead of nonsense, this is what he saw: *The townsfolk were as rugged as the harsh New England coastline. They had characters of granite, able to withstand the punishments of nature, as if they had learned the techniques of survival from the sturdy rocks along the shore, impervious to tidal onslaughts.*

Eric flinched. He knew he hadn't typed those words. What's more, he never could have *forced* himself to type them. They were terrible. Redundancy was everywhere, and Lord, those strained commercial images. The sentences were hackwork, typical of gushy best-sellers.

Anger seized him. He typed frantically, determined to discover what was happening. His writer's block had disappeared. The notion of best-sellers had inspired him to write a column, scorning the outrageous decadence of fiction that was cynically designed to pander to the basest common taste.

But what he read was: *Deep December snows enshrouded Fletcher's Cove. The land lay dormant, frozen. January. February. The townsfolk huddled, imprisoned near the stoves and hearths inside their homes. They scanned the too-familiar faces of their forced companions. While the savage wind howled past their bedroom windows, wives and husbands soon grew bored with one another. March came with its early thaw. Then April, and the land became alive again. But as the warm spring air rekindled nature, so within the citizens of Fletcher's Cove, strong passions smoldered.*

Eric stumbled toward the scotch. This time, he ignored the glass and drank straight from the bottle. He shook, nauseous, scared to death. As the tasteless scotch dribbled from his lips, his mind spun. He clutched the kitchen counter for support. In his delirium, he thought of only three explanations. One, he'd gone insane. Two, he was so drunk that, like the wino on the stairs, he was hallucinating. Three, the hardest to accept, this wasn't an ordinary typewriter.

The way it looks should tell you that.

Good God.

The telephone's harsh ring jolted him. He nearly slipped from the counter. Fighting for balance, he teetered toward the living room. The phone was one more thing he'd soon lose, he knew. For two months, he'd failed to pay the bill. The way his life was going, he suspected that this call was from the telephone company, telling him it was canceling his service.

He fumbled to pick up the phone. Hesitant, he said, "Hello," but those two syllables slurred, combining as one. ". . . Lo," he said, then repeated it in confusion. ". . . Lo?"

"Is that you, Eric?" a man's loud, nasal voice asked him. "You sound different. Are you sick? You've got a cold?" The editor of *Village Mind.*

"No, I was working on my column." Eric attempted to control the drunken thickness in his voice. "The phone surprised me."

"On your column? Listen, Eric, I could break this to you gently, but I know you're strong enough to take it on the chin. Forget about your column. I won't need it."

"What? You're canceling my—" Eric felt his heart skip.

"Hey, not just your column. Everything. The *Village Mind* is folding. It's kaput. Bankrupt. Hell, why beat around the bush? It's broke."

His editor's clichés had always bothered Eric, but now he felt too stunned to be offended. "Broke?" Terror flooded through him.

"Absolutely busted. See, the IRS won't let me write the magazine off. They insist it's a tax dodge, not a business."

"Fascists!"

"To be honest, Eric, they're right. It *is* a tax dodge. You should see the way I juggle my accounts."

Now Eric was completely certain he'd gone insane. He couldn't actually be hearing this. The *Village Mind* a fraud, a con game? "You can't be serious!"

"Hey, look, don't take this hard, huh? Nothing personal. It's business. You can find another magazine. Got to run, pal. See you sometime."

Eric heard the sudden drone of the dial tone. Its dull monotony amplified inside his head. His stomach churned. The system. Once again the system had attacked him. Was there nothing sacred, even art?

He dropped the phone back on its cradle. Hopelessly, he rubbed his throbbing forehead. If he didn't get his check tomorrow, his phone would be disconnected. He'd be dragged from his apartment. The police would find his starved, emaciated body in the gutter. Either that or— Eric cringed—he'd have to find a steady—here he swallowed with great difficulty—job.

He panicked. Could he borrow money from his friends? He heard their scornful laughter. Could he beg more money from his mother? He imagined her disowning him.

It wasn't fair! He'd pledged his life to art, and he was starving while those hacks churned out their trashy best-sellers and were millionaires! There wasn't any justice!

A thought gleamed. An idea clicked into place. A trashy best-seller? Something those hacks churned out? Well, in his kitchen, waiting on the counter, was a hideous contraption that a while ago had churned like crazy.

That horrific word again. Like crazy? Yes, and *he*

was crazy to believe that what had happened in his drunken fit was more than an illusion.

Better see a shrink, he told himself.

And how am I supposed to pay him?

Totally discouraged, Eric tottered toward the scotch in the kitchen. Might as well get blotto. Nothing else will help.

He stared at the grotesque typewriter and the words on the paper. Although the letters were now blurred by alcohol, they nonetheless were readable, and, more important, they seemed actual. He swigged more scotch, tapping at keys in stupefaction, randomly, no longer startled when the gushy words made sense. It was a sign of his insanity, he told himself, that he could stand here at this kitchen counter, hitting any keys he wanted, and not be surprised by the result. No matter what the cause or explanation, he apparently was automatically composing the outrageous saga of the passions and perversions of the folks in Fletcher's Cove.

"Yes, Johnny," Eric told the television personality, then smiled with humble candor. "*Fletcher's Cove* burst out of me in one enormous flash of inspiration. Frankly, the experience was scary. I'd been waiting all my life to tell that story, but I wasn't sure I had the talent. Then one day I took a chance. I sat down at my faithful battered typewriter. I bought it in a junk shop, Johnny. That's how poor I was. And fate or luck or something was on *my* side for a change. My fingers seemed to dance across the keys. The story leapt out from me toward the page. A day doesn't go by that I don't thank the Lord for how He's blessed me."

Johnny tapped a pencil on his desk with practiced ease. The studio lights blazed. Eric sweated underneath his thousand-dollar sharkskin suit. His two-hundred-dollar designer haircut felt stiff from hairspray. In the glare, he squinted but couldn't see the audience, although he sensed their firm approval of his wonderful rags-to-riches success. America was validated. One day, there'd be a shrine to honor its most cherished saint: Horatio Alger.

"Eric, you're too modest. You're not just our country's most admired novelist. You're also a respected critic, not to mention that a short story of yours won a prestigious literary prize."

Prestigious? Eric inwardly frowned. Hey, be careful, Johnny. With a word that big, you'll lose our audience. I've got a book to sell.

"Yes," Eric said, admiring his host's sophisticated light gray hair. "The heyday of the *Village Mind*. The good old days in Greenwich Village. That's a disadvantage of success. I miss the gang down at Washington Square. I miss the coffeehouses and the nights when we'd get together, reading stories to one another, testing new ideas, talking till after dawn."

Like hell I miss them, Eric thought. That dump I lived in. That fat-assed Simmons. He can have his cockroach colony and those winos on the stairs. The *Village Mind*? A more descriptive title would have been the *Village Idiot*. And literary prize? The Subway Press awarded prizes every month. Sure, with the prizes and a quarter, you could buy a cup of coffee.

"You'll admit success has its advantages," Johnny said.

Eric shrugged disarmingly. "A few more creature comforts."

"You're a wealthy man."

You bet I'm wealthy, Eric thought. Two million bucks for the hardback. Four million for the paperback. Two million for the movie, and another million from the book club. Then the British rights, the other foreign rights in twenty countries. Fifteen million was the total. Ten percent went to his agent. Five percent to his publicity director. After that, the IRS held out its hand. But Eric had been clever. Oil and cattle, real estate—he coveted tax shelters. His trips to Europe, he wrote off as research. He'd incorporated. His estate, his jet, his yacht, he wrote off as expenses. After all, a man in his position needed privacy to write, to earn more money for the government. Taking advantage of every tax dodge he could find, he pocketed $9 million. Not bad for a forty-buck investment, although, to hedge against inflation, Eric wished he'd found a way to keep a few more million. Well, I can't complain.

"But Johnny, money isn't everything. Oh, sure, if someone wants to give it to me, I won't throw the money in the Hudson River." Eric laughed and heard the audience respond in kind. Their laughter was good-natured. You can bet they wouldn't turn down money, either. "No, the thing is, Johnny, the reward I most enjoy comes when I read the letters from my fans. The pleasure they've received from *Fletcher's Cove* is more important than material success. It's what this business is about. The reading public."

Eric paused. The interview had gone too smoothly. Smoothness didn't sell his book. What people wanted was a controversy.

Beneath the blazing lights, his underarms sweated in profusion. He feared he'd stain his sharkskin suit and ruin it, but then he realized he could always buy another one.

"I know what Truman Capote says, that *Fletcher's Cove* is hardly writing—it's mere typing. But he's used that comment several times before, and if you want to know what I think, he's done several *other* things too many times before."

The audience began to laugh, but this time cruelly.

"Johnny, I'm still waiting for that novel he keeps promising. I'm glad I didn't hold my breath."

The audience laughed more derisively. If Truman had been present, they'd have stoned him.

"To be honest, Johnny, I think Truman's lost his touch with that great readership out there. The middle of America. I've tasted modern fiction, and it makes me gag. What people want are bulging stories filled with glamour, romance, action, and suspense. The kind of thing Dickens wrote."

The audience applauded with approval.

"Eric," Johnny said, "you mentioned Dickens. But a different writer comes to mind. A man whose work was popular back in the fifties. Winston Davis. If I hadn't known you wrote *Fletcher's Cove*, I'd have sworn it was something new by Davis. But, of course, that isn't possible. The man's dead—a tragic boating accident when he was only forty-eight. Just off Long Island, I believe."

"I'm flattered you thought of Davis," Eric said. "In fact, you're not the only reader who's noticed the comparison. He's an example of the kind of author I admire. His enormous love of character and plot. Those small towns in New England he immortalized. The richness of his prose. I've studied everything Davis wrote. I'm trying to continue his tradition. People want true, honest, human stories."

Eric hadn't even *heard* of Winston Davis until fans began comparing his book with Davis's. Puzzled, Eric had gone to the New York Public Library. He'd squirmed with discomfort as he'd tried to struggle through half a dozen books by Davis. Eric couldn't finish *any* of them. Tasteless dreck. Mind-numbing trash. The prose was deadening, but Eric recognized it. The comparison was valid. *Fletcher's Cove* was like a book by Winston Davis. Eric had frowned as he'd left the library. He'd felt that tingle again. Despite their frequent appearances throughout *Fletcher's Cove,* he'd never liked coincidences.

"One last question," Johnny said. "Your fans are anxious for another novel. Can you tell us what the new one's about?"

"I'd like to, but I'm superstitious, Johnny. I'm afraid to talk about a work while it's in progress. I can tell you this, though." Eric glanced around suspiciously, as if he feared that spies from rival publishers were lurking in the studio. He shrugged and laughed. "I guess I can say it. After all, who'd steal a title after several million people have heard me stake a claim to it? The new book is called *Parson's Grove.*" He heard a sigh of rapture from the audience. "It takes place in a small town in Vermont, and . . . well, I'd better not go any further. When the book is published, everyone can read it."

"Totally fantastic," Eric's agent said. His name was Jeffrey Amgott. He was in his thirties, but his hair was gray and thin from worry. He frowned constantly. His stomach gave him trouble, and his motions were so hurried that he seemed to be on speed. "Perfect. What you said about Capote—guaranteed to sell another hundred thousand copies."

"I figured," Eric said. Outside the studio, he climbed in the limousine. "But you don't look happy."

The Carson show was taped in the late afternoon, but the smog was so thick, it looked like twilight.

"We've got problems," Jeffrey said.

"I don't see what. Here, have a drink to calm your nerves."

"And wreck my stomach? Thanks, but no thanks. Listen, I've been talking to your business manager."

"I hear it coming. You both worry too damn much."

"But you've been spending money like you're printing it. That jet, that yacht, that big estate. You can't afford them."

"Hey, I've got nine million bucks. Let me live a little."

"No, you don't."

Eric stared. "I beg your pardon."

"You haven't got nine million dollars. All those trips to Europe. That beach house here in Malibu, the place in Bimini."

"I've got investments. Oil and cattle."

"The wells went dry. The cattle died from hoof-and-mouth disease."

"You're kidding me."

"My stomach isn't kidding. You've got mortgages on those estates. Your Ferrari isn't paid for. The Learjet isn't paid for, either. You're flat broke."

"I've been extravagant, I grant you."

Jeffrey gaped. "Extravagant? *Extravagant?* You've lost your mind is what you've done."

"You're my agent. Make another deal for me."

"I did already. What's the matter with you? Have you lost your memory with your mind? A week from now, your publisher expects a brand-new book from you. He's offering three million dollars for the hardback rights. I let him have the book. He lets me have the money. That's the way the contract was arranged. Have you forgotten?"

"What's the problem, then? Three million bucks will pay my bills."

"But where the hell's the book? You don't get any money if you don't deliver the manuscript."

"I'm working on it."

Jeffrey moaned. "Dear God, you mean it isn't finished yet? I asked you. No, I pleaded with you. Please stop partying. Get busy. Write the book, and then have all the parties you want. What is it? All those women, did they sap your strength, your brains, or what?"

"You'll have the book a week from now."

"Oh, Eric, I wish I had your confidence. You think writing's like turning on a tap? It's work. Suppose you get a block. Suppose you get the flu or something. How can anybody write a novel in a week?"

"You'll have the book. I promise, Jeffrey. Anyway, if I'm a little late, it doesn't matter. I'm worth money to the publisher. He'll extend the deadline."

"Damn it, you don't listen. Everything depends on timing. The new hardback's been announced. It should have been delivered and edited months ago. The release of the paperback of *Fletcher's Cove* is tied to it. The stores are expecting both books. The printer's waiting. The publicity's set to start. If you don't deliver, the publisher will think you've made a fool of him. You'll lose your media spots. The book club will get angry, not to mention your foreign publishers, who've announced the new book in their catalogs. They're depending on you. Eric, you don't understand. Big business. You don't disappoint big business."

"Not to worry." Eric smiled to reassure him. "Everything's taken care of. Robert Evans invited me to a party tonight, but after that, I'll get to work."

"God help you, Eric. Hit those keys, man. Hit those keys."

At 3:00 A.M., the Learjet soared from LAX. Above the city, Eric peered down toward the grids of streetlights and gleaming freeways in the darkness.

Might as well get started, he decided with reluctance.

Cocaine that he'd snorted on the way to the airport gave him energy.

As the engine's muffled roar came through the fuselage, he reached inside a cabinet and lifted out the enormous typewriter. He took it everywhere with him, afraid that something might happen to it if it was unattended.

Struggling, he set it on a table. He'd given orders to the pilot not to come back to the passenger compartment. A thick bulkhead separated Eric from the cockpit. Here, as at his mansion up the Hudson, Eric did his typing in strict secrecy.

The work was boring, really. Toward the end of *Fletcher's Cove,* he hadn't even faced the keyboard. He'd watched a week of television while he let his fingers tap whatever letters they happened to select. After all, it didn't make a difference what he typed. The strange machine did the composing. At the end of every television program, he'd read the last page the machine had typed, hoping to see *The End.* And one day, finally, those closing words appeared before him.

After the success of *Fletcher's Cove,* he'd started typing again. He'd read the title *Parson's Grove* and worked patiently for twenty pages. Unenthusiastically. What he'd learned from his experience was that he'd never liked writing, that instead he liked to talk about it and be called a writer, but the pain of work did not appeal to him. And this way, when his mind wasn't engaged, the work was even less appealing. To be absolutely honest, Eric thought, I should have been a prince.

He'd put off typing *Parson's Grove* as long as possible. The money came so easily, he didn't want to suffer even the one week he'd calculated would be necessary to complete the manuscript.

But Jeffrey had alarmed him. There's no money? Then I'd better go back to the gold mine. The goose that laid the golden egg. Or what was it a writer's helper used to be called? Amanuensis. Sure, that's what I'll call you, Eric told his weird machine. From now on, you'll be my amanuensis. He couldn't believe he was actually a millionaire—at least on paper—flying in his own Learjet, en route to New York and the *Today* show. This can't be really happening.

It was, though. And if Eric wanted to continue his fine life, he'd better type like hell for one week to produce his second book.

The jet streaked through the night. He shoved a sheet of paper into his amanuensis. Bored, he sipped a glass of Dom Pérignon. He selected a cassette of *Halloween* and put it in his VCR. Watching a monitor where some kid stabbed his big sister, Eric started typing.

Chapter Three. . . . Ramona felt a rapture. She had never known such pleasure. Not her husband, not her lover had produced such ecstasy within her. Yes, the milkman . . .

Eric yawned. He watched a nut escape from an asylum. He watched some crazy doctor try to find the nut. A baby-sitter screamed a lot. The nut got killed a half dozen times but still survived because apparently he was the boogeyman.

Without once looking at the keyboard, Eric typed.

The stack of pages grew beside him. He finished drinking his fifth glass of Dom Pérignon. *Halloween* ended. He watched *Alien* and an arousing woman in her underwear who'd trapped herself inside a shuttle with a monster. Somewhere over Indiana—Eric later calculated where and when it happened—he glanced at a sheet of paper he'd just typed and gasped when he discovered that the prose was total nonsense.

He fumbled through the stack of paper, realizing that for half an hour he'd been typing gibberish.

He paled. He gaped. He nearly vomited.

"Good God, what's happened?"

He typed madly: *Little Bo Peep has lost her sheep.*

Those words were what he read.

He typed *The quick brown fox.*

And *that* was what he read.

He scrambled letters, and the scramble faced him.

By the time he reached La Guardia Airport, he had a two-inch stack of frantic gibberish beside him, and to make things worse, the typewriter jammed. He heard a nauseating crunch inside it, and the keys froze solidly. He couldn't make them type even gibberish. It's got a block, he thought, then moaned. Dear God, it's broken, busted, wrecked.

We both are.

He tried slamming it to free the keys, but all he managed to do was hurt his hands. Jesus, I'd better be careful. I might break more parts inside. Drunkenly, he set a blanket over it and struggled from the jet to put it in the limousine that waited for him. He wasn't due at the

television interviews until the next day. As the sun glared
blindingly, he rubbed his haggard whisker-stubbled face
and in panic told the chauffeur, "Manhattan. Find a shop
that fixes typewriters."

The errand took two hours through stalled trucks, accidents, and detours. Finally the limousine double-
parked on Thirty-second Street, and Eric stumbled with
his burden toward a store with Olivettis in the window.

"I can't fix this," the young serviceman informed
him.

Eric moaned. "You've got to."

"See this brace inside. It's cracked. I don't have
any parts for something strange like this." The serviceman looked horrified by the sheer ugliness of the machine. "I'd have to weld the brace. But buddy, look, a
piece of junk this old, it's like a worn-out shirt. You
patch an elbow, and the shirt tears at the patch. You
patch the new hole, and the shirt tears at the new patch.
When you're through, you haven't got a shirt. You've
just got patches. If I weld this brace, the heat'll weaken
this old metal, and the brace'll crack in other places.
You'll keep coming back till you've got more welds
than metal. Anyway, a weird design like this, I wouldn't
want to fool with it. Believe me, buddy, I don't understand this thing. You'd better find the guy who built it.
Maybe *he* can fix it. Maybe he's got extra parts. Say,
don't I know you?"

Eric frowned. "I beg your pardon?"

"Aren't you famous? Weren't you on the Carson
show?"

"No, you're mistaken," Eric told him furtively. He

glanced at his gold Rolex and saw that it was almost noon. Good God, he'd lost the morning. "I've got to hurry."

Eric grabbed the broken typewriter and tottered from the building toward the limousine. The traffic's blare unnerved him.

"Greenwich Village," Eric blurted to the bored chauffeur. "As fast as you can get there."

"In this traffic? Sir, it's noon. And this is midtown."

Eric's stomach soured. He trembled, sweating. When the driver reached the Village, Eric gave directions in a frenzy. He kept glancing at his watch. At almost twenty after one, he had a sudden fearful thought. Oh, God, suppose the place is closed. Suppose the old guy's dead or out of business.

Eric cringed. But then he squinted through the windshield, seeing the dusty windows of the junk shop down the street. He scrambled from the limousine before it stopped. He grabbed the massive typewriter, and although adrenaline spurred him, his knees wobbled as he fumbled at the creaky junk shop door and lurched inside the musty, narrow, shadowed room.

The old guy stood exactly where he'd been the last time Eric had walked in: hunched across a battered desk, a half an inch of cigarette between his yellowed fingers, scowling at a racetrack form. He even wore the same frayed sweater with the buttons missing. Cobweb hair. Sallow face.

The old guy peered up from the *Racing Form*. "All sales are final. Can't you read the sign?"

Off balance from his burden, Eric cocked his head in disbelief. "You still remember me?"

"You bet I do. I can't forget that piece of trash. I told you I don't take returns."

"But that's not why I'm here."

"Then why'd you bring that damn thing back? Good God, it's ugly. I can't stand to look at it."

"It's broken."

"Yeah, it figures."

"I can't get it fixed. The serviceman won't touch it. He's afraid he'll break it even more."

"So throw it in the garbage. Sell it as scrap metal. It weighs enough. You'll maybe get a couple dollars."

"But I like it!"

"Have you always had bad taste?"

"The serviceman suggested the guy who built it might know how to fix it."

"And if cows had wings—"

"Look, tell me where you got it!"

"How much is the information worth to you?"

"A hundred bucks!"

The old man looked suspicious. "I won't take a check."

"In cash! For God's sake, hurry!"

"Where's the money?"

The old man took several hours. Eric paced and smoked and sweated. Finally the old man came groaning up from his basement with some scribbles on a scrap of paper.

"An estate. Out on Long Island. Some guy died. He drowned, I think. Let's see." The old man struggled to decipher what he'd scrawled on the scrap of paper. "Yeah, his name was Winston Davis."

Eric clutched the battered desk; his stomach fluttered; his heart skipped several beats. "No, that can't be."

"You mean you know this guy? This Winston Davis."

Eric tasted dust. "I've heard of him. He was a novelist." His voice was hoarse.

"I hope he didn't try to write his novels on that thing. It's like I told you when you bought it. I tried every way I knew to make them keep it. But the owners sold the dead guy's stuff in one big lump. They wouldn't split the package. Everything or nothing."

"On Long Island?"

"The address is on this paper."

Eric grabbed it, frantically picked up the heavy typewriter, and stumbled toward the door.

"Say, don't I know your face?" the old man asked. "Weren't you on the Carson show last night?"

The sun had almost set as Eric found his destination. All the way across Long Island, he'd trembled fearfully. He realized now why so many readers had compared his work with that of Winston Davis. Davis had once owned this same machine. He'd typed his novels on it. The machine had done the actual composing. That's why Eric's work and Davis's were similar. Their novels had the same creator. Just as Eric kept the secret, so had Davis, evidently never telling even his close friends or his family. When Davis died, the family had guessed that this old typewriter was nothing more than junk, and they'd sold it with some other junk around the house. If they'd known about the secret, surely they'd have kept this golden goose, this gold mine.

But it wasn't any gold mine now. It was a hunk of junk, a broken hulk of bolts and levers.

"Here's the mansion, sir," the totally confused chauffeur told Eric.

Frightened, Eric studied the big open gates, the smooth wide lawn, the huge black road that curved up to the massive house. It's like a castle, Eric thought. Apprehensively, he told the driver, "Go up to the front."

Suppose there's no one home, he thought. Suppose they don't remember. What if someone else is living there?

He left his burden in the car. At once both hesitant and frantic, he walked up the marble front steps toward the large oak door. His fingers shook. He pressed a button, heard the echo of a bell inside, and was surprised when someone opened the door.

A gray-haired woman in her sixties. Kindly, well dressed, pleasant-looking.

Smiling, with a feeble voice, she asked how she could help him.

Eric stammered, but the woman's gentle gaze encouraged him, and soon he spoke to her with ease, explaining that he knew her husband's work and admired it.

"How good of you to remember," she said.

"I was in the neighborhood. I hoped you wouldn't mind if I stopped by. To tell you how I felt about his novels."

"Wouldn't mind? No, I'm delighted. So few readers take the time to care. Won't you come in?"

The mansion seemed to Eric like a mausoleum— cold and echoing.

"Would you like to see my husband's study? Where he worked?" the aging woman asked.

They went along a chilly marble hall. The old woman opened an ornate door and gestured toward the sacristy, the sanctum.

It was wonderful. A high, wide, spacious room with priceless paintings on the walls—and bookshelves, thick, soft carpeting, big windows that faced the whitecapped ocean, where three sunset-tinted sailboats scudded in the evening breeze.

But the attraction of the room was in its middle—a large, gleaming teakwood desk, and, like a chalice at its center, an old Smith-Corona from the fifties.

"This is where my husband wrote his books," the old woman told him proudly. "Every morning—eight until noon. Then we'd have lunch, and we'd go shopping for our dinner, or we'd swim or use the sailboat. In the winter, we took long walks by the water. Winston loved the ocean in the winter. He . . . I'm babbling. Please, forgive me."

"No, it's quite all right. I understand the way you feel. He used this Smith-Corona?"

"Every day."

"I ask, because I bought a clunky typewriter the other day. It looked so strange, it appealed to me. The man who sold it told me your husband used to own it."

"No, I . . ."

Eric's chest cramped. His heart sank in despair.

"Wait, I remember now," the gray-haired woman said, and Eric held his breath.

"That awful ugly one," she said.

"Yes, that describes it."

"Winston kept it in a closet. I kept telling him to throw it out, but Winston said his friend would never forgive him."

"Friend?" The word stuck like a fish bone in Eric's throat.

"Yes, Stuart Donovan. They often sailed together. One day, Winston brought that strange machine home. 'It's antique,' he said. 'A present. Stuart gave it to me.' Well, it looked like junk to me. But friends are friends, and Winston kept it. When he died, though . . ." The old woman's voice changed pitch, sank deeper, seemed to crack. "Well, anyway, I sold it with some other things I didn't need."

Eric left the car. The sun had set. The dusk loomed thickly around him. He smelled salty sea air in this quaint Long Island coastal village. He stared at the sign above the shop's door: DONOVAN'S TYPEWRITERS—NEW AND USED—REBUILT, RESTORED. His plan had been to find the shop and come back in the morning when it opened. But amazingly, a light glowed faintly through the drawn blind of the window. Although a card on the door said CLOSED, a shadow moved behind the shielded window.

Eric knocked. A figure shuffled close. An ancient

gentleman pulled up the blind and squinted out toward Eric.

"Closed," the old man told him faintly through the window.

"No, I have to see you. It's important."

"Closed," the man repeated.

"Winston Davis."

Although the shadow had begun to turn, it stopped. Again pulling the blind, the ancient gentleman peered out.

"Did you say Winston Davis?"

"Please, I have to talk to you about him."

Eric heard the lock snick open. The door swung slowly inward. The old man frowned at him.

"Is your name Stuart Donovan?"

The old man nodded. "Winston? We were friends for many years."

"That's why I have to see you."

"Then come in," the old man told him, puzzled. Short and frail, he leaned on a wooden cane. He wore a double-breasted suit, a thin silk tie. The collar of his shirt was too large for his shrunken neck. He smelled of peppermint.

"I have to show you something," Eric said. Hurrying back from the limousine, he lugged his ugly typewriter toward the shop.

"Why, that's . . ." The old man's eyes widened in surprise.

"I know. It was your gift to Winston."

"Where . . ."

"I bought it in a junk shop."

Wearied by his grief, the old man groaned.

"It's broken," Eric said. "I've brought it here for you to fix."

"Then you know about . . . ."

"Its secret. Absolutely. Look, I need it. I'm in trouble if it isn't fixed."

"You sound like Winston." The old man's eyes blurred with memories of long ago. "A few times, when it broke, he came to me in total panic. 'Contracts. Royalties. I'm ruined if you can't repair it,' he'd say to me. I always fixed it, though." The old man chuckled nostalgically.

"And will you do the same for me? I'll pay you anything."

"Oh, no, my rate's the same for everyone. I was about to leave. My wife has supper waiting. But this model was my masterpiece. I'll look at it. For Winston. Bring it over to the counter."

Eric set it down and rubbed his aching arms. "What I don't understand is why you didn't keep this thing. It's worth a fortune."

"I had others."

Eric stiffened with surprise.

"Then, too," the old man said, "I've always had sufficient money. Rich folks have too many worries. Winston, for example. Toward the end, he was a nervous wreck, afraid that this typewriter would break beyond repair. It ruined him. I wish I hadn't given it to him. But he was good to me. He always gave me ten percent of everything he earned."

"I'll do the same for you. Please, fix it. Help me."

"I'll see what the problem is."

The old man tinkered, hummed, hawed, and poked. He took off bolts and tested levers.

Eric bit his lips. He chewed his fingernails.

"I know what's wrong," the old man said.

"That brace is cracked."

"Oh, that's a minor problem. I have other braces. I can easily replace it."

Eric sighed with relief. "Then if you wouldn't mind . . ."

"The keys are stuck because the brace is cracked," the old man said. "Before the keys stuck, though, this model wasn't typing what you wanted. It wasn't composing."

Eric feared he'd throw up. He nodded palely.

"See, the trouble is," the old man said, "this typewriter ran out of words. It used up every word it had inside it."

Eric fought the urge to scream. This can't be happening, he told himself. "Then put more words inside it."

"Don't I wish I could. But once the words are gone, I can't put new ones in. I don't know why that happens, but I've tried repeatedly, and every time I've failed. I have to build a brand-new model."

"Do it, then. I'll pay you anything."

"I'm sorry, but I can't. I've lost the knack. I made five successful models. The sixth and seventh failed. The eighth was a complete disaster. I stopped trying."

"Try again."

"I can't. You don't know how it weakens me. The effort. Afterward, my brain feels empty. I need every word I've got."

"Goddamn it, try!"

The old man shook his head. "You have my sympathy."

Beyond the old man, past the counter, in the workshop, Eric saw another model. Knobs and levers, bolts.

"I'll pay a million dollars for that other one."

The old man slowly turned to look. "Oh, that one. No, I'm sorry. That's my own. I built it for my children. Now they're married. They have children of their own, and when they visit, my grandchildren like to play with it."

"I'll double what I offered."

Eric thought about his mansion on the Hudson, his estates in Bimini and Malibu, his yacht, his jet, his European trips, and his Ferrari.

"Hell, I'll triple what I offered."

Six more days, he thought. I've got to finish that new book by then. I'll just have time to do it. If I type every day and night.

"You've got to let me have it."

"I don't need the money. I'm an old man. What does money mean to me? I'm sorry."

Eric lost control. He scrambled past the counter, racing toward the workshop. He grabbed the other model. When the old man tried to take it from him, Eric pushed. The old man fell, clutching Eric's legs.

"It's mine!" the old man wailed. "I built it for my children! You can't have it!"

"Four! Four million dollars!" Eric shouted.

"Not for all the money in the world!"

The old man clung to Eric's legs.

"Damn it!" Eric said. He set the model on the counter, grabbed the old man's cane, and struck his head. "I need it! Don't you understand!"

He struck again and again and again.

The old man shuddered. Blood dripped from the cane.

The shop was silent.

Eric stared at what he'd done. Stumbling back, he dropped the cane and put his hands to his mouth.

And then he realized. "It's mine."

He wiped his fingerprints from everything he'd touched. He exchanged the models so his broken one sat on the workshop table. His chauffeur wouldn't know what had happened. It was likely he'd never learn. The murder of an old man in a tiny village on Long Island— there was little reason for publicity. True, Mrs. Davis might recall her evening visitor, but would she link this murder with her visitor? And anyway, she didn't know who Eric was.

He took his chance. He grabbed his prize, and despite its weight, he ran.

His IBM word processor sat on the desk in his study. For pure show. He never used it, but he needed it to fool his guests, to hide the way he actually composed. He vaguely heard the limousine drive from the mansion toward the city. He turned on the lights. Hurrying toward his desk, he shoved the IBM away and set down his salvation. Six more days. Yes, he could do the job. A lot of champagne and television. Stiff joints in his aching fingers after all the automatic typing. He could do it, though.

He poured a brimming glass, needing it. He turned the Late Show on. He lit a cigarette, and as *The Body Snatcher*'s credits began, he desperately started typing.

He felt shaky, scared, and shocked by what had happened. But he had another model. He could keep his yacht, his jet, his three estates. The parties could continue. Now that Eric thought about it, he'd even saved the $4 million he would have paid the old man for this model.

Curious, on impulse, Eric glanced at what he'd typed so far.

And began to scream.

Because his random typing had become something different, as he'd expected. But not the gushy prose of *Parson's Grove*. Something far more different.

See Jack run. See Jill run. See Spot chase the ball.

("I built it for my children. Now they're married. They have children of their own, and when they visit, my grandchildren like to play with it.")

He screamed so loudly, he couldn't hear the clatter as he typed.

See Spot run up the hill. See Jill run after Spot. See Jack run after Jill.

The neighbors half a mile away were wakened by his shrieks. They feared he was being murdered, so they called 911, and when the state police broke into the house, they found Eric typing, screaming.

They weren't sure which sight was worse—the man

or the machine. But when they dragged him from the monstrous typewriter, one of the state policemen glanced down at the page.

See Jill climb the tree. See Jack climb the tree. See Spot bark at Jack.

Then farther down—they soon discovered what it meant—*See Eric murder Mr. Donovan. See Eric club the old man with the cane. See Eric steal me. Now see Eric go to jail.*

Perhaps it was a trick of light, or maybe it was the consequence of the machine's peculiar keyboard. For whatever reason, the state policeman later swore—he told only his wife—the damned typewriter seemed to grin.

A Trap for the Unwary

*D*ennis Etchison is both a gifted fiction writer and a respected editor of short-story anthologies. In 1991, for the third volume of his Masters of Darkness series, he asked me and a number of other contributors—Clive Barker, Stephen King, Dean Koontz, Joyce Carol Oates, and more—to choose a favorite from the stories we had written. He also requested that we compose an afterword, explaining our choice. This is the afterword I submitted.

HOW DOES A WRITER CHOOSE A STORY, AMONG MANY, that typifies what he or she has been trying to accomplish? Prior to selecting "But at My Back I Always Hear" (1983), I reread several others and finally settled on this one, not because it's my most horrific (although I did find my skin go cold, but not to the frigid degree that was caused by "For These and All My Sins" or the middle section of my novel *Testament*) and not because its style is experimental (as is that of "The Hidden Laughter"), but precisely because this story *is* typical, an example of a technique and various themes I've returned to again and again.

Let's deal with the technique first. Like many novelists, I find the discipline, the *compression*, of a story enormously difficult. There's an irony here. In the early seventies, my initial effort at fiction was *First Blood*, but after I sent it to my agent, I had a nightmare that so compelled me I wrote it *verbatim*, a story called "The Dripping," which was purchased by *Ellery Queen's Mystery Magazine* and became my first sale, two weeks before my agent phoned to tell me a publisher had accepted *First Blood*. Other writers will understand. "The Dripping," to me, will always be special. A validation of my dreams.

But as I labored on my next book (the dreaded second-novel syndrome: *Can I possibly do it again?*), short-story nightmares failed to visit me. And as that second novel, *Testament*, continued to give me problems, to aggravate my insecurity, I craved the satisfaction of writing another short, microcosmic, "I can do it with luck in a couple of days" validation of my ambition to be a hypnotist, a magician, a teller of tales.

I was then a professor of literature at the University of Iowa, and by chance, preparing for a class, I picked up Robert Browning's "My Last Duchess" and felt a prickle of revelation. You see, "The Dripping" had been a first-person narrative, but I've always been suspicious of first-person narratives because of my admiration for Henry James.

The master, commenting on his consummate horror novel, *The Turn of the Screw*, had called his tale "a trap for the unwary"—because its first-person technique made it impossible to decide if the narrator was telling the truth about the ghosts she encountered or if she was hopelessly insane. James, in fact, disdained the first-person technique, calling the device a trick in which the only interest for the reader was to decide if the "I" of the story was self-deluded, a liar, or crazy. So how could I, devoted to the master, feel justified in following my instincts to repeat, to build on, what I'd done in "The Dripping" if the viewpoint I felt compelled to use had been dismissed by one of my literary heroes?

Robert Browning's "My Last Duchess" supplied the answer. It's called a "dramatic monologue," a technique he's given credit for creating, not in a play (where a soliloquy's an accepted convention) but on a page, in a poem! "That's my last Duchess painted on the wall," Browning begins, or rather, his narrator does. And I thought, Who is the speaker addressing? And how did the reader happen to receive these words? The technique is unbelievable, artificial, yet wonderfully effective. Around the same time, I fell in love with the novels of James M. Cain. "They threw me off the hay truck about noon." That's how *The Postman Always Rings Twice* begins, one of the all-time great first sentences, in one of the greatest thrillers ever written. But *Cain's* narrator wasn't addressing an imagined audience viewing a stage. No, that damned fate-controlled aggressor/victim was writing his story as a form of confession while he waited, tough and controlled, to be executed for murder.

So I asked myself, Why not pretend you never read James? Why not concentrate on Browning and Cain? And that decision broke my block about writing short stories. I embraced the first-person technique. It's direct. It's intimate. It's vivid. And it allows a writer to compress. The tormented narrator blurts out his tale of horror. Until the end of "But at My Back I Always Hear," the story is due to Browning. But when the hero-victim picks up the pen and paper in his hotel room and reveals that all along he's been writing his tale of terror, as a document, so the people who find his body will understand his predestined doom, that's Cain, and God bless him. He showed me the way.

Now about theme. For reasons too complex to elaborate in this brief space, I'm obsessed about security. That topic is manifest in all of my work. The worst horror I could ever imagine was to lose my family, to lose a *member* of my family, to be separated from those I love. In real life, that horror became all too real. On June 27, 1987, my wonderful fifteen-year-old son, Matthew, died (after six months of unbelievable agony) from bone cancer. I described that ordeal in a book called *Fireflies*. But in "The Dripping" and other stories before Matthew's death, I was already terrified by versions of that ultimate horror. The narrator in "But at My Back I Always Hear" loses everything he cherishes. Not because it's his fault. *But because of fate.* Because sometimes things don't work out. Because, God help me, life isn't fair.

Then, too, I *was* a professor of literature, and I *did* have a student who claimed I was sending sexual telepathic messages to her. She did keep calling, threatening, haunting—not only me (I can deal with that) but also my *family.* Most of "But at My Back I Always Hear" is true. Except that the student is still alive and, for all I know, lurking.

Finally, after I moved from where I was raised in Canada to graduate school in Pennsylvania and then to the University of Iowa, I fell in love with the boundless sky and incredibly fertile beauty of my adopted state. I call it "exotic." Watch the movie *Field of Dreams* to understand what I mean. It occurred to me that horror didn't have to fester in the traditional Hawthorne-invented gloom of New England, or in the oppressive ghettos of decaying major cities, but in bright sunlight, in the midst of splendor. Remember Cary Grant racing desperately to escape the machine-gun bullets from the "innocent" crop duster in Hitchcock's *North by Northwest?* I began to envision a series of stories that would take advantage of the broad Midwest and Highway 80 and the space, the sublime, hence terrifying, *space* between one isolated community and another. I explored that notion in several stories: "The Storm," "For These and All My Sins," and others. Even the *time-zone* changes are fraught with danger.

So if you desperately need security (as the hero of "But at My Back I Always Hear" does and as its *author* does), you choose this story as representative of your

work. My alter-ego professor sacrifices his life and his
soul for his family. Good man. I understand him all too
well. Because given the chance, I would gladly have sacrificed *my* life and soul to save my son.

But at My Back
I Always Hear

SHE PHONED AGAIN LAST NIGHT. AT 3:00 A.M., THE WAY she always does. I'm scared to death. I can't keep running. On the hotel register downstairs, I lied about my name, address, and occupation. Although I'm here in Johnstown, Pennsylvania, I'm from Iowa City, Iowa. I teach—or used to teach, until three days ago—American literature at the university. I can't risk going back there. But I don't think I can hide much longer. Each night, she comes closer.

From the start, she scared me. I went to school at eight to prepare my classes. After going through the side door of the English building, I went up a stairwell to my third-floor office, which was isolated by a fire door from all the other offices. My colleagues used to joke that I'd been banished, but I didn't care, for in my far-off corner, I could concentrate. Few students interrupted me. Regardless of the busy noises past the fire door, I sometimes felt that there was no one else inside the building. And indeed at 8:00 A.M., I often *was* the only person in the building.

That day, I was wrong, however. Clutching my heavy briefcase, I trudged up the stairwell. My scraping footsteps echoed off the walls of pale red cinder block, the stairs of pale green imitation marble. First floor. Second floor. The fluorescent lights glowed coldly. Then the stairwell angled toward the third floor, and I saw her waiting on a chair outside my office. Pausing, I frowned up the stairs at her. I felt uneasy.

Eight A.M., for you, is probably not early. You've been up for quite a while so that you can get to work on time or get your children off to school. But 8:00 A.M., for college students, is the middle of the night. They don't like morning classes. When their schedules force them to attend one, they don't crawl from bed until they absolutely have to, and they don't come stumbling into class until I'm just about to start my lecture.

I felt startled, then, to find her waiting ninety minutes early. She sat tensely: lifeless dull brown hair, a shapeless dingy sweater, baggy faded jeans with patches on the knees and frays around the cuffs. Her eyes were haunted and wild, deep and dark.

I climbed the last few steps and stopped before her. "Do you want an early conference?"

Instead of answering, she nodded bleakly.

"You're concerned about a grade I gave you?"

This time, though, in pain, she shook her head from side to side.

Confused, I fumbled with my key and opened the office, stepping in. The room was small and narrow: a desk, two chairs, a wall of bookshelves, and a window. As I sat behind the desk, I watched her slowly come inside. She glanced around uncertainly. Distraught, she shut the door.

That made me nervous. When a female student shuts the door, I start to worry that a colleague or a student might walk up the stairs and hear a female voice and wonder what's so private that I want to keep the door closed. Although I should have told her to reopen it, her frantic eyes aroused such pity in me that I sacrificed my principle, deciding her torment was so personal that she could talk about it only in strict secrecy.

"Sit down." I smiled and tried to make her feel at ease, although I myself was not at ease. "What seems to be the difficulty, Miss . . . I'm sorry, but I don't recall your name."

"Samantha Perry. I don't like Samantha, though." She fidgeted. "I've shortened it to . . ."

"Yes? To what?"

"To Sam. I'm in your nine-thirty Tuesday-Thursday class." She bit her lip. "You spoke to me."

I frowned, not understanding. "You mean what I taught seemed vivid to you?"

"Mr. Ingram, no. I mean you *spoke* to me. You stared at me while you were teaching. You ignored the other students. You directed what you said to *me*. When you talked about Hemingway, how Frederic Henry wants to go to bed with Catherine"—she swallowed—"you were asking me to go to bed with you."

I gaped. To disguise my shock, I quickly lit a cigarette. "You're mistaken."

"But I *heard* you. You kept staring straight at *me*. I felt all the other students knew what you were doing."

"I was only lecturing. I often look at students' faces to make sure they pay attention. You received the wrong impression."

"You weren't asking me to go to bed with you?" Her voice sounded anguished.

"No. I don't trade sex for grades."

"But I don't care about a grade!"

"I'm married. Happily. I've got two children. Anyway, suppose I did intend to proposition you. Would I do it in the middle of a class? I'd be foolish."

"Then you never meant to . . ." She kept biting her lip.

"I'm sorry."

"But you speak to me! Outside class, I hear your voice! When I'm in my room or walking down the street! You talk to me when I'm asleep! You say you want to go to bed with me!"

My skin prickled. I felt frozen. "You're mistaken. Your imagination's playing tricks."

"But I hear your voice so clearly! When I'm studying or—"

"How? If I'm not there."

"You send your thoughts! You concentrate and put your voice inside my mind!"

Adrenaline scalded my stomach. I frantically sought an argument to disillusion her. "Telepathy? I don't believe in it. I've never tried to send my thoughts to you."

"Unconsciously?"

I shook my head from side to side. I couldn't bring myself to tell her: Of all the female students in her class, she looked so plain, even if I weren't married, I'd never have wanted to have sex with her.

"You're studying too hard," I said. "You want to do so well, you're preoccupied with me. That's why you think you hear my voice when I'm not there. I try to make my lectures vivid. As a consequence, you think I'm speaking totally to you."

"Then you shouldn't teach that way!" she shouted. "It's not fair! It's cruel! It's teasing!" Tears streamed down her face. "You made a fool of me!"

"I didn't mean to."

"But you did! You tricked me! You misled me!"

"No."

She stood so quickly that I flinched, afraid she'd lunge at me or scream for help and claim I'd tried to rape her. That damned door. I cursed myself for not insisting she leave it open.

Sobbing, she rushed toward it. She pawed at the knob and stumbled out, hysterically retreating down the stairwell.

Shaken, I stubbed out my cigarette, grabbing another. My chest tightened as I heard the dwindling echo of her racking sobs, the awkward scuffle of her dimming footsteps, then the low, deep rumble of the outside door.

Silence settled over me.

An hour later, I found her waiting in class. She'd wiped her tears. The only signs of what had happened were her puffy red eyes. She sat alertly, pen to paper. I carefully didn't face her as I spoke. She seldom glanced up from her notes.

After class, I asked my graduate assistant if he knew her.

"You mean Sam? Sure, I know her. She's been getting D's. She had a conference with me. Instead of asking how to get a better grade, though, all she did was talk about you, pumping me for information. She's got quite a thing for you. Too bad about her."

"Why?"

"Well, she's so plain, she doesn't have many friends. I doubt she goes out much. There's a problem with her father. She was vague about it, but I had the sense her three sisters are so beautiful that Daddy treats her as the ugly duckling. She wants very much to please him. He ignores her, though. He's practically disowned her. You remind her of him."

"Who? Of her father?"

"She admits you're ten years younger than he, but she says you look exactly like him."

I felt heartsick.

Two days later, I found her waiting for me—again at 8:00 A.M.—outside my office.

Tense, I unlocked the door. As if she heard my thought, she didn't shut it this time. Sitting before my desk, she didn't fidget. She just stared at me.

"It happened again," she said.

"In class, I didn't even look at you."

"No, afterward, when I went to the library." She drew

an anguished breath. "And later—I ate supper in the dorm. I heard your voice so clearly, I was sure you were in the cafeteria."

"What time was that?"

"Five-thirty."

"I was having cocktails with the dean. Believe me, Sam, I wasn't sending messages to you. I didn't even *think* of you."

"I couldn't have imagined it! You wanted me to go to bed with you!"

"I wanted research money from the dean. I thought of nothing else. My mind was totally involved in trying to convince him. When I didn't get the money, I was too annoyed to concentrate on anything else but getting drunk."

"Your voice—"

"It isn't real. If I sent thoughts to you, wouldn't I admit what I was doing? When you asked me, wouldn't I confirm the message? Why would I deny it?"

"I'm afraid."

"You're troubled by your father."

"What?"

"My graduate assistant says you identify me with your father."

She went ashen. "That's supposed to be a secret!"

"Sam, I asked him. He won't lie to me."

"If you remind me of my father, if I want to go to bed with you, then I must want to go to bed with—my father! You must think I'm disgusting!"

"No, I think you're confused. You ought to find some help. You ought to see a—"

But she never let me finish. Weeping again, ashamed, hysterical, she bolted from the room.

And that's the last I ever saw of her. An hour later, when I started lecturing, she wasn't in class. A few days later, I received a "drop" slip from the registrar, informing me she'd canceled all her classes.

I forgot her.

Summer came. Then fall arrived. November. On a rainy Tuesday night, my wife and I stayed up to watch the close results of the national election, worried for our presidential candidate.

At 3:00 A.M., the phone rang. No one calls that late unless . . .

The jangle of the phone made me bang my head as I reached for a beer in the fridge. I rubbed my throbbing skull and swung in alarm as Jean, my wife, came from the living room and squinted toward the kitchen phone.

"It might be just a friend," I said. "Election gossip."

But I worried about our parents. Maybe one of them was sick or . . .

I watched uneasily as Jean picked up the phone.

"Hello?" She listened apprehensively. Frowning, she put her hand across the mouthpiece. "It's for you. A woman."

"What?"

"She's young. She asked for Mr. Ingram."

"Damn, a student."

"At three A.M.?"

I almost didn't think to shut the fridge. Annoyed, I yanked the pop tab off the can of beer. My marriage is successful. I'll admit we've had our troubles. So has every couple. But we've faced those troubles, and we're happy. Jean is thirty-five, attractive, smart, and patient. But her trust in me was clearly tested at that moment. A woman had to know me awfully well to call at 3:00 A.M.

"Let's find out." I grabbed the phone. To prove my innocence to Jean, I roughly said, "Yeah, what?"

"I heard you." The female voice was frail and plaintive, trembling.

"Who *is* this?" I asked angrily.

"It's me."

I heard a low-pitched crackle on the line.

"Who the hell is *me*? Just tell me what your name is."

"Sam."

My knees went weak. I slumped against the wall.

Jean stared. "What's wrong?" Her eyes narrowed with suspicion

"Sam, it's three A.M. What's so damned important that you can't wait to call me during office hours?"

"Three? It can't be. No, it's one."

"It's three. For God's sake, Sam, I know what time it is."

"Please, don't get angry. On my radio, the news announcer said it was one o'clock."

"Where *are* you, Sam?"

"At Berkeley."

"California? Sam, the time-zone difference. In the Midwest, it's two hours later. Here, it's three o'clock."

". . . I guess I forgot."

"But that's absurd. Have you been drinking? Are you drunk?"

"No, not exactly."

"What the hell does *that* mean?"

"Well, I took some pills. I'm not sure what they were."

"Oh Jesus."

"Then I heard you. You were speaking to me."

"No. I told you that your mind's playing tricks. The voice isn't real. You're imagining—"

"You called to me. You said you wanted me to go to bed with you. You wanted me to come to you."

"To Iowa? No. You've got to understand. Don't do it. I'm not sending thoughts to you."

"You're lying! Tell me why you're lying!"

"I don't want to go to bed with you. I'm glad you're in Berkeley. Stay there. Get some help. Lord, don't you realize? Those pills—they make you hear my voice. They make you hallucinate."

"I . . ."

"Trust me, Sam. Believe me. I'm not sending thoughts to you. I didn't even know you'd gone to Berkeley. You're two thousand miles away from me. What you're suggesting is impossible."

She didn't answer. All I heard was low-pitched static.

"Sam—"

The dial tone abruptly droned. My stomach sank. Appalled, I kept the phone against my ear. I swallowed dryly, shaking as I set the phone back on its cradle.

Jean glared. "Who was that? She wasn't any *Sam.* She wants to go to bed with you? At three A.M.? What games have you been playing?"

"None." I gulped my beer, but my throat stayed dry. "You'd better sit down. I'll get a beer for you."

Jean clutched her stomach.

"It's not what you think. I promise I'm not screwing anybody. But it's bad. I'm scared."

I handed Jean a beer.

"I don't know why it happened. But last spring, at eight A.M., I went to school and . . ."

Jean listened, troubled. Afterward, she asked for Sam's description, somewhat mollified to learn that she was plain and pitiful.

"The truth?" Jean asked.

"I promise you."

Jean studied me. "You did nothing to encourage her?"

"I guarantee it. I wasn't aware of her until I found her waiting for me."

"But unconsciously?"

"Sam asked me that, too. I was only lecturing the best way I know how."

Jean kept her eyes on me. She nodded, glancing toward her beer. "Then she's disturbed. There's nothing you can do for her. I'm glad she moved to Berkeley. In your place, I'd have been afraid."

"I *am* afraid. She spooks me."

At a dinner party the next Saturday, I told our host and hostess what had happened, motivated more than just by the need to share my fear with someone else, for while the host was both a friend and colleague, he was married to a clinical psychologist. I needed professional advice.

Diane, the hostess, listened with slim interest until halfway through my story, when she suddenly sat straight and peered at me.

I faltered. "What's the matter?"

"Don't stop. What else?"

I frowned and finished, waiting for Diane's reaction. Instead, she poured more wine. She offered more lasagna.

"Something bothered you."

She tucked her long black hair behind her ears. "It could be nothing."

"I need to know."

Diane nodded grimly. "I can't make a diagnosis merely on the basis of your story. I'd be irresponsible."

"But hypothetically . . ."

"And *only* hypothetically. She hears your voice. That's symptomatic of a severe disturbance. Paranoia, for example. Schizophrenia. The man who shot John Lennon heard a voice. And so did Manson. So did Son of Sam."

"My God," Jean said. "Her name. Sam." Jean set her fork down loudly.

"The parallel occurred to me," Diane said. "Chuck, if she identifies you with her father, she might be dangerous to Jean and to the children."

"Why?"

"Jealousy. To hurt the equivalent of her mother and her rival sisters."

I felt sick. The wine turned sour in my stomach.

"There's another possibility. No more encouraging. If you continue to reject her, she could be dangerous to you. Instead of dealing with her father, she might redirect her rage and jealousy toward you. By killing you, she'd be venting her frustration toward her father."

I felt panicked. "For the *good* news?"

"Understand, I'm speaking hypothetically. Possibly she's lying to you, and she doesn't hear your voice. Or, as you guessed, the drugs she takes might make her hallucinate. There could be many explanations. Without seeing her, without the proper tests, I wouldn't dare to judge her symptoms. You're a friend, so I'm compromising. Possibly she's homicidal."

"Tell me what to do."

"For openers, I'd stay away from her."

"I'm *trying*. She called from California. She's threatening to come back here to see me."

"Talk her out of it."

"I'm no psychologist. I don't know what to say to her."

"Suggest she get professional advice."

"I tried that."

"Try again. But if you find her at your office, don't go in the room with her. Find other people. Crowds protect you."

"But at eight A.M., there's no one in the building."

"Think of some excuse to leave her. Jean, if she comes to the house, don't let her in."

Jean paled. "I've never seen her. How could I identify her?"

"Chuck described her. Don't take chances. Don't trust anyone who might resemble her, and keep a close watch on the children."

"*How?* Rebecca's twelve. Sue's nine. I can't insist they stay around the house."

Diane turned her wineglass, saying nothing.

"Oh, dear Lord," Jean said.

The next few weeks were hellish. Every time the phone rang, Jean and I jerked, startled, staring at it. But the calls were from our friends or from our children's friends or from some insulation/magazine/home-siding salesman. Every day, I mustered courage as I climbed the stairwell to my office. Silent prayers were answered. Sam was never there. My tension dissipated. I began to feel she no longer was obsessed with me.

Thanksgiving came—the last day of peace I've known. We went to church. Our parents live too far away for us to share the feast with them. But we invited friends to dinner. We watched football. I helped Jean make the dressing for the turkey. I made both the pumpkin pies. The friends we'd invited were my colleague and his wife, the clinical psychologist. She asked if my student had continued to harass me. Shaking my head from side to side, I grinned and raised my glass in special thanks.

The guests stayed late to watch a movie with us. Jean and I felt pleasantly exhausted, mellowed by good food, good drink, good friends, when after midnight we washed all the dishes, went to bed, made love, and drifted wearily to sleep.

The phone rang, shocking me awake. I fumbled toward the bedside lamp. Jean's eyes went wide with fright.

She clutched my arm and pointed toward the clock. It was 3:00 A.M.

The phone kept ringing.

"Don't," Jean said.

"Suppose it's someone else."

"You know it isn't."

"If it's Sam and I don't answer, she might come to the house instead of phoning."

"For God's sake, make her stop."

I grabbed the phone, but my throat wouldn't work.

"I'm coming to you," the voice wailed.

"Sam?"

"I heard you. I won't disappoint you. I'll be there soon."

"No. Wait. Listen."

"I've been listening. I hear you all the time. The anguish in your voice. You're begging me to come to you, to hold you, to make love to you."

"That isn't true."

"You say your wife's jealous of me. I'll convince her she isn't being fair. I'll make her let you go. Then we'll be happy."

"Sam, where are you? Still in Berkeley?"

"Yes. I spent Thanksgiving by myself. My father didn't want me to come home."

"You have to stay there, Sam. I didn't send my voice. You need advice. You need to see a doctor. Will you do that for me? As a favor?"

"I already did. But Dr. Campbell doesn't understand. He thinks I'm imagining what I hear. He humors me. He doesn't realize how much you love me."

"Sam, you have to talk to him again. You have to tell him what you plan to do."

"I can't wait any longer. I'll be there soon. I'll be with you."

My heart pounded frantically. I heard a roar in my head. I flinched as the phone was yanked away from me.

Jean shouted to the mouthpiece, "Stay away from us! Don't call again! Stop terrorizing—"

Jean stared wildly at me. "No one's there. The line went dead. I hear just the dial tone."

I'm writing this as quickly as I can. I don't have much more time. It's almost three o'clock.

That night, we didn't try to go back to sleep. We couldn't. We got dressed and went downstairs, where, drinking coffee, we decided what to do. At eight, as soon as we got the kids dressed and into the car, we drove to the police.

They listened sympathetically, but there was no way they could help us. After all, Sam hadn't broken any law. Her calls weren't obscene; it was difficult to prove harassment; she'd made no overt threats. Unless she harmed us, there was nothing the police could do.

"Protect us," I insisted.

"How?" the sergeant asked.

"Assign an officer to guard the house."

"For how long? A day, a week, a month? That woman might not even bother you again. We're overworked and understaffed. I'm sorry—I can't spare an officer whose only duty is to watch you. I can send a car to check the house from time to time. No more than that.

But if this woman does show up and bother you, then call us. We'll take care of her."

"But that might be too late!"

Back at home, we made the children stay inside. Sam couldn't have arrived from California yet, but what else could we do? I don't own any guns. If all of us stayed together, we had some chance for protection.

That was Friday. I slept lightly. 3:00 A.M., the phone rang. It was Sam, of course.

"I'm coming."

"Sam, where are you?"

"Reno."

"You're not flying?"

"No, I can't."

"Turn back, Sam. Go to Berkeley. See that doctor."

"I can't wait to see you."

"Please—"

The dial tone was droning.

The first thing in the morning, I phoned Berkeley information. Sam had mentioned Dr. Campbell. But the operator couldn't find him in the Yellow Pages.

"Try the university," I blurted. "Student Counseling."

I was right. A Dr. Campbell was a university psychiatrist. On Saturday, I couldn't reach him at his office, but a woman answered at his home. He wouldn't be available until the afternoon. At four o'clock, I finally got through to him.

"You have a patient named Samantha Perry," I began.

"I did. Not anymore."

"I know. She's left for Iowa. She wants to see me. I'm afraid. I think she might be dangerous."

"Well, you don't have to worry."

"She's not dangerous?"

"Potentially, she was."

"But tell me what to do when she arrives. You're treating her. You'll know what I should do."

"No, Mr. Ingram, she won't come to see you. On Thanksgiving night. Actually, it was Friday morning, at one A.M., she killed herself. An overdose of drugs."

My vision failed. I clutched the kitchen table to prevent myself from falling. "That's impossible."

"I saw the body. I identified it."

"But she phoned that night."

"What time?"

"At three A.M. Central time."

"Or one o'clock in California. No doubt after or before she took the drugs. She didn't leave a note, but she phoned you."

"She gave no indication—"

"She mentioned you quite often. She was morbidly attracted to you. She had an extreme, unhealthy certainty that she was telepathic, that you put your voice inside her mind."

"I know that! Was she paranoid or homicidal?"

"Mr. Ingram, I've already said too much. Although she's dead, I can't violate her confidence."

"But I don't think she's dead."

"I beg your pardon."

"If she died on Friday morning, then tell me how she phoned again on *Saturday* morning?"

The line hummed. I sensed the doctor's hesitation. "Mr. Ingram, you're upset. You don't know what you're saying. You've confused the nights."

"I'm telling you she called again early this morning!"

"And I'm telling you she died on *Friday*. Either someone's tricking you, or else . . ." The doctor swallowed with discomfort.

"Or?" I trembled. "*I'm* the one who's hearing voices?"

"Mr. Ingram, don't upset yourself. You're honestly confused."

I slowly put the phone down, terrified. "I'm sure I heard her voice."

That night, Sam called again. At 3:00 A.M. From Salt Lake City. When I handed Jean the phone, all she heard was the dial tone.

"But you know the goddamn phone rang!" I insisted.

"Maybe a short circuit. Chuck, I'm telling you there was no one on the line."

Then the next night. 3:00 A.M. Cheyenne, Wyoming. Coming closer. But she couldn't be if she was dead.

The student newspaper at the university subscribes to all the other major student newspapers. Monday, Jean and I took the children with us and drove to its office. Friday's copy of the Berkeley campus newspaper had arrived. In desperation, I searched its pages. "There!" A two-inch item. Sudden student death. Samantha Perry. Tactfully, no cause was given.

Outside in the parking lot, Jean said, "Now do you believe she's dead?"

"Then tell me why I hear her voice! I've got to be crazy if I think I hear a corpse!"

"You're feeling guilty that she killed herself because of you. You shouldn't. There was nothing you could do to stop her. You've been losing too much sleep. Your imagination's taking over."

"You admit you heard the phone ring!"

"Yes, it's true. I can't explain that. If the phone's broken, we'll have it fixed. To put your mind at rest, we'll get a new, unlisted number."

I felt better. After several drinks, I even got some sleep.

But the next night, again the phone rang. 3:00 A.M. I jerked awake. Cringing, I insisted that Jean answer it. But she heard just the dial tone. I grabbed the phone. Of course, I heard Sam's voice.

"I'm almost there. I'll hurry. I'm in Omaha."

"This number isn't listed!"

"But you told me the new one. Your wife's the one who changed it. She's trying to keep us apart. I'll make her sorry. Darling, I can't wait to be with you."

I screamed. Jean jerked away from me.

"Sam, you've got to stop!" I shouted into the phone. "I spoke to Dr. Campbell!"

"No. He wouldn't dare. He wouldn't violate my trust."

"He told me you were dead!"

"I couldn't live without you. Soon we'll be together."

My shrieks woke the children. I was so hysterical that Jean had to call for an ambulance. Two attendants struggled to sedate me.

Omaha was one day's drive from where we live. Jean came to visit me in the hospital on Tuesday.

"Are you feeling better?" She frowned at the restraints that held me down.

"Please, you have to humor me," I said. "All right? Suspect I've gone crazy, but for God's sake, humor me. I can't prove what I'm thinking, but I know you're in danger. I am, too. You have to get the children and leave town. You have to hide somewhere. Tonight at three A.M. she'll reach the house."

Jean studied me with pity.

"Promise me!" I said.

Jean saw the anguish on my face and nodded.

"Maybe she won't try the house," I said. "She seems to know everything. She might know I'm in the hospital. She might come here. I have to get away. I'm not sure how, but later, when you're gone, I'll find a way to get out of these restraints."

Jean peered at me, distressed. Her voice sounded totally discouraged. "Chuck."

"I'll check the house. If you're still there, you'll make me more upset."

"I promise. I'll take Susan and Rebecca. We'll drive somewhere."

"I love you."

Jean began to cry. "I won't know where you are."

"If I survive this, I'll get word to you."

"But how?"

"The English Department. I'll leave a message with the secretary."

Jean leaned down to kiss me, crying, certain I'd lost my mind.

I reached the house shortly after dark. As Jean had promised, she'd left with the children. I got in my sports car and raced to the interstate.

A Chicago hotel, where at 3:00 A.M. Sam phoned from Iowa City. She'd heard my voice. She said I'd told her where I was. She was hurt and angry. "Tell me why you're running."

I fled from Chicago, driving until I absolutely had to rest. I checked in here at this hotel in Johnstown, Pennsylvania. I can't sleep. I've got an awful feeling. Last night, Sam repeated, "Soon you'll join me." In the desk, I found this stationery.

God, it's 3:00 A.M. I pray that I'll see the sun come up.

It's almost four o'clock. She didn't phone. I can't believe I escaped. I keep staring at the phone.

It's four o'clock. Dear Christ, I hear the ringing.

Finally I've realized. Sam killed herself at one. In Iowa, the time-zone difference made it three. But I'm in

Pennsylvania. In the East. A different time zone. One o'clock in California would be *four* o'clock, not three, in Pennsylvania.

Now.

The ringing persists. But I've realized something else. This hotel's unusual, designed to seem like a home.

The ringing?

God help me, it isn't the phone. It's the doorbell.

The Storm

*A*s I mentioned in my afterword for "But at My Back I Always Hear," there is something about the flat, wide, open spaces of the Midwest that can cause fright as much as awe. When I lived in Pennsylvania, I thought I knew how bad a thunderstorm could be. But no weather there prepared me for the terror of an Iowa thunderstorm. As a character in this story points out, some Iowa storms can be seven miles high. When the weather forecasters announce a thunderstorm warning, you pay attention. Green skies. Eighty-mile-an-hour winds. Look out. One summer, lightning struck my house three times. In the middle of the night, while I lay in bed awake, feeling thunder shake the windows, I decided to write a story about it. "The Storm" was included in The Year's Best Fantasy Stories *of 1984.*

GAIL SAW IT FIRST. SHE CAME FROM THE HOWARD Johnson toward the heat haze in the parking lot where our son, Jeff, and I were hefting luggage into our station wagon. Actually, Jeff supervised. He gave me his excited ten-year-old advice about the best place for this suitcase and that knapsack. Grinning at his sun-bleached hair and nut brown freckled face, I told him I could never have done the job without him.

It was 8:00 A.M., Tuesday, August 2, but even that early, the thermometer outside our motel unit had risen to eighty-five. The humidity was thick and smothering. Just from my slight exertion with the luggage, I'd sweated through my shirt and jeans, wishing I'd thought to put on shorts. To the east, the sun blazed, white and swollen, the sky an oppressive chalky blue. This would be one day when the station wagon's air conditioning would be not just a comfort but a necessity.

My hands were sweat-slick as I shut the hatch. Jeff nodded, satisfied with my work, then grinned beyond me. Turning, I saw Gail coming toward us. When she left the brown parched grass, her brow creased as her sandals touched the heat-softened asphalt parking lot.

"All set?" she asked.

Her smooth white shorts and cool blue top emphasized her tan. She looked trim and lithe and wonderful. I'm not sure how she did it, but she seemed completely unaffected by the heat. Her hair was soft and golden. Her subtle trace of makeup made the day seem somehow cooler.

"Ready. Thanks to Jeff," I told her.

Jeff grinned up proudly.

"Well, I paid the bill. I gave them back the key," Gail said. "Let's go." She paused. "Except . . ."

"What's wrong?"

"Those clouds." She pointed past my shoulder.

I turned and frowned. In contrast to the blinding eastern sky, pitch-black clouds seethed on the western horizon. They roiled and churned. In the distance, lightning flickered like a string of flashbulbs, the thunder rumbling hollowly.

"Now where the hell did *that* come from?" I said. "It wasn't there before I packed the car."

Gail squinted toward the thunderheads. "You think we should wait till it passes?"

"It isn't close." I shrugged.

"But it's coming fast." Gail bit her lip. "And it looks bad."

Jeff grabbed my hand. I glanced at his worried face.

"It's just a storm, son."

Jeff surprised me, though. I'd misjudged what worried him.

"I want to go back home," he said. "I don't want to wait. I miss my friends. Please, can't we leave?"

I nodded. "I'm on your side. Two votes out of three, Gail. If you're really scared, though . . ."

"No. I . . ." Gail drew a breath and shook her head. "I'm being silly. It's just the thunder. You know how storms bother me." She ruffled Jeff's hair. "But I won't make us wait. I'm homesick, too."

We'd spent the past two weeks in Colorado, fishing, camping, touring ghost towns. The vacation had been perfect. But as eagerly as we'd gone, we were just as eager to be heading back. Last night, we'd stopped here in North Platte, a small, quiet town off Interstate 80, halfway through Nebraska. Now, today, we hoped we could reach home in Iowa City by nightfall.

"Let's get moving, then," I said. "It's probably a local storm. We'll drive ahead of it. We'll never see a drop of rain."

Gail tried to smile. "I hope."

Jeff hummed as we got in the station wagon. I steered toward the interstate, went up the eastbound ramp, and set the cruise control for the speed limit of fifty-five. Ahead, the morning sun glared through the windshield. After I tugged down the visors, I turned on the air conditioner, then the radio. The local weatherman said it was hot and hazy.

"Hear that?" I said. "He didn't mention a storm. No need to worry. Those are only heat clouds."

I was wrong. From time to time, I checked the rearview mirror, and the clouds loomed thicker, blacker, closer, seething toward us down the interstate. Ahead, the sun kept blazing fiercely. Jeff wiped his sweaty face. I set the air conditioner on the DESERT setting, but it didn't seem to help.

"Jeff, reach in the ice chest. Grab us each a Coke."

He grinned. But I suddenly felt uneasy, realizing too late that he'd have to turn to open the chest in the rear compartment.

"Gosh," he murmured, staring back, awestruck.

"What's the matter?" Gail swung around before I could stop her. "Oh my God, the clouds."

They were angry midnight chasing us. Lightning flashed. Thunder jolted.

"They still haven't reached us," I said. "If you want, I'll try outrunning them."

"Do *something*."

I switched off the cruise control and sped to sixty, then sixty-five. The strain of squinting toward the white-hot sky ahead of us gave me a piercing headache. I put on my sunglasses.

But all at once I didn't need them. Abruptly the clouds caught up to us. The sky went totally black. We drove in roiling darkness.

"Seventy. I'm doing seventy," I said. "But the clouds are moving faster."

"Almost a hurricane," Gail said. "That isn't possible. Not in Nebraska."

"I'm scared," Jeff said.

He wasn't the only one. Lightning blinded me, stabbing to the right and left of us. Thunder shook the car. Then the air became an eerie dirty shade of green, and I started thinking about tornadoes.

"Find a place to stop!" Gail shouted.

But there wasn't one. We'd already passed the exit for the next town, Kearney. I searched for a roadside park, but a sign said REST STOP, THIRTY MILES. I couldn't just pull off the highway. On the shoulder, if the rain obscured another driver's vision, we could all be hit and killed. No choice. I had to keep on driving.

"At least it isn't raining," I said.

The clouds unloaded. No preliminary sprinkle. Massive raindrops burst around us, gusting, roaring, pelting.

"I can't see!" I flicked the windshield wipers to their highest setting. They flapped in sharp, staccato triple time. I peered through murky, undulating, windswept waves of water, struggling for a clear view of the highway.

I was going too fast. When I braked, the station wagon fishtailed. We skidded on the slippery pavement. I couldn't breathe. The tires gripped. I felt the jolt. Then the car was in control.

I slowed to forty, but the rain heaved with such force against the windshield, I still couldn't see.

"Pull your seat belts tight."

Although I never found that rest stop, I got lucky when a flash of lightning showed a sign, the exit for a town called Grand Island. Shaking from tension, I eased down the off-ramp. At the bottom, across from me, a Best Western motel was shrouded with rain. We left a wake through the flooded parking lot and stopped under the motel's canopy. My hands were stiff from clenching the steering wheel. My shoulders ached. My eyes felt swollen, raw.

Gail and Jeff got out, rain gusting under the canopy as they ran inside. I had to move the car to park it in the lot. I locked the doors, but although I sprinted, I was drenched and chilled when I reached the motel's entrance.

Inside, a small group stared past me toward the storm—two clerks, two waitresses, a cleaning lady. I trembled.

"Mister, use this towel," the cleaning lady said. She took one from a pile on her cart.

I thanked her, wiping my dripping face and soggy hair.

"See any accidents?" a waitress asked.

With the towel around my neck, I shook my head no.

"A storm this sudden, there ought to be accidents," the waitress said, as if doubting me.

I frowned when she said "sudden." "You mean it's just starting here?"

A skinny clerk stepped past me to the window. "Not too long before you came. A minute maybe. I looked out this window, and the sky was bright. I knelt to tie my shoe. When I stood up, the clouds were here—as black as night. I don't know where they came from all of a sudden, but I never saw it rain so hard so fast."

"But—" I shivered, puzzled. "The storm hit us back near Kearney. We've been driving in it for an hour."

"You were on the edge of it, I guess," the clerk said, spellbound by the devastation outside. "It followed you."

My cold, wet shirt clung to me, but I felt a deeper chill.

"Looks like we've got other customers," the second clerk said, pointing out the window.

Other cars splashed through the torrent in the parking lot.

"Yeah, we'll be busy, that's for sure," the clerk said. He switched on the lights, but they didn't dispel the outside gloom.

The wind howled.

I glanced around the lobby, suddenly noticing that Gail and Jeff weren't in sight. "My wife and son."

"They're in the restaurant," the second waitress said, smiling to reassure me. "Through that arch. They ordered coffee for you. Hot and strong."

"I need it. Thanks."

Dripping travelers stumbled in.

We waited an hour. Although the coffee was as hot as promised, it didn't warm me. In the air conditioning, my soggy clothes stuck to the chilly chrome and plastic seat. A bone-deep, freezing numbness made me sneeze.

"You need dry clothes," Gail said. "You'll catch pneumonia."

I'd hoped the storm would stop before I went out for the clothes. But even in the restaurant, I felt the thunder rumble. I couldn't wait. My muscles cramped from shivering. "I'll get a suitcase." I stood.

"Dad, be careful." Jeff looked worried.

Smiling, I leaned down and kissed him. "Son, I promise."

Near the restaurant's exit, one of the waitresses I'd talked to came over. "You want to hear a joke?"

I didn't, but I nodded politely.

"On the radio," she said. "The local weatherman. He claims it's hot and clear."

I shook my head, confused.

"The storm." She laughed. "He doesn't know it's raining. All his instruments, his radar and his charts, he hasn't brains enough to look outside and see what kind of day it is. If anything, the rain got worse." She laughed again. "The biggest joke—that dummy's my husband."

I laughed to be agreeable and went to the lobby.

It was crowded. More rain-drenched travelers pushed in, cursing the weather. They tugged at dripping clothes and bunched before the motel's counter, wanting rooms.

I squeezed past them, stopping at the big glass door, squinting out at the wildest rain I'd ever seen. Above the exclamations of the crowd, I heard the shriek of the wind.

My hand reached for the door.

It hesitated. I really didn't want to go out.

The skinny desk clerk suddenly stood next to me. "It could be you're not interested," he said.

I frowned, surprised.

"We're renting rooms so fast, we'll soon be all full up," he said. "But fair is fair. You got here first. I saved a room. In case you plan on staying."

"I appreciate it. But we're leaving soon."

"You'd better take another look."

I did. Lightning split a tree. The window shook from thunder.

A steaming bath, I thought. A sizzling steak. Warm blankets while my clothes get dry.

"I changed my mind. We'll take that room."

All night, thunder shook the building. Even with the drapes shut, I saw brilliant streaks of lightning. I slept fitfully, waking with a headache. 6:00 A.M., it was still raining.

On the radio, the weatherman sounded puzzled. As the lightning's static garbled what he said, I learned that Grand Island was suffering the worst storm in its history. Streets were flooded, sewers blocked, basements overflowing. An emergency had been declared, the damage in the millions. But the cause of the storm seemed inexplicable. The weather pattern made no sense. The front was tiny, localized, and stationary. Half a mile outside Grand Island—north and south, east and west—the sky was cloudless.

That last statement was all I needed to know. We quickly dressed and went downstairs to eat. We checked out shortly after seven.

"Driving in this rain?" The desk clerk shook his head. He had the tact not to tell me I was crazy.

"Listen to the radio," I answered. "Half a mile away, the sky is clear."

I'd have stayed if it hadn't been for Gail. Her fear of storms—the constant lightning and thunder—made her frantic.

"Get me out of here."

And so we went.

And almost didn't reach the interstate. The car was hubcap-deep in water. The distributor was damp. I nearly killed the battery before I got the engine started. The brakes were soaked. They failed as I reached the local road. Skidding, blinded, I swerved around the blur of an abandoned truck, missing the entrance to the interstate. Backing up, I barely saw the ditch in time. But finally we headed up the ramp, rising above the flood, doing twenty down the highway.

Jeff was white-faced. I'd bought some comics for him, but he was too scared to read them.

"The odometer," I told him. "Watch the numbers. Half a mile, and we'll be out of this."

I counted tenths of a mile with him. "One, two, three . . ."

The storm grew darker, stronger.

"Four, five, six . . ."

The numbers felt like broken glass wedged in my throat.

"But Dad, we're half a mile away. The rain's not stopping."

"Just a little farther."

But instead of ending, it got worse. We had to stop in Lincoln. The next day, the storm persisted. We pressed on to Omaha. We could normally drive from Colorado to our home in Iowa City in two leisurely days.

But *this* trip took us seven long, slow, agonizing days. We had to stop in Omaha and then Des Moines and towns whose names I'd never heard of. When we at last reached home, we felt so exhausted, so frightened, we left our bags in the car and stumbled from the garage to bed.

The rain slashed against the windows. It drummed on the roof. I couldn't sleep. When I peered out, I saw a waterfall from the overflowing eaves. Lightning struck an electricity pole. I settled to my knees and recollected every prayer I'd ever learned and then invented stronger ones.

The electricity was fixed by morning. The phone still

worked. Gail called a friend and asked a question. As she listened to the answer, I was startled by the way her face shrank and her eyes receded. Mumbling "Thanks," she set the phone down.

"It's been dry here," she said. "Then last night at eight, the storm began."

"But that's when we arrived. My God, what's happening?"

"Coincidence." Gail frowned. "The storm front moved in our direction. We kept trying to escape. Instead, we only followed it."

The fridge was bare. I told Gail I'd get some food and warned Jeff not to go outside.

"But Dad, I want to see my friends."

"Watch television. Don't go out till the rain stops."

"It won't end."

I froze. "What makes you say that?"

"Not today it won't. The sky's too dark. The rain's too hard."

I nodded, relaxing. "Then call your friends. But don't go out."

When I opened the garage door, I watched the torrent. Eight days since I'd seen the sun. Damp clung on me. Gusts angled toward me.

I drove from the garage and was swallowed.

Gail looked overjoyed when I came back. "It stopped for forty minutes." She grinned with relief.

"Not where I was."

The nearest supermarket was half a mile away. Despite my umbrella and raincoat, I'd been drenched when

I lurched through the hissing automatic door of the supermarket. Fighting to catch my breath, I'd fumbled with the inside-out umbrella and muttered to a clerk about the goddamn endless rain.

The clerk hadn't known what I meant. "But it started just a minute ago."

I shuddered, but not from the water dripping off me.

Gail heard me out and paled. Her joy turned into frightened disbelief. "As soon as you came back, the storm began again."

I flinched as the bottom fell out of my soggy grocery bag. Ignoring the cans and boxes of food on the floor, I hurried to find a weather station on the radio. But the announcer's static-garbled voice sounded as bewildered as his counterparts throughout Nebraska.

His report was the same. The weather pattern made no sense. The front was tiny, localized, and stationary. Half a mile away, the sky was cloudless. In a small circumference, however, Iowa City was enduring its most savage storm on record. Downtown streets were . . .

I shut off the radio.

Thinking frantically, I told Gail I was going to my office at the university to see if I had any mail. But my motive was quite different, and I hoped she wouldn't think of it.

She started to speak as Jeff came into the kitchen, interrupting us, his eyes bleak with cabin fever. "Drive me down to Freddie's, Dad?"

I didn't have the heart to tell him no.

At the school, the parking lot was flecked with rain. There weren't any puddles. I live a mile away. I went in the English building and asked a secretary, although I knew what she'd tell me.

"No, Mr. Price. All morning it's been clear. The rain's just beginning."

In my office, I phoned home.

"The rain stopped," Gail said. "You won't believe how beautiful the sky is, bright and sunny."

I stared from my office window toward a storm so black and ugly that I barely saw the whitecaps on the angry, churning river.

Fear coiled in my guts, then hissed and struck.

The pattern was always the same. No matter where I went, the storm went with me. When I left, the storm left, as well. It got worse. Nine days of it. Then ten. Eleven. Twelve. Our basement flooded, as did all the other basements in the district. Streets eroded. There were mud slides. Shingles blew away. Attics leaked. Retaining walls fell over. Lightning struck the electricity poles so often, the food spoiled in our freezer. We lit candles. If our stove hadn't used gas, we couldn't have cooked. As in Grand Island, an emergency was declared, the damage so great that it couldn't be calculated.

What hurt the most was seeing the effect on Gail and Jeff. The constant chilly dampness gave them colds. I sneezed and sniffled, too, but didn't care about myself because Gail's spirits sank the more it rained. Her eyes became a dismal gray. She had no energy. She put on sweaters and rubbed her listless, aching arms.

Jeff went to bed much earlier than usual. He slept later. He looked thin. His eyes had dark circles.

And he had nightmares. As lightning cracked, his screams woke us. Again the electricity wasn't working. We used flashlights as we hurried to his room.

"Wake up, Jeff! You're only dreaming!"

"The Indian!" Moaning, he rubbed his frightened eyes.

Thunder rumbled, making Gail jerk.

"What Indian?" I said.

"He warned you."

"Son, I don't know what—"

"In Colorado." Gail turned sharply, startling me with the hollows the darkness cast on her cheeks. "The weather dancer."

"You mean that witch doctor?"

On our trip, we'd stopped in a dingy desert town for gas and seen a meager group of tourists studying a roadside Indian display. A shack, rickety tables, beads and drums and belts. Skeptical, I'd walked across. A scruffy Indian, who looked to be at least a hundred, dressed in threadbare, faded vestments, had chanted gibberish while he danced around a circle of rocks in the dust.

"What's going on?" I asked a woman aiming a camera.

"He's a medicine man. He's dancing to make it rain and end the drought."

I scuffed the dust and glanced at the burning sky. My head ached from the heat and the long, oppressive drive. I'd seen too many sleazy roadside stands, too many Indians ripping off tourists, selling overpriced, inauthentic artifacts. Imperfect turquoise, shoddy silver. They'd turned their back on their heritage and prostituted their traditions.

I didn't care how much they hated us for what we'd done to them. What bothered me was that behind their stoical faces, they laughed as they duped us.

Whiskey fumes wafted from the ancient Indian as he clumsily danced around the circle, chanting.

"Can he do it?" Jeff asked. "Can he make it rain?"

"It's a gimmick," I said. "Watch these tourists put money in that so-called native bowl he bought at Sears."

The tourists heard me, their rapt faces suddenly suspicious.

The old man stopped performing. "Gimmick?" He glared.

"I didn't mean to speak so loudly. I'm sorry if I ruined your routine."

"I made that bowl myself."

"Of course you did."

He lurched across, the whiskey fumes stronger. "You don't think my dance can make it rain?"

"I couldn't care less if you fool these tourists, but my son should know the truth."

"You want convincing?"

"I said I was sorry."

"White men always say they're sorry."

Gail came over, glancing furtively around. Embarrassed, she tugged at my sleeve. "The gas tank's full. Let's go."

I backed away.

"You'll see it rain! You'll pray it stops!" the old man shouted.

Jeff looked terrified, and that made me angry. "Shut your mouth! You scared my son!"

"He wonders if I can make it rain? Watch the sky! I dance for *you* now! When the lightning strikes, remember me!"

We got in the car. "That crazy coot. Don't let him bother you. The sun cooked his brain."

"All right, he threatened me. So what?" I asked. "Gail, you surely can't believe he sent this storm. By dancing? Think. It isn't possible."

"Then tell me why it's happening."

"A hundred weather experts tried but can't explain it. How can I?"

"The storm's linked to you. It never leaves you."

"It's . . ."

I meant to say "coincidence," but the word had lost its meaning and died in my throat. I studied Gail and Jeff, and in the glare of the flashlights, I realized they blamed me. We were adversaries, both of them against me.

"The rain, Dad. Can't you make it stop?"

I cried when he whispered, "Please."

Department of Meteorology. It consisted of a full professor, one associate, and one assistant. I'd met the full professor at a cocktail party several years ago. We sometimes played tennis together. On occasion, we had lunch. I knew his office hours and braved the storm to go see him.

Again the parking lot was speckled with increasing raindrops when I got there. I ran through raging wind and shook my raincoat in the lobby of his building. I'd phoned ahead. He was waiting.

Forty-five, freckled, almost bald. In damn fine shape, though, as I knew from many tennis games I'd lost.

"The rain's back." He shook his head disgustedly.

"No explanation yet?"

"I'm supposed to be the expert. Your guess would be as good as mine. If this keeps up, I'll take to reading tea leaves."

"Maybe superstition's . . ." I wanted to say "the answer," but I couldn't force myself.

"What?" He leaned ahead.

I rubbed my aching forehead. "What causes thunderstorms?"

He shrugged. "Two different fronts collide. One's hot and moist. The other's cold and dry. They bang together so hard that they explode. The lightning and thunder are the blast. The rain's the fallout."

"But in *this* case?"

"That's the problem. We don't have two different fronts. Even if we did, the storm would move because of vacuums the winds create. But this storm stays right here. It only shifts a half a mile or so and then comes back. It's forcing us to reassess the rules."

"I don't know how to say this." But somehow I told him. Everything.

He frowned. "And you believe this?"

"I'm not sure. My wife and son do. Is it possible?"

He put some papers away. He poured two cups of coffee. He did everything but rearrange his bookshelves.

"Is it possible?" I said.

"If you repeat this, I'll deny it."

"How much crazier can—"

"In the sixties, when I was in grad school, I went on a field trip to Mexico. The mountain valleys have such complicated weather patterns, they're perfect for a dissertation. One place gets so much rain that the villages are flooded. Ten miles away, another valley gets no rain whatsoever. In one valley I studied, something had gone wrong. It normally had lots of rain. For seven years, though, it had been completely dry. The valley next to it, normally dry, was getting all the rain. No explanation. God knows, I worked hard to find one. People were forced to leave their homes and go where the rain was. In this seventh summer, they stopped hoping the weather would behave the way it used to. They wanted to return to their valley, so they sent for special help. A weather dancer. He claimed to be a descendant of the Mayans. He arrived one day and paced the valley, praying to all the compass points. Where they intersected in the valley's middle, he arranged a wheel of stones. He put on vestments. He danced around the wheel. One day later, it was raining, and the weather pattern went back to the way it used to be. I told myself he'd been lucky, that he'd somehow read the signs of nature and danced when he was positive it would rain. But I saw those clouds rush in, and they were strange. They didn't move on until the streams were flowing and the wells were full. Coincidence? Special knowledge? Who can say? But it troubles me when I think about what happened in that valley."

"Then the Indian I met could cause this storm?"

"Who knows? Look, I'm a scientist. I trust in facts. But sometimes *superstition*'s a word we use for science we don't understand."

"What happens if the storm continues, if it doesn't stop?"

"Whoever lives beneath it will have to move, or else they'll die."

"But what if it follows someone?"

"You really believe it would?"

"It does!"

He studied me. "You ever hear of a superstorm?"

Dismayed, I shook my head.

"On rare occasions, several storms will climb on top of one another. They can tower as high as seven miles."

I felt my heart lurch.

"But this storm's already climbed that high. It's heading up to ten miles now. It'll soon tear houses from foundations. It'll level everything. A stationary half-mile-wide tornado."

"If I'm right, though, if the old man wants to punish me, I can't escape. Unless my wife and son are separate from me, they'll die, too."

"Assuming you're right. But I have to emphasize. There's no scientific reason to believe your theory."

"I think I'm crazy."

* * *

Eliminate the probable, then the possible. What's left must be the explanation. Either Gail and Jeff would die or they'd have to leave me. But I couldn't bear losing them.

I knew what I had to do. I struggled through the storm to get back home. Jeff was feverish. Gail kept coughing, glaring at me in accusation.

They argued when I told them, but in desperation, they agreed.

"If what we think is true," I said, "once I'm gone, the storm'll stop. You'll see the sun again."

"But what about you? What'll happen?"

"Pray for me."

The interstate again, heading west. The storm, of course, went with me.

Iowa. Nebraska. It took me three insane, disastrous weeks to get to Colorado. Driving through rain-swept mountains was a nightmare. But I finally reached that dingy desert town. I found that sleazy roadside stand.

No trinkets, no beads. As the storm raged, turning dust to mud, I searched the town, begging for information. "That old Indian. The weather dancer."

"He took sick," a store owner said.

"Where is he?"

"How should I know? Try the reservation."

It was fifteen miles away. The road was serpentine, narrow, and mucky. I passed rocks so hot that they steamed from rain. The car slid, crashing into a ditch, resting on its driveshaft. I ran through lightning and thunder, drenched and moaning when I stumbled to the largest building on the reservation. It was low and wide, made from stone. I pounded on the door. A man in a uniform opened it, the agent for the government.

I told him.

He frowned with suspicion. Turning, he spoke a different language to some Indians in the office. They answered.

He nodded. "You must want him bad," he said, "if you came out here in this storm. You're almost out of time. The old man's dying."

In the reservation's hospital, the old man lay motionless under sheets, an IV in his arm. Shriveled, he looked like a dry, empty corn husk. He slowly opened his eyes. They gleamed with recognition.

"I believe you now," I said. "Please, make the rain stop."

He breathed in pain.

"My wife and son believe. It isn't fair to make them suffer. Please." My voice rose. "I shouldn't have said what I did. I'm sorry. Make it stop."

The old man squirmed.

I sank to my knees, kissed his hand, and sobbed. "I know I don't deserve it. But I'm begging you. I've learned my lesson. Stop the rain."

The old man studied me and slowly nodded. The doctor tried to restrain him, but the old man's strength was extraordinary. He crawled from bed. He hobbled. Slowly, in evident pain, he chanted and danced.

The lightning and thunder worsened. Rain slashed the windows. The old man strained to dance harder. The frenzy of the storm increased. Its strident fury soared. It reached a crescendo, hung there—and stopped.

The old man fell. Gasping, I ran to him and helped the doctor lift him into bed.

The doctor scowled. "You almost killed him."

"He isn't dead?"

"No thanks to you."

But that was the word I used: "Thanks." To the old man and the powers in the sky.

I left the hospital. The sun, a once-common sight, overwhelmed me.

Four days later, back in Iowa, I got the call. The agent from the government. He thought I'd want to know. That morning, the old man had died.

I turned to Gail and Jeff. Their colds were gone. From warm, sunny weeks while I was away, their skin was brown again. They seemed to have forgotten how the nightmare had nearly destroyed us, more than just our lives, our love. Indeed, they were now skeptical about the Indian and told me that the rain would have stopped, no matter what I did.

But they hadn't been in the hospital to see him dance. They didn't understand.

I set the phone down and swallowed with sadness. Stepping from our house—it rests on a hill—I peered in admiration toward the glorious sky.

I turned and faltered.

To the west, a massive cloud bank approached, dark and thick and roiling. Wind began, bringing a chill.

September 12. The temperature was seventy-eight. It dropped to fifty, then thirty-two.

The rain had stopped. The old man had done what I'd asked. But I hadn't counted on his sense of humor.

He had stopped the rain, all right.

But I had a terrible feeling that the snow would never end.

For These and
All My Sins

*I*f there's a touch of humor in the final line of "The Storm," there's nothing at all humorous in this next story about the Midwest: a gross-out shocker. Although the story was published in 1984, its origin is eleven years earlier. In the summer of 1973, I spent thirty-five days on a survival course in the Wind River Range of Wyoming. The course was conducted by Paul Petzoldt's National Outdoor Leadership School and trained its students in a variety of mountaineering skills: climbing, camping without a trace, crossing wild streams, living in snow caves, scavenging, and so on. At the end of the course, our food was taken away from us. We were each allowed to keep a compass, a map, and a canteen. We were shown a spot on the map, fifty miles away, over the Continental Divide, and told that three days later a truck would be waiting to pick us up.

How did we eat? We weren't supposed to. The idea

was to replicate an emergency situation. Scavenging uses more energy than is supplied by the plants that are scavenged, so that was out. We could have caught and eaten fish, which would have provided adequate protein, but that would have been as a last measure. The idea was to prove to us that we could go three days without food, in strenuous conditions, and still be functional at the end. I was weak and light-headed when we came over the mountains and reached the dusty trailhead that was our destination, but I could have gone a day or two longer, and I certainly had acquired confidence about the outdoors. The course completed, I set out toward Iowa along Interstate 80, but my old four-cylinder Porsche 912 developed engine trouble, and in the Nebraska panhandle, I had to leave the highway, hoping to find a mechanic. That's when I came to this very unusual, very scary town. While the story is fictional, the setting is not.

THERE WAS A TREE. I REMEMBER IT. I SWEAR I'D BE able to recognize it. Because it looked so unusual.

It stood on my left, in the distance, by Interstate 80. At first, it was just a blur in the shimmering heat haze, but as I drove closer, its skeletal outline became distinct. Skeletal: That's what struck me at first as being strange. After all, in August, even in the sun-parched Nebraska panhandle, trees (the few you see) are thick with leaves, but this one was bare.

So it's dead, I thought. So what? Nothing to frown about. But then I noticed the second thing about it, and I guess I'd subconsciously been reacting before I even realized what its silhouette resembled.

Stronger than resembled.

I felt uneasy. The tree was very menorah-like, a giant counterpart of the candelabrum used for Jewish religious services. Nine candles in a row. Except in this case, the candles were barren branches standing straight. I shrugged off an eerie tingle. It's just a freak, an accident of nature, I concluded, although I briefly wondered if someone had pruned the tree to give it that distinctive appearance and in the process had unavoidably killed it.

But coincidence or not, the shape struck me as being uncanny—a religious symbol formed by a sterile tree ironically blessing a drought-wracked western plain. I thought of *The Waste Land*.

For the past two weeks, I'd been camping with friends in the Wind River Range of Wyoming. Fishing, exploring, rock climbing, mostly sitting around our cook fire, drinking, reminiscing. After our long-postponed reunion, our time together had gone too quickly. Again we'd separated, heading our different ways across the country, back to wives and children, jobs and obligations. For me, that meant Iowa City, home, and the university. As much as I wanted to see my family again, I dreaded the prospect of still another fall semester, preparing classes, grading freshmen papers.

Weary from driving (eight hours east since a wrenching emotional farewell breakfast), I glanced from the weird menorah tree and realized I was doing seventy. Slow down, I told myself. You'll end up getting a ticket.

Or killed.

And that's when the engine started shuddering. I drive a secondhand Porsche 912, the kind with four cylin-

ders, from the sixties. I bought it cheap because it needed
a lot of bodywork, but despite its age, it usually worked
like a charm. The trouble is, I didn't know the carburetors
had to be adjusted for the thinner air of a higher altitude,
so when I'd reached the mountains in Wyoming, the engine had sputtered, the carburetors had overflowed, and
I'd rushed to put out a devastating fire on the engine. In
Lander, Wyoming, a garage had repaired the damage
while I went camping with my friends, but when I'd
come back to get it, the accelerator hadn't seemed as re-
sponsive as it used to be. All day, the motor had sounded
a little noisier than usual, and now as it shuddered, it
wasn't just noisy; it was thunderous. Oh, Christ, I
thought. The fire must have cracked the engine block.
Whatever was wrong, I didn't dare go much farther. The
steering wheel was jerking in my hands. Scared, I slowed
to thirty. The roar and shudder persisted. I needed to find
a mechanic fast.

   I said this happened in Nebraska's panhandle.
Imagine the state as a wide rectangle. Cut away the
bottom-left corner. The remaining *top*-left corner—
that's the panhandle, just to the east of Wyoming. It's
nothing but broad, flat, open range. Scrub grass, sagebrush, tumbleweed. The land's as desolate as when the
pioneers struggled across it a hundred years ago. A couple more hours into Nebraska, I wouldn't have worried
too much. Towns start showing up every twenty miles
or so. But heading through the panhandle, I hadn't seen
a sign for a town in quite a while. Despite the false security of the four-lane interstate, I might as well have
been on the moon.

As a consequence, when I saw the off-ramp, I didn't think twice. Thanking whatever god had smiled on me, I struggled with the spastic tremors of the steering wheel and exited, wincing as the engine not only roared but crackled, as if bits of metal were breaking off inside and scraping, gouging. There wasn't a sign for a town at this exit, but I knew there had to be a reason for the off-ramp. Reaching a stop sign, I glanced right and left along a two-lane blacktop but saw no buildings either way. So which direction? I asked myself. On impulse, I chose the left and crossed the bridge above the interstate, only then realizing I was heading toward the menorah tree.

Again I felt that eerie tingle. But the shuddering roar of the engine distracted me. The accelerator heaved beneath my foot, sending spasms up my leg. The car could barely do twenty miles an hour now. I tried to control my nervous breathing, vaguely sensing the tree as I passed it.

On my left. I'm sure of it. I wasn't so preoccupied that I wouldn't remember. The tree was on the left of the unmarked two-lane road.

I'm positive. I know I'm not wrong.

I drove. And drove. The Porsche seemed ready to fall apart at any moment, jolting, rattling. The road stretched ahead, leading nowhere, seemingly forever. With the menorah tree behind me, nothing relieved the dismal prairie landscape. Anytime now, I thought. I'll see some buildings. Just another mile or so—if the car can manage that far.

It did, and another mile after that, but down to fifteen now. My stomach cramped. I had the terrible sense I should have gone the other way along this road. For all I knew, I'd have reached a town in a minute. But now I'd gone so far in this direction, I had to keep going. I wasn't sure the car could fight its way back to the interstate.

When I'd first seen the menorah tree, the clock on my dashboard had shown it was almost 5:00 P.M. As I glanced at the clock again, I winced when I saw it was near 6:00. Christ, just a few more hours of light, and even if I found a garage, the chances were it wouldn't stay open after six o'clock. Premonitions squeezed my chest. I should have stayed on the interstate, I thought. There at least, if the car broke down, I could have flagged down someone going by and asked them to send a tow truck. Here, I hadn't seen any traffic. Visions of a night spent at the side of the road in my disabled car were dismally matched by the wearying prospect of the long hike back to the interstate. I'd been planning to drive all night in hopes of reaching home in Iowa City by noon tomorrow, but if my luck kept turning sour, I might not get there for at best another day, and likely more, supposing the engine was as bad as the roar made it seem. I had to find a phone and tell my wife not to worry when I didn't reach home at the time I'd said I would. My thoughts became more urgent. I had to—

That's when I saw the building. In the distance. Hard to make out, a vague rectangular object, but unmistakably a building, its metal roof reflecting the glint of the lowering sun. Then I saw another building, and another. Trees. Thank God, a town. My heart pounded almost as hard as the engine rattled. I clutched the steering wheel, frantically trying to control it, lurching past a water tower and an empty cattle pen. The buildings became distinct: houses, a car lot, a diner.

And a service station, where I lurched to a raw-nerved stop, my hands still shaking from the vibrations of the steering wheel. I shut off the engine, grateful for the sudden quiet, and noticed two men at the pump, their backs to me. Self-conscious about my beard stubble and my sweat-drenched clothes, I got out wearily to ask directions.

The fact that they had their backs to me should have told me right away that something was wrong. I'd made such a racket pulling up, it wasn't normal for them not to turn, curious, wondering what the hell was coming.

But they didn't, and I was too exhausted for my instincts to jangle, warning me. Stiff-legged, I approached them. "Excuse me," I said. "I guess you can tell I've got some trouble. Is the mechanic still on duty?"

Neither turned or answered.

They must have heard me, I thought. All the same, I repeated louder, "The mechanic. Is he still on duty?"

No response.

For Christ sake, are they deaf or what? So I walked around to face them.

Even as they pivoted to show me their backs again, I gaped. Because I'd seen a brief glimpse of their faces. Oh my God. I felt as if an ice-cold needle had pierced my spine. I'd never seen a leper. All the same, from what I'd read, I imagined a leper might have been less ugly than what I was looking at. *Ugly* isn't strong enough to describe what I saw. Not just the swollen goiter bulging from each throat like an obscene Adam's apple. Not just the twisted jaws and cheekbones or the massive lumps on their foreheads. Or the distended lips and misshapen nostrils. Worse, their skin itself seemed rotten, gray and mushy. Like festering open sores.

I nearly gagged. My throat contracted so that I couldn't breathe. Get control, I told myself. Whatever's wrong with them, it's not their fault. Don't gape like a six-year-old who's never seen someone malformed before. Obviously, that's why they didn't want to look at me. Because they hated the disgusted reaction, the awful sickened stare.

They faced the door to the service station now, and I certainly wasn't about to walk in front of them again, so I repeated, "The mechanic. Where is he?"

As one, they each raised their right arm and pointed horribly twisted fingers toward the right, toward a gravel road that led out of town, parallel to the interstate miles away.

Well, damn it, I thought. I'm sorry about what's happened to you. I wish there was some way to help you, but right now I need to help myself, and you two guys are rude.

I stalked away, my head beginning to ache, my throat feeling raw. A quick glance at my watch showed it was seven o'clock. The sun, of course, was lower. If I didn't find a mechanic soon . . .

Across the street, on the corner, I saw a restaurant. Perhaps too kind a description. Greasy spoon would have been more accurate. The windows looked grimy. The posters for Pepsi and Schlitz looked ten years old. BAR-B-

CUE, a dingy neon sign said. Why not shorten it, I thought, to BBC, which if you change the C to G stands for botulism and bad gas?

And why not stop with the jokes? You might be eating there tonight.

That's almost funny now. Eating, I mean. Dear God, I don't know how long I can stand this.

. . . So I walked across the dusty street and opened the fly-covered, creaky screen door, peering in at five customers. "Hey, anybody know where—"

The words caught in my throat. My mind reeled. Because the customers had already shifted, turning, with their backs to me—and *these* had humps and twisted spines and shoulders wrenched in directions nature had never intended. In shock, I hurriedly glanced at the waitress behind the counter, and she'd turned her back, as well. The mirror, though. The goddamn mirror. Her face reflecting off it seemed the result of a hideous genetic experiment. She had no jaw. And only one eye. I stumbled back, letting the door swing shut with a creak and a bang, my mind still retaining the terrible impression of—it couldn't be—two slits where there should have been a nose.

I'll make this quick. Everywhere I went, growing ever more apprehensive, I found monsters. The town was like a hundred horror movies squeezed together. Lon Chaney's worst makeup inventions almost seemed normal by comparison. The island of Dr. Moreau would have been a resort for beauty-contest winners.

Jesus.

Eight o'clock. The eastern sky was turning gray. The

western horizon was the red of blood. I wondered if I'd gone insane. A town of monsters, no one speaking to me, everyone turning away, most pointing toward the gravel road that headed east out of town.

Appalled, I scrambled into the Porsche, turned the key, and the rest hadn't done the car any good. If anything, the engine roared and shuddered more extremely. Stomach scalding, I prayed. Although the Porsche shook and protested, it blessedly managed to move.

A town, I thought. Maybe there's another town a few miles along that gravel road. Maybe that's why they pointed down there.

I rattled and heaved and jolted out of town, switching on my emergency flashers, although I didn't know why, since I'd seen no traffic. All the same, with dusk coming on, it didn't hurt to be careful.

A quarter mile. Then half a mile. That's as far as I got before the engine failed completely. It's probable that only one cylinder was working by then. I'd hear a bang, then three silent beats, then another bang and three more silent beats. With every bang, the car crept forward a little. Then it finally wheezed and coasted to a stop. The motor pinged from the heat. A Porsche doesn't have a radiator, but I swear I heard a hiss.

And that was that, stuck in the middle of nowhere, a town of horrors behind me, an empty landscape ahead of me, and an interstate God knew how far away.

With night approaching.

On the prairie.

I've said I was frightened. But then I got mad. At my luck and the guy in Lander who'd "fixed" my car, at my-

self and my stupidity for having left the highway, not to
mention my failure to think ahead when I was back in
town. I should have bought some soft drinks anyhow,
some candy bars and potato chips or something—anything to keep from starving all night out here in the dark.
A beer. Hell, considering the way I felt, a six-pack. Might
as well get shit-faced.

Angry, I stepped from the car. I leaned against a
fender and lit a cigarette and cursed. Eight-thirty now.
Dusk thickened. What was I going to do?

I try to convince myself I was being logical. By nine
o'clock, I'd made my choice. The town was only half a
mile away. Ten minutes' walk at most. If that stupid Bar-
B-Cue had stayed open, I could still get some beer and
chips. At the moment, I didn't care how revolting those
people looked. I'd be damned if I was going to spend the
night out here with my stomach rumbling. That'd be one
discomfort too many.

So I walked, and when I reached the outskirts, night
at last had fallen. The lights were on in the Bar-B-Cue; at
least my luck hadn't failed entirely. Or so I thought, because the lights quickly went off as I got closer. Swell, I
thought in disgust.

The place stayed dark.

But then the door creaked open. The waitress—a
vague white shape—stepped out. She locked the door behind her. I almost asked if she'd mind waiting so I could
buy some food. Naturally, I assumed she hadn't seen me.
That's why she surprised me when she turned.

I blinked, astonished. In contrast with the way the
town had treated me, she actually spoke. Her voice was

frail and wispy, the words slurred, suggestive of a cleft palate or a hair lip. "I saw you," she said. "Through the window. Coming back." Maybe I imagined it, but her whispered cadence sounded musical.

And this is important, too. Although we faced each other, the street had no lights, and the darkness had thickened enough that I couldn't see her features. For the first time since I'd arrived in town, I felt as if I was having a normal conversation. It wasn't hard to pretend, as long as I forced myself not to remember the horror of what she looked like.

I managed a shrug, a laugh of despair. "My car broke down. I'm stuck out there." Although I knew she couldn't see my gesture, I pointed down the pitch-dark road. "I hoped you'd still be open so I could get something to eat."

She didn't answer for a moment. Then abruptly she said, "I'm sorry. The owner closed a half hour ago. I stayed to clean up and get things ready for tomorrow. The grill's cold."

"But just some beer? Potato chips or something?"

"Can't. The cash register's empty."

"But I don't care about change. I'll pay you more than the stuff is worth."

Again she didn't answer for a moment. "Beer and potato chips?"

"Please." My hopes rose. "If you wouldn't mind."

"While you spend the night in your car?"

"Unless there's a hotel."

"There isn't. You need a decent meal, a proper place to sleep. Considering the trouble you're in."

She paused. I remember the night was silent. Not even crickets sang.

"I live alone," she said, her cadence even more musical. "You can sleep on the sofa in the living room. I'll broil a steak for you."

"I couldn't," I said. The thought of seeing her face again filled me with panic.

"I won't turn the lights on. I won't disgust you."

I lied. "It's just that I don't want to inconvenience you."

"No trouble." She sounded emphatic. "I want to help. I've always believed in charity."

She began to walk away. Paralyzed, I thought about it. For sure, the steak sounded good. And the sofa. A hell of a lot better than sleeping hunched in the car.

But Jesus, the way she looked.

And maybe my attitude was painfully familiar to her. How would I feel, I wondered, if I were deformed and people shunned me? Charity. Hadn't she said she believed in charity? Well, maybe it was time I believed in it myself. I followed her, less motivated by the steak and the sofa than by my determination to be kind.

She lived three blocks away, on a street as dark as the one we'd left. The houses were still, no sounds, no sign of anyone. It was the strangest walk of my life.

From what I could tell in the dark, she lived in an old two-story Victorian house. The porch floor squeaked as we crossed it to go inside. And true to her word, she didn't turn on the lights.

"The living room's through an arch to your left," she

said. "The sofa's against the wall straight ahead. I'll fix the steak."

I thanked her and did what she said. The sofa was deep and soft. I hadn't realized how tired I was until I leaned back. In the dark, I heard the sizzle of the steak from somewhere at the back of the house. I assume she turned the kitchen lights on to cook it, but I didn't see even the edge of a glow. Then the fragrance of the beef drifted toward me. Echoing footsteps came near.

"I should have asked how well-done you like it. Most customers ask for medium rare." Her wispy voice sounded like wind chimes.

"Great." I no longer cared if she was ugly. By then I was ravenous.

In the dark, she cautiously set up a tray, brought the steak, bread and butter, A.1. sauce, and a beer. Although awkward because I couldn't see, I ate amazingly fast. I couldn't get enough of it. *Delicious* couldn't describe it. Mouth-watering. Taste-bud-expanding. Incredible.

I sopped up sauce and steak juice with my final remnant of bread, stuffed it in my mouth, washed it down with my final sip of beer, and sagged back, knowing I'd eaten the best meal of my life.

Throughout, she'd sat in a chair across the room and hadn't spoken once.

"That was wonderful," I said. "I don't know how to thank you."

"You already have."

I wasn't sure what she meant. My belly felt reassuringly packed to the bursting point.

"You haven't asked," she said.

I frowned. "Asked what? I don't understand."

"You do. You're dying to ask. I know you are. They always are."

"They?"

"Why the people here are horribly deformed."

I felt a chill. In truth, I had been tempted to ask. The town was so unusual, the people so strange, I could barely stifle my curiosity. She'd been so generous, though, I didn't want to draw attention to her infirmity and be rude. At once, her reflection in the mirror at the Bar-B-Cue popped up terribly in my mind. No chin. One eye. Flat slits where there should have been a nose. Oozing sores.

I almost vomited. And not just from the memory. Something was happening in my stomach. It churned and complained, growling, swelling larger, as if it were crammed with a million tiny darting hornets.

"Sins," she said.

I squirmed, afraid.

"Long ago," she said, "in the Middle Ages, certain priests used to travel from village to village. Instead of hearing confessions, they performed a ceremony to cleanse the souls of the villagers. Each member of the group brought something to eat and set it on a table in front of the priest. At last, an enormous meal awaited him. He said the necessary words. All the sins of the village were transferred into the food."

I swallowed bile, unaccountably terrified.

"And then he ate the meal. Their sins," she said. "He stuffed himself with sins."

Her tone was so hateful, I wanted to scream and run.

"The villagers knew he'd damned himself to save

their souls. For this, they gave him money. Of course, there were disbelievers, who maintained the priest was nothing more than a cheat, a con man tricking the villagers into feeding him and giving him money. They were wrong."

I heard her stand.

"Because the evidence was clear. The sins had their effect. The evil spread through the sin-eater's body, festering, twisting, bulging to escape."

I heard her doing something in the corner. I tensed from the sound of scratching.

"And not just priests ate sins," she said. "Sometimes special women did it, too. But the problem was, suppose the sin-eater wanted to be redeemed, as well? How could a sin-eater get rid of the sins? Get rid of the ugliness. By passing the sins along, of course. By having them eaten by someone else."

"You're crazy," I said. "I'm getting out of here."

"No, not just yet."

I realized the scratching sound was a match being struck. A tiny flame appeared. My stomach soured in pulsing agony.

"A town filled with sin-eaters," she said. "Monsters shunned by the world. Bearable only to one another. Suffering out of charity for the millions of souls who've been redeemed."

She lit a candle. The light grew larger in the room. I saw her face and gaped again, but this time for a different reason. She was beautiful. Stunning. Gorgeous. Her skin seemed to glow with sensuality.

It also seemed to shimmer, to ripple, to—

"No. My God," I said. "You put something in my food."

"I told you."

"Not that foolishness." I tried to stand, but my legs felt like plastic. My body seemed to expand, contract, and twist. My vision became distorted, as if I were peering at fun-house mirrors. "LSD? Was that it? Mescalin? I'm hallucinating." Each word echoed more loudly, yet seemed to murmur from far away.

I cringed as she approached, growing more beautiful with every step.

"And it's been so long," she said. "I've been so ugly. So long since anyone wanted me."

Reality cracked. The universe spun. She stripped off her uniform, showing her breasts, her . . . Her body was . . .

Despite the torture in my stomach, the insanity of my distorted senses, I wanted her. I suddenly needed her as desperately as anything I'd ever coveted.

Passion was endless, powerful, frantic. Rolling, we bumped the tray, sending glass and plate, knife and fork and steak sauce crashing down. A lamp fell, shattering. My naked back slammed against the sharp edge of a table, making me groan. Not from pain. I screamed in ecstasy.

And just before I came with an explosive burst, as if from the core of my soul, as if after foisting her sins upon me, she needed something from me in return, I felt her drawing me close to her, down, ever down.

She moaned and pleaded, "Eat me. Eat me!"

I lost consciousness. The Nebraska state police claimed they found me wandering naked down the middle of Interstate 80 at one o'clock in the afternoon two days later. They said I was horribly sunburned. I don't know. I don't remember. All I recall is waking up in the hospital in Iowa City.

In the psych ward.

The doctors lied. They claimed I wasn't ugly. Then why would they have locked me up and taken the mirrors away? Why would the nurses have flinched when they came in with guards to feed me? They thought they were so smart, but I knew the truth. Despite the thick wire screen across the window, at night I saw my reflection. I don't have a chin. There's only one eye. In place of a nose, I've got two flat, repulsive slits. I'm being punished. I understand that now. For all the evil in the world.

I used to be a Catholic, but I don't go to church anymore. When I was young, though, learning to go to confession, the nuns made me learn a speech to say to the priest in the booth: "Bless me, Father, for I have sinned. My last confession was . . ." And then I'd tell him how long ago, and then I'd confess, and then I'd finish by saying, "I'm sorry for these and all my sins." I am, you know. I'm sorry. Except I didn't commit them. The sins aren't mine.

My wife and children came to visit. I refused to let them see me. I couldn't bear to see the sickened reaction in their eyes.

"How could a sin-eater get rid of the sins?" That's what she said to me. "By passing the sins along, of course. By having them eaten by someone else."

I've known for several weeks now what I had to do. It was simply a matter of pretending to be calm, of waiting for my chance. I hope the guard wasn't badly hurt. I tried not to hit him too hard. But his head made a terrible sound when I cracked it against the wall.

I've been very clever. I've stolen three cars, and I've never kept one long enough for the state police to catch me. It's taken me two days to return.

That's why the tree's so important. It's my landmark, you see. Remember, the off-ramp had no sign. The tree's all I had to give me direction.

But I'm puzzled. Oh, I found the tree all right, its branches in the shape of the menorah candelabrum. And it's so distinctive, I can't believe there'd be another like it. But I swear it had eight upright branches then, and it was bare.

But now it's got nine.

And leaves have sprouted.

Dear God, help me. Save me.

I pressed the accelerator to the floor, racing along the two-lane blacktop. As before, the road stretched forever. Doubt made me frantic. I tried not to glance at the rearview mirror. All the same, I weakened, and my ugliness made me wail.

I saw the building in the distance, the glint of sunlight off the metal roof. I whimpered, rushing closer. And I found the town again. Exactly the same. The water tower. The cattle pen (but it's full now). The service station, the Bar-B-Cue.

I don't understand, though. Everyone's normal. I see no goiters, no hunchbacks, no twisted limbs and festering sores. They stare as I drive past. I can't stand to see their shock and disgust.

. . . I've found her house. I'm in here waiting.

In the hospital, the doctors said I was having delusions. They agreed my initial suspicion might have been correct—that some chemical in my food could have made me hallucinate, and now the effects of the drug persist, making me think I'm ugly, distorting my memory of the trip. I wish I could believe that. I even wish I could believe I've gone crazy. Anything would be better than the truth.

But I know what it is. She *did* it. She made me eat her sins. But damn it, I'll get even with her. I'll make her take them back.

I've been writing this in her living room while I glance hurriedly out the window. In case something happens to me, so people will understand. It wasn't my fault.

But she'll come home soon. Yes, she will. And then

I hear a car door. On the street, someone's stepping from a station wagon.

Oh, sweet Christ, at last. But no, it's not one person. Two. A man and a woman.

And the woman isn't the one I want.

What *happened*? Did she leave?

They'll come in. They'll find me.

I don't care. I can't bear this anymore. I have to pass the sins along. I have to . . .

I found a knife in the kitchen. See, I don't know the words. I don't know how to put my sins in the food.

But I remember the last thing she said to me. I know how to do it. I have to use the knife and a fork and make them—

Eat me.

Black and White and Red All Over

*T*he following three stories were written as a group and published together in 1985 as part of the Night Visions series. Their common theme is ambition and the dark side of success. Each is about a specific occupation—in this first case, a paperboy. I have a special fondness for this story because when my son, Matt, was twelve, he liked to earn extra money delivering newspapers. He had more than an adequate allowance, but like the chatty, likable boy you're about to meet, he was determined to be an entrepreneur. Because the route required him to get up every morning at 5:30, my wife and I couldn't resist helping. Often, before dawn, I set out with Matt, and in winter, that help was especially appreciated. It was appreciated even more when, over the space of a year, two paperboys disappeared in a neighboring city. Those boys were never found. As you might expect, the route had its tense mo-

ments, and part of the purpose of this story is to commu-
nicate how alone a paper carrier can feel early in the
morning. These days, the job is usually done by adults in
cars, but if you're in one of those rare places where boys
or girls still deliver the paper, next time your carrier
comes to the door, give a big tip.

YOU PROBABLY READ ABOUT ME IN THE PAPER THIS
morning. Fact is, if you live near the corner of Benton
and Sunset, I'm the kid who normally delivers it to you.
Course, I couldn't bring it to you today, being in the hospital and all with my arm busted and my skull what the
doctor says is fractured. My dad took over for me. To tell
the truth, I kinda miss doing the route. I've been delivering three years now, since I was nine, and it gets to be a
habit, even if I do have to wake up at 5:30 A.M., Christmas and New Year's and every day. But if you think I
slept in this morning, you're wrong. The nurses wake you
up early here, just the same as if my mom was nudging
me to crawl out of bed and make sure I put on my long
johns before I take the papers, 'cause it's awful cold these
snowy mornings. You have to walk the route instead of
riding your bike, and that takes a half hour longer, especially with the sky staying dark so long, and sometimes
you can't see the numbers on the houses when you're
looking for where a new customer lives.

The way this works, the *Gazette* has this guy in a
truck come along and drop a bundle in front of my house,
and my dad goes out to get the bundle and fold the papers
in my sack while I get dressed. A lot of times, there'll be
this card with the name of a new customer or else the

name of a customer who doesn't want the paper anymore, and then my mom and I'll have to add or subtract the name from my list and figure out how much the customer owes me, especially if he's starting or stopping in the middle of a week. It's pretty complicated, but my dad says it teaches me how to run a business, and the extra money comes in handy for buying CDs or playing video games, even if I do have to put a third of what I earn away in my bank account.

But I was telling you about my customers. You'd be surprised how close a kid can feel to the people he delivers the paper to. They wake up early and rush to get ready for work or whatever, and I figure the only fun they have is when they sit down at breakfast to read what happened while they were sleeping. It's sorta like catching up on gossip, I guess. They depend on me, and I've never been late delivering the papers, and the only times I've missed are when I was sick or like now from what happened yesterday morning. The bandages around my head feel itchy, and the cast on my arm's awful heavy. The nurses have written lots of jokes on it, though, so I'm looking forward to going back to school in two or three weeks, the doctor says, and showing it to all the kids.

You get to notice things about your customers, stuff a guy wouldn't think of unless he delivers papers. Like after a big football game—you can't believe how many people are awake with all the lights on before I even get there, waiting for the paper so they can find out something new about the game they already heard or went to or watched on TV. Or like this house on Gilby Street where for a week or so I had to hold my breath when I came up the sidewalk past the shrubs because of the worst scuzzy smell, like something really rotten. Even when I held my breath, it almost made me sick. Like the bad potatoes Mom found in the cellar last month. Nobody was picking up the papers I left. They just kept piling up beside the door, and after I told my dad, he looked at my mom kinda strange and said he'd better go over to see what was wrong. I could tell he figured maybe somebody was dead, and I guess I wondered that myself, but the way things turned out, those people were just on vacation, which is why the papers kept piling up, and the smell was only from these plastic bags of garbage they'd forgotten to put out and some dogs had torn open at the side of the house. That smell really made me nervous for a while, though.

And then there's the Carrigans. He lost his job at the mill last summer, and his wife likes fancy clothes, and they're always yelling about money when I'm next door playing with Ralph or when I come around to collect or even at six in the morning when I bring them the paper. Imagine that, getting up way before dawn to argue. Or what about old Mr. Blanchard? His wife's old, too, and she's sick with what my mom says is cancer, and I haven't seen Mrs. Blanchard in a couple months, but old Mr. Blanchard, he's up when I put the paper under the mat. I can see through his living room window where the light's on in the kitchen, and he's sitting at the table, hunched over, holding his head, and his shoulders are shaking. Even out front, I can hear him sobbing. It makes my throat tight. He always wears this old lumpy gray sweater. I'd feel sorry for him no matter what, but he cries like it's tearing his chest apart.

And then there's Mr. Lang. He's got this puffy face and a red-veined nose and squinty, angry eyes. He's always complaining about how much the paper costs and claims I'm cheating him by coming around more often than I should to collect, which of course I've never done. Two months ago, he started swearing at me, so I'm afraid to go over there. My dad says it's the whiskey makes him act like that, and now my dad collects from him. The last time my dad came back from there, he said Mr. Lang's not bad if you get to know him and realize he doesn't like his life, but I don't care. I want my dad to keep collecting from him.

I guess I was spooked by what you read about that happened in Granite Falls two months ago when Mr. Lang swore at me. That paperboy who disappeared. His parents waited for him to come home from his Sunday-morning route, and after they got calls from customers wanting to know where the paper was, his dad went out looking and found his sackful of papers a block away in an empty lot behind some bushes. You remember how the police and the neighbors went out searching, and the paper he worked for put his picture on the front page and offered a reward if anybody knew where he was, but they didn't find him. The police said he might've run away, but that didn't make any sense to me. It was too darn cold to run away, and where would he go? My dad says he read how the police even seemed to think the parents might have done something to him themselves and how the parents got so mad that they wanted to sue the police for saying that. One man was cruel enough to phone the parents and pretend he had the boy and ask for money, but the police traced the calls, and the man didn't have him. Now the man says it was just a joke, but I read where he's in lots of trouble.

Granite Falls. That's not too far from here. My dad said some nut from there could easily drive to other towns like ours. I wasn't going to give up my route, though, just because of what happened there. Like I said, I'm used to the money I make and going downtown on Saturdays to buy a new CD. But I felt kinda fluttery in my stomach. I sure didn't want to disappear myself. I'm old enough to know about the creepy things perverts do to kids. So my dad went with me the next few mornings on my route, and I took a flashlight when I started going alone again, and I delivered the papers fast, believe me. You can't guess what the wind scraping through bushes behind you in the dark can make you feel when it's early and there's nobody around to shout to for help. But after a month when nothing happened, I started feeling easier, ashamed of myself for getting scared like I was a little kid. I slipped back into my old routine, delivering the papers half-asleep, looking forward to the homemade Orange Julius my mom always has waiting for me when I get back from the route. I read the comics in the *Gazette* before I catch an extra hour of sleep till it's time for school. After being out in the snow, those blankets feel great.

Three weeks ago, another paperboy disappeared, this time right here in Crowell, and you remember how the neighbors searched the same as in Granite Falls, and his picture was in the *Gazette,* and the parents offered a reward, but they didn't find him, only his sack of papers stuffed behind some bushes like the last time. The police said it looked like the same MO. That's fancy police talk for "pattern." But heck, you don't have to go to police school to figure out that both kids disappeared the same way. And one kid might have run away, but not two of them, leastways not in the snow.

Oh, yeah, that's something I forgot to mention. Both mornings when the kids disappeared, it was snowing real hard, so there weren't any tracks except for the neighbors searching. No kid runs away in a blizzard, I'll tell you. The rest of us paperboys nearly went on what my dad calls a strike. Actually, it was our parents wanted us to quit delivering. They demanded police protection for us, but the police said we were overreacting, we shouldn't panic, and anyway, there weren't enough police to protect us all. The *Gazette* said if we stopped delivering, the paper would go out of business. They asked our parents to keep a close watch on us, and they made us sign a contract agreeing to give up seventy-five cents a month, so the paper could insure us in case something happened to us on the route.

Well, that made my dad twice as mad. He told me to quit, and I almost did, but I couldn't stop thinking of all the money I like to spend on Saturdays. My dad says I was born a capitalist and I'll probably grow up to vote Republican—whatever that means—but I told him I won a ribbon last year on the sixth-grade track team, and I could run faster than any pervert, I bet. Well, he just laughed and shook his head and told me he'd go out with me every morning, but my mom looked like she was going to cry. I guess moms are like that, always worrying. Besides, I said, I only have to worry if it's snowing. That's the only time the kids disappeared. My dad said that made sense, but all my mom said was, "We'll see," which is always bad news, like if you ask for a friend to stay overnight and your mom says, "We'll see," you figure she means no.

But she didn't. The next morning, my dad went with me on the route, and it was one of those sharp, cold times when your boots squeak on the snow and the air's so clean that you can hear a car start up three blocks away. I knew for sure I'd hear any pervert if he tried sneaking up on me, and anyway, my dad was with me, and all the other carriers had it as easy as I did. Still, every morning I got up praying it wasn't snowing, and lots of times it had snowed in the night but stopped, and when I saw the house across from ours clear in the streetlight, I felt like somebody had taken a rope from around my chest.

So we went on like that, getting up really early and doing the papers, and once my dad got the flu, so my mom went with me. You can believe it, she was nervous, more than me I guess. You should have seen us rushing to finish the route all the time we were looking over our shoulders. Mr. Carrigan was yelling at his wife like always, and Mr. Blanchard was crying for his own wife, and Mr. Lang was drinking beer when he opened his door and scared me, getting his paper. I almost wet my pants, no fooling. He asked if I wanted to step in and get warm, but I backed off, saying, "No, Mr. Lang, no thank you," holding up my hands and shaking my head. I forgot about his stairs behind me. I bet I'd have broken my arm even sooner than now if he'd shoveled them. But the snow made them soft, and when I tumbled to the bottom, I landed in a drift. He tried to help me, but I jumped up and ran away.

Then last Sunday I woke up, and even before I looked out, I knew from the shriek of the wind that it was snowing. My heart felt hard and small. I almost couldn't move. I tasted this sour stuff from my stomach. I couldn't see the house across the street. The snow was flying so thick and strong that I couldn't even see the maple tree in our front yard. As warm as I'd been in bed, I shivered like I was outside and the wind was stinging through my pajamas. I didn't want to go, but I knew that'd be all the excuse my mom'd need to make me quit, so I forced myself. I dressed real quick, long underwear and the rest, and put on my down-filled coat that almost doesn't fit me anymore and my mitts and ski mask, and it wasn't just my mom or dad who went with me that time, but both of them, and I could tell they felt as scared as I was.

Nothing happened, as far as we knew. We finished the route and came home and made hot chocolate. All our cheeks were red, and we went back to sleep, and when we woke up, my dad turned on the radio. I guess you know what we heard. Another paperboy had disappeared, right here in Crowell. That's an MO if I ever heard of one. Three carriers gone, and two of them from town, and all three when it was snowing.

The storm kept on, so this time there weren't even any tracks from the police and the neighbors searching. They couldn't find his sack of papers. A couple of people helping out had to go to the hospital because of frostbite. The missing boys didn't live on our side of town, but even so, my dad went over to help. With the streets so drifted, he couldn't drive—he had to walk. When he came back after dark with his parka all covered with snow, he said it was horrible out there. He couldn't get warm. He just kept sitting hunched in front of the fireplace, throwing logs on, rubbing his raw-looking hands, and shivering. My mom kept bringing him steaming drinks that she called hot toddies, and after an hour, he slumped back snoring. Mom and me had to help him up to bed. Then Mom took me back downstairs and sat with me in the living room and told me I had to quit.

I didn't argue. Crowell's got forty thousand people. If you figure three-quarters of them get the paper and most of the carriers have forty customers, that's 750 paperboys. I worked that out on my dad's pocket calculator. Kinda surprising—that many paperboys—if you're not a carrier yourself. But if you're on the streets at 5:30 A.M. every day like I am, then you see a lot of us. There's a kid on almost every corner, walking up somebody's driveway, leaving a paper in front of a door. Not counting the kid in Granite Falls, that's two missing carriers out of 750. That might make the odds seem in my favor, but the way I figured it, and my mom said it, too, that many paperboys only gave the nut a lot of choices. I like to play video games and all, but the money I earned wasn't worth disappearing the way those other boys did, with my papers stuffed behind some bushes, which is where they found the third kid's papers, like the others, when the snow stopped. After we put my dad to bed and my mom

looked out the living room window, she made a funny
noise in her throat. I walked to her and saw the house
across the street, all shimmery, covered with snow and
glinting from the streetlight. Any other time, it would've
looked peaceful, like a Christmas card. But I felt sick,
like all that white had something ugly underneath. I was
standing on a vent for the furnace, and I heard the gas
burner turn on. Warm air rushed up my pajama leg. All
the same, I shivered.

I've told you I quit. But my dad says we've got
something called a body clock inside us. It comes from
being used to a regular routine, like when you know even
if you don't have your watch on that it's time for your favorite TV program or you know you'd better get home
'cause your mom'll have supper ready. I wasn't going to
deliver papers, but I woke up at the same time as usual,
even if Mom didn't wake me. For just a second, I told
myself I'd better hurry. Then I remembered I wasn't
going to deliver the papers anymore. I slumped back in
bed and tried to go back to sleep, but I kept squinting at
the digital clock Mom and Dad gave me last Christmas,
and the red numbers kept changing, getting later: 5:40,
then 5:45. At last I couldn't bear feeling guilty, like I'd
done something wrong even though I hadn't. I crawled
from bed and opened my curtains and peered at the dark
snow in our driveway. I could see the tire tracks on the
street where the guy from the *Gazette* had pulled up and
thrown my bundle. It was all by itself in the driveway,
sunk in the snow. It was wrapped in a garbage bag to keep
it dry, this big black shape with all this white around it.

I kept staring at it, and the *Gazette* office hadn't been

open the day before, on Sunday. Even on Monday, they're not open till eight o'clock, so there wasn't any way for the paper to know I'd quit. I kept thinking of my customers getting up, looking forward to reading the paper at breakfast, going to the door, not finding it. Then I thought of all the calls we'd soon be getting, forty of them, wanting to know where their paper was. The more I thought about it, the more I felt worse, till I reminded myself of what my dad always says: "There's only one way to do a job, and that's the right way." I put on my long johns, my jeans and sweater and parka. I woke up my dad, whose face looked old all of a sudden, I guess from being out in the storm searching the day before. I told him I had to deliver the papers, and he just blinked at me, then nodded with his lips pursed like he didn't agree but he understood.

My mom made a fuss, as you'd expect, but my dad got dressed and went with me. I wasn't sure if I was shaking from the cold or from being scared. It wasn't snowing, though, and even shivering I knew I'd be all right. We hurried. We'd started a half hour late, but we got the papers to every customer without seeing any tire tracks in their driveway to tell us they'd left for work already. A couple places, we met a customer shoveling drifts, puffing frost from his mouth from the work, and every one of them looked glad to see me, like they'd been sure they weren't going to get a paper and here I'd been as dependable as ever. They grinned and promised me a tip when I came around next time to collect, and I guess I grinned, too. It made me feel warm all of a sudden. Even Mr. Lang, who's normally so hard to get along with, came out and patted me on the back the way the track coach some-times does. My dad and I did the route the fastest we ever had, and when we got home, my mom had pancakes ready and syrup hot from the Radarange. I guess I'd never been so hungry. My dad even gave me a little cof-fee in a glass. I sipped it, feeling its steam on my nose, ac-tually liking the bitter taste. Then my dad clicked his cup against my glass, and I felt like I'd grown in the night. My chest never felt so big, and even my mom had to admit we'd done the right thing.

But that didn't change what had happened. At eight o'clock, just before I left for school, my mom phoned the paper and told them I was quitting. When I went outside, I felt relieved, like something heavy had been taken off my back, but that didn't last long. A block from school, my stomach started getting hard, and I couldn't stop thinking I'd lost something or like the track season was over or I'd missed a movie I was looking forward to. It's funny how you get used to things, even a job, which I know isn't supposed to be fun—that's why it's called a job—but I liked being a paperboy, earning money and all, and I could tell I was going to feel empty now from not doing it.

All morning, I couldn't concentrate on what the teacher said. She asked if I was sick, but I told her I was only tired, I was sorry, I'd be okay. I tried my best to act interested, and when I got home for lunch, my mom said the paper had called to ask if they could send somebody over to talk to us around suppertime. She'd done her hardest to tell them no, but I guess they insisted, 'cause someone was coming anyhow, and I ate my hamburger fast from being curious and excited about getting attention.

The afternoon was the longest I ever remember. After school, I didn't care about hanging around with the guys. I just stayed at home and played video games and watched the clock on the TV recorder. My dad came home from work a little after five o'clock. He was just opening a can of beer when the doorbell rang. I don't know why, but my arm muscles hurt when he went to the door, and it was Sharon from the paper. She's the one who came to the house and explained how to do my route when I first got started. Lots of times, she stopped at the house to give me extra cards for figuring out how much my customers owed me. Once she brought me the fifty dollars' worth of movie passes that I won from going around the neighborhood and convincing the most new customers than any other carrier in town to take the *Gazette* in the morning instead of the *Chronicle* from Granite Falls, which is the evening paper, but you know that, I guess.

Sharon's younger than my mom. She's got a ponytail and rosy cheeks, and she reminds me of the student teacher from the college here in town who's helping my regular teacher. Sharon always shows more interest in talking to me instead of to my parents. She makes me feel special and grown-up, and she always smiles and tells me I'm the best carrier she's got. But last Monday, she wasn't smiling. She looked like she hadn't slept all night, and her cheeks were pale. She said so many carriers had quit and no new carriers wanted to take their place that the paper was worried, like it might go out of business. She said her boss had told her to go around to all the carriers that had quit and tell them the paper would pay them three dollars extra a week if they stayed, but my mom wouldn't let me answer for myself. My mom said no. But it was like Sharon hadn't heard. She said the *Gazette* would promise that any morning it snowed, the papers didn't have to be delivered, and I could see my dad agreed it was a good idea, but my mom kept shaking her head from side to side. Then Sharon rushed on and said at least let her have a few days to find a replacement for me, which was going to be hard because I was so dependable, and that made my heart beat funny. Please give her a week, she said. If she couldn't find somebody else by next Monday, then I could go ahead and quit and she wouldn't bother us again. But at least let her have the chance—her voice sounded thick and choky—because her boss said if she couldn't find kids to do the routes he'd get somebody else to do her job.

Her eyes looked moist, like she'd been out in the wind. All of a sudden I felt crummy, like I'd let her down. I wanted to make myself small. I couldn't face her. For the first time, she paid more attention to my parents than to me, blinking at my mom, then my dad, sorta pleading, and my mom didn't seem to breathe. Then she did, long and deep, like she felt real tired. She said my dad and her would have to talk about it, so they went to the kitchen, and I tried not to look at Sharon while I heard them whispering, and when they came back, my mom said okay, for a week, till Sharon could find a replacement, but no longer. In the meantime, if it was snowing, I wasn't going out to deliver the papers. Sharon almost cried then. She kept saying thanks, and after she left, my mom said she hoped we weren't making a mistake, but I knew I wasn't. I figured out what had been bothering me—not quitting, but doing it so fast, without making sure my customers got their paper and explaining to them and saying good-bye. I was going to miss them. Funny how you get used to things.

The next morning, I didn't feel nervous as much as glad to have the route back, at least for a few more days. It was one of the last times I'd see my customers' houses that early, and I tried to memorize what it was like, taking the paper to the Carrigans, who still kept arguing, and Mr. Blanchard crying for his wife, and Mr. Lang still drinking beer for breakfast. My dad went with me that Tuesday, and you could see other parents helping their kids do the routes. I'd never seen so many people out so early, and in the cold, their whispers and their boots squeaking were as clear as the sharp reflection of the streetlights off the drifts. Nothing happened, though the police kept looking for the boys who'd disappeared. And Wednesday, nothing happened, either. The fact is, by Saturday, everything had gone pretty much back to normal. It was never snowing in the morning, and my dad says people have awful short memories, 'cause we heard how a lot of paperboys who'd quit had asked for their routes back and a lot of other kids had asked for the routes that needed a carrier. I know in my own case I'd stopped feeling scared. Pretty much the opposite. I kept thinking about Monday and how it was closer all the time and maybe I could convince my mom to let me go on delivering.

Saturday was clear. When my dad came in from the

driveway, carrying the bundle of papers, he said it wasn't hardly cold at all out there. I looked through the kitchen window toward the thermometer on the side of the house, and the light from the kitchen reached it in the dark. The red line was almost at 32. I wouldn't need my ski mask, though I made sure to take my mitts, and we packed the papers in my sack, and we went out. That early, the air smelled almost sweet from being warmer than usual, and under my long johns, I started to sweat. We went down Benton, then over to Sunset, and started up Gilby. That's the hardest street 'cause it's got this steep hill. In summer, I'm always puffing when I ride my bike to the top, and in winter, I have to stop a minute going up with my heavy boots and coat on. How we did it was that my dad took one side of the street and I took the other. We could see each other because of the streetlights, and by splitting the work, we'd do the route twice as fast. But we'd got a note about a new customer that morning, and my dad couldn't find the house number. I kept delivering papers, going up the hill, and the next thing I knew, I'd reached the top. I looked back down, and my dad was a shadow near the bottom.

It wasn't snowing, so I figured I'd do a few more papers. My next customer was over on Crossridge. If you went by car, you had to drive back down Gilby hill, then go a block over to Crossridge, then drive all the way up to the top of the other hill. But if you went on foot or bike, you could cut through this sidewalk that one of my customers has in his yard, connecting Gilby and Crossridge, so I went through there and left the paper.

And I suddenly felt frozen-scared 'cause flurries

began to fall. I'd been looking at the dark sky from time to time. There wasn't a moon, but the stars had been bright, twinkling real pretty. I looked up fast now, and I couldn't see the stars. All I saw were these thick black clouds. I swear even in the dark I could see 'em. They were twisting and heaving like something was inside rolling and straining to bust loose. The flurries got bigger. I should've remembered from school. Thirty-two: That's the perfect temperature for getting snow. My legs felt limp. I wasn't walking right from being scared. I tried to run, but I lost my balance and almost fell. The snow came fast now. I couldn't even see the clouds because of it. It was falling so thick that I couldn't even see the houses across the street. A wind started, and then it got worse and screechy. My cheeks hurt like something was burning them, but it wasn't heat. It was cold. The air had been sweet and warm, but now it was freezing, and the wind stung, and the snow felt like tiny bits of ice-cold broken glass.

I swung to look for Dad, but I couldn't see the houses next to me. The snow kept pelting my face, and the wind bit, so I kept blinking and tears filled my eyes. I wiped them with my mitts. That only made them blurry. Snow froze to my cheeks and hair. I moaned, wishing I'd worn my ski mask. The shriek of the wind was worse. I tried to yell for my dad, but the gusting snow pushed the words back into my mouth. Then I couldn't see the sidewalk. I couldn't see my mitts in front of my face. All I saw was a wall of moving white. As cold as I felt, deep in my bones, my stomach burned. The more it felt hot, the more I shook. I yelled once more for my dad and in a panic stumbled to find him.

I didn't know I was off the sidewalk till I hit Mr. Carrigan's fence. It's sharp and pointy, like metal spears. When I banged against it, one of the points jabbed my chest. I felt it gouge me even through the padding of my coat. It pushed all the air out of me. I fell back into a drift and it felt like I was in quicksand, going deeper, scrambling to stand, but my heavy sack of papers held me down, and the snow kept piling on me. It went down my neck, like a cold hand on my back. It stung so hard that I jumped up screaming, but the wind shrieked louder, and all I saw was the swirling snow around me in the dark.

I ran, but I must've got turned around, 'cause nothing was where it should've been. Invisible bushes slashed my face. I smacked against a tree, and I guess that's how my nose got broken, but I didn't feel it, 'cause I was too scared. I just kept running, yelling for my dad, and when I didn't bump into anything, I guessed I was in the street, but I know now it was the vacant lot next to Mr. Carrigan's place. Somebody's digging a foundation for a new house, and it was like the ground disappeared. I was suddenly falling—it seemed like forever—and I landed so hard that I bit my lip right through. You ought to see the stitches. My dad says sometimes when something terrible happens to you, you don't feel it on account of what he calls shock. He says your body has a limit to what it can stand, and then it shuts out the pain. That must've been what happened, 'cause my chest and my nose and my lip got numb, and all I wanted was to find my dad and get back home. I wanted my mom.

I crawled from the hole, and somehow I knew there was someone close. With my eyes full of tears, I could barely see the snow, but then this dark shape rushed at me, and I knew it was my dad, except it wasn't. In the comics, when someone gets hit on the head, they always show stars. And that's what I saw, stars, bright in the snow, and I knew I'd been hit, but I didn't feel it. My dad says shock can do that, too. Something can happen to you that would normally slam you flat, but if you're scared, you somehow get the strength not to fall.

I almost did, though. Everything got blurry and began to spin, and this is the strange part. I got hit so hard that I dropped my sack of papers. The sack fell open, and as clear as day I saw my papers in a drift, the black ink with white all around it. Then the papers were splattered with red. You know that old joke? What's black and white and read all over? A newspaper. Only this is spelled different. The red was the blood from my head. I turned to run, and that's when the shadow grabbed my arm.

I kept turning, and even in the shriek of the wind, I heard the crack as clear as if my dad had taken a piece of kindling and snapped it across his knee for the fireplace, but the snap was from my arm, and I felt it twist at the elbow, pointing toward my shoulder. The next thing I was on my back, and the snow stopped gusting long enough for me to gape up at old Mr. Blanchard kneeling beside me, raising the claw end of a hammer.

I moved my head as he brought it down, so the claws glanced past my scalp, tearing away some hair. I kicked, and this time the hammer whacked my collarbone. I screamed. The claws of the hammer plunged toward the spot between my eyes.

And another hand shot from the storm, grabbing Mr. Blanchard's arm. Before I passed out, I saw my dad yank the hammer away from him and jerk him to his feet. My dad shouted stuff at him I'd never heard before. I mean terrible words I don't want to remember and I won't repeat. Then my dad was shaking Mr. Blanchard, and Mr. Blanchard's head was flopping back and forth, and the next thing I knew, I was here in the hospital with the bandages around my head and my nose and mouth swollen and my arm in this cast.

My dad tried to explain it to me. I think I understand, but I'm not sure. Mr. Blanchard's wife died three months ago. I thought she was still alive, but I was wrong. He and his wife, they never had any children, and my dad says he felt so alone without her that he wanted somebody around the house to take care of, like a son, so the first boy he took home was from Granite Falls that time two months ago when he went to visit his wife's sister. Then he wanted another son and another, so he took home those two boys from here, making sure it was snowing so he could hide his tracks, but then he wanted all the sons he could get. It makes me sick to think about it, how after he realized the boys were dead he took them out to his garage and stacked them under a sheet of canvas in the corner, "like cordwood" a reporter said. It's been cold enough that the bodies got hard and frozen. Otherwise they would've smelled like that other house I told you about. I wonder now if all the times I saw Mr. Blanchard crying it was because of his wife being dead or because he realized he was doing wrong but he couldn't stop himself. A part of me feels sorry for him, but another part keeps thinking about those missing boys and how scared they must've been when Mr. Blanchard came at them in the storm, and what he looked like when he knelt beside me, raising that hammer. I have a feeling I'll remember that till I grow up. I've said the nurses wake me early here, the same as if my mom was getting me up to do my route. I guess I lied. The nurses didn't wake me. I woke myself, screaming, remembering the claws of the hammer and the blood on my papers. The nurses ran in, and someone's been sitting with me ever since. My mom or my dad is always here, and they say my collarbone is broken, too, but what hurts worst is my arm.

The *Gazette* sent Sharon over, though I know she'd have come on her own. She's writing down what I say, but I'm not sure why, 'cause she's also got a tape recorder turned on. You ought to see her smiling when I talk about her. She says she's going to put my story in the paper, and her boss is going to pay me for it. I can sure use the money, 'cause the doctor says I won't be delivering papers for quite a while. I guess even after everything that's happened I'll go back to my route. After all, we know why those boys disappeared, and there can't be that many crazy people like Mr. Blanchard, though my dad says he's beginning to wonder. He just read about a girl carrier in Ashville that had somebody try to pull her into a car. What's going on that even kids who deliver papers can't feel safe? My dad says pretty soon nobody'll want to go outside.

Well, never mind. I told Sharon I've been talking for

quite a while. I'm getting sleepy, and I don't believe the paper will print all this, but she says my story's what they call an exclusive, and maybe some other papers will pick it up. My mom says she hopes I won't start acting temperamental—whatever that means—now that I'm famous, but I don't feel famous. I feel sore. I hope my customers enjoy reading what I said, though, 'cause I like them, and I hope they remember what they promised about giving me a tip on account of there's a new video game I want to buy. My dad came in and heard this last part. He said it again. I must've been born a businessman and I'll probably grow up to vote Republican. I still don't know what a Republican is, but I've been thinking. Maybe if I go around to a few houses and show them the bandages around my head and the cast on my arm, they'll subscribe to the paper. There's a new contest on. The kid who finds the most new customers gets a year's free pass to the movies. Now if only they'll throw in the popcorn.

Mumbo Jumbo

*T*his middle story about the dark side of
success concerns a different occupation:
sports—specifically, football. The main character of the previous story was a boy; here, we have a
teenager. The third story is about an adult. The plot was inspired by a newspaper account of an Iowa high school
football team that had a controversial ritual before each
game. Odd how the stars of high school seldom remain
stars in later life. Do they peak too early? Or is something
extra needed to go all the way?

THAT'S WHAT THEY CALLED IT: MUMBO JUMBO. YOU
wouldn't think they could have kept it a secret all those
years. But Coach Hayes made them promise, and he
wasn't someone you crossed, so there weren't even any
rumors. I didn't know the thing existed until my junior
year in high school, when I tried out for the football team.

I promised myself I'd be honest. Trying out wasn't my idea. It was Joey's. Sure, I liked to throw a football around as much as any other guy. But showing up for practice after classes every day?

"And don't forget the pain, Joey. You know what I'm talking about? Coach Hayes makes the team run two miles double time before each practice. That's not counting all the jumping jacks and push-ups and sit-ups and God knows how many other ups he makes them do. For starters. Before they get down to the rough stuff. Agony, Joey. That's what I'm talking about. You're sure you know what you want to get us in for?"

We were having cherry Cokes and fries down at the Chicken Nest near the school. A lot of good times. Of course, the Nest's torn down now. Seven years ago, the city made it a parking lot. But I remember Joey bracking through a straw at the bottom of his Coke, squinting at me across the table. "Joining the team would be something to do," he said. "If we make it, of course."

"Oh, that's no problem. We'd make it all right."

"I'm not so sure."

"Come on." I ate a fry with catsup on it. "We're big guys, and we're in shape."

"We're overweight. And Danny, we're not in shape. This morning, I had to pull in my gut to button my jeans. Anyway, that's not the point. I told you, playing with the team would be something to do. We can't just hang around here or down in your rec room all the time."

"What's wrong with playing records and—"

"Nothing. But it's not enough."

I stopped eating fries and frowned at him. "What are you talking about?"

"Don't you get the feeling we're not going anywhere?"

I shook my head, confused. I'd never heard Joey talk that way before.

"Left out," he said. "All the extra stuff they do at school. The student council, the way they're always included in what's going on."

"That stuck-up Bill Stedman. Ever since he got elected president last year, he walks around like he owns the goddamned school."

"And the plays the drama club puts on, and the debating team, and—"

"All that's candy-ass. What's with you? You want to be an actor now?"

"I don't know what I want to be." Joey rubbed his forehead. "But I want to be *something*. Those guys on the football team. They look like . . ."

"What?"

"Like they enjoy being good at what they do. They look damned proud. You can tell they're glad to belong."

"But all that pain."

His eyes had been bright. They seemed to be looking at something far away. Then all at once they came back to normal. He gave me that sly grin of his. "But there's a payoff. Those football players date the sexiest girls in school. All those muscles give the cheerleaders the hots."

I grinned right back. "Why didn't you say so? Now I get it. Why hang around here when there's a chance to date Rebecca Henderson?"

"Or her girlfriend, huh?"

We started laughing so hard that the waitress told us to shut up or leave, and that's how we came to try out for the football team, and how I learned about Mumbo Jumbo.

These days, I've got a beer gut, and I puff if I walk up a couple flights of stairs, and my doctor says my cholesterol count's too high. Cholesterol. You should have seen us back then. Granted, what Joey had said was right. We were overweight and soft. But we soon changed all that. The conversation I just described took place the week before school started, and Joey had us lifting weights and running laps even before Coach Hayes announced the dates for tryouts. When we showed up on the football field behind the gym that first Saturday of the school term, asking to join the team, Coach Hayes took his cap off, scratched his head, and wondered if we were kidding.

"No, we mean it," Joey said. "We really want to join."

"But you guys know my rules. You can't be on the team unless your scholastic average is B."

"Then we'll study harder. We'll raise our grades."

"Or waste my time, not to mention the team's. Your record speaks for itself. I've got no patience with guys who don't commit themselves."

"We'll try. We promise," Joey said. "Please. It's important to us."

"But look at the flab on you two. Sure, you're tall enough."

"Six feet," Joey said. "Danny's a quarter inch taller."

"But how are you going to keep up with the other guys? Look at Welsh over there. He's been working out all summer."

I glanced at Welsh, who was running through the holes in a double row of tires laid out on the field. He made it easily. Me, I'd have been groaning on my way to the hospital.

"You'll give up as soon as thing's get tough," Coach Hayes said. "Why pretend different?"

"All we're asking for is a chance," Joey said.

Coach Hayes rubbed a big, tanned calloused hand across his mouth. "A chance? Okay, I'll give you one. The same chance the other boys have. Show me you can keep up with the training. Get in shape, and earn decent grades. We'll see."

"That's all we want. Coach, thanks."

"One hundred percent. Remember, I won't accept less. If you guys get on the team and then stop trying, you'll wish you hadn't asked to join."

"One hundred percent."

"And Danny, what about you? You haven't said anything."

I nodded, wondering what the hell I was doing there. "Yeah, right, one hundred percent."

It was more like 200 percent—of torture. The weight lifting and sprints Joey and I had been doing were a joke compared with what Coach Hayes soon made us do. Even the guys who'd stayed in shape all summer had trouble keeping up with the routines. That two-mile double-time warm-up nearly killed me. And the calisthenics—I threw up when I got home and smelled the meat loaf my mom had cooked.

The next morning, Sunday, my knees felt so stiff that I hobbled when I crawled out of bed. I groaned to Joey on the phone, "This isn't going to work. I'm telling you, I can't make the tryout today. I feel like shit."

"Danny," my mother said from the kitchen. "Watch your language."

"You think you feel worse than me?" Joey asked. "All night I dreamed I was doing sit-ups. My stomach's got rocks in it."

"Then let's not go."

"We're going. We promised. I won't break my word."

"But what's the point? Even a date with Rebecca Henderson isn't worth the agony we'll be going through."

"Rebecca Henderson? Who cares? The team," he said. "I want to make the team."

"But I thought—"

"I said that just to get you interested. Listen, Danny, we've got a chance to belong to something special, to be good at something, better than anybody else. I'm tired of being a fuckup."

On the phone in the background, I heard Joey's mother tell him to watch his language.

"But my back feels—"

"We've been friends a long time, right?"

"Since we started grade school."

"And we've done everything together, right? We went to the movies together, and we went swimming together, and we—"

"I get the idea. But—"

"So I'm asking you, let's do this together, too. I don't want to lose your friendship, Danny. I don't want to do this by myself."

Inside, I felt warm, knowing what he was trying to tell me. Sure, it was sappy, but I guess I loved him like a brother.

"Okay," I said. "If it means that much to you."

"It means that much."

When we showed up that afternoon behind the gym, Coach Hayes blinked. "Wonders never cease."

"We told you we're serious," Joey said.

"And sore?"

"You bet."

"Legs feel like they've been run over by a truck?"

"A steamroller."

Coach Hayes grinned. "Well, at least you're honest. Even the pros admit they hurt. The trick is to do the job no matter how much it hurts."

I silently cursed.

"We won't let you down," Joey said.

"We'll see. Danny, you sure don't say much. Everybody, let's get started. Double-time around the track. After that, I've got a few new exercises for you."

Inwardly, I groaned.

After the first mile, I nearly threw up again.

But it's funny. I guess you can get used to anything. Monday morning, I felt awful. I mean really wretched. There wasn't a part of me that didn't ache.

And Tuesday morning was worse. I don't want to remember Wednesday morning. Plus, we didn't hang around the Chicken Nest anymore or go down to my rec room, playing records. We didn't have time. And I felt so tired, all I wanted to do was watch the tube.

But I had to hit the books. Every night after supper, Joey phoned to make sure I was studying. What I missed most were those cherry Cokes and fries, but Coach Hayes insisted we stay off them. We could eat spaghetti but no mashed potatoes, beef was okay, but the next day had to be chicken or fish. My mother went crazy trying to figure out the menus. For the life of me, I didn't understand the diet. But along about Saturday, after a week of tryouts, I started feeling not too bad. Oh, I still ached, but it was a different kind of ache. Solid and tight, pulling me in. And my mind felt brighter, clearer.

The first quiz I took, I got an A.

Two Sundays later, Coach Hayes lined us up after our workout. The bunch of us stood there facing him, breathing hard, sweating.

"Freddie," Coach Hayes told the kid beside me. "Sorry. You just don't have enough weight. The West High team'd mash you into the field. Maybe next year. For what it's worth, you're nimble enough to get on the track team." He shifted his glance. "Pete, you'd make a good tackle. Harry, I like the way you block."

And so on. Down until only Joey and I were left.

Coach Hayes spread his legs, put his hands on his hips, and scowled. "As for you two guys, I've never seen a more miserable pair of . . ."

Joey made a choking sound.

"But I guess you'll do."

Joey breathed out sharply.

I cheered.

"We made it." Joey grinned with excitement. "I can't believe we're on the team!"

We stood on the corner where we always separated on the way home.

I laughed. "It's the first thing I ever really tried for."

"And got! We're on the team!"

"I owe you. I couldn't have done it without you," I said.

"Same goes here."

"But I'd have quit if you hadn't . . ."

"Naw. I was close to quitting a couple times myself," Joey said.

I didn't think so. He'd wanted it more than I had.

"I'd better go. My mom'll have supper ready," I said.

"Yeah, mine will, too. I'll meet you a half hour early tomorrow so we can study for that science quiz."

"You bet." I didn't add what I was thinking.

Joey added it for me. "Now comes the hard part."

He was right. What we'd been doing until then were only exercises and sloppy scrimmage. Now we really got down to business.

"I've diagrammed these plays for you to memorize." Coach Hayes aimed a pointer against a blackboard in the social studies room after Monday's final bell. "I'll soon give you plenty more. You'll have to learn about game psychology, how to fake out the other team. And you'll have to build team spirit. That's as important as anything else. I want you guys to hang around with one another, go to movies together, eat lunch together. I want you all to understand one another until you can guess what Joey or Pete or Danny will do on the field. Anticipate one another. That's the secret."

But Coach Hayes had another secret. I didn't learn about it until our first game, and that was two weeks away. In the meantime, the pressure kept building. Harder, longer exercise sessions. Practice games until my shoulder ached so bad, I thought I'd dislocate it throwing the ball.

That's right. Throwing the ball. I guess Coach Hayes had been more impressed with us than he let on. After trying different guys in different positions, he'd actually picked me as a quarterback and Joey as a receiver.

"You two think alike. Let's see if you can make it work for you."

Sure, I was proud. But there were still grades to keep up and even more plays to memorize. I had no time to think about Rebecca Henderson. The school, the team, and winning were all that mattered, Coach Hayes told us.

Six-thirty Friday night, we showed up at the locker room and put on our uniforms. I felt shaky already. The other guys hardly spoke. Their faces were pale. Coach Hayes didn't help any when he started bitching about how good the other team was.

"Covington High's gonna stomp us. You guys aren't ready. You look like a bunch of losers. Eight winning seasons, and now I'm stuck being nursemaid to a bunch of sissies. I can't take the embarrassment of going out there with you. Pussies."

He went on like that, sounding meaner, more insulting as he went along, until he had us so mad that I wanted to shout at him to shut the fuck up. I knew what he was doing—using reverse psychology to work us up, so we'd take out our anger on the other team—but all of us respected Coach Hayes so much and wanted him to like us so much that hearing him put us down made me feel like we'd been fools. You bastard, I thought.

Joey kept glancing from Coach Hayes to me, his face in pain.

At once, the insults stopped. Coach Hayes glared and nodded. "All right." He walked to a wooden cabinet at the far end of the room.

It was always locked. I'd often wondered what was in there. Now he put a key in the lock and turned it, and behind me I heard a kid who'd been on last year's team whisper, "Mumbo Jumbo."

Next to me, Joey straightened. Those who'd been on last year's team started fidgeting, and somebody else whispered, "Mumbo Jumbo."

Coach Hayes opened the cabinet's door. I couldn't see what was in there because he stood in front of it, his back to us.

Then he slowly stepped away.

Several guys breathed in.

I was looking at a statue. It wasn't big, a foot tall, if that. Maybe four inches thick. Pale brown, like the color of a cardboard box. It was made from some kind of stone, not shiny and smooth, but dull and gritty-looking, like the stone was sand squeezed together. It had tiny holes here and there.

The statue was a man, distorted, creepy. He had a round bald head and huge bulging lips. His stomach was so swollen, he looked pregnant. He sat with his legs crossed. His hands in his lap hid his dong. His navel was an upright slit. He reminded me of pictures I'd seen of Chinese idols. But he also reminded me of those weird statues on Easter Island (we'd studied some of this in history class) and those ugly ones in ruins in Mexico. You know, the Aztecs, the Mayans, and all that.

The guys who'd been on last year's team didn't act surprised, but they sure looked spellbound. The rest of us didn't know what the hell was going on.

"Boys, I'd better explain. For our new members anyhow. This is . . . I don't know what you'd call him. Our mascot, I suppose. Or maybe better, our team's good-luck charm."

"Mumbo Jumbo," a kid from last year murmured.

"For quite a few years now, we've gone through a little ritual before each game." Coach Hayes slid a table into the middle of the room. Its legs scraped on the concrete floor. "Just as we're going out to play, I set the statue on this table. We walk around it twice. We each put our right hand on the statue's head. Then we go out there, kick the other team's butt, and win."

What kind of shit is this? I thought.

Coach Hayes seemed to read my mind. "Oh, sure, I know it's silly. Childish." He grinned in embarrassment. "But I've been having the team do it so often now, and we've had so many winning seasons, I'm almost afraid to stop. Mind you, I don't think for a second that touching old Mumbo Jumbo's head does us any good. But, well, when you've got a good thing going, why change the pattern? It's not as if I'm superstitious. But maybe some of you guys are. Maybe stopping the ritual would throw off your timing. Why not leave well enough alone?"

He studied us, letting what he'd said sink in. Boy, I thought, he doesn't miss a trick. Anything to psych us up. For Christ's sake, a lucky statue.

"There's just one other thing. A few outsiders might not understand the odd things we sometimes have to do to gear ourselves up for a game. They might object to what they thought was—who knows what?—voodoo or something. So we've always had this rule. No one talks about Mumbo Jumbo outside this room. We don't give away our little secrets."

I understood now why I hadn't heard about the statue before, even from the guys who'd been on last year's team. In a way, Joey and I hadn't been officially on the team until tonight, when we went out to play.

"I mean it," Coach Hayes said. "If any of you guys blab about this, I'll boot you off the team." He glared. "Do I have your word?"

A few guys mumbled "Sure."

"I didn't hear you. Say it! Promise!"

We did what he said.

"Louder!"

We shouted it.

"All right." Coach Hayes took the statue from the cabinet and set it on the table. Up close, the thing looked even uglier.

We walked around it twice, put our right hand on its head (I felt stupid as hell), then ran out onto the football field and—

This is what happened. I didn't believe it then. Now, through the haze of all these years, I try to convince myself that my memory's playing tricks. But it happened. That's the terrible part, knowing the truth deep down, but too late.

Five minutes into the game, no score, Coach Hayes sent me out as quarterback. In the huddle, I called a passing play, nothing fancy, just something basic to get the feel of being in the game. So we got set. I grabbed the ball, and all of a sudden it wasn't like in practice. This was the real thing, what all the pain and throwing up and weeks of work had been about, and Covington High's players looked like they wanted to kick in my teeth and make me swallow them. Our receivers ran out. Covington's interceptors stayed with them. My heart thundered. Frantic, I skipped back to get some room and gain some time, straining to see if anybody was in the open. Covington's blockers charged at me. It couldn't have taken five seconds, but it seemed even shorter, like a flash. A swirl of bodies lunged at me. My hands felt sweaty on the ball. Slick. I had the terrible fear I was going to drop it.

Then I saw Joey. He'd managed to get in the open. He was sprinting toward Covington's goal line, on the left, glancing back across his shoulder, hands up, wanting the ball. I snapped back my arm and shot the ball forward, perfect, exactly the way Coach Hayes had taught me, one smooth, powerful motion.

I pivoted sideways so I wouldn't get crushed by Covington's blockers, staring at the ball spinning through the air like a bullet, my heart in my throat, shouting to Joey.

And that's when I froze. I don't think I've ever felt that cold. My blood was like ice, my spine packed with snow. Because that end of the field, to the left, near Covington's goal line, was empty. Joey wasn't there. Nobody was.

But I'd seen him. I'd aimed the ball to him. I swear to God he'd been there. How the—

Joey was over to the right, streaking away from Covington's men, suddenly in the open. To this day, I still don't know how he gained so much yardage so fast. In a rush, he was charging toward the left, toward the goal line.

And that ball fell in his hands so easily, so neatly. . . .

The fans assumed we'd planned it, a fake-out tactic, a brilliant play. Coach Hayes later said the same, or claimed he believed it. When Joey sprinted across the goal line, holding the ball up in triumph, the kids from our school broke out in a cheer so loud, I didn't hear it as much as feel it, like a wall of sound shoving against me, pressing me.

I threw up my hands, yelling to get rid of my excitement. But I knew. It wasn't any fakeout play. It wasn't brilliant. It had almost been a massive screwup. But it had worked. Almost as if . . .

(I saw Joey there. I know it. On the left, near the goal line. Except he hadn't been there.)

. . . as if we'd intended it to happen. Or it had been meant to happen.

Or we'd been unbelievably lucky.

I started shaking then. I couldn't stop. I wasn't steady enough to play for the next ten minutes. Sitting on the bench, I kept seeing the play again in my mind, Joey in two spots at once.

Maybe I'd hoped so hard that I saw what I'd prayed I'd see.

But it felt spooky.

Coach Hayes came over to where I hunched on the bench. "Something the matter?"

I clutched my helmet. "I guess I'm just not used to . . ." What? ". . . a real game instead of practice. I've never helped score a touchdown before."

"You'll help score plenty more."

I felt a tingle in my gut.

The game was full of miracles like that: plays that shouldn't have worked but did. Incredible timing. With five minutes to go in the game and the score thirty-five to nothing in our favor, Coach Hayes walked along our bench and murmured to the defensive squad, "The next time they're close to our goal line, let them score. Hold back, but don't make it obvious."

Joey and I frowned at each other.

"But—" somebody said.

"No buts. Do what you're told," Coach Hayes said. "It's demoralizing for them if they don't get at least a few points. We want to let them feel they had a chance. Good sportsmanship."

Nobody dared to argue with him. Our defensive squad sure looked troubled, though.

"And be convincing," Coach Hayes said.

And that's why Covington scored when our guys failed to stop an end run.

The school had an after-game dance in the gym. Everybody kept coming up to me and Joey and the rest of the team, congratulating us, slapping us on the back. Rebecca Henderson even agreed to dance with me. But she'd come with some girlfriends and wouldn't let me take her home. "Maybe next time," she said.

Believe it or not, I didn't mind. In fact, I was so preoccupied that I didn't remember to ask her out for Saturday night. What I wanted to do was talk to Joey. By ourselves.

A little after midnight, we started home. A vague smell of autumn in the air. Smoke from somebody's fireplace. Far off, a dog barked, the only sound except for the scrape of our shoes as we walked along. I shoved my hands in the pockets of my green-and-gold varsity jacket and finally said what was on my mind. "Our first play? When I threw you the ball and you scored?"

Joey didn't answer right away. I almost repeated what I'd said.

"Yeah, what about it?" His voice was soft.

I told him what I thought I'd seen.

"The coach says we think alike." Joey shrugged. "What he calls anticipation. You guessed that's where I was headed."

"Sure. It's just . . ." I turned to him. "We won so easily."

"Hey, I've got bruises on my—"

"I don't mean we didn't work. But we were so damned lucky. Everything clicked together."

"That's why Coach Hayes kept drilling us. To play as a team. All the guys did what they'd been taught to do."

"Like clockwork. Yeah. Everybody in the right place at the right time."

"So what's bugging you? You thought you saw me in one place while I was in another? You're not the only one who thought he was seeing things. When we started that play, I saw you snap the ball toward that empty slot in the field, so I faked out the guy covering me and ran like hell to get there ahead of the ball. Know what? As I started running, I suddenly realized you hadn't even thrown the ball yet. You were still looking for an opening. I saw what you were going to do, not what you'd already done."

I felt a chill.

"Anticipation. No big deal. Hell, luck had nothing to do with it. Coach Hayes had us psyched up. The old adrenaline started burning. I ran to where I guessed you'd throw."

I tried to look convinced. "It must be I'm not used to all the excitement."

"Yeah, the excitement."

Even in the dark, his eyes glowed.

"There's a lot of room for improvement," Coach Hayes said at Saturday's game analysis. "We missed a chance for at least two interceptions. Our blocking's got to be quicker, harder."

He surprised me. The score had been so misbalanced,

our plays so nearly perfect, I figured we'd done as well as we could.

He made the team practice Sunday afternoon and every day after school. "Just because we won our first game doesn't mean we can afford to slack off. Overconfidence makes losers."

We still had to stay on that crazy diet of his. In my fantasies, I dreamed of mountains of cherry Cokes and fries with catsup. For sure, we had to keep our grades up. The end of the week, he went around to all our teachers and asked how we'd done on our quizzes. "Let your studies slide," he warned us, "and you don't play."

Friday night, we packed our equipment in the school bus and drove across town to meet West High. We used the girls' locker room in the gym, and after we'd dressed, Coach Hayes insulted us again. He set down a small wooden case (it had a big lock on it) in the middle of the room, opened it, and took out Mumbo Jumbo. The thing looked twice as ugly as before, scowling, with those big bulging lips and that upright slit for a navel.

But we knew the routine and walked around it twice and put a hand on the statue's head (I still felt stupid). Then we went out and won forty-two to six. Those six points wouldn't have been scored except that again Coach Hayes made us let them get a touchdown. And again that spooky thing happened. Coach Hayes let me play in the second quarter. I got the ball and looked for an opening. There was Joey, far down the field, ready to catch it. And there was Joey, twenty yards in front of where I saw him, trying to get away from a West High player.

My mouth hung open. My hands felt numb. I couldn't

breathe. At once, something snapped inside me, and the next thing I knew, I'd thrown the ball.

Joey raced from where he'd been trying to dodge the West High player. He ran toward the other Joey who was in the open. The two Joeys came together. And of course he caught the ball.

Our fans went nuts, screaming, cheering.

Joey crossed the goal line and jumped up and down. Even halfway down the field, despite the noise, I heard him whoop. Our guys were slapping me on the ass. I tried to look as excited as they were.

The next time I walked to our bench, Coach Hayes said, "Nice pass."

We studied each other for a second. I couldn't tell if he knew how startled I'd been out there, and why.

"Well, Joey's the one who caught it," I said.

"That's right. Team spirit, Danny. Everybody's in this together. All the same, nice pass."

Beside him, close, its lock shut, was the box.

We played eight games that season. Sometimes I had nightmares about them—double images of Joey or other players, the images coming together. I felt as if everything happened twice, as if I could see what was going to happen before it did.

Impossible.

But that's how it seemed. One night, I scared my mom and dad when I woke up screaming. I didn't tell them what the nightmare was about. I didn't talk to Joey about it, either. After that first time I'd tried to, I sensed that he didn't want to listen.

"We're winners. Jesus, it feels good," he said.

And the scores were always lopsided. We always let the other team score a few points when we were way in front.

Except one time. The sixth game, the one against Central High. Coach Hayes didn't call us names that night before the game. In the locker room, he sat in a corner, watching us put on our uniforms, and the guys started glancing at one another, nervous, sensing something was wrong.

"It's tonight," a kid from last year said, his voice tense.

I didn't understand.

Coach Hayes stood up. "Get out there, and give it your best."

Joey looked surprised. "But what about " He turned to the cabinet at the end of the locker room. "Mumbo—"

"Time to go." Coach Hayes sounded gruff. "Do what you're told. They're waiting."

"But—"

"What's the matter with you, Joey? Don't you want to play tonight?"

Joey's face turned an angry red. His jaw stood out. With a final look at the cabinet, he stalked from the locker room.

It could be you've already guessed. We didn't just lose that night. They trounced us. Hell, we never scored a point. Oh, we played hard. After all the training we'd been through, we knew what we were doing. But the other team played harder.

And it was the only game when I wasn't spooked, when I didn't see two images of Joey or what would happen before it actually did.

The after-game dance was a flop.

And Joey was mad as hell. Walking home with me, he kept slamming his fists together. "It's Coach Hayes's fault. He changed the routine. He got us used to him making us pissed at him before the game, calling us names and all that shit. We weren't prepared. We weren't worked up enough to go out there and win."

I tried to calm him down. "Hey, it's just one loss. We're still the winning team in the league."

He spun so fast, he scared me. "He didn't even bring out that dumb-ass statue! He wanted us to look like fools out there! He wanted us to lose!"

"I can't believe that."

"Maybe you like being a loser! I don't!"

He surged ahead of me. When I reached the corner where we always talked for a bit before splitting up, he was already heading down his street.

"Joey!" I wasn't sure what I wanted to say to him. It didn't matter. He didn't shout back.

And maybe you've guessed the rest of it, too. The next game, everything was back to normal. Or abnormal, depending on how you look at it. Coach Hayes cussed us out before the game. He set Mumbo Jumbo in the middle of the locker room.

"Why didn't you do it the last time?" Joey demanded. "We could've won!"

"You think so?" Coach Hayes squinted. "Maybe you'd have won. Then again, maybe not."

"You know we could've! You wanted us to—"

"Joey, it seems to me you've got things turned around. You're supposed to get mad at the other team, not me. I'm on your side, remember."

"Not last time you weren't."

Coach Hayes stood awfully straight then, his eyes blazing. "I'll forget you said that. Listen, I'll explain this only once. Last time, I broke the routine to make a point. It doesn't matter what tricks I use in the locker room to prepare you for a game. What counts is how you play. And last time you guys didn't give your best. It's your fault you didn't win, not mine. You got that?"

Joey glared.

"Besides, it's good for you to lose once in a while."

"Bullshit!"

"Don't try my patience. It's good for you to lose because it makes you try harder next time. It makes you hungrier. It makes you appreciate how sweet it is to be a winner. Don't say another word. Believe me, if you want to play tonight, don't say another word."

We walked around Mumbo Jumbo, touched him, and started the game. Of course, I saw things again. And, of course, we won, finally letting the other team score.

One more week, the final game. And after touching Mumbo Jumbo, we won that, too. City High's ninth winning season. Yet another gleaming trophy stood in the glass case in the lobby near the principal's office.

*   *   *

A lot had happened. My parents couldn't get over my B's and A's. They raised my allowance. They let me borrow the family car more often. Rebecca Henderson and I started going steady.

And Joey and I continued drifting apart. He was obsessed with being a star, with having attention directed at him all the time. So when the football season was over, he couldn't get used to being treated the same as everybody else. He tried out for the basketball team—Mr. Emery, the science teacher, coached it—but he didn't make the squad. "So what?" he said, but you could tell how disappointed he was. "They lose more games than they win. Who wants to be a loser?" He hated how everybody crowded around the new student council president. He finally decided to try out for the drama club—It figures, I thought, being onstage, everybody looking at you—and he made it. He didn't get the starring role in the big production they always put on in December, but he did have a half-decent part. He had to fake a German accent and play a maniac doctor called Einstein in a murder comedy called *Arsenic and Old Lace*. I took Rebecca to it, and I have to say Joey did okay, not great, but pretty good. I mean, at least he made me laugh at the jokes, and I hoped that now he'd be satisfied, although I heard later how he was always grumbling in rehearsals about not being onstage enough and wanting more lines.

I'll skip to all the trouble—the following year, our last one at City High. Our grades had put Joey and me on the junior honor role. He and I had stayed in shape all summer. Rebecca and I were spending even more time together. Maybe she was the reason I tried out for the football team again, even though I hated the prospect of seeing that ugly statue again, not to mention getting spooked seeing that other stuff on the field. But I knew we wouldn't have gotten together if I hadn't been a football player, and I didn't want things to change between us, so I tried out again and made the team.

Joey did, too, and his reasons were obvious—getting attention, being a star.

Coach Hayes did everything the same. I dragged myself home after practice each day. I heard the same old speeches about grades and diet. I listened to him cuss us out before the starting game (but he didn't make me mad anymore), and watched him bring out Mumbo Jumbo. "Our mascot," he explained, swearing us to secrecy, the same routine (but that squat, ugly brown thing still made me feel creepy). And on the field, I saw the double images again and felt the chill creep up my spine. If it hadn't been for Rebecca cheering on the sidelines, I'd have . . .

But I didn't, and because of that, sometimes I think I might have caused what happened, partly anyhow.

We won, of course. In fact, it seemed too easy. Maybe that was why at the next game Coach Hayes didn't cuss us out and didn't show us Mumbo Jumbo.

As soon as I noticed he was changing the pattern, I said to myself, It's tonight, only then realizing I'd heard the same thing last year from a kid who'd been on the team the year before that. The kid had graduated now, and I suddenly realized that next year, after my own graduation, some other kid would repeat what I'd just said. And I wondered how many others had said it before me.

"No!" Joey shouted, furious.

"One more word and you're benched!" Coach Hayes shouted back.

Joey shut up. But leaving the locker room, I heard him mutter, "Goddamn him. I'll show him. We don't need that frigging statue. We'll win anyhow."

But we didn't. And I didn't see the double images. And Joey went nearly out of his mind with rage. He didn't go to the after-game dance, and he didn't say a word at Saturday's game analysis or Sunday's practice. All he did was keep glaring at Coach Hayes.

And me? How did I help cause all the trouble? I got curious is all. I started thinking about patterns.

And patterns.

So what do you do when you're curious? What I did, I went to the school newspaper. Your school probably had one just like ours. The student reporters were the same bunch who put together the yearbook and belonged to the creative writing club. A gossip column, a hit parade column, a humor column. Plenty of announcements. A report from the student council.

And a sports column.

All of this stuff was typed on stencils and run off on a mimeograph machine. Three pages, on both sides, orange sheets stapled together. The *City High Examiner.* Original, huh? It came out every Monday morning. I think the school administration set aside money for it mostly because of the weekly "Report from the Principal." School spirit and all that.

Anyhow, I decided to do some checking, so I went to

the newspaper office, which was also the yearbook office. A cluttered room on the third floor between the typing classroom and the janitor's closet. The place smelled sickish-sweet, like that white liquid goop you put on stencils to hide your typing mistakes. The editor was a kid named Albert Webb, and I guess he'd seen too many newspaper movies. He was always talking about the "student council beat" and the "drama club beat" and "going to press." All of us called him "Scoop," and he took it as a compliment instead of a put-down.

He was sitting at a desk, shoving his glasses back on his nose, glancing back and forth from a handwritten sheet of paper to the stencil he was typing. He had a pen behind his ear and a zit on his chin. He turned as I walked in.

"How's tricks, Scoop?"

"I just got the word on the nominations for homecoming queen."

"Nobody's supposed to know that till next week's assembly."

"No kidding." He grinned. "Maybe you'll be interested. Rebecca Henderson's one of them."

"My, my." I grinned right back. "Somebody's got good taste. So listen, have you got any old editions of the paper?"

"All the ones I edited. Plus a bunch from a couple editors before me."

"How far back do they go?"

He was proud. "Fifteen years."

"Hey, swell. So where do you keep them?"

"In the morgue."

"Huh?"

"That's what newspapers call where they store old issues. Over there." He pointed past some boxes to a rickety bookshelf in one corner.

"You mind?"

He spread his arms. "Hey, be my guest. What do you want to look at them for?"

I'd figured he'd ask. "A couple of us on the football team have been thinking about a reunion game with former players. An exhibition thing. You know, the old guys against the new."

"Yeah?" Scoop's eyes brightened. He reached for his pencil.

"Now wait a minute. We're still just talking, Scoop. If you put this in the paper and it doesn't happen, you'll look dumb. You might even screw up our chances of convincing those guys."

"Right." He nodded. "I'll make you a deal. You look at the former issues, but if the plans for the game look definite, let me know so I can break the story."

"Anything you say."

So I went to the corner and started sorting through the papers. They smelled like a moldy cellar. I almost sneezed.

Fifteen years of them. How many weeks in a school year? Forty? A lot of issues. But looking through them wasn't as hard as you'd think. See, the only issues I wanted were the ones during the football season. And I only wanted the issues since Coach Hayes had come to the school eleven years ago. It took me less than half an hour. And this is what I learned.

The first two seasons when Hayes had coached had

been awful. Worse than that. Disastrous. The team had never won a game. A total zip.

But after that? Winning season after winning season.

With these facts in common. The games we'd won had had lopsided scores in our favor, but the opposing team had always managed to get on the board. And every season, we'd lost one game, the first or the seventh or the third, no consistent pattern there. And the teams that had beaten us varied. But the score had always been zero for us.

Because he hadn't brought out Mumbo Jumbo?

I know that's crazy. Next thing, you'll figure I believe in horoscopes and fortune-telling and all that crap. But I swear it made me wonder, and remember, you weren't on the field to see those creepy double images. In my place, you'd have started to wonder, too.

By then, Scoop was leaning over my shoulder, squinting at the paper in front of me.

"Something the matter, Scoop?"

"Just nosy."

"Yeah."

"I see you're reading about the game the team lost three years ago."

"I wasn't playing then."

"I know. But I was a cub reporter for the paper then. I was there that night. I remember thinking how weird that game was."

"Oh?"

"All those perfect games, and then a real dog."

"Well, nobody plays good every game. Hey, thanks, Scoop. Anything I can do for you, just—"

"Let me know about the reunion game."

"Believe me, you'll be the first."

And that's what started things. With some bad moves from a new kid on the team, a guy named Price. See, he wouldn't keep his grades up. Maybe he was just stupid. He soon started acting that way.

Coach Hayes followed through on his threat. No grades, no play. So Price got kicked off the team.

But Price had a father with a beer gut who'd been a jock when he was in high school, and when Price started whining, the father went wacko over what he said was an insult to his kid. "I don't care about his grades. You think I want him to grow up with ulcers, trying to be a brain? Football's been good for me. It gave me character, and I know it's good for my boy's."

No major problem. Just your basic asshole father sticking up for his kid. But Coach Hayes wouldn't budge, and that's when Price broke the rule.

You might remember reading about it back then, and I'm not talking about the high school paper, but the local *Courier.* Then the major paper in the state. Then . . . FATHER OF HIGH SCHOOL FOOTBALL PLAYER ACCUSES TEAM OF DEVIL WORSHIP.

Well, you can imagine, there wasn't any stopping it after that. The city council wanted to know what the hell was going on. The school board demanded an explanation. The principal got angry phone calls.

My father put down the *Courier* and frowned at me. "Is this story about the statue true? Mumbo Jumbo?"

"It's not like Price says. It's just a mascot."

"But you touch it before you go out to play?"

"Hey, it's nothing. It's only sort of for good luck."

My father frowned harder.

The other guys on the team got the same bit from their parents. Joey told me his father was so upset that he wanted Joey to quit.

"Are you going to?" I asked.

"Are you kidding? Christ, no. The team means too much to me."

Or winning does, I thought.

By then, the week was over. Friday night had come around. Another game. One of the first-aid guys came down to the locker room, excited. "The bleachers are packed! A record crowd!" Sure, all the publicity. Everybody wanted to see the team with the voodoo statue.

At first, I thought Coach Hayes would leave it in the cabinet. Because of the controversy. But as soon as he started insulting us, I knew he didn't intend to break the routine. Looking back to that night, I wonder if he guessed that he wouldn't have many more chances to bring it out. He meant to take advantage of every one of them.

So he went to the cabinet. I held my breath as he unlocked it. The publicity made me self-conscious. Certainly all the talk about devil worship made me nervous about the double images I'd seen.

I watched as he opened the door.

His throat made a funny sound, and when he stepped to the side, I understood why.

"Where is it?" Joey blurted.

Several players gasped.

"Where's Mumbo Jumbo?" Joey's cleats scraped on

the concrete floor as he stalked to the empty cabinet. "What happened to—"

Coach Hayes looked stunned. All at once, his neck bulged. "Harcourt." His lips curled. He made the principal's name sound like a curse. "The school board must have told him—"

"But the cabinet was locked," someone said.

"The janitor could have opened it for him." Coach Hayes stomped across the room toward the door.

And suddenly stopped, as if he'd realized something. "We've got a game to play. I can't chase after him while—" Turning, he stared at us. "Get out there and show them. I'll find the statue. You can bet on that."

So we went out, and maybe because we'd been spooked, the other team killed us. We couldn't do anything right. Fumbles, interceptions, major penalties. It must have been the worst game any team from City High ever played. The fans started hissing, booing. A man shouted, "Devil worship, my ass! These guys don't need a voodoo statue! They need a miracle!" The more we screwed up, the more we lost confidence and screwed up worse. I saw Rebecca wiping tears from her eyes and felt so humiliated that I couldn't wait for the game to end so I could hide in the locker room.

Coach Hayes kept scurrying around, talking to the principal and anybody else he suspected, gesturing angrily. They shook their heads no. By the end of the game, he still hadn't found the statue.

We sat in the locker room, bitter, silent, when somebody knocked on the door.

I was closest.

"Open it," Coach Hayes said.

So I did.

And stared at Mumbo Jumbo on the floor. There wasn't anyone in the hall.

Sure, we heard rumors, but we could never prove that the other team had taken it. We even heard that stealing the statue had been the rival coach's idea, a practical joke on his good old friend Coach Hayes.

Scoop put all this in the school newspaper Monday morning. Don't ask me how he found out. He must have been a better reporter than any of us gave him credit for. He even had a drawing of the statue, so accurate that whoever had stolen it must have shown it to him. Or maybe Scoop was the one who stole it.

Whoever. I feel partly responsible for the story he wrote. I must have made him curious that time I went to see him and asked to look at the back issues of the paper. Maybe he checked and found out I'd handed him a line about a reunion game.

For whatever reason, he went through the same issues I'd looked at, and he noticed the same pattern. Two losing seasons, then all of a sudden an unbroken string of winners. Because of Mumbo Jumbo? He didn't come right out and link the statue with the team's success, but you could tell he was trying to raise the question. In every winning season, we'd lost only one game, and our score had always been zero. In our winning games, however, we'd always had a lopsided spread in our favor, but the other team had always somehow managed to gain a few points. Coincidence, Scoop asked, or was there a better explanation? For evidence, he quoted from an interview he'd had with Price. He didn't bother mentioning that he had no witness for what had happened in the locker room in the years when Price wasn't on the team. His whole story was like that, making guesses seem like facts. Then he talked about Friday's game and how in the years since Coach Hayes had been showing the statue, this was the first time we'd lost two games in one season. Perhaps because somebody stole the statue Friday night? Scoop repeated the rumor that the rival team had been responsible for the theft. We'd probably never know the truth, he said. He'd already described the few tiny holes in the statue, "the size of a pin, one of them over the statue's heart." Now several paragraphs later, he ended the story by mourning the rival coach, who'd died from a heart attack on his way home from the game.

I wanted to get my hands on Scoop and strangle the little shit. All everybody in the lunchroom talked about was how creepy it would be if the statue had really caused that coach's death, if someone had stuck a pin in Mumbo Jumbo's chest.

I don't know if Coach Hayes wanted to strangle Scoop, but he sure wanted him expelled. Every kid at school soon heard about the argument Coach Hayes'd had in the principal's office, his shouts booming down the hall, "Irresponsible! Libelous!" Scoop was smart enough to stay home sick all week.

By next Friday's game, though, Scoop was the least of our problems. The churches in town got worked up over Mumbo Jumbo. I read in the local paper how the school had received at least a dozen letters from local ministers, priests, and rabbis. One of the letters was quoted: ". . . superstition . . . unwholesome atmosphere . . . Satanism . . . counterproductive to education." My parents were so upset that they didn't want me to play in the game that night. I told them I couldn't let the other guys down, and as far as education was concerned, what about the B's and A's I'd been bringing home? If anything, the team had been good for me.

But this superstition crap was beginning to get to me, maybe because I still felt bothered by the weird things I'd been seeing on the field, things that seemed to happen before they happened. Could the statue really have made me see them? Or was Joey right, and I was only caught up in the speed and excitement of the game?

Enough already, I thought. Mumbo Jumbo. That described it all right. It's a lot of bullshit. I had no way to know, of course, that this would be the last time Coach Hayes would be allowed to bring out the statue. I did know this—I was sick of touching that creepy thing, and if I needed it to make me a good football player, I didn't belong in the game.

So after we dressed in the locker room and Coach Hayes insulted us and brought out the statue, I didn't touch it as the other guys did when we went out to play.

My right arm still aches when the temperature drops below freezing. The cast stayed on for almost three months. I hadn't been on the field more than thirty seconds, my first play of the game. I got the ball and pulled my arm back to throw, but I couldn't find an opening. And I never saw the four guys who hit me, all together at once, really plowing into me, knocking my wind out, taking me down, my arm cocked behind my shoulder, all that weight on it. I fainted. But not before I heard the cracks.

Saturday morning, Joey came to visit me in the hospital. He'd scored three touchdowns, he said. Through a swirl of pain, I tried to seem excited for him.

"Did we win?" I asked.

"Does the Pope live in Italy?" His grin dissolved. "I'm sorry about your arm."

"Thanks."

"How long are they going to keep you here?"

"Till tomorrow afternoon."

He fidgeted. "Well, look, I'll visit you at home."

I nodded, feeling sleepy from the painkiller a nurse had given me. Rebecca came in, and Joey left.

He and I drifted further apart after that. He had the team, and I had my broken arm. After the football season, he got a big role in a murder mystery the drama club put on, *Ten Little Indians*. Everybody said he was wonderful in it. I have to admit he was.

And me? I guess I let things slide. I couldn't take notes or do class assignments with my writing arm in a cast. Rebecca helped as much as she could, but she had to do her own work, too. I started getting C's again. I also got back in the habit of going down to the Chicken Nest, with Rebecca this time instead of Joey. Those cherry Cokes and fries with catsup can really put weight on you, especially if you're not exercising.

The city newspaper reported on the meeting between the school board and Coach Hayes. They asked him to explain. He found the statue at a rummage sale, he said.

Its owner claimed it was a fertility symbol that the Mayans or the Polynesians or whoever (the name of the group kept changing) had used in secret rituals. Coach Hayes said he hadn't believed that—not when its price was fifteen dollars. But he'd been looking for a gimmick, he said, something to work up team spirit, especially after two horrible seasons. A kind of mascot. If the team believed the statue brought them good luck, if the statue gave them confidence, so what? No harm was done. Besides, he said, he sometimes didn't bring the statue out—to teach the players to depend on themselves. The team had lost on those occasions, true, but as a consequence, they'd tried harder next time. There was nothing mysterious about it. A dramatic gimmick, that's all. The point was, it had worked. The team had been winning championships over since. School spirit had never been better.

"What about the statue's name?" a school board member asked.

"That came later. In the third winning season. One of the players made a joke. I forget what it was. Something about good luck and all that mumbo jumbo. The phrase sort of stuck."

The school board heard him out. They held up the stacks of letters from angry parents and clergy. Their decision was final.

To show that they were willing to compromise, they let him put the statue in the glass case in the school's front lobby, along with the trophies the team had won.

The rest of the season was brutal. We lost every game. Sitting with Rebecca on the sidelines, trying to show enthusiasm for the team, I felt terrible for Joey. You could see how depressed he was, not being a winner.

West High won the championship. Monday, the big news was that over the weekend somebody had smashed the glass in the trophy case and stolen Mumbo Jumbo. Nobody knew who had it, although all of us suspected Coach Hayes. He resigned that spring. I'm told he teaches now in upstate New York. I think about him often.

Joey's grades were good enough that Yale accepted him on a scholarship. With my C's, I won't even tell you what college accepted me. I didn't go anyhow. Rebecca got pregnant that summer. In those days, abortions weren't easy to arrange. I'm not sure I'd have wanted her to have one anyhow. The child, a daughter, breaks my heart with love every time I look at her. Rebecca and I got married that Halloween. Both sets of parents were good about it. We couldn't have made a go of it without their help.

We have three children now, two girls and a boy. It's tough to pay the rent and feed and dress and give them everything we want to. Both Rebecca and I have jobs. She's a secretary at our high school. I work at the chemical plant in town.

And Joey? You know him as Joseph "Footwork" Summers. He played receiver for Yale and was picked up by the NFL. You saw him play twice in the Super Bowl. For sure, you saw him in plenty of beer commercials. The one where he beats up five motorcycle guys, then walks to the bar and demands a beer is famous.

"What kind?" the bartender asks. "What those guys were drinking?"

And Joey says, "That stuff's for losers. When I say I want a beer, I mean the best."

And you know what brand he means. The commercial got him into the movies. I saw *Dead Heat* last week and loved it. The action was great. His acting gets better and better.

But a part of me . . .

I'll try to explain. Three years ago, Joey came back to town to see his folks. Imagine how surprised I was when he called me up. I mean, he hadn't exactly been keeping in touch. He asked me over to his parents' house for a beer—he really drinks the brand he advertises—and while I was there, he took me up to his old bedroom. A lot of good memories. He gestured toward his battered dresser. I was so busy looking at him (hell, he's a movie star, after all) that I didn't know what he meant at first.

Then I really looked.

And there it was. In his open suitcase. Mumbo Jumbo. As ugly and shitty and creepy as ever. I felt spooked, the way I used to.

Abruptly I realized what had happened. "No. You don't mean . . . You're the one who stole it?"

He just grinned.

"But I thought it was Coach Hayes. I thought . . ."

He shook his head. "No, me."

My stomach felt hollow. I don't remember what we talked about after that. To tell you the truth, the conversation was kind of awkward. I finished my beer and went home. And Joey returned to Hollywood.

But this is what I think. The other night, my son and I were watching a movie on television. *David Copperfield.*

I never watch that kind of stuff, but my son had a book report due, and he hadn't read the book, so he was cheating, sort of, watching the movie. And I was helping him.

At the end, after David Copperfield becomes a success and all his friends have turned out losers, there's a part in this movie where you hear what he's thinking. "It isn't enough to have the luck," he says. "Or the talent. You've got to have the character."

Maybe so. But I keep thinking about Mumbo Jumbo and how, when I didn't touch the statue, I got my arm broken in the game. That was a turning point. If I'd stayed on the team and kept my grades up, could I have gone to Yale like Joey? Could I have been a winner, too?

I keep thinking about Coach Hayes and his winning streak. Was that streak caused by the statue? I can't believe it.

But . . .

I remember Joey—the movie star—pointing at the statue he stole from the glass case in the school's front lobby. In his senior year. And everything kept getting better for him after that.

Then I think about myself. I love my kids and my wife.

But I felt so tired tonight when I got home from work. . . . The bills . . . My son needs braces on his teeth, and . . .

Maybe Joey understood. Maybe David Copperfield was wrong.

Maybe it doesn't take talent. Or character.

Maybe all it takes is Mumbo Jumbo.

The Road
to Damascus

I n my foreword to this collection, I told you about
Philip Klass and the influence he had on my fiction. I also mentioned a second writer who made
a difference. In fact, if not for him, I would never have become a writer at all: Stirling Silliphant.

A little background. Earlier, I explained that my father
died in World War II and that my mother, unable to work
and simultaneously look after me, put me in an orphanage
when I was around four. Part of me wonders if the woman
who finally came to get me was the woman who had left
me. But let's assume she was. Still unable to watch me at
home while earning a living, she arranged for me to live on
a Mennonite farm. There, my confusion about where I belonged intensified. Seasons passed. Every Friday, I was
put on a bus into town, where my mother waited for me at
the terminal. Every Sunday, I got on a bus to go back to the
farm. When a child boarding on a different farm was killed

by a car as he walked along the highway, my mother decided to keep me with her.

By now, she had remarried—to give me a father, she later said. I was desperate for the affection of a male authority figure, and her new husband wasn't prepared to fill the role. He looked visibly uncomfortable if I called him Father. In the years that followed, I thought of him as a stranger. The marriage itself wasn't a success. My mother and my stepfather argued so much that my memories of my youth are mostly about fear. Many nights, their arguments were so loud that I worried about my safety. Imitating scenes in movies, I stuffed pillows under my blankets, making them look as if I slept there. Then I crawled under my bed and dozed fitfully in what I hoped was a protected space.

We lived above a bar and, later, a hamburger joint. There wasn't enough money for a television or a phone. For Saturday-night entertainment, I listened to "Gunsmoke" and "Tarzan" on the radio while watching drunks fight in the alley below me. On one occasion, my mother went out to use the pay phone in the alley, only to have a stray bullet shatter the booth's glass.

As I grew older, I discovered movies. In those days, movie theaters were palaces, and audiences didn't jabber endlessly. To earn the money to see a film, I set up pins in bowling alleys. Occasionally, I stood at a crowded bus stop and pretended that I'd lost my bus fare. Someone was always kind enough to give me the fifteen cents, which I immediately spent getting into a movie theater.

And there I sat, hour after hour, in the silvery darkness, watching film after film (they had double features in those days), sometimes staying to see the movies twice. It didn't matter to me what kind of movies they were, although, I confess, I wasn't crazy about the ones with a lot of kissing. What did matter was that I was distracted from reality.

In retrospect, it seems logical that I would have wanted to become a storyteller, to distract others from their realities. But at the time, I was too confused to know what I wanted. I ran with a street gang. I treated grade school as an interruption of my spare time. High school was a little better. Our finances improved. We moved to a small house in the suburbs. The family arguments were fewer. Still, by the time I entered grade eleven, I was going nowhere.

That fall of 1960, with little interest in anything except pool halls and eight hours of television a day, I found myself (like a minor-league Saul on his way to Damascus) struck by a bolt of light that changed my life. Even now, I can be specific about the time and date—8:30 P.M., Friday, October 7. The light was from my television and the first episode of a series called Route 66.

The show was about two young men who, in Jack Kerouac fashion, drove a Corvette across the United States in search of America and themselves. One of them was Tod, a rich kid from New York whose father had recently died, leaving such massive debts that, when the creditors finished, the only thing left was Tod's sports car. His partner, Buz, was a tough street kid from Hell's Kitchen, who had worked for Tod's father on the New York docks and had become friends with Tod. Because Route 66 *was then the principal highway across the United States, the title was perfect. And because the series was as much about Amer-*

ica as it was about Tod and Buz, the producers decided to film each episode on the locations that the characters were supposed to be visiting, although many were far from Route 66: Boston, Philadelphia, Biloxi, Santa Fe, and Oregon City, for example.

The first episode, "Black November," involved a small southern town haunted by a grisly secret from years earlier—the ax murder of a German prisoner of war and the minister who tried to protect him. I'd never seen a story like it, not merely the mystery, suspense, and action (a scene involving a power saw remains vivid in my mind) but also the appeal of the characters and the reality of the writing. I waited eagerly for the next Friday night to come around, and the next Friday night, and the next. There was something about the way the characters talked, the emotions they expressed, and the values they believed in that affected me deeply, awakening my mind.

For the first time in my life, I began to study credits. Who on earth was responsible for this wonderful experience? One episode would be about shrimp boats in the Gulf of Mexico, with a plot that paralleled Shakespeare's The Taming of the Shrew. Another involved street gangs in Los Angeles, with poetic dialogue amid the squalor. Still another would be about crop dusting in Phoenix, with tragic overtones of Greek myth. Back then, I didn't know anything about Sartre or existentialism or the philosophy of the Beat Generation. But even if I couldn't put a name to what I was experiencing, it made me feel emotionally and intellectually alive. Martin Milner and George Maharis were the stars. Still, despite their considerable acting talents, I felt uncharacteristically attracted to whoever had *invented the dramatic situations and put the words (sometimes spellbinding speeches that lasted five minutes) in the actors' mouths. Herbert B. Leonard was the producer. Sam Manners was the production chief. Okay. But still . . . Then I realized that one other name appeared prominently in the credits of almost every episode: Stirling Silliphant, writer. My, my. A new thought.*

That grade-eleven student, who formerly had no ambition whatsoever, managed to find the address of Screen Gems, the company listed at the end of the credits. Unable to type, I sent a handwritten letter—scrawled would be a more accurate word—to Stirling Silliphant and asked how I could learn to do the wonderful things that he was doing. One week later (I still recall my amazement), I received an answer from him—two densely typed pages that began with an apology for having taken so long to get back to me. He'd have written to me sooner, he explained, but when my letter arrived, he'd been out at sea in a boat. He revealed no secrets and indeed refused to look at anything I might write (partly because of my inexperience and partly for legal reasons), but he did tell me this: The way to be a writer is to write and write and write and . . .

Millions of words later, I'm still writing. If not for Stirling, I would never have gone on to college. I wouldn't have gotten a B.A., let alone an M.A. and a Ph.D., wouldn't have met Philip Klass, wouldn't have written First Blood. *One of my greatest thrills came on a summer afternoon in 1972 when Stirling phoned to thank me for having sent him a copy of* First Blood *and to say that he'd liked it, that he was gratified to have been an inspiration. "If I were a cat," he said, "I'd purr."*

We stayed in touch but never met until the summer of 1985, when he suggested that I come to Los Angeles and spend the Fourth of July weekend with him. Twenty-five years after I first experienced his work, I finally got to meet him, a stocky, broad-smiled, gentle-featured man with short gray hair and a generous good nature. It was like coming face-to-face with the father I'd never known. Finally, in a closing of the circle, he took my novel The Brotherhood of the Rose to NBC and suggested that they do a miniseries of it. In 1989, when the series was broadcast after the Super Bowl, the most coveted time slot on television, I was struck with awe when I watched the credits and again saw the magical words: Executive Producer Stirling Silliphant.

Shortly afterward, Stirling told me that in one of his former lives he had lived in Thailand and that now he was going home. He had a Beverly Hills garage sale, moved to Bangkok, and had the luxury of writing whatever he wanted, with no deadlines except his own. We often talked about my going there to visit him, but our various schedules kept conflicting. My only contact with him was via frequent faxes. Regret is a terrible emotion. At a little after 8:00 A.M. on the morning of April 26, 1996 (as with the debut of Route 66, I can be very specific about this moment), I was eating breakfast, listening to the news on National Public Radio, when the announcer informed me, "Academy Award–winning screenwriter Stirling Silliphant died this morning from prostate cancer. He was seventy-eight." My Cheerios stuck in my throat. It was two days after my birthday. The man I thought of as my father was gone.

Stirling was as determined a writer as I ever encountered. He once had two wisdom teeth extracted in the morning and was hitting the typewriter keys by noon. He worked almost every day and was religious about meeting deadlines. Legendary for being prolific and fast, he was hesitant to show a complete list of his credits because he was certain that no one would believe that anyone could write that much. I've never been prolific or fast, but at his best, his action-filled scripts were inventive, compelling, and thoughtful: his Oscar-winning screenplay In the Heat of the Night, for example, not to mention his television work for Naked City. I have tried to follow his example.

Thus, my first contact with Hollywood was positive. The troubled street kid who became addicted to movies as an antidote to the darkness of his life found that the dreams those movies inspired could, with hard work, be fulfilled. But many who've been exposed to Hollywood have had the opposite experience. Too often, writers are treated with indifference, at best, and malicious contempt, at worst. They're stonewalled, misled, or blatantly lied to. Some producers can't imagine showing courtesy to anyone they don't have to impress. Their inability to relate to others borders on the sociopathic. That never happened to me on any of the projects based on my works, but I certainly came across it in other contexts, enough so that I eventually decided to write about the downside of dreams in Hollywood. This is the final story in my trilogy about the paradoxes of ambition and the dark side of success. The series began with a paperboy. It moved on to a teenaged football player. It now concludes with an adult who tells us about the heartbreak of the movie business. I haven't updated the fi-

nancial figures in this story. After the $200 million price tag of Titanic, I'm amazed to look back at how comparatively cheaply a film could once get made. The following story was a finalist for the World Fantasy Award as the best novella of 1985.

Dead Image

"YOU KNOW WHO HE LOOKS LIKE, DON'T YOU?"

Watching the scene, I just shrugged.

"Really, the resemblance is amazing," Jill said.

"Mmm."

We were in the studio's screening room, watching yesterday's dailies. The director—and I use the term loosely—had been having troubles with the leading actor, if acting's what you could say that good-looking bozo does. Hell, he used to be a male model. He doesn't act. He poses. It wasn't enough that he wanted 8 million bucks and fifteen upfront points to do the picture. It wasn't enough that he changed my scene so the dialogue sounded as if a moron had written it. No, he had to keep dashing to his trailer, snorting more coke (for "creative inspiration," he said), then sniffling after every sentence in the big speech of the picture. If this scene didn't work, the audience wouldn't understand his motivation for leaving his girlfriend after she became a famous singer, and believe me, nothing's more unforgiving than an audience when it gets confused. The word of mouth would kill us.

"Come on, you big dumb son of a bitch," I muttered. "You make me want to blow my nose just listening to you."

The director had wasted three days doing retakes, and the dailies from yesterday were worse than the ones from the two days before. Sliding down in my seat, I groaned. The director's idea of fixing the scene was to have a team of editors work all night patching in reaction shots from the girl and the guys in the country-western band she sang with. Every time Mr. Wonderful sniffled— cut, we saw somebody staring at him as if he were Jesus.

"Jesus," I moaned to Jill. "Those cuts distract from the speech. It's supposed to be one continuous shot."

"Of course, this is rough, you understand," the director told everyone from where he sat in the back row of seats, near the door. To make a quick getaway, if he had any sense. "We haven't worked on the dubbing yet. That sniffling won't be on the release print."

"I hope to God not," I muttered.

"Really. Just like him," Jill said next to me.

"Huh? Who?" I turned to her. "What are you talking about?"

"The guitar player. The kid behind the girl. Haven't you been listening?" She kept her voice low enough that no one else could have heard her.

That's why I blinked when the studio VP asked from

somewhere in the dark to my left, "Who's the kid behind the girl?"

Jill whispered, "Watch the way he holds that beer can."

"There. The one with the beer can," the VP said.

Except for the lumox sniffling on the screen, the room was silent.

The VP spoke louder. "I said, who's the—"

"I don't know." Behind us, the director cleared his throat.

"He must have told you his name."

"I never met him."

"How the hell, if you . . ."

"All the concert scenes were shot by the second-unit director."

"What about these reaction shots?"

"Same thing. The kid only had a few lines. He did his bit and went home. Hey, I had my hands full making Mr. Nose Candy feel like the genius he thinks he is."

"There's the kid again," Jill said.

I was beginning to see what she meant now. The kid looked a lot like—

"James Deacon," the VP said. "Yeah, that's who he reminds me of."

Mr. Muscle Bound had managed to struggle through the speech. I'd recognized only half of it—partly because the lines he'd added made no sense, mostly because he mumbled. At the end, we had a close-up of his girlfriend, the singer, crying. She'd been so heartless clawing her way to the top that she'd lost the one thing that mattered—the man who'd loved her. In theory, the audience was supposed to feel so sorry for her that they'd be crying along with her. If you ask me, they'd be in tears all right—from rolling around in the aisles with laughter. On the screen, Mr. Beefcake turned and trudged from the rehearsal hall, as if his underwear was too tight. He had his eyes narrowed manfully, ready to pick up his Oscar.

The screen went dark. The director cleared his throat again. He sounded nervous. "Well?"

The room was silent.

The director sounded more nervous. "Uh . . . so what do you think?"

The lights came on, but they weren't the reason I suddenly had a headache.

Everybody turned toward the VP, waiting for the word of God.

"What I think," the VP said, nodding wisely, "is that we need a rewrite."

"This fucking town." I gobbled Di-Gel as Jill drove us home. The Santa Monica freeway was jammed, as usual. We had the top down on the Porsche, so we got a really good dose of car exhaust.

"They won't blame the star. After all, he charged eight million bucks, and next time he'll charge more if the studio pisses him off." I winced from heartburn. "They'd never think to blame the director. He's a goddamned artist, as he keeps telling everybody. So who does that leave? The underpaid schmuck who wrote what everybody changed."

"Take it easy. You'll raise your blood pressure." Jill turned off the freeway.

"Raise my blood pressure? Raise my— It's already raised! Any higher, I'll have a stroke!"

"I don't know what you're so surprised about. This happens on every picture. We've been out here fifteen years. You ought to be used to how they treat writers."

"Whipping boys. That's the only reason they keep us around. Any director, producer, or actor in town is a better writer. Just ask them; they'll tell you. The only problem is, they can't read, let alone write, and they just don't seem to have the time to sit down and put all their wonderful thoughts on paper."

"But that's how the system works, hun. There's no way to win, so either you love this business or leave it."

I scowled. "About the only way to make a decent picture is to direct as well as write it. Hell, I'd star in it, too, if I wasn't losing my hair from pulling it out."

"And twenty million bucks," Jill said.

"Yeah, that would help, too—so I wouldn't have to grovel in front of those studio heads. But hell, if I had twenty million bucks to finance a picture, what would I need to be a writer for?"

"You know you'd keep writing, even if you had a hundred million."

"You're right. I must be nuts."

"Wes Crane," Jill said.

I sat at the word processor, grumbling as I did the rewrite. The studio VP had decided that Mr. Biceps wasn't going to leave his girlfriend. Instead, his girlfriend was going to realize how much she'd been ignoring him and give up her career for love. "There's an audience out there dying for a movie against women's lib," he said. It was all I could do not to throw up.

"Wes who?" I kept typing on the keyboard.

"Crane. The kid in the dailies."

I turned to where she stood at the open door to my study. I must have blinked stupidly, because she got that patient look on her face.

"The one who looks like James Deacon. I got curious. So for the hell of it, I phoned the casting office at the studio."

"All right, so you found out his name. So what's the point?"

"Just a hunch."

"I still don't get it."

"Your script about mercenary soldiers."

I shrugged. "It still needs a polish. Anyway, it's strictly on spec. When the studio decides we've ruined this picture sufficiently, I have to do that Napoléon miniseries for ABC."

"You wrote that script on spec because you believed in the story, right? It's something you really wanted to do."

"The subject's important. Soldiers of fortune employed by the CIA. Unofficially, America's involved in a lot of foreign wars."

"Then fuck the miniseries. I think the kid would be wonderful as the young mercenary who gets so disgusted that he finally shoots the dictator who hired him."

I stared. "You know, that's not a bad idea."

"When we were driving home, didn't you tell me the

only way to film something decent was to direct the thing yourself?"

"And star in it." I raised my eyebrows. "Yeah, that's me. But I was just making a joke."

"Well, lover, I know you couldn't direct any worse than that asshole who ruined your stuff this morning. I've got the hots for you, but you're not good-looking enough for even a character part. That kid is, though. And the man who discovers him . . ."

". . . can write his own ticket. If he puts the package together properly."

"You've had fifteen years of learning the politics."

"But if I back out on ABC . . ."

"Half the writers in town wanted that assignment. They'll sign someone else in an hour."

"But they offered a lot of dough."

"You just made four hundred thousand on a story the studio ruined. Take a flier, why don't you? This one's for your self-respect."

"I think I love you," I said.

"When you're sure, come down to the bedroom."

She turned and left. I watched the doorway for a while, then swung my chair to face the picture window and thought about mercenaries. We live on a bluff in Pacific Palisades. You can see the ocean forever. But what I saw in my head was the kid in the dailies. How he held that beer can.

Just like James Deacon.

Deacon. If you're a film buff, you know the guy I'm talking about. The farm boy from Oklahoma. Back in the middle fifties. At the start, a juvenile delinquent, almost went to reform school for stealing cars. But a teacher managed to get him interested in high school plays. Deacon never graduated. Instead, he borrowed a hundred bucks and hitchhiked to New York, where he camped on Lee Strasberg's doorstep till Strasberg agreed to give him a chance in the Actors Studio. A lot of brilliant actors came out of that school. Brando, Newman, Clift, Gazzara, McQueen. But some say Deacon was the best of the lot. A bit part on Broadway. A talent scout in the audience. A screen test. The rest, as they say, is history. The part of the younger brother in *The Prodigal Son*. The juvenile delinquent in *Revolt on Thirty-second Street*. Then the wildcat oil driller in *Birthright*, where he upstaged half a dozen major stars. There was something about him. Intensity, sure. You could sense the pressure building in him, swelling inside his skin, wanting out. And authenticity. God knows, you could tell how much he believed the parts he was playing. He actually was those characters.

But mostly, the camera simply loved him. That's the way they explain a star out here. Some good-looking guys come across as plain on the screen. And some plain ones look gorgeous. It's a question of taking a three-dimensional face and making it two-dimensional for the screen. What's distinctive in real life gets muted, and vice versa. There's no way to figure if the camera will like you. It either does or doesn't. And it sure liked Deacon.

What's fascinating is that he also looked as gorgeous in real life. A walking movie. Or so they say. I never met him, of course. He was before my time. But the word in the industry was that he couldn't do anything wrong. That was even before his three movies were released. A guaranteed superstar.

And then?

Cars. If you think of his life as a tragedy, cars were the flaw. He loved to race them. I'm told his body had practically disintegrated when he hit the pickup truck at a hundred miles an hour on his way to drive his modified Corvette at a racetrack in northern California. Maybe you heard the legend. That he didn't die but was so disfigured that he's in a rest home somewhere to spare his fans the disgust of how he looks. But don't believe it. Oh, he died all right. Just like a shooting star, he exploded. And the irony is that, since his three pictures hadn't been released by then, he never knew how famous he would become.

But what I was thinking was, if a star could shine once, maybe it can shine again.

"I'm looking for Wes. Is he around?"

I'd phoned the Screen Actors Guild to get his address. For the sake of privacy, sometimes all the Guild gives out is the name and phone number of an actor's agent, and what I had in mind was so tentative that I didn't want the hassle of dealing with an agent right then.

But I got lucky. The Guild gave me an address.

The place was in a canyon north of the Valley. A dusty, winding road led up to an unpainted house with a sundeck supported on stilts and half a dozen junky cars in front, along with a dune buggy and a motorcycle. Seeing those clunkers, I felt self-conscious in the Porsche.

Two guys and a girl were sitting on the steps. The girl had a butch cut. The guys had hair to their shoulders.

They wore sandals, shorts, and that's all. The girl's breasts were as brown as nutmeg.

The three of them stared right through me. Their eyes looked big and strange.

I opened my mouth to repeat the question.

But the girl beat me to it. "Wes?" She sounded groggy. "I think . . . out back."

"Hey, thanks." But I made sure I had the Porsche's keys in my pocket before I plodded past sagebrush toward where she managed to point.

The back of the house had a sundeck, too, and as I turned the corner, I saw him up there, leaning against the rail, squinting toward the foothills.

I tried not to show surprise. In person, Wes looked even more like Deacon. Lean, intense, hypnotic. Around twenty-one, the same age Deacon had been when he made his first movie. Sensitive, brooding, as if he suffered secret tortures. But tough-looking, also, projecting the image of someone who'd been emotionally savaged once and wouldn't allow it to happen again. He wasn't tall, and he sure was thin, but he radiated such energy that he made you think he was big and powerful. Even his clothes reminded me of Deacon. Boots, faded jeans, a denim shirt with the sleeves rolled up and a pack of cigarettes tucked in the fold. And a battered Stetson with the rim curved up to meet the sides.

Actors love to pose, of course. I'm convinced that they don't even go to the bathroom without giving an imaginary camera their best profile. And the way this kid leaned against the rail, staring moodily toward the foothills, was certainly photogenic.

But I had the feeling it wasn't a pose. His clothes didn't seem a deliberate imitation of Deacon. He wore them too comfortably. And his brooding silhouette didn't seem calculated, either. I've been in the business long enough to know. He dressed and leaned that way naturally. That's the word they use for a winner in this business. He was a natural.

"Wes Crane?" I asked.

He turned and looked down at me. At last, he grinned. "Why not?" He had a vague country-boy accent. Like Deacon.

"I'm David Sloane."

He nodded.

"Then you recognize the name?"

He shrugged. "Sounds awful familiar."

"I'm a screenwriter. I did *Broken Promises*, the picture you just finished working on."

"I remember the name now. On the script."

"I'd like to talk to you."

"About?"

"Another script." I held it up. "There's a part in it that I think might interest you."

"So you're a producer, too?"

I shook my head no.

"Then why come to me? Even if I like the part, it won't do us any good."

I thought about how to explain. "I'll be honest. It's a big mistake as far as negotiating goes, but I'm tired of bullshit."

"Cheers." He raised a beer can to his lips.

"I saw you in the dailies this morning. I liked what I

saw. A lot. What I want you to do is read this script and tell me if you want the part. With your commitment and me as director, I'd like to approach a studio for financing. But that's the package. You don't do it if I don't direct. And I don't do it unless you're the star."

"So what makes you think they'd accept me?"

"My wife's got a hunch."

He laughed. "Hey, I'm out of work. Anybody offers me a job, I take it. Why should I care who directs? Who are you to me?"

My heart sank.

He opened another beer can. "Guess what, though? I don't like bullshit, either." His eyes looked mischievous. "Sure, what have I got to lose? Leave the script."

My number was on the front of it. The next afternoon, he called.

"This script of yours? I'll tell you the same thing you said to me about my acting. I liked it. A lot."

"It still needs a polish."

"Only where the guy's best friend gets killed. The hero wouldn't talk so much about what he feels. The fact is, he wouldn't say anything. No tears. No outburst. This is a guy who holds himself in. All you need is a close-up on his eyes. That says it all. He stares down at his buddy. He picks up his M16. He turns toward the palace. The audience'll start to cheer. They'll know he's set to kick ass."

Most times when an actor offers suggestions, my stomach cramps. They get so involved in the part, they forget about the story's logic. They want more lines. They want to emphasize their role till everybody else in the picture looks weak. Now here was an actor who wanted his largest speech cut out. He was thinking story, not ego. And he was right. That speech had always bothered me. I'd written it ten different ways and still hadn't figured out what was wrong.

Till now.

"The speech is out," I said. "It won't take fifteen minutes to redo the scene."

"And then?"

"I'll go to the studio."

"You're really not kidding me? You think there's a chance I can get the part?"

"As much chance as I have to direct it. Remember the arrangement. We're a package. Both of us, or none."

"And you don't want me to sign some kind of promise?"

"It's called a binder. And you're right. You don't have to sign a thing."

"Let me get this straight. If they don't want you to direct but they offer me the part, I'm supposed to turn them down. Because I promised you?"

"Sounds crazy, doesn't it?" The truth was, even if I had his promise in writing, the studio lawyers could have it nullified if Wes claimed he'd been misled. This town wouldn't function if people kept their word.

"Yeah, crazy," Wes said. "You've got a deal."

In the casting office at the studio, I asked a thirtyish thin-faced woman behind a counter, "Have you got any film on an actor named Crane? Wes Crane?"

She looked at me strangely. Frowning, she opened a

filing cabinet and sorted through some folders. She nodded, relieved. "I knew that name was familiar. Sure,
we've got a screen test on him."

"What? Who authorized it?"

She studied a page. "Doesn't say."

And I never found out, and that's one of many things
that bother me. "Do you know who's seen the test?"

"Oh, sure, we have to keep a record." She studied another page. "But I'm the only one who looked at it."

"You?"

"He came in one day to fill out some forms. We got
to kidding around. It's hard to describe. There's something about him. So I thought I'd take a look at his test."

"And?"

"What can I say? I recommended him for that bit part
in *Broken Promises*."

"If I want to see that test, do you have to check with
anybody?"

She thought about it. "You're still on the payroll for
Broken Promises, aren't you?"

"Right."

"And Crane's in the movie. It seems a legitimate request." She checked a schedule. "Use screening room
four. In thirty minutes. I'll send down a projectionist with
the reel."

So I sat in the dark and watched the test and first felt
the shiver that I'd soon know well. When the reel was
over, I didn't move for quite a while.

The projectionist came out. "Are you all right, Mr.
Sloane? I mean, you're not sick or anything?"

"No. Thanks. I'm . . ."

"What?"

"Just thinking."

I took a deep breath and went back to the casting office.

"There's been a mistake. That wasn't Crane's test."

The thin-faced woman shook her head. "There's no mistake."

"But that was a scene from *The Prodigal Son*. James Deacon's movie. There's been a switch."

"No, that was Wes Crane. It's the scene he wanted to do. The set department used something that looked like the hayloft in the original."

"Wes . . ."

"Crane," she said. "Not Deacon."

We stared.

"And you liked it?" I asked.

"Well, I thought he was ballsy to choose that scene— and pull it off. One wrong move, he'd have looked like an idiot. Yeah, I liked it."

"You want to help the kid along?"

"Depends. Will it get me in trouble?"

"Exactly the opposite. You'll earn brownie points."

"How?"

"Just phone the studio VP. Tell him I was down here asking to watch a screen test. Tell him you didn't let me because I didn't have authorization. But I acted upset, so now you've had second thoughts, and you're calling him to make sure you did the right thing. You don't want to lose your job."

"So what will that accomplish?"

"He'll get curious. He'll ask whose test it was. Just tell him the truth. But use these words. 'The kid who looks like James Deacon.'"

"I still don't see . . ."

"You will." I grinned.

I called my agent and told him to plant an item in *Variety* and *The Hollywood Reporter.* "Oscar-winning scribe David Sloane currently prepping his first behind-the-lens chore on *Mercenaries,* top-lining James Deacon look-alike Wes Crane."

"What's going on? Is somebody else representing you? I don't know from chicken livers about *Mercenaries.*"

"Lou, trust me."

"What's the studio?"

"All in good time."

"You son of a bitch, if you expect me to work for you when somebody else is getting the commission—"

"Believe me, you'll get your ten percent. But if anybody calls, tell them they have to talk to me. You're not allowed to discuss the project."

"Discuss it? How the hell can I discuss it when I don't know a thing about it?"

"There. You see how easy it'll be?"

Then I drove to a video store and bought a tape of *The Prodigal Son.*

I hadn't seen the movie in years. That evening, Jill and I watched it fifteen times. Or at least a part of it that often. Every time the hayloft scene was over, I rewound the tape to the start of the scene.

"For God's sake, what are you doing? Don't you want to see the whole movie?"

"It's the same." I stared in astonishment.

"What do you mean, 'the same'? Have you been drinking?"

"The hayloft scene. It's the same as in Wes Crane's screen test."

"Well, of course. You told me the set department tried to imitate the original scene."

"I don't mean the hayloft." I felt that tingle again. "See, here in *The Prodigal Son*, Deacon does most of the scene sprawled on the floor of the loft. He has the side of his face pressed against those bits of straw. I can almost smell the dust and the chaff. He's talking more to the floor than he is to his father, behind him."

"I see it. So what are you getting at?"

"That's identical in Wes Crane's test. One continuous shot with the camera at the floor. Crane has his cheek against the wood. He sounds the same as Deacon. Every movement, every pause, even that choking noise right here as if the character's about to start sobbing—they're identical."

"But what's the mystery about it? Crane must have studied this section before he decided to use it in his test."

I rewound the tape.

"No, not again," Jill said.

The next afternoon, the studio VP phoned. "I'm disappointed in you, David."

"Don't tell me you didn't like the rewrite on *Broken Promises*."

"The rewrite? The . . . Oh, yes, the rewrite. Great, David, great. They're shooting it now. Of course, you understand I had to make a few extra changes. Don't worry, though. I won't ask to share the writing credit with you." He chuckled.

I chuckled right back. "Well, that's a relief."

"What I'm calling about are the trades today. Since when have you become a director?"

"I was afraid of this. I'm not allowed to talk about it."

"I asked your agent. He says he didn't handle the deal."

"Well, yeah, it's something I set up on my own."

"Where?"

"Walt, I really can't talk about it. Those items in the trades surprised the hell out of me. They might screw up the deal. I haven't finished the negotiations yet."

"With this kid who looks like James Deacon."

"Honestly, I've said as much as I can, Walt."

"I'll tell you flat out. I don't think it's right for you to try to sneak him away from us. I'm the one who discovered him, remember. I had a look at his screen test yesterday. He's got the makings of a star."

I knew when he'd screened that test. Right after the woman in the casting department phoned him to ask if I had a right to see the test. One thing you can count on in this business: Everybody's so paranoid, they want to know what everybody else is doing. If they think a trend is developing, they'll stampede to follow it.

"Walt, I'm not exactly trying to sneak him away from you. You don't have him under contract, do you?"

"And what's this project called *Mercenaries*? What's that all about?"

"It's a script I did on spec. I got the idea when I heard about the ads at the back of *Soldier of Fortune* magazine."

"*Soldier of* . . . David, I thought we had a good working relationship."

"Sure. That's what I thought, too."

"Then why didn't you talk to me about this story? Hey, we're friends, after all. Chances are, you wouldn't have had to write it on spec. I could have given you some development money."

And after you'd finished mucking with it, you'd have turned it into a musical, I thought. "Well, I guess I figured it wasn't for you. Since I wanted to direct and use an unknown in the lead."

Another thing you can count on in this business: Tell a producer that a project isn't for him, and he'll feel so left out that he'll want to see it. That doesn't mean he'll buy it. But at least he'll have the satisfaction of knowing that he didn't miss out on a chance for a hit.

"Directing, David? You're a writer. What do you know about directing? I'd have to draw the line on that. But using the kid as a lead. I considered that yesterday after I saw his test."

Like hell you did, I thought. The test only made you curious. The items in the trades today are what gave you the idea.

"You see what I mean?" I asked. "I figured you wouldn't like the package. That's why I didn't take it to you."

"Well, the problem's hypothetical. I just sent the head of our legal department out to see him. We're offering the kid a long-term option."

"In other words, you want to fix it so no one else can use him, but you're not committing yourself to star him in a picture, and you're paying him a fraction of what you think he might be worth."

"Hey, ten thousand bucks isn't pickled herring. Not from his point of view. So maybe we'll go to fifteen."

"Against?"

"A hundred and fifty thousand if we use him in a picture."

"His agent won't go for it."

"He doesn't have one."

That explained why the Screen Actors Guild had given me Wes's home address and phone number instead of an agent's.

"I get it now," I said. "You're doing all this just to spite me."

"There's nothing personal in this, David. It's business. I tell you what. Show me the script. Maybe we can put a deal together."

"But you won't accept me as a director."

"Hey, with budgets as high as they are, the only way I can justify our risk with an unknown actor is by paying him next to nothing. If the picture's a hit, he'll screw us next time anyhow. But I won't risk the money I'm saving by using an inexperienced director who'd probably run the budget into the stratosphere. I see this picture coming in at fifteen million tops."

"But you haven't even read the script. It's got several

big action scenes. Explosions. Helicopters. Expensive special effects. Twenty-five million minimum."

"That's just my point. You're so close to the concept that you wouldn't want to compromise on the special effects. You're not directing."

"Well, as you said before, it's hypothetical. I've taken the package to somebody else."

"Not if we put him under option. David, don't fight me on this. Remember, we're friends."

Paramount phoned an hour later. Trade gossip travels fast. They'd heard I was having troubles with my studio and wondered if we could take a meeting to discuss the project they'd been reading about.

I said I'd get back to them. But now I had what I wanted—I could truthfully say that Paramount had been in touch with me. I could play the studios off against each other.

Walt phoned back that evening. "What did you do with the kid? Hide him in your closet?"

"Couldn't find him, huh?"

"The head of our legal department says the kid lives with a bunch of freaks way the hell out in the middle of nowhere. The freaks don't communicate too well. The kid isn't there, and they don't know where he went."

"I'm meeting him tomorrow."

"Where?"

"Can't say, Walt. Paramount's been in touch."

Wes met me at a taco stand he liked in Burbank. He'd been racing his motorcycle in a meet, and when he pulled up in his boots and jeans, his T-shirt and leather jacket, I shivered from déjà vu. He looked exactly as Deacon had looked in *Revolt on Thirty-second Street.*

"Did you win?"

He grinned and raised his thumb. "Yourself?"

"Some interesting developments."

He barely had time to park his bike before two men in suits came over. I wondered if they were cops, but their suits were too expensive. Then I realized. The studio. I'd been followed from my house.

"Mr. Hepner would like you to look at this," the blue suit told Wes. He set a document on the roadside table.

"What is it?"

"An option for your services. Mr. Hepner feels that the figure will interest you."

Wes shoved it over to me. "What's it mean?"

I read it quickly. The studio had raised the fee. They were offering fifty thousand now against a quarter of a million.

I told him the truth. "In your position, it's a lot of cash. I think that at this point you need an agent."

"You know a good one?"

"My own. But that might be too chummy."

"So what do you think I should do?"

"The truth? How much did you make last year? Fifty grand's a serious offer."

"Is there a catch?"

I nodded. "Chances are, you'll be put in *Mercs.*"

"And?"

"I don't direct."

Wes squinted at me. This would be the moment I'd

always cherish. "You're willing to let me do it?" he asked.

"I told you that I can't hold you to our bargain. In your place, I'd be tempted. It's a good career move."

"Listen to him," the gray suit said.

"But do you *want* to direct?"

I nodded. Until now, all the moves had been predictable. But Wes himself was not. Most unknown actors would grab at the chance for stardom. They wouldn't care what private agreements they ignored. Everything depended on whether Wes had a character similar to Deacon's.

"And no hard feelings if I go with the studio?" he asked.

I shrugged. "What we talked about was fantasy. This is real."

He kept squinting at me. All at once, he turned to the suits and slid the option toward them. "Tell Mr. Hepner that my friend here has to direct."

"You're making a big mistake," the blue suit said.

"Yeah, well, here today, gone tomorrow. Tell Mr. Hepner I trust my friend to make me look good."

I exhaled slowly. The suits looked grim.

I'll skip the month of negotiations. There were times when I sensed that Wes and I had both thrown away our careers. The key was that Walt had taken a stand, and pride wouldn't let him budge. But when I offered to direct for union scale (and let the studio have the screenplay for the minimum the Writers Guild would allow, and Wes agreed to the Actors Guild minimum), Walt had a deal that he couldn't refuse. Greed budged him in our favor. He bragged about how he'd outmaneuvered us.

We didn't care. I was making a picture I believed in, and Wes was on the verge of being a star.

I did my homework. I brought the picture in for $12 million. These days, that's a bargain. The rule of thumb says that you multiply the picture's cost by three (to account for studio overhead, bank interest, promotion, this and that), and you've got the break-even point.

So we were aiming for $36 million in ticket sales. Worldwide, we did $120 million. Now a lot of that went to the distributors, the folks that sell you popcorn. And a lot of that went into some mysterious black hole of theater owners who don't report all the tickets they sell and foreign chains that suddenly go bankrupt. But after the sale to HBO and CBS, after the income from tapes and discs and showings on airlines, the studio had a solid $40 million profit in the bank. And that, believe me, qualifies as a hit.

We were golden. The studio wanted another Wes Crane picture yesterday. The reviews were glowing. Both Wes and I were nominated for—but didn't receive—an Oscar. "Next time," I told Wes.

And now that we were hot, we demanded fees that were large enough to compensate for the pennies we'd been paid on the first one.

Then the trouble started.

You remember that Deacon never knew he was a star. He died with three pictures in the can and a legacy that he never knew would make him immortal. But what you probably don't know is that Deacon became more difficult as he went from picture to picture. The theory is that he sensed the power he was going to have, and he couldn't handle it. Because he was making up for his troubled youth. He was showing people that he wasn't the fuckup his foster parents and his teachers (with one exception) said he was. But Deacon was so intense—and so insecure—that he started reverting. Secretly, he felt that he didn't deserve his predicted success. So he did become a fuckup, as predicted.

On his next-to-last picture, he started showing up three hours late for the scenes he was supposed to be in. He played expensive pranks on the set, the worst of which was lacing the crow's lunch with a laxative that shut down production for the rest of the day. His insistence on racing cars forced the studio to pay exorbitant premiums to the insurance company that covered him during shooting. On his last picture, he was drunk more often than not, swilling beer and tequila on the set. Just before he died in the car crash, he looked twenty-two going on sixty. Most of his visuals had been completed, just a few close-ups remaining, but since a good deal of *Birthright* was shot on location in the Texas oil fields, his dialogue needed rerecording to eliminate background noises on the sound track. A friend of his who'd learned to imitate Deacon's voice was hired to dub several key speeches. The audience loved the finished print, but they didn't realize how much of the film depended on careful editing, emphasizing other characters in scenes where

Deacon looked so wasted that his footage couldn't be used.

So naturally, I wondered—if Wes Crane looked like Deacon and sounded like Deacon, dressed like Deacon and had Deacon's style, would he start to behave like Deacon? What would happen when I went to Wes with a second project?

I wasn't the only one offering stories to him. The scripts came pouring in.

I learned this from the trades. I hadn't seen him since Oscar night in March. Whenever I called his place, either I didn't get an answer or a spaced-out woman's voice told me Wes wasn't home. In truth, I'd expected him to have moved from that dingy house near the desert. The gang who lived there reminded me of the Manson clan. But then I remembered that he hadn't come into big money yet. The second project would be the gold mine. And I wondered if he was going to stake the claim only for himself.

His motorcycle was parked outside our house when Jill and I came back from a Writers Guild screening of a new Clint Eastwood movie. This was at sunset, with sailboats silhouetted against a crimson ocean. Wes was sitting on the steps that wound up through a rose garden to our house. He held a beer can. He was wearing jeans and a T-shirt again, and the white of that T-shirt contrasted beautifully with his tan. But his cheeks looked gaunter than when I'd last seen him.

Our exchange had become a ritual.

"Did you win?"

He grinned and raised a thumb. "Yourself?"

I grinned right back. "I've been trying to get in touch with you."

He shrugged. "Well, yeah, I've been racing. I needed some downtime. All that publicity, and . . . Jill, how are you?"

"Fine, Wes. You?"

"The second go-round's the hardest."

I thought I understood. Trying for another hit. But now I wonder.

"Stay for supper?" Jill asked.

"I'd like to, but . . ."

"Please, do. It won't be any trouble."

"Are you sure?"

"The chili's been cooking in the Crock-Pot all day. Tortillas and salad."

Wes nodded. "Yeah, my mom used to like making chili. That's before my dad went away and she got to drinking."

Jill's eyebrows narrowed. Wes didn't notice; he was staring at his beer can.

"Then she didn't do much cooking at all," he said. "When she went to the hospital . . . This was back in Oklahoma. Well, the cancer ate her up. And the city put me in a foster home. I guess that's when I started running wild." Brooding, he drained his beer can and blinked at us as if remembering we were there. "A home-cooked meal would go good."

"It's coming up," Jill said.

But she still looked bothered, and I almost asked her what was wrong. She went inside.

Wes reached in a paper sack beneath a rosebush.

"Anyway, buddy." He handed me a beer can. "You want to make another movie?"

"The trades say you're much in demand." I sat beside him, stared at the ocean, and popped the tab on the beer can.

"Yeah, but aren't we supposed to be a team? You direct and write. I act. Both of us, or none." He nudged my knee. "Isn't that the bargain?"

"It is if you say so. Right now, you've got the clout to do anything you want."

"Well, what I want is a friend. Someone I trust to tell me when I'm fucking up. Those other guys, they'll let you do anything if they think they can make a buck, even if you ruin yourself. I've learned my lesson. Believe me, this time I'm doing things right."

"In that case," I said, vaguely puzzled.

"Let's hear it."

"I've been working on something. We start with several givens. The audience likes you in an action role. But you've got to be rebellious, antiestablishment. And the issue has to be controversial. What about a bodyguard—he's young, he's tough—who's supposed to protect a famous movie actress? Someone who reminds us of Marilyn Monroe. Secretly, he's in love with her, but he can't bring himself to tell her. And she dies from an overdose of sleeping pills. The cops say it's suicide. The newspapers go along. But the bodyguard can't believe she killed herself. He discovers evidence that it was murder. He gets pissed at the cover-up. From grief, he investigates further. A hit team nearly kills him. Now he's twice as pissed. And what he learns is that the man who ordered the murder—it's an election year, the actress was writing a tell-all about her famous lovers—is the president of the United States."

"I think"—he sipped his beer—"it would play in Oklahoma."

"And Chicago and New York. It's a backlash about big government. With a sympathetic hero."

He chuckled. "When do we start?"

And that's how we made the deal on *Grievance*.

I felt excited all evening, but later—after we'd had a pleasant supper and Wes had driven off on his motorcycle—Jill stuck a pin in my swollen optimism.

"What he said about Oklahoma, about his father running away, his mother becoming a drunk and dying from cancer, about his going to a foster home . . ."

"I noticed it bothered you."

"You bet. You're so busy staring at your keyboard that you don't keep up on the handouts about your star."

I put a bowl in the dishwasher. "So?"

"Wes comes from Indiana. He's a foundling, raised in an orphanage. The background he gave you isn't his."

"Then whose . . ."

Jill stared at me.

"My God, not Deacon's."

So there it was, like a hideous face popping out of a box to leer at me. Wes's physical resemblance to Deacon was accidental, an act of fate that turned out to be a godsend for him. But the rest—the mannerisms, the clothes, the voice—was truly deliberate. I know what you're thinking—I'm contradicting myself. When I first met him, I thought his style was too natural to be a conscious imitation. And when I realized that his screen test was identical in every respect to Deacon's hayloft scene in *The Prodigal Son,* I didn't believe that Wes had callously reproduced the scene. The screen test felt too natural to be an imitation. It was a homage.

But now I knew better. Wes was imitating all right. But chillingly, what Wes had done went beyond conventional imitation. He'd accomplished the ultimate goal of every Method actor. He wasn't playing a part. He wasn't pretending to be Deacon. He actually *was* his model. He'd so immersed himself in a role, which at the start was no doubt consciously performed, that now he *was* the role. Wes Crane existed only in name. His background, his thoughts, his very identity, weren't his own anymore. They belonged to a dead man.

"What the hell is this?" I asked. "*The Three Faces of Eve? Sybil?*"

Jill looked at me nervously. "As long as it isn't *Psycho.*"

What was I to do? Tell Wes he needed help? Have a heart-to-heart and try to talk him out of his delusion? All we had was the one conversation to back up our theory, and anyway, he wasn't dangerous. The opposite. His manners were impeccable. He always spoke softly, with humor. Besides, actors use all kinds of ways to psych themselves up. By nature, they're eccentric. The best thing to do, I thought, is wait and see. With another picture about to start, there wasn't any sense in making trouble. If his delusion became destructive . . .

But he certainly wasn't difficult on the set. He showed up a half hour early for his scenes. He knew his lines. He spent several evenings and weekends—no charge—rehearsing with the other actors. Even the studio VP admitted that the dailies looked wonderful.

About the only sign of trouble was his mania for racing cars and motorcycles. The VP had a fit about the insurance premiums.

"Hey, he needs to let off steam," I said. "There's a lot of pressure on him."

And on me, I'll admit. I had a budget of $25 million this time, and I wasn't going to ruin things by making my star self-conscious.

Halfway through the shooting schedule, Wes came over. "See, no pranks. I'm being good this time."

"Hey, I appreciate it." What the fuck did he mean by "this time"?

You're probably thinking that I could have stopped what happened if I'd cared more about him than I did for the picture. But I did care—as you'll see. And it didn't matter. What happened was as inevitable as tragedy.

Grievance became a bigger success than *Mercenaries*. A worldwide $200 million gross. *Variety* predicted an even bigger gross for the next one. Sure, the next one— number three. But at the back of my head, a nasty voice was telling me that for Deacon, three had been the unlucky number.

I left a conference at the studio and was walking toward my new Ferrari in the executive parking lot when someone shouted my name. Turning, I peered through the Burbank smog at a longhaired, bearded man wearing beads, a serape, and sandals, who was running over to me. I wondered what he wore, if anything, beneath the dangling serape.

I recognized him—Donald Porter, the friend of Deacon who'd played a bit part in *Birthright* and imitated Deacon's voice on some of the sound track after Deacon had died. Porter had to be in his forties now, but he dressed as if the sixties had never ended and hippies still existed. He'd starred and directed in a hit youth film twenty years ago—a lot of drugs and rock and sex. For a while, he'd tried to start his own studio in Santa Fe, but the second picture he directed was a flop, and after fading from the business for a while, he'd made a comeback as a character actor. The way he was dressed, I didn't understand how he'd passed the security guard at the gate. And because we knew each other—I'd once done a rewrite on a television show he was featured in—I had the terrible feeling he was going to ask me for a job.

"I heard you were on the lot. I've been waiting for you," Porter said.

I stared at his skinny bare legs beneath his serape.

"This, man?" He gestured comically at himself. "I'm in the new TV movie they're shooting here. *The Electric Kool-Aid Acid Test.*"

I nodded. "Tom Wolfe's book. Ken Kesey. Don't tell me you're playing—"

"No. Too old for Kesey. I'm Neal Cassidy. After he

split from Kerouac, he joined up with Kesey, driving the bus for the Merry Pranksters. You know, it's all a load of crap, man. Cassidy never dressed like this. He dressed like Deacon. Or Deacon dressed like him."

"Well, good. Hey, great. I'm glad things are going well for you." I turned toward my car.

"Just a second, man. That's not what I wanted to talk to you about. Wes Crane. You know?"

"No, I . . ."

"Deacon, man. Come on. Don't tell me you haven't noticed. Shit, man. I dubbed Deacon's voice. I knew him. I was his *friend*. Nobody else knew him better. Crane sounds more like Deacon than I did."

"So?"

"It isn't possible."

"Because he's better?"

"Cruel, man. Really. Beneath you. I have to tell you something. I don't want you thinking I'm on drugs again. I swear I'm clean. A little grass. That's it." His eyes looked as bright as a nova. "I'm into horoscopes. Astrology. The stars. That's a good thing for a movie actor, don't you think? The stars. There's a lot of truth in the stars."

"Whatever turns you on."

"You think so, man? Well, listen to this. I wanted to see for myself, so I found out where he lives, but I didn't go out there. Want to know why?" He didn't let me answer. "I didn't have to. 'Cause I recognized the address. I've been there a hundred times. When Deacon lived there."

I flinched. "You're changing the subject. What's that got to do with horoscopes and astrology?"

"Crane's birth date."

"Well?"

"It's the same as the day Deacon died."

I realized I'd stopped breathing. "So what?"

"More shit, man. Don't pretend it's coincidence. It's in the stars. You know what's coming. Crane's your bread and butter. But the gravy train'll end four months from now."

I didn't ask.

"Crane's birthday's coming up. The anniversary of Deacon's death."

And when I looked into it, there were other parallels. Wes would be twenty-four—Deacon's age when he died. And Wes would be close to the end of his third movie—about the same place as Deacon was in his third movie when he . . .

We were doing a script I'd written, *Rampage,* about a young man from a tough neighborhood who goes back there to teach. A local street gang harasses him and his wife, until the only way he can survive is by reverting to the violent life (he once led his own gang) that he ran away from.

It was Wes's idea to have the character renew his fascination with motorcycles. I have to admit that the notion had commercial value, given Wes's well-known passion for motorcycle racing. But I also felt apprehensive, especially when he insisted on doing his own stunts.

I couldn't talk him out of it. As if his model behavior on the first two pictures had been too great a strain on him, he snapped to the opposite extreme—showing up late, drinking on the set, playing expensive pranks. One joke involving firecrackers started a blaze in the costume trailer.

It all had the makings of a death wish. His absolute identification with Deacon was leading him to the ultimate parallel.

And just like Deacon in his final picture, Wes began to look wasted. Hollow-cheeked, squinty, stooped from lack of food and sleep. His dailies were shameful.

"How the hell are we supposed to ask an audience to pay to see this shit?" the studio VP asked.

"I'll have to shoot around him. Cut to reaction shots from the characters he's talking to." My heart lurched.

"That sounds familiar," Jill said.

I knew what she meant. I'd become the director I'd criticized on *Broken Promises*.

"Well, can't you control him?" the VP asked.

"It's hard. He's not quite himself these days."

"Damn it, if you can't, maybe another director can. This garbage is costing us forty million bucks."

The threat made me seethe. I almost told him to take his forty million bucks and . . .

Abruptly I understood the leverage he'd given me. I straightened. "Relax. Just let me have a week. If he hasn't improved by then, I'll back out gladly."

"Witnesses heard you say it. One week, pal, or else."

In the morning, I waited for Wes in his trailer. As usual, he showed up late for his first shot.

At the open trailer door, he had trouble focusing on me. "If it isn't teach." He shook his head. "No, wrong.

It's me who's supposed to play the teach in—what's the name of this garbage we're making?"

"Wes, I want to talk to you."

"Hey, funny thing. The same goes for me with you. Just give me a chance to grab a beer, okay?" Fumbling, he shut the trailer door behind him and lurched through shadows toward the miniature fridge.

"Try to keep your head clear. This is important," I said.

"Right. Sure." He popped the tab on a beer can and left the fridge door open while he drank. He wiped his mouth. "But first I want a favor."

"That depends."

"I don't have to ask, you know. I can just go ahead and do it. I'm trying to be polite."

"What is it?"

"Monday's my birthday. I want the day off. There's a motorcycle race near Sonora. I want to make a long weekend out of it." He drank more beer.

"We had an agreement once."

He scowled. Beer dribbled down his chin.

"I write and direct. You star. Both of us, or none."

"Yeah. So? I've kept the bargain."

"The studio's given me a week. To shape you up. If not, I'm off the project."

He sneered. "I'll tell them I don't work if you don't."

"Not that simple, Wes. At the moment, they're not that eager to do what you want. You're losing your clout. Remember why you liked us as a team?"

He wavered blearily.

"Because you wanted a friend. To keep you from

making the same mistakes again. To keep you from fucking up. Well, Wes, that's what you're doing. Fucking up."

He finished his beer and crumpled the can. He curled his lips, angry. "Because I want a day off on my birthday?"

"No, because you're getting your roles confused. You're not James Deacon. But you've convinced yourself that you are, and Monday you'll die in a crash."

He blinked. Then he sneered. "So what are you, a fortune-teller now?"

"A half-baked psychiatrist. Unconsciously, you want to complete the legend. The way you've been acting, the parallel's too exact."

"I told you the first time we met—I don't like bull-shit!"

"Then prove it. Monday, you don't go near a motor-cycle, a car . . . hell, even a go-cart. You come to the studio sober. You do your work as well as you know how. I drive you over to my place. We have a private party. You and me and Jill. She promises to make your favorite meal: T-bones, baked beans, steamed corn. Homemade birthday cake. Chocolate. Again, your favorite. The works. You stay the night. In the morning, we put James Deacon behind us and . . . ."

"Yeah? What?"

"You achieve the career Deacon never had."

His eyes looked uncertain.

"Or you go to the race and destroy yourself and break the promise you made. You and me together. A team. Don't back out of our bargain."

He shuddered as if he was going to crack.

*   *   *

In a movie, that would have been the climax—how he didn't race on his birthday, how we had the private party and he hardly said a word and went to sleep in our guest room.

And survived.

But this is what happened. On the Tuesday after his birthday, he couldn't remember his lines. He couldn't play to the camera. He couldn't control his voice. Wednesday was worse.

But I'll say this. On his birthday, the anniversary of Deacon's death, when Wes showed up sober and treated our bargain with honor, he did the most brilliant acting of his career. A zenith of tradecraft. I often watch the video of those scenes with profound respect.

And the dailies were so truly brilliant that the studio VP let me finish the picture.

But the VP never knew how I faked the rest of it. Overnight, Wes had totally lost his technique. I had enough in the can to deliver a print—with a lot of fancy editing and some uncredited but very expensive help from Donald Porter. He dubbed most of Wes's final dialogue.

"I told you. Horoscopes. Astrology," Donald said.

I didn't believe him until I took four scenes to an audio expert I know. He specializes in putting voices through a computer and making visual graphs of them.

He spread the charts in front of me. "Somebody played a joke on you. Or else you're playing one on me."

I felt so unsteady that I had to press my hands on his desk when I asked him, "How?"

"Using this first film, Deacon's scene from *The Prodigal Son*, as the standard, this second film is close. But this third one doesn't have any resemblance."

"So where's the joke?"

"In the fourth. It matches perfectly. Who's kidding who?"

Deacon had been the voice on the first. Donald Porter had been the voice on the second. Close to Deacon's, dubbing for Wes in *Rampage*. Wes himself had been the voice on the third—the dialogue in *Rampage* that I couldn't use because Wes's technique had gone to hell.

And the fourth clip? The voice that was identical to Deacon's, authenticated, verifiable. Wes again. His screen test. The imitated scene from *The Prodigal Son*.

Wes dropped out of sight. For sure, his technique had collapsed so badly that he would never again be a shining star. I kept phoning him, but I never got an answer. So, for what turned out to be the second-to-last time, I drove out to his dingy place near the desert. The Manson lookalikes were gone. Only one motorcycle stood outside. I climbed the steps to the sunporch, knocked, received no answer, and opened the door.

The blinds were closed. The place was in shadow. I went down a hall and heard strained breathing. Turned to the right. And entered a room.

The breathing was louder, more strident and forced.

"Wes?"

"Don't turn on the lights."

"I've been worried about you, friend."

"Don't . . ."

But I did. And what I saw made me swallow vomit.

He was slumped in a chair. Seeping into it would be more accurate. Rotting. Decomposing. His cheeks had holes that showed his teeth. A pool that stank of decaying vegetables spread on the floor around him.

"I should have gone racing on my birthday, huh?" His voice whistled through the gaping flesh in his throat.

"Oh, shit, friend." I started to cry. "Jesus Christ, I should have let you."

"Do me a favor, huh? Turn off the light now. Let me finish this in peace."

I had so much to say to him. But I couldn't. My heart broke.

"And buddy," he said, "I think we'd better forget about our bargain. We won't be working together anymore."

"What can I do to help? There must be something I can—"

"Yeah, let me end this the way I need to."

"Listen, I—"

"Leave," Wes said. "It hurts me too much to have you here, to listen to the pity in your voice."

"But I care about you. I'm your friend. I—"

"That's why I know you'll do what I ask"—the hole in his throat made another whistling sound—"and leave."

I stood in the darkness, listening to other sounds he made: liquid rotting sounds. "A doctor. There must be something a doctor can—"

"Been there. Done that. What's wrong with me, no doctor's going to cure. Now if you don't mind . . ."

"What?"

"You weren't invited. Get out."

I waited another long moment. ". . . Sure."

"Love you, man," he said.

". . . Love you."

Dazed, I stumbled outside. Down the steps. Across the sand. Blinded by the sun, unable to clear my nostrils of the stench in that room, I threw up beside the car.

The next day, I drove out again. The last time. Jill went with me. He'd moved. I never learned where.

And this is how it ended, the final dregs of his career. His talent was gone, but how his determination lingered.

Movies. Immortality.

See, special effects are expensive. Studios will grasp at any means to cut the cost.

He'd told me, "Forget about our bargain." I later discovered what he meant—he worked without me in one final feature. He wasn't listed in the credits, though. *Zombies from Hell.* Remember how awful Bela Lugosi looked in his last exploitation movie before they buried him in his Dracula cape?

Bela looked great compared to Wes. I saw the zombie movie in an eightplex out in the Valley. It did great business. Jill and I almost didn't get a seat.

Jill wept, as I did.

This fucking town. Nobody cares how it's done, as long as it packs them in.

The audience cheered when Wes stalked toward the leading lady.

And his jaw fell off.

Orange Is for Anguish, Blue for Insanity

*I*n 1986, a year after the previous story was published, I made a decision that surprised me as much as it did anyone else. Since 1970, I had been teaching American literature at the University of Iowa. I had risen through the ranks, gaining tenure and a full professorship. I thoroughly enjoyed teaching. It was a delight to be around young people eager to learn. The stimulation of the university environment and of my colleague friends had been a constant in my life for sixteen years.

Then I woke up one morning and recognized that I didn't have the energy to devote myself to two full-time professions any longer. I had been working seven days a week for as long as I could remember. Balancing my teaching responsibilities with my writing needs had often required me to get up before dawn and to stay awake after my family went to sleep. The idea of a day off or of a free weekend *wasn't in my universe. But while teaching was my love, writing was my passion, and when the burden of fatigue finally overwhelmed me, there wasn't any doubt what "the mild-mannered professor with the bloody-minded visions," as one critic called me, would do. In the fall of 1986, I resigned from the university.*

The adjustment was painful. After all, academia had been a crucial part of my life for even longer than my years at Iowa—all the way back to 1966, when I'd entered graduate school at Penn State. Although I now had the luxury to write full-time, I continued to feel the tug of the classroom. Often I reconsidered my decision. But in a matter of months, neither writing nor teaching mattered any longer.

In January of 1987, my son was diagnosed with bone cancer. From then until his death in June, the nightmarish roller coaster of emotions and pain through which Matt suffered made me fear for my sanity. This can't be happening, I told myself. It isn't real. But despairingly, it was, and I found myself wanting to escape from reality. While sitting in Matt's intensive-care room, watching his septic-shock-ravaged, comatose body, I was surprised to discover that the novel I was holding was by Stephen King. Stephen is a friend. He knew Matt and kindly sent him letters, along with rock tapes, to try to distract him from his ordeal. Even so, it seemed odd to me that in the midst of real-life horror, I was reading made-up horror. Then it occurred to me that the made-up horror was paradoxically providing a barrier from real-life horror. I recalled how fans often wrote to me, describing disasters in their lives—deaths, marriage breakups, lost jobs, fires, floods, car accidents—telling me that a book of mine had helped them make it through the night. As the subject of my doctoral dissertation, John Barth, once said, "Reality is a nice place to visit, but you wouldn't want to live there."

While these thoughts went through my mind, another friend, Douglas Winter, a multiple-talent fiction writer/ critic/anthologist/attorney, asked if I would contribute to an anthology he was putting together, Prime Evil. Writing was the last thing I wanted to do, and yet, with Doug's encouragement, when I wasn't visiting Matt in the hospital, I wrote the following novella, which was suggested by my fascination with the paintings of van Gogh. A tale about insanity, it helped to keep me sane. It received the Horror Writers Association's award for the best novella of 1988.

VAN DORN'S WORK WAS CONTROVERSIAL, OF COURSE. The scandal his paintings caused among Parisian artists in the late 1800s provided the stuff of legend. Disdaining conventions, thrusting beyond accepted theories, Van Dorn seized upon the essentials of the craft to which he'd devoted his soul. Color, design, and texture. With those principles in mind, he created portraits and landscapes so different, so innovative, that their subjects seemed merely an excuse for Van Dorn to put paint onto canvas. His brilliant colors, applied in passionate splotches and swirls, often so thick that they projected an eighth of an inch from the canvas, in the manner of a bas-relief, so dominated the viewer's perception that the person or scene depicted seemed secondary to technique.

Impressionism, the prevailing avant-garde theory of the late 1800s, imitated the eye's tendency to perceive the edges of peripheral objects as blurs. Van Dorn went one step further and so emphasized the lack of distinction among objects that they seemed to melt together, to merge into an interconnected, pantheistic universe of color. The branches of a Van Dorn tree became ectoplasmic tentacles, thrusting toward the sky and the grass, just as tentacles from the sky and grass thrust toward the tree, all melding into a radiant swirl. He seemed to address himself not to the illusions of light but to reality itself, or at least to his theory of it. The tree *is* the sky, his technique asserted. The grass is the tree, and the sky the grass. All is one.

Van Dorn's approach proved so unpopular among theorists of his time that he frequently couldn't buy a meal in exchange for a canvas upon which he'd labored for months. His frustration produced a nervous breakdown. His self-mutilation shocked and alienated such onetime friends as Cézanne and Gauguin. He died in squalor and obscurity. Not until the 1920s, thirty years after his death, were his paintings recognized for the genius they displayed. In the 1940s, his soul-tortured character became the subject of a best-selling novel, and in the 1950s, a Hollywood spectacular. These days, of course, even the least of his efforts can't be purchased for less than $3 million.

Ah, art.

It started with Myers and his meeting with Professor Stuyvesant. "He agreed . . . reluctantly."

"I'm surprised he agreed at all," I said. "Stuyvesant hates Post-Impressionism and Van Dorn in particular.

Why didn't you ask someone easy, like old man Bradford?"

"Because Bradford's academic reputation sucks. I can't see writing a dissertation if it won't be published, and a respected dissertation director can make an editor pay attention. Besides, if I can convince Stuyvesant, I can convince anyone."

"Convince him of what?"

"That's what Stuyvesant wanted to know," Myers said.

I remember that moment vividly, the way Myers straightened his lanky body, pushed his glasses close to his eyes, and frowned so hard that his curly red hair scrunched forward on his brow.

"Stuyvesant said that, even disallowing his own disinclination toward Van Dorn—God, the way that pompous asshole talks—he couldn't understand why I'd want to spend a year of my life writing about an artist who'd been the subject of countless books and articles. Why not choose an obscure but promising Neo-Expressionist and gamble that *my* reputation would rise with his? Naturally, the artist Stuyvesant recommended was one of his favorites."

"Naturally," I said. "If he named the artist I think he did . . ."

Myers mentioned the name.

I nodded. "Stuyvesant's been collecting him for the past five years. He hopes the resale value of the paintings will buy him a town house in London when he retires. So what did you tell him?"

Myers opened his mouth to answer, then hesitated.

With a brooding look, he turned toward a print of Van Dorn's swirling *Cypresses in a Hollow,* which hung beside a ceiling-high bookshelf crammed with Van Dorn biographies, analyses, and bound collections of reproductions. He didn't speak for a moment, as if the sight of the familiar print—its facsimile colors incapable of matching the brilliant tones of the original, its manufacturing process unable to re-create the exquisite texture of raised, swirled layers of paint on canvas—still took his breath away.

"So what did you tell him?" I asked again.

Myers exhaled with a mixture of frustration and admiration. "I said that what the critics wrote about Van Dorn was mostly junk. He agreed, with the implications that the paintings invited no less. I said that even the gifted critics hadn't probed to Van Dorn's essence. They were missing something crucial."

"Which is?"

"Exactly. Stuyvesant's next question. You know how he keeps relighting his pipe when he gets impatient. I had to talk fast. I told him I didn't know what I was looking for, but there's something"—Myers gestured toward the print—"something there. Something nobody's noticed. Van Dorn hinted as much in his diary. I don't know what it is, but I'm convinced his paintings hide a secret." Myers glanced at me.

I raised my eyebrows.

"Well, if nobody's noticed," Myers said, "it *must* be a secret, right?"

"But if *you* haven't noticed . . ."

Compelled, Myers turned toward the print again, his

tone filled with wonder. "How do I know it's there? Because when I look at Van Dorn's paintings, I *sense* it. I *feel* it."

I shook my head. "I can imagine what Stuyvesant said to that. The man deals with art as if it's geometry, and there aren't any secrets in——"

"What he said was, if I'm becoming a mystic, I ought to be in the School of Religion, not Art. But if I wanted enough rope to hang myself and strangle my career, he'd give it to me. He likes to believe he has an open mind, he said."

"That's a laugh."

"Believe me, he wasn't joking. He has a fondness for Sherlock Holmes, he said. If I thought I'd found a mystery and could solve it, by all means do so. And at that, he gave me his most condescending smile and said he would mention it at today's faculty meeting."

"So what's the problem? You got what you wanted. He agreed to direct your dissertation. Why do you sound so——"

"Today there *wasn't* any faculty meeting."

"Oh." My voice dropped. "You're screwed."

Myers and I had started graduate school at the University of Iowa together. That had been three years earlier, and we'd formed a strong-enough friendship to rent adjacent rooms in an old apartment building near campus. The spinster who owned it had a hobby of doing watercolors—she had no talent, I might add—and rented only to art students so they would give her lessons. In Myers's case, she had made an exception. He wasn't a painter, as I was. He was an art historian. Most painters work instinctively. They're not skilled at verbalizing what they want to accomplish. But words and not pigment were Myers's specialty. His impromptu lectures had quickly made him the old lady's favorite tenant.

After that day, however, she didn't see much of him. Nor did I. He wasn't at the classes we took together. I assumed he spent most of his time at the library. Late at night, when I noticed a light beneath his door and knocked, I didn't get an answer. I phoned him. Through the wall I heard the persistent, muffled ringing.

One evening I let the phone ring eleven times and was just about to hang up when he answered. He sounded exhausted.

"You're getting to be a stranger," I said.

His voice was puzzled. "Stranger? But I just saw you a couple of days ago."

"Two weeks ago, you mean."

"Oh, shit," he said.

"I've got a six-pack. You want to—"

"Yeah, I'd like that." He sighed. "Come over."

When he opened his door, I don't know what startled me more, the way Myers looked or what he'd done to his apartment.

I'll start with Myers. He had always been thin, but now he looked gaunt, emaciated. His shirt and jeans were rumpled. His red hair was matted. Behind his glasses, his eyes looked bloodshot. He hadn't shaved. When he closed the door and reached for a beer, his hand shook.

His apartment was filled with, covered with—I'm not sure how to convey the dismaying effect of so much brilliant clutter—Van Dorn prints. On every inch of the walls. The sofa, the chairs, the desk, the TV, the bookshelves. And the drapes, and the ceiling, and, except for a narrow path, the floor. Swirling sunflowers, olive trees, meadows, skies, and streams surrounded me, encompassed me, seemed to reach out for me. At the same time, I felt swallowed. Just as the blurred edges of objects within each print seemed to melt into one another, so each print melted into the next. I was speechless amid the chaos of color.

Myers took several deep gulps of beer. Embarrassed by my stunned reaction to the room, he gestured toward the vortex of prints. "I guess you could say I'm immersing myself in my work."

"When did you eat last?"

He looked confused.

"That's what I thought." I walked along the narrow path among the prints on the floor and picked up the phone. "The pizza's on me." I ordered the largest supreme the nearest Pepi's had to offer. They didn't deliver beer, but I had another six-pack in my fridge, and I had the feeling we'd be needing it.

I set down the phone. "Myers, what the hell are you doing?"

"I told you."

"Immersing yourself? Give me a break. You're cutting classes. You haven't showered in God knows how long. You look like hell. Your deal with Stuyvesant isn't worth destroying your health. Tell him you've changed your mind. Get an easier dissertation director."

"Stuyvesant's got nothing to do with this."

"Damn it, what *does* it have to do with? The end of comprehensive exams, the start of dissertation blues?"

Myers gulped the rest of his beer and reached for another can. "No, blue is for insanity."

"What?"

"That's the pattern." Myers turned toward the swirling prints. "I studied them chronologically. The more Van Dorn became insane, the more he used blue. And orange is his color of anguish. If you match the paintings with the personal crises described in his biographies, you see a corresponding use of orange."

"Myers, you're the best friend I've got. So forgive me for saying I think you're off the deep end."

He swallowed more beer and shrugged, as if to say he didn't expect me to understand.

"Listen," I said. "A personal color code, a connection between emotion and pigment, that's bullshit. I should know. You're the historian, but I'm the painter. I'm telling you, different people react to colors in different ways. Never mind the advertising agencies and their theories that some colors sell products more than others. It all depends on context. It depends on fashion. This year's 'in' color is next year's 'out.' But an honest-to-God great painter uses whatever color will give him the greatest effect. He's interested in creating, not selling."

"Van Dorn could have used a few sales."

"No question. The poor bastard didn't live long enough to come into fashion. But orange is for anguish and blue means insanity? Tell that to Stuyvesant, and he'll throw you out of his office."

Myers took off his glasses and rubbed the bridge of his nose. "I feel so . . . Maybe you're right."

"There's no maybe about it. I *am* right. You need food, a shower, and sleep. A painting's a combination of color and shape that people either like or they don't. The artist follows his instincts, uses whatever techniques he can master, and does his best. But if there's a secret in Van Dorn's work, it isn't a color code."

Myers finished his second beer and blinked in distress. "You know what I found out yesterday?"

I shook my head.

"The critics who devoted themselves to analyzing Van Dorn . . ."

"What about them?"

"They went insane, the same as he did."

"*What?* No way. I've studied Van Dorn's critics. They're as conventional and boring as Stuyvesant."

"You mean the mainstream scholars. The safe ones. I'm talking about the truly brilliant ones. The ones who haven't been recognized for their genius, just as Van Dorn wasn't recognized."

"What happened to them?"

"They suffered. The same as Van Dorn."

"They were put in an asylum?"

"Worse than that."

"Myers, don't make me ask."

"The parallels are amazing. They each tried to paint. In Van Dorn's style. And just like Van Dorn, they stabbed out their eyes."

* * *

I guess it's obvious by now—Myers was what you might call "high-strung." No negative judgment intended. In fact, his excitability was one of the reasons I liked him. That and his imagination. Hanging around with him was never dull. He loved ideas. Learning was his passion. And he passed his excitement on to me.

The truth is, I needed all the inspiration I could get. I wasn't a bad artist. Not at all. On the other hand, I wasn't a great one, either. As I neared the end of grad school, I had painfully come to realize that my work would never be more than "interesting." I didn't want to admit it, but I'd probably end up as a commercial artist in an advertising agency.

That night, however, Myers's imagination wasn't inspiring. It was scary. He was always going through phases of enthusiasm. El Greco, Picasso, Pollock. Each had preoccupied him to the point of obsession, only to be abandoned for another favorite, then another. When he'd fixated on Van Dorn, I'd assumed it was merely one more infatuation.

But the chaos of Van Dorn prints in his room made clear he'd reached a greater excess of compulsion. I was skeptical about his insistence that there was a secret in Van Dorn's work. After all, great art can't be explained. You can analyze its technique, you can diagram its symmetry, but ultimately there's a mystery words can't communicate. Genius can't be summarized. As far as I could tell, Myers had been using the word *secret* as a synonym for indescribable brilliance.

When I realized he literally meant that Van Dorn had a secret, I was appalled. The distress in his eyes was equally appalling. His references to insanity, not only in Van Dorn but in his critics, made me worry that Myers himself was having a breakdown. Stabbed out their eyes, for Christ's sake?

I stayed up with Myers till 5:00 A.M., trying to calm him, to convince him he needed a few days' rest. We finished the six-pack I'd brought, the six-pack in my refrigerator, and another six-pack I bought from an art student down the hall. At dawn, just before Myers dozed off and I staggered back to my room, he murmured that I was right. He needed a break, he said. Tomorrow he'd call his folks. He'd ask if they'd pay his plane fare back to Denver.

Hungover, I didn't wake up until late afternoon. Disgusted that I'd missed my classes, I showered and managed to ignore the taste of last night's pizza. I wasn't surprised when I phoned Myers and got no answer. He probably felt as shitty as I did. But after sunset, when I called again, then knocked on his door, I started to worry. His door was locked, so I went downstairs to get the landlady's key. That's when I saw the note in my mail slot.

> Meant what I said. Need a break. Went home.
> Will be in touch. Stay cool. Paint well. I love
> you, pal. Your friend forever,
>
> Myers

My throat ached. He never came back. I saw him only twice after that. Once in New York, and once in . . .

* * *

Let's talk about New York. I finished my graduate project, a series of landscapes that celebrated Iowa's big-sky, rolling, dark-earthed, wooded hills. A local patron paid fifty dollars for one of them. I gave three to the university's hospital. The rest are who knows where.

Too much has happened.

As I predicted, the world wasn't waiting for my good but not great efforts. I ended where I belonged, as a commercial artist for a Madison Avenue advertising agency. My beer cans are the best in the business.

I met a smart, attractive woman who worked in the marketing department of a cosmetics firm. One of my agency's clients. Professional conferences led to personal dinners and intimate evenings that lasted all night. I proposed. She agreed.

We'd live in Connecticut, she said. Of course.

When the time was right, we might have children, she said.

Of course.

Myers phoned me at the office. I don't know how he knew where I was. I remember his breathless voice.

"I found it," he said.

"Myers?" I grinned. "Is it really— *How are you? Where have—*"

"I'm telling you. I found it!"

"I don't know what you're—"

"Remember? Van Dorn's secret!"

In a rush, I did remember—the excitement Myers could generate, the wonderful, expectant conversations of my youth—the days and especially the nights when ideas and the future beckoned. "Van Dorn? Are you still—"

"Yes! I was right! There *was* a secret!"

"You crazy bastard, I don't care about Van Dorn. But I care about you! Why did you— I never forgave you for disappearing."

"I had to. Couldn't let you hold me back. Couldn't let you—"

"For your own good!"

"So *you* thought. But I was right!"

"Where *are* you?"

"Exactly where you'd expect me to be."

"For the sake of old friendship, Myers, don't piss me off. *Where are you?*"

"The Metropolitan Museum of Art."

"Will you stay there, Myers? While I catch a cab? I can't wait to see you."

"I can't wait for you to see what *I* see!"

I postponed a deadline, canceled two appointments, and told my fiancée I couldn't meet her for dinner. She sounded miffed. But Myers was all that mattered.

He stood beyond the pillars at the entrance. His face was haggard, but his eyes were like stars. I hugged him. "Myers, it's so good to—"

"I want you to see something. Hurry."

He tugged at my coat, rushing.

"But where have you been?"

"I'll tell you later."

We entered the Post-Impressionist gallery. Bewildered, I followed Myers and let him anxiously seat me on a bench before Van Dorn's *Fir Trees at Sunrise*.

I'd never seen the original. Prints couldn't compare. After a year of drawing ads for feminine beauty aids, I was devastated. Van Dorn's power brought me close to tears.

For my visionless skills. For the youth I'd abandoned a year before.

"Look!" Myers said. He raised his arm and gestured toward the painting.

I frowned. I looked.

It took time—an hour, two hours—and the coaxing vision of Myers. I concentrated. And then, at last, I saw.

Profound admiration changed to . . .

My heart raced. As Myers traced his hand across the painting one final time, as a guard who had been watching us with increasing wariness stalked forward to stop him from touching the canvas, I felt as if a cloud had dispersed and a lens had focused.

"Jesus," I said.

"You see? The bushes, the trees, the branches?"

"Yes! Oh God, yes! Why didn't I—"

"Notice before? Because it doesn't show up in the prints," Myers said. "Only in the originals. And the effect's so deep, you have to study them—"

"Forever."

"It seems that long. But I knew. I was right."

"A secret."

When I was a boy, my father—how I loved him—took me mushroom hunting. We drove from town, climbed a barbed-wire fence, walked through a forest, and reached a slope of dead elms. My father told me to search the top of the slope while he checked the bottom.

An hour later, he came back with two large paper sacks filled with mushrooms. I hadn't found even one.

"I guess your spot was lucky," I said.

"But they're all around you," my father said.

"All around me? Where?"

"You didn't look hard enough."

"I crossed this slope five times."

"You searched, but you didn't really see," my father said. He picked up a long stick and pointed it toward the ground. "Focus your eyes toward the end of the stick."

I did.

And I've never forgotten the hot excitement that surged through my stomach. The mushrooms appeared as if by magic. They'd been there all along, of course, so perfectly adapted to their surroundings, their color so much like dead leaves, their shape so much like bits of wood and chunks of rock, they'd been invisible to ignorant eyes. But once my vision adjusted, once my mind reevaluated the visual impressions it received, I saw mushrooms everywhere, seemingly thousands of them. I'd been standing on them, walking over them, staring at them, but hadn't realized.

I felt an infinitely greater shock when I saw the tiny faces Myers made me recognize in Van Dorn's *Fir Trees at Sunrise*. Most were smaller than a quarter of an inch, hints and suggestions, dots and curves, blended perfectly with the landscape. They weren't exactly human, although they did have mouths, noses, and eyes. Each mouth was a gaping black maw, each nose a jagged gash, the eyes dark sinkholes of despair. The twisted faces seemed to be screaming in total agony. I could almost hear their anguished shrieks, their tortured wails. I thought of damnation. Of hell.

As soon as I noticed the faces, they emerged from the swirling texture of the painting in such abundance that the landscape became an illusion, the grotesque faces reality. The fir trees turned into an obscene cluster of writhing arms and pain-racked torsos.

I stepped back in shock an instant before the guard would have pulled me away.

"Don't touch the——" the guard said.

Myers had already rushed to point at another Van Dorn, the original *Cypresses in a Hollow.* I followed, and now that my eyes knew what to look for, I saw small tortured faces in every branch and rock. The canvas swarmed with them.

"Jesus."

"And this!"

Myers hurried to *Sunflowers at Harvest Time,* and again, as if a lens had changed focus, I no longer saw flowers, but anguished faces and twisted limbs. I lurched back, felt a bench against my legs, and sat.

"You were right," I said.

The guard stood nearby, scowling.

"Van Dorn did have a secret," I said. I shook my head in astonishment.

"It explains everything," Myers said. "These agonized faces give his work depth. They're hidden, but we *sense* them. We *feel* the anguish beneath the beauty."

"But why would he——"

"I don't think he had a choice. His genius drove him insane. It's my guess that this is how he literally saw the world. These faces are the demons he wrestled with. The festering products of his insanity. And they're not just an illustrator's gimmick. Only a genius could have painted them for all the world to see and yet have so perfectly infused them into the landscape that *no one* would see. Because he took them for granted in a terrible way."

"No one? *You* saw, Myers."

He smiled. "Maybe that means I'm crazy."

"I doubt it, friend." I returned his smile. "It does mean you're persistent. This'll make your reputation."

"But I'm not through yet," Myers said.

I frowned.

"So far, all I've got is a fascinating case of optical illusion. Tortured souls writhing beneath, perhaps producing, incomparable beauty. I call them 'secondary images.' In your ad work, I guess they'd be called 'subliminal.' But this isn't commercialism. This is a genuine artist who had the brilliance to use his madness as an ingredient in his vision. I need to go deeper."

"What are you talking about?"

"The paintings here don't provide enough examples. I've seen his work in Paris and Rome, in Zurich and London. I've borrowed from my parents to the limits of their patience and my conscience. But I've seen, and I know what I have to do. The anguished faces began in 1889, when Van Dorn left Paris in disgrace. His early paintings were abysmal. He settled in La Verge, in the south of France. Six months later, his genius suddenly exploded. In a frenzy, he painted. He returned to Paris. He showed his work, but no one appreciated it. He kept painting, kept showing. Still no one appreciated it. He returned to La Verge, reached the peak of his genius, and went totally insane. He had to be committed to an asylum, but not before he stabbed out his eyes. That's my dissertation. I intend to parallel his course. To match his paintings to the events in his life, to show how the faces increased and became more severe as his madness worsened. I want to dramatize the turmoil in his soul as he imposed his twisted vision on each landscape."

It was typical of Myers to take an excessive attitude and make it even more excessive. Don't misunderstand. His discovery was important. But he didn't know when to stop. I'm not an art historian, but I've read enough to know that what's called "psychological criticism," the attempt to analyze great art as a manifestation of neuroses, is considered off-the-wall. If Myers handed Stuyvesant a psychological dissertation, the pompous bastard would have a fit.

That was one misgiving I had about what Myers planned to do with his discovery. Another troubled me more. "I intend to parallel his course," he'd said. After we left the museum and walked through Central Park, I realized how literally Myers meant it.

"I'm going to southern France," he said.

I stared in surprise. "You don't mean—"

"La Verge? That's right. I want to write my dissertation there."

"But—"

"What place could be more appropriate? It's the village where Van Dorn suffered his nervous breakdown and eventually went insane. If it's possible, I'll even rent the same room *he* did."

"Myers, this sounds too far-out, even for you."

"But it makes perfect sense. I need to immerse myself. I need atmosphere, a sense of history. So I can put myself in the mood to write."

"The last time you immersed yourself, you crammed your room with Van Dorn prints, didn't sleep, didn't eat, didn't bathe. I hope—"

"I admit I got too involved. But last time, I didn't know what I was looking for. Now that I've found it, I'm in good shape."

"You look strung out to *me*."

"An optical illusion." Myers grinned.

"Come on, I'll treat you to drinks and dinner."

"Sorry. Can't. I've got a plane to catch."

"You're leaving *tonight*? But I haven't seen you since—"

"You can buy me that dinner when I finish the dissertation."

I never did. I saw him only one more time. Because of the letter he sent two months later. Or asked his nurse to send. She wrote down what he'd said and added an explanation of her own. He'd blinded himself, of course.

You were right. Shouldn't have gone. But when
did I ever take advice? Always knew better,
didn't I? Now it's too late. What I showed you
that day at the Met—God help me, there's so

much more. Found the truth. Can't bear it.
Don't make my mistake. Don't look ever again,
I beg you, at Van Dorn's paintings. Can't stand
the pain. Need a break. Going home. Stay cool.
Paint well. Love you, pal. Your friend forever,

Myers

In her postscript, the nurse apologized for her English. She sometimes took care of aged Americans on the Riviera, she said, and had had to learn the language. But she understood what she heard better than she could speak it or write it, and she hoped that what she'd written made sense. It didn't, but that wasn't her fault. Myers had been in great pain, sedated with morphine, not thinking clearly, she said. The miracle was that he'd managed to be coherent at all.

Your friend was staying at our only hotel. The
manager says that he slept little and ate even
less. His research was obsessive. He filled his
room with reproductions of Van Dorn's work.
He tried to duplicate Van Dorn's daily schedule.
He demanded paints and canvas, refused all
meals, and wouldn't answer his door. Three
days ago, a scream woke the manager. The door
was blocked. It took three men to break it
down. Your friend used the sharp end of a
paintbrush to stab out his eyes. The clinic here
is excellent. Physically, your friend will recover,

although he will never see again. But I worry
about his mind.

Myers had said he was going home. It had taken a
week for the letter to reach me. I assumed his parents
would have been informed immediately by phone or
telegram. He was probably back in the States by now. I
knew his parents lived in Denver, but I didn't know their
first names or address, so I got in touch with information
and phoned every Myers in Denver until I made contact.
Not with his parents, but with a family friend watching
their house. Myers hadn't been flown to the States. His
parents had gone to the south of France. I caught the next
available plane. Not that it matters, but I was supposed to
be married that weekend.

La Verge is fifty kilometers inland from Nice. I hired
a driver. The road curved through olive-tree orchards and
farmland, crested cypress-covered hills, and often skirted
cliffs. Passing one of the orchards, I had the eerie convic-
tion that I'd seen it before. Entering La Verge, my déjà vu
strengthened. The village seemed trapped in the nine-
teenth century. Except for phone poles and power lines, it
looked exactly as Van Dorn had painted it. I recognized
the narrow cobbled streets and rustic shops that Van Dorn
had made famous. I asked directions. It wasn't hard to
find Myers and his parents.

The final time I saw my friend, the undertaker was
putting the lid on his coffin. I had trouble sorting out the
details, but despite my burning tears, I gradually came to
understand that the local clinic was as good as the nurse

had assured me in her note. All things being equal, he would have lived.

But the damage to his mind had been another matter. He'd complained of headaches. He'd also become increasingly distressed. Even morphine hadn't helped. He'd been left alone only for a minute, appearing to be asleep. In that brief interval, he had managed to stagger from his bed, grope across the room, and find a pair of scissors. Yanking off his bandages, he'd jabbed the scissors into an empty eye socket and tried to ream out his brain. He'd collapsed before accomplishing his purpose, but the damage had been sufficient. Death had taken two days.

His parents were pale, incoherent with shock. I somehow controlled my own shock enough to try to comfort them. Despite the blur of those terrible hours, I remember noticing the kind of irrelevance that signals the mind's attempt to reassert normality. Myers's father wore Gucci loafers and a gold Rolex watch. In grad school, Myers had lived on a strict budget. I had no idea he came from wealthy parents.

I helped them make arrangements to fly his body back to the States. I went to Nice with them and stayed by their side as they watched the crate that contained his coffin being loaded onto the baggage compartment of the plane. I shook their hands and hugged them. I waited as they sobbed and trudged down the boarding tunnel. An hour later, I was back in La Verge.

I returned because of a promise. I wanted to ease his parents' suffering—and my own. Because I'd been his friend. "You've got too much to take care of," I had said to his parents. "The long trip home. The arrangements for the funeral." My throat had felt choked. "Let me help. I'll settle things here, pay whatever bills he owes, pack up his clothes, and . . ." I had taken a deep breath. "And his books and whatever else he had and send them home to you. Let me do that. I'd consider it a kindness. Please. I need to do *something*."

True to his ambition, Myers had managed to rent the same room taken by Van Dorn at the village's only hotel. Don't be surprised that it was available. The management used it to promote the hotel. A plaque announced the historic value of the room. The furnishings were the same style as when Van Dorn had stayed there. Tourists, to be sure, had paid to peer in and sniff the residue of genius. But business had been slow this season, and Myers had wealthy parents. For a generous sum, coupled with his typical enthusiasm, he had convinced the hotel's owner to let him have that room.

I rented a different room—more like a closet—two doors down the hall, and then, my eyes still burning from tears, I went into Van Dorn's musty sanctuary to pack my dear friend's possessions. Prints of Van Dorn paintings were everywhere, several splattered with dried blood. Heartsick, I made a stack of them.

That's when I found the diary.

During grad school, I had taken a course in Post-Impressionism that emphasized Van Dorn, and I'd read a facsimile edition of his diary. The publisher had photocopied the handwritten pages and bound them, adding an introduction, translation, and footnotes. The diary had been cryptic from the start, but as Van Dorn became more feverish about his work, as his nervous breakdown became more severe, his statements deteriorated into riddles. His handwriting—hardly neat, even when he was sane—went quickly out of control and finally turned into almost indecipherable slashes and curves as he rushed to unloose his frantic thoughts.

I sat at a small wooden desk and paged through the diary, recognizing phrases I had read years before. With each passage, my stomach turned colder. Because this diary *wasn't* the published photocopy. Instead, it was a notebook, and although I wanted to believe that Myers had somehow, impossibly, gotten his hands on the original diary, I knew I was fooling myself. The pages in this ledger weren't yellow and brittle with age. The ink hadn't faded until it was brown more than blue. The notebook had been purchased and written in recently. It wasn't Van Dorn's diary. It belonged to *Myers*. The ice in my stomach turned to lava.

Glancing sharply away from the ledger, I saw a shelf beyond the desk and a stack of other notebooks. Apprehensive, I grabbed them and, in a fearful rush, flipped through them. My stomach threatened to erupt. Each notebook was the same, the words identical.

My hands shook as I looked again to the shelf, found the facsimile edition of the original, and compared it with the notebooks. I moaned, imagining Myers at this desk, his expression intense and insane as he reproduced the diary word for word, slash for slash, curve for curve. Eight times.

Myers had indeed immersed himself, straining to put

himself into Van Dorn's disintegrating frame of mind. And in the end, he'd succeeded. The weapon Van Dorn had used to stab out his eyes had been the sharp end of a paintbrush. In the mental hospital, Van Dorn had finished the job by skewering his brain with a pair of scissors. Like Myers. Or vice versa. When Myers had finally broken, had he and Van Dorn been horribly indistinguishable?

I pressed my hands to my face. Whimpers squeezed from my convulsing throat. It seemed forever before I stopped sobbing. My consciousness strained to control my anguish. ("And orange is his color of anguish," Myers had said.) Rationality fought to subdue my distress. ("The critics who devoted themselves to analyzing Van Dorn," Myers had said. "The ones who haven't been recognized for their genius, just as Van Dorn wasn't recognized. They suffered. . . . And just like Van Dorn, they stabbed out their eyes.") Had they done it with a paintbrush? I wondered. Were the parallels that exact? And in the end, had they, too, used scissors to skewer their brains?

I scowled at the prints I'd been stacking. Many still surrounded me—on the walls, the floor, the bed, the windows, even the ceiling. A swirl of colors. A vortex of brilliance.

Or at least I once had thought of them as brilliant. But now, with the insight Myers had given me, with the vision I'd gained in the Metropolitan Museum, I saw behind the sun-drenched cypresses and hay fields, the orchards and meadows, toward their secret darkness, toward the minuscule twisted arms and gaping mouths, the black dots of tortured eyes, the blue knots of writhing bodies. ("Blue is for insanity," Myers had said.)

All it took was a slight shift of perception, and there *weren't* any orchards and hay fields, only a terrifying gestalt of souls in hell. Van Dorn had indeed invented a new stage of Impressionism. He'd impressed upon the splendor of God's creation the teeming images of his own disgust. His paintings didn't glorify. They abhorred. Everywhere Van Dorn had looked, he'd seen his own private nightmare. Blue was for insanity, indeed, and if you fixated on Van Dorn's insanity long enough, you, too, became insane. ("Don't look ever again, I beg you, at Van Dorn's paintings," Myers had said in his letter.) In the last stages of his breakdown, had Myers somehow become lucid enough to try to warn me? ("Can't stand the pain. Need a break. Going home.") In a way I'd never expected, he had indeed gone home.

Another startling thought occurred to me. ("The critics who devoted themselves to analyzing Van Dorn. They each tried to paint. In Van Dorn's style," Myers had said a year ago.) As if attracted by a magnet, my gaze swung across the welter of prints and focused on the corner across from me, where two canvas originals leaned against the wall. I shivered, stood, and haltingly approached them.

They'd been painted by an amateur. Myers was an art *historian,* after all. The colors were clumsily applied, especially the splotches of orange and blue. The cypresses were crude. At their bases, the rocks looked like cartoons. The sky needed texture. But I knew what the black dots among them were meant to suggest. I understood the purpose of the tiny blue gashes. The miniature anguished faces and twisted limbs were implied, even if Myers had lacked the talent to depict them. He'd contracted Van Dorn's madness. All that had remained were the terminal stages.

I sighed from the pit of my soul. As the village's church bell rang, I prayed that my friend had found peace.

It was dark when I left the hotel. I needed to walk, to escape the greater darkness of that room, to feel at liberty, to think. But my footsteps and inquiries led me down a narrow cobbled street toward the village's clinic, where Myers had finished what he had started in Van Dorn's room. I asked at the desk and five minutes later introduced myself to an attractive dark-haired woman in her thirties.

The nurse's English was more than adequate. She said her name was Clarisse.

"You took care of my friend," I said. "You sent me the letter he dictated, and you added a note of your own."

She nodded. "He worried me. He was so distressed."

The fluorescent lights in the vestibule hummed. We sat on a bench.

"I'm trying to understand why he killed himself," I said. "I think I know, but I'd like your opinion."

Her eyes, a bright, intelligent hazel, suddenly were guarded. "He stayed too long in his room. He studied too much." She shook her head and stared toward the floor. "The mind can be a trap. It can be a torture."

"But he was excited when he came here?"

"Yes."

"Despite his studies, he behaved as if he'd come on vacation?"

"Very much."

"Then what made him change? My friend was unusual, I agree. What we call 'high-strung.' But he *enjoyed* doing research. He might have looked sick from too much work, but he thrived on learning. His body was nothing, but his mind was brilliant. What tipped the balance, Clarisse?"

"Tipped the . . ."

"Made him depressed instead of excited. What did he learn that made him—"

She stood and looked at her watch. "Forgive me. I stopped work twenty minutes ago. I'm expected at a friend's."

My voice hardened. "Of course. I wouldn't want to keep you."

Outside the clinic, beneath the light at its entrance, I stared at my own watch, surprised to see that it was almost 11:30 P.M. Fatigue made my knees ache. The trauma of the day had taken away my appetite, but I knew I should try to eat, and after walking back to the hotel's dining room, I ordered a chicken sandwich and a glass of Chablis. I meant to eat in my room, but I never got that far. Van Dorn's room and the diary beckoned.

The sandwich and wine went untasted. Sitting at the desk, surrounded by the swirling colors and hidden horrors of Van Dorn prints, I opened a notebook and tried to understand.

A knock at the door made me turn.

Again I glanced at my watch, astonished to find that hours had passed like minutes. It was almost 2:00 A.M.

The knock was repeated, gentle but insistent. The manager?

"Come in," I said in French. "The door isn't locked."

The knob turned. The door swung open.

Clarisse stepped in. Instead of her nurse's uniform, she now wore sneakers, jeans, and a tight-fitting sweater whose yellow accentuated the hazel in her eyes.

"I apologize," she said in English. "I must have seemed rude at the clinic."

"Not at all. You had an appointment. I was keeping you."

She shrugged self-consciously. "I sometimes leave the clinic so late, I don't have a chance to see my friend."

"I understand perfectly."

She drew a hand through her lush long hair. "My friend got tired. As I walked home, passing the hotel, I saw a light up here. On the chance it might be you . . ."

I nodded, waiting.

I had the sense that she'd been avoiding it, but now she turned toward the room. Toward where I'd found the dried blood on the prints. "The doctor and I came as fast as we could when the manager phoned us that afternoon." Clarisse stared at the prints. "How could so much beauty cause so much pain?"

"Beauty?" I glanced toward the tiny gaping mouths.

"You mustn't stay here. Don't make the mistake your friend did."

"Mistake?"

"You've had a long journey. You've suffered a shock. You need to rest. You'll wear yourself out, as your friend did."

"I was just looking through some things of his. I'll be packing them to send them back to America."

"Do it quickly. You mustn't torture yourself by thinking about what happened here. It isn't good to surround yourself with the things that disturbed your friend. Don't intensify your grief."

"Surround myself? My friend would have said 'immerse.' "

"You look exhausted. Come." She held out her hand. "I'll take you to your room. Sleep will ease your pain. If you need some pills to help you . . ."

"Thanks. But a sedative won't be necessary."

Clarisse continued to offer her hand. I took it and went to the hallway.

For a moment, I stared back toward the prints and the horror within the beauty. I said a silent prayer for Myers, shut off the lights, and locked the door.

We went down the hall. In my room, I sat on the bed.

"Sleep long and well," Clarisse said.

"I hope."

"You have my sympathy." She kissed my cheek.

I touched her shoulder. Her lips shifted toward my own. She leaned against me.

We sank toward the bed. In silence, we made love.

Sleep came like her kisses, softly smothering.

But in my nightmares, there were tiny gaping mouths.

*   *   *

Sunlight glowed through my window. With aching eyes, I looked at my watch. Half past ten. My head hurt. Clarisse had left a note on my bureau.

Last night was sympathy. To share and ease your grief. Do what you intended. Pack your friend's belongings. Send them to America. Go with them. Don't make your friend's mistake. Don't, as you said *he* said, "immerse" yourself. Don't let beauty give you pain.

I meant to leave. I truly believe that. I phoned the front desk and asked the concierge to send up some boxes. After I showered and shaved, I went to Myers's room, where I finished stacking the prints. I made another stack of books and another of clothes. I packed everything into the boxes and looked around to make sure I hadn't forgotten anything.

The two canvases that Myers had painted still leaned against a corner. I decided not to take them. No one needed to be reminded of the delusions that had overcome him.

All that remained was to seal the boxes, to address and mail them. But as I started to close the flap on a box, I saw the notebooks inside.

So much suffering, I thought. So much waste.

Once more I leafed through a notebook. Various passages caught my eye. Van Dorn's discouragement about his failed career. His reasons for leaving Paris to come to La Verge—the stifling, backbiting artists' community, the snobbish critics and their sneering responses to his early efforts. *Need to free myself of convention. Need to void myself of aesthete politics, to shit it out of me. To find what's never been painted. To feel instead of being told what to feel. To see instead of imitating what others have seen.*

I knew from the biographies how impoverished Van Dorn's ambition had made him. In Paris, he'd literally eaten slops thrown into alleys behind restaurants. He'd been able to afford his quest to La Verge only because a successful but very conventional (and now ridiculed) painter friend had loaned him a small sum of money. Eager to conserve his endowment, Van Dorn had walked all the way from Paris to the south of France.

In those days, you have to remember, this valley had been an unfashionable area of hills, rocks, farms, and villages. Limping into La Verge, Van Dorn must have been a pathetic sight. He'd chosen this provincial town precisely because it *was* unconventional, because it offered mundane scenes so in contrast with the salons of Paris that no other artist would dare to paint them.

Need to create what's never been imagined, he'd written. For six despairing months, he tried and failed. He finally quit in self-doubt, then suddenly reversed himself and, in a year of unbelievably brilliant productivity, gave the world thirty-eight masterpieces. At the time, of course, he couldn't trade any canvas for a meal. But the world knows better now.

He must have painted in a frenzy. His suddenly found energy must have been enormous. To me, a would-be artist with technical facility but only conventional eyes, he achieved the ultimate. Despite his suffering, I en-

vied him. When I compared my maudlin, Wyeth-like de-
pictions of Iowa landscapes to Van Dorn's trend-setting
genius, I despaired. The task awaiting me back in the
States was to imitate beer cans and deodorant packages
for magazine ads.

I continued flipping through the notebook, tracing
the course of Van Dorn's despair and epiphany. His victory had a price, to be sure. Insanity. Self-blinding. Suicide. But I had to wonder if perhaps, as he died, he'd have
chosen to reverse his life if he'd been able. He must have
known how remarkable, how truly astonishing, his work
had become.

Or perhaps he didn't. The last canvas he'd painted
before stabbing his eyes had been of himself. A lean-
faced, brooding man with short, thinning hair, sunken
features, pallid skin, and a scraggly beard. The famous
portrait reminded me of how I always thought Christ
would have looked just before he was crucified. All that
was missing was the crown of thorns. But Van Dorn had
a different crown of thorns. Not around him, but *within*
him. Disguised among his scraggly beard and sunken features, the tiny gaping mouths and writhing bodies told it
all. His suddenly acquired vision had stung him too
much.

As I read the notebook, again distressed by Myers's
effort to reproduce Van Dorn's agonized words and handwriting exactly, I reached the section where Van Dorn described his epiphany: *La Verge! I walked! I saw! I feel!
Canvas! Paint! Creation and damnation!*

After that cryptic passage, the notebook—and Van

Dorn's diary—became totally incoherent. Except for the persistent refrain of severe and increasing headaches.

I was waiting outside the clinic when Clarisse arrived to start her shift at three o'clock. The sun was brilliant, glinting off her eyes. She wore a burgundy skirt and a turquoise blouse. Mentally, I stroked their cottony texture.

When she saw me, her footsteps faltered. Forcing a smile, she approached.

"You came to say good-bye?" She sounded hopeful.

"No. To ask you some questions."

Her smile disintegrated. "I mustn't be late for work."

"This'll take just a minute. My French vocabulary needs improvement. I didn't bring a dictionary. The name of this village. La Verge. What does it mean?"

She hunched her shoulders as if to say the question was unimportant. "It's not very colorful. The literal translation is 'the stick.' "

"That's all?"

She reacted to my frown. "There are rough equivalents. 'The branch.' 'The switch.' A willow, for example, that a father might use to discipline a child." She looked uncomfortable. "It can also be a slang term for *penis*."

"And it doesn't mean anything else?"

"Indirectly. The synonyms keep getting further from the literal sense. A *wand*, perhaps. Or a *rod*. The kind of forked stick that people who claim they can find water hold ahead of them when they walk across a field. The stick is supposed to bend down if there's water."

"We call it a divining rod. My father once told me

he'd seen a man who could actually make one work. I always suspected the man just tilted the stick with his hands. Do you suppose this village got its name because long ago someone found water here with a divining rod?"

"Why would anyone have bothered when these hills have so many streams and springs? What makes you interested in the name?"

"Something I read in Van Dorn's diary. The village's name excited him for some reason."

"But *anything* could have excited him. He was insane."

"Eccentric. But he didn't become insane until after that passage in his diary."

"You mean, his *symptoms* didn't show themselves until after that. You're not a psychiatrist."

I had to agree.

"Again, I'm afraid I'll seem rude. I really must go to work." Clarisse hesitated. "Last night . . ."

"Was exactly what you described in the note. A gesture of sympathy. An attempt to ease my grief. You didn't mean it to be the start of anything."

"Please do what I asked. Please leave. Don't destroy yourself like the others."

"*Others?*"

"Like your friend."

"No, you said 'others.' " My words were rushed. "Clarisse, tell me."

She glanced up, squinting as if she'd been cornered. "After your friend stabbed out his eyes, I heard talk around the village. Older people. It could be merely gossip that became exaggerated with the passage of time."

"What did they say?"

She squinted harder. "Twenty years ago, a man came here to do research on Van Dorn. He stayed three months and had a breakdown."

"He stabbed out his eyes?"

"Rumors drifted back that he blinded himself in a mental hospital in England. Ten years before, another man came. He jabbed scissors through an eye, all the way into his brain."

I stared, unable to control the spasms that racked my shoulder blades. "What the hell is going on?"

I asked around the village. No one would talk to me. At the hotel, the manager told me he'd decided to stop renting Van Dorn's room. I had to remove Myers's belongings at once.

"But I can still stay in *my* room?"

"If that's what you wish. I don't recommend it, but even France is still a free country."

I paid the bill, went upstairs, moved the packed boxes from Van Dorn's room to mine, and turned in surprise as the phone rang.

The call was from my fiancée.

When was I coming home?

I didn't know.

What about the wedding this weekend?

The wedding would have to be postponed.

I winced as she slammed down the phone.

I sat on the bed and couldn't help recalling the last time I'd sat there, with Clarisse standing over me, just before we'd made love. I was throwing away the life I'd tried to build.

For a moment, I came close to calling my fiancée back, but a different sort of compulsion made me scowl toward the boxes, toward Van Dorn's diary. In the note Clarisse had added to Myers's letter, she'd said that his research had become so obsessive that he'd tried to re-create Van Dorn's daily habits. Again it occurred to me—at the end, had Myers and Van Dorn become indistinguishable? Was the secret to what had happened to Myers hidden in the diary, just as the suffering faces were hidden in Van Dorn's paintings? I grabbed one of the ledgers. Scanning the pages, I looked for references to Van Dorn's daily routine. And so it began.

I've said that except for telephone poles and electrical lines, La Verge seemed caught in the previous century. Not only was the hotel still in existence but so were Van Dorn's favorite tavern and the bakery where he had bought his morning croissant. A small restaurant he favored remained in business. On the edge of the village, a trout stream where he sometimes sat with a midafternoon glass of wine still bubbled along, although pollution had long since killed the trout. I went to all of them, in the order and at the time Van Dorn had recorded in his diary.

Breakfast at eight, lunch at two, a glass of wine at the trout stream, a stroll to the countryside, then back to the room. After a week, I knew the diary so well, I didn't need to refer to it. Mornings had been Van Dorn's time to paint. The light was best then, he'd written. And evenings were a time for remembering and sketching.

It finally came to me that I wouldn't be following the schedule exactly if I didn't paint and sketch when Van Dorn had done so. I bought a notepad, canvas, pigments, a palette, whatever I needed, and for the first time since leaving graduate school, I tried to *create*. I used local scenes that Van Dorn had favored and produced what you'd expect: uninspired versions of Van Dorn's paintings. With no discoveries, no understanding of what had ultimately undermined Myers's sanity, tedium set in. My finances were almost gone. I prepared to give up.

Except . . .

I had the disturbing sense that I'd missed something. A part of Van Dorn's routine that wasn't explicit in the diary. Or something about the locales themselves that I hadn't noticed, although I'd been painting them in Van Dorn's spirit, if not with his talent.

Clarisse found me sipping wine on the sunlit bank of the now-troutless stream. I felt her shadow and turned toward her silhouette against the sun.

I hadn't seen her for two weeks, since our uneasy conversation outside the clinic. Even with the sun in my eyes, she looked more beautiful than I remembered.

"When was the last time you changed your clothes?" she asked.

A year ago, I had said the same thing to Myers.

"You need a shave. You've been drinking too much. You look awful."

I sipped my wine and shrugged. "Well, you know what the drunk said about his bloodshot eyes. 'You think they look bad to you? You should see them from *my* side.'"

"At least you can joke."

"I'm beginning to think that *I'm* the joke."

"You're definitely not a joke." She sat beside me. "You're becoming your friend. Why don't you leave?"

"I'm tempted."

"Good." She touched my hand.

"Clarisse?"

"Yes?"

"Answer some questions one more time?"

She studied me. "Why?"

"Because if I get the right answers, I might leave."

She nodded slowly.

Back in town, in my room, I showed her the stack of prints. I almost told her about the faces they contained, but her brooding features stopped me. She thought I was disturbed enough as it was.

"When I walk in the afternoons, I go to the settings Van Dorn chose for his paintings." I sorted through the prints. "This orchard. This farm. This pond. This cliff. And so on."

"Yes, I recognize these places. I've seen them all."

"I hoped if I saw them, maybe I'd understand what happened to my friend. You told me he went to them, as well. Each of them is within a five-kilometer radius of the village. Many are close together. It wasn't difficult to find each site. Except for one."

She didn't ask which. Instead, she tensely rubbed her arm.

When I'd taken the boxes from Van Dorn's room, I'd also removed the two paintings Myers had attempted. Now I pulled them from where I'd tucked them under the bed.

"My friend did these. It's obvious he wasn't an artist. But as crude as they are, you can see they both depict the same area."

I slid a Van Dorn print from the bottom of the stack.

"*This* area," I said. "A grove of cypresses in a hollow, surrounded by rocks. It's the only site I haven't been able to find. I've asked the villagers. They claim they don't know where it is. Do *you* know, Clarisse? Can you tell me? It must have some significance if my friend was fixated on it enough to try to paint it *twice*."

Clarisse scratched a fingernail across her wrist. "I'm sorry."

"What?"

"I can't help you."

"Can't or won't? Do you mean you don't know where to find it, or you know but you won't tell me?"

"I said I can't help."

"What's wrong with this village, Clarisse? What's everybody trying to hide?"

"I've done my best." She shook her head, stood, and walked to the door. She glanced back sadly. "Sometimes it's better to leave well enough alone. Sometimes there are reasons for secrets."

I watched her go down the hall. "Clarisse . . ."

She turned and spoke a single word: "North." She

was crying. "God help you," she added. "I'll pray for your soul." Then she disappeared down the stairs.

For the first time, I felt afraid.

Five minutes later, I left the hotel. In my walks to the sites of Van Dorn's paintings, I had always chosen the easiest routes—east, west, and south. Whenever I'd asked about the distant tree-lined hills to the north, the villagers had told me there was nothing of interest in that direction, nothing at all to do with Van Dorn. What about cypresses in a hollow? I had asked. There weren't any cypresses in those hills, only olive trees, they'd answered. But now I knew.

La Verge was in the southern end of an oblong valley, squeezed by cliffs to the east and west. I rented a car. Leaving a dust cloud, I pressed my foot on the accelerator and headed north toward the rapidly enlarging hills. The trees I'd seen from the village were indeed olive trees. But the lead-colored rocks among them were the same as in Van Dorn's painting. I sped along the road, veering up through the hills. At the top, I found a narrow space to park and rushed from the car. But which direction to take? On impulse, I chose left and hurried among the rocks and trees.

My decision seems less arbitrary now. Something about the slopes to the left was more dramatic, more aesthetically compelling. A greater wildness in the landscape. A sense of depth, of substance. Like Van Dorn's work.

My instincts urged me forward. I'd reached the hills at quarter after five. Time compressed eerily. At once, my watch showed ten past seven. The sun blazed crimson, descending toward the bluffs. I kept searching, letting the grotesque landscape guide me. The ridges and ravines were like a maze, every turn of which either blocked or gave access, controlling my direction. That's the sense I had—I was being controlled. I rounded a crag, scurried down a slope of thorns, ignored the rips in my shirt and the blood streaming from my hands, and stopped on the precipice of a hollow. Cypresses, not olive trees, filled the basin. Boulders jutted among them and formed a grotto.

The basin was steep. I skirted its brambles, ignoring their scalding sting. Boulders led me down. I stifled my misgivings, frantic to reach the bottom.

This hollow, this basin of cypresses and boulders, this thorn-rimmed funnel, was the image not only in Van Dorn's painting but in the canvases Myers had attempted. But why had this place so affected them?

The answer came as quickly as the question. I heard before I saw, although hearing doesn't accurately describe my sensation. The sound was so faint and high-pitched, it was almost beyond the range of detection. At first, I thought I was near a hornet's nest. I sensed a subtle vibration in the otherwise still air of the hollow. I felt an itch behind my eardrums, a tingle on my skin. The sound was actually many sounds, each identical, merging, like the collective buzz of a swarm of insects. But this was high-pitched. Not a buzz, but more like a distant chorus of shrieks and wails.

Frowning, I took another step toward the cypresses. The tingle on my skin intensified. The itch behind my eardrums became so irritating that I raised my hands to the sides of my head. I came close enough to see within the trees, and what I noticed with terrible clarity made me panic. Gasping, I stumbled back. But not in time. What shot from the trees was too small and fast for me to identify.

It struck my right eye. The pain was excruciating, as if the white-hot tip of a needle had pierced my retina and lanced my brain. I clamped my right hand across that eye and screamed.

I continued stumbling backward, agony spurring my panic. But the sharp, hot pain intensified, surging through my skull. My knees bent. My consciousness dimmed. I fell against the slope.

It was after midnight when I managed to drive back to the village. Although my eye no longer burned, my panic was more extreme. Still dizzy from having passed out, I tried to keep control when I entered the clinic and asked where Clarisse lived. She had invited me to visit, I claimed. A sleepy attendant frowned but told me. I drove desperately toward her cottage, five blocks away.

Lights were on. I knocked. She didn't answer. I pounded harder, faster. At last I saw a shadow. When the door swung open, I lurched into the living room. I barely noticed the negligee Clarisse clutched around her, or the open door to her bedroom, where a startled woman sat up in bed, held a sheet to her breasts, and stood quickly to shut the bedroom door.

"What the hell do you think you're doing?" Clarisse demanded. "I didn't invite you in! I didn't—"

I managed the strength to talk: "I don't have time to explain. I'm terrified. I need your help."

She clutched her negligee tighter.

"I've been stung. I think I've caught a disease. Help me stop whatever's inside me. Antibiotics. An antidote. Anything you can think of. Maybe it's a virus, maybe a fungus. Maybe it acts like bacteria."

"What happened?"

"I told you, no time. I'd have asked for help at the clinic, but they wouldn't have understood. They'd have thought I'd had a breakdown, the same as Myers. You've got to take me there. You've got to make sure I'm injected with as much of any and every drug that might possibly kill this thing."

The panic in my voice overcame her doubt. "I'll dress as fast as I can."

As we rushed to the clinic, I described what had happened. Clarisse phoned the doctor the moment we arrived. While we waited, she put disinfectant drops in my eye and gave me something for my rapidly developing headache. The doctor showed up, his sleepy features becoming alert when he saw how distressed I was. True to my prediction, he reacted as if I'd had a breakdown. I shouted at him to humor me and saturate me with antibiotics. Clarisse made sure it wasn't just a sedative he gave me. He used every compatible combination. If I thought it would have worked, I'd have swallowed Drano.

What I'd seen within the cypresses were tiny gaping mouths and minuscule writhing bodies, as small and camouflaged as those in Van Dorn's paintings. I know now that Van Dorn wasn't imposing his insane vision on reality. He wasn't an Impressionist after all. At least not in his *Cypresses in a Hollow*. I'm convinced *Cypresses* was his first painting after his brain became infected. He was literally depicting what he had seen on one of his walks. Later, as the infection progressed, he saw the gaping mouths and writhing bodies like an overlay on everything else he looked at. In that sense, too, he wasn't an Impressionist. To him, the gaping mouths and writhing bodies *were* in all those later scenes. To the limits of his infected brain, he painted what to him *was* reality. His art was representational.

I know, believe me. Because the drugs didn't work. My brain is as diseased as Van Dorn's . . . or Myers's. I've tried to understand why they didn't panic when they were stung, why they didn't rush to a hospital to make a doctor comprehend what had happened. My conclusion is that Van Dorn had been so desperate for a vision to enliven his paintings that he gladly endured the suffering. And Myers had been so desperate to understand Van Dorn that, when stung, he'd willingly taken the risk to identify even more with his subject until, too late, he had realized his mistake.

Orange is for anguish, blue for insanity. How true. Whatever infects my brain has affected my color sense. More and more, orange and blue overpower the other colors I know are there. I have no choice. I see little else. My paintings are *rife* with orange and blue.

My paintings. I've solved another mystery. It always puzzled me how Van Dorn could have suddenly been seized by such energetic genius that he painted thirty-eight masterpieces in one year. I know the answer now. What's in my head, the gaping mouths and writhing bodies, the orange of anguish and the blue of insanity, cause such pressure, such headaches, that I've tried everything to subdue them, to get them out. I went from codeine to Demerol to morphine. Each helped for a time, but not enough. Then I learned what Van Dorn understood and Myers attempted. Painting the disease somehow gets it out of you. For a time. And then you paint harder, faster. Anything to relieve the pain. But Myers wasn't an artist. The disease had no release and reached its terminal stage in weeks instead of Van Dorn's year.

But *I'm* an artist—or used to hope I was. I had skill but not a vision. Now, God help me, I've got a vision. At first, I painted the cypresses and their secret. I accomplished what you'd expect. An imitation of Van Dorn's original. But I refuse to suffer pointlessly. I vividly recall the portraits of Midwestern landscapes I produced in graduate school. The dark-earthed Iowa landscape. The attempt to make an observer feel the fecundity of the soil. At the time, the results were ersatz Wyeth. But not anymore. The twenty paintings I've so far stored away aren't versions of Van Dorn, either. They're my own creations. Unique. A combination of the disease and my experience. Aided by powerful memory, I paint the river that flows through Iowa City. Blue. I paint the cornfields that cram the rolling big-sky country outside town. Orange. I paint my innocence. My youth. With my ultimate discovery hidden within them. Ugliness lurks within the beauty. Horror festers in my brain.

*   *   *

Clarisse at last told me about the local legend. In the Middle Ages, when La Verge was founded, she said, a meteor streaked from the sky. It lit the night. It burst upon the hills north of here. Flames erupted. Trees were consumed. The hour was late. Few villagers saw it. The site of the impact was too far away for those few witnesses to rush that night to see the crater. In the morning, the smoke had dispersed. The embers had died. Although the witnesses tried to find the meteor, the lack of the roads that now exist hampered their search through the tangled hills, to the point of discouragement. A few among the few witnesses persisted. The few of the few of the few who had accomplished their quest staggered back to the village, babbling about headaches and tiny gaping mouths. Using sticks, they scraped disturbing images in the dirt and eventually stabbed out their eyes. Over the centuries, legend has it, similar self-mutilations occurred whenever someone returned from seeking the crater in those hills. The unknown had power then. The hills acquired the negative force of taboo. No villager, then or now, intruded on what came to be called "the place where God's wand touched the earth." A poetic description of a blazing meteor's impact. La Verge.

I don't conclude the obvious: that the meteor carried spores that multiplied in the crater, which became a hollow eventually filled with cypresses. No—to me, the meteor was a cause, but not an effect. I saw a pit among the cypresses, and from the pit, tiny mouths and writhing bodies resembling insects—how they wailed!—spewed. They clung to the leaves of the cypresses, flailed in anguish as they fell back, and instantly were replaced by other spewing, anguished souls.

Yes. Souls. For the meteor, I insist, was just the cause. To me, the effect was the opening of hell. The tiny wailing mouths are the damned. As *I* am damned. Desperate to survive, to escape from the ultimate prison we call hell, a frantic sinner lunged. He caught my eye and stabbed my brain, the gateway to my soul. My soul. It festers. I paint to remove the pus.

I talk. That helps somehow. Clarisse writes it down while her female lover rubs my shoulders.

My paintings are brilliant. I'll be recognized as a genius, the way I had always dreamed.

At such a cost.

The headaches grow worse. The orange is more brilliant. The blue more disturbing.

I try my best. I urge myself to be stronger than Myers, whose endurance lasted only weeks. Van Dorn persisted for a year. Maybe genius is strength.

My brain swells. How it threatens to split my skull. The gaping mouths blossom.

The headaches! I tell myself to be strong. Another day. Another rush to complete another painting.

The sharp end of my paintbrush invites. Anything to lance my seething mental boil, to jab my eyes for the ecstasy of relief. But I have to endure.

On a table near my left hand, the scissors wait.

But not today. Or tomorrow.

I'll outlast Van Dorn.

The Beautiful Uncut Hair of Graves

After Matt's death in June of 1987, I collapsed. The day-after-day, month-after-month tension of watching his painful decline had weakened the part of my brain that controls stress. A circuit breaker failed. No matter what I tried to do—take a walk, watch television, read, eat—my body was in a constant state of emergency. Stress chemicals rushed unchecked through me. Panic attacks repeatedly hit me. My mind swirling, my heart racing, all I could do was lie on my back and stare at the ceiling.

Gradually, with the love of my family and friends, I began to climb from the darkness. But the gap of three years between the publication of The League of Night and Fog *in 1987 and* The Fifth Profession *in 1990 gives an idea of the black hole that almost swallowed me. It took even longer for me to return to short fiction. The following story's unusual technique communicates the psychological state I was in. If you've ever taken a fiction-writing class, you know that there are three main viewpoints: first person, third person limited, and third person omniscient. Each has strengths and weaknesses. But there is a fourth viewpoint, one that is almost never used because of its limitations: the second person. Instead of "I" or "he" and "she," the author tells the story as "you." It's unconventional and problematic, but why not try it? I thought. Just once. To violate a taboo. To add to the lack of convention, I decided to use the present tense. But for a purpose. After all, the way a story is told ought to have something to do with its subject matter. Here, the main character is so stunned by what he has gone through that he feels detached from himself and thinks of himself as "you." Past horrors are constantly being replayed in the present tense of his savaged mind. "The Beautiful Uncut Hair of Graves" received the Horror Writers Association's award for the best novella of 1991.*

DESPITE THE RAIN, YOU'VE BEEN TO THE CEMETERY YET again, ignoring the cold autumn gusts slanting under your bowed umbrella, the drenched drab leaves blowing against your soaked pant legs and shoes.

Two graves. You shiver, blinking through tears toward the freshly laid sod. There aren't any tombstones. There won't be for a year. But you imagine what the markers will look like, each birth date different, the death dates—God help you—the same. Simon and Esther Weinberg. Your parents. You silently mouth the kaddish prayers that Rabbi Goldstein recited at the funeral. Losing strength, you turn to trudge back to your rain-beaded car, to throw your umbrella on the passenger seat and jab the button marked DEFROSTER, to try to control your trembling hands and somehow suppress your chest-swelling rage, your heart-numbing grief.

Eyes swollen from tears, you manage to drive back to your parents' home. An estate on Lake Michigan, north of Chicago, the mansion feels ghostly, hollow without its proper occupants. You cross the enormous vestibule and enter the oak-paneled study. One wall is lined with books, another with photographs of your precious father shaking hands with local and national dignitaries, even a president. As you sit at the massive desk to resume sorting through your father's papers, the last of them, the documents unsealed from your parents' safe-deposit box, your wife appears in the study's doorway, a coffee cup in her hand. She slumps against the wall and frowns as she did when you obeyed your repeated, so intense compulsion to go back—yet *again*—to the cemetery.

"Why?" she asks.

You squint up from the documents. "Isn't it obvious? I feel the need to be with them."

"That's not what I meant," Rebecca says. She's forty-nine, tall, with dark hair, a narrow face, and pensive eyes. "All the work you've been doing. All the documents and the meetings. All the phone calls. Can't you let yourself relax? You look terrible."

"How the hell should I look? My father's chest was crushed. My mother's head was . . . The drunken bastard who hit their car got away with just a few stitches."

"Not what I meant," Rebecca repeats. Using two hands, both of them shaky, she raises the coffee cup to her lips. "Don't make sympathy sound like an accusation. You've got *every* right to look terrible. It's bad enough to lose *one* parent, let alone *two at once,* and the way they died was"—she shakes her head—"obscene. But what you're doing, your compulsion to . . . I'm afraid you'll push yourself until you collapse. Don't torture yourself. Your father assigned an executor for his estate, a perfectly competent lawyer from his firm. Let the man do his job. I grant, you're a wonderful attorney, but right now it's time to let someone else take charge. For God's sake, Jacob—and if not for God, then for me—get some rest."

You sigh, knowing she means well and wants only what's best for you. But she doesn't understand: You *need* to keep busy; you *need* to distract yourself with minutiae so that your mind doesn't snap from confronting the full horror of losing your parents.

"I'm almost finished," you say. "Just a few more documents from the safe-deposit box. Then I promise I'll try to rest. A bath sounds . . . Lord, I still can't believe . . . How much I miss . . . Pour me a scotch. I think my nerves need numbing."

"I'll have one with you."

As Rebecca crosses the study toward the liquor cabinet, you glance down toward the next document: a faded copy of your birth certificate. You shake your head. "Dad kept *everything*. What a pack rat." Your tone is bittersweet, your throat tight with affection. "That's why his estate's so hard to sort through. It's so difficult to tell what's important, what's sentimental, and what's just . . ."

You glance at the next document, almost set it aside,

take another look, frown, feel what seems to be a frozen fishhook in your stomach, and murmur, "God." Your breathing fails.

"Jacob?" Your wife turns from pouring the scotch and hurriedly sets down the bottle, rushing toward you. "What's wrong? Your face. You're as gray as—"

You keep staring toward the document, feeling as if you've been punched in the ribs, the wind knocked out of you. Rebecca crouches beside you, touching your face. You swallow and manage to breathe. "I . . ."

"*What?* Jacob, tell me. What's the matter?"

"There has to be some mistake." You point toward the document.

Rebecca hurriedly reads it. "I don't understand. It's crammed with legal jargon. A woman's promising to give up two children for adoption, is that what this means?"

"Yes." You have trouble speaking. "Look at the date."

"August fifteen, 1938."

"A week before my birthday. Same year." You sound hoarse.

"So what? That's just a coincidence. Your father did all kinds of legal work, probably including adoptions."

"But he wouldn't have kept a business affidavit with his personal papers in his private safe-deposit box. Here, at the bottom, look at the place where this was notarized."

"Redwood Point, California."

"Right," you say. "Now check this copy of my birth certificate. The place of birth is . . ."

"Redwood Point, California." Rebecca's voice drops. "Still think it's just a coincidence?"

"It has to be. Jacob, you've been under a lot of strain, but this is *one* strain you don't have to deal with. You know you're not adopted."

"Do I? *How?*"

"Well, it's . . ."

You gesture impatiently.

"I mean, it's something a person takes for granted," Rebecca says.

"Why?"

"Because your parents would have told you."

"*Why?* If they didn't need to, why would they have taken the chance of shocking me? Wasn't it better for my parents to leave well enough alone?"

"Listen to me, Jacob. You're letting your imagination get control of you."

"Maybe." You stand. Your legs unsteady, you cross to the liquor cabinet and finish pouring the drinks that Rebecca had started preparing. *"Maybe."* You swallow an inch of the drink. Made deliberately strong, it burns your throat. "But I won't know for sure, will I? Unless I find out why my father kept that woman's adoption agreement with his private papers, and how it happened that I was born one week later and in the same place that the woman signed and dated her consent form."

"So what?" Rebecca rubs her forehead. "Don't you see? It doesn't make a difference! Your parents loved you! *You* loved *them.* Suppose, despite Lord knows how many odds, suppose your suspicion turns out to be correct. What will it change? It won't make your grief any less. It won't affect a lifetime of love."

"It might affect a lot of things."

"Look, finish your drink. It's Friday. We still have time to go to temple. If ever you needed to focus your spirit, it's now."

In anguish, you swallow a third of your drink. "Take another look at that adoption consent. The woman agrees to give up *two* babies. If I *was* adopted, that means somewhere out there I've got a brother or a sister. A *twin*."

"A stranger to you. Jacob, there's more to being a brother or a sister than just the biological connection."

Your stomach recoils as you gulp the last of your drink. "Keep looking at the consent form. At the bottom. The woman's name."

"Mary Duncan."

"A Scot."

"So?" Rebecca asks.

"Go to temple? Think about it. Have you ever heard of any Scot who . . . It could be I wasn't born Jewish."

Your uncle's normally slack-jowled features tighten in confusion. "Adopted? What on earth would make you think—"

You sit beside him on the sofa in his living room and explain as you show him the documents.

His age-wrinkled brow contorts. He shakes his bald head. "Coincidence."

"That's what my wife claims."

"Then listen to her. And listen to *me*. Jacob, your father and I were as close as two brothers can possibly be. We kept no secrets from each other. Neither of us ever did anything important without first asking the other's opinion. When Simon—may he rest in peace—decided to marry your mother, he discussed it with *me* long before he talked to our parents. Believe me, trust me, if he and Esther had planned to adopt a child, *I'd have been told.*"

You exhale, wanting to believe but tortured by doubts. "Then why . . ." Your skull throbs.

"Tell me, Jacob."

"All right, let's pretend it *is* a coincidence that these documents were together in my parents' safe-deposit box. Let's pretend that they're unrelated matters. But why? As far as I know, Dad always lived here in Chicago. I never thought about it before, but why wasn't I born here instead of in California?"

Your uncle strains to concentrate. Weary, he shrugs. "That was so long ago. Nineteen"—he peers through his glasses toward your birth certificate—"thirty-eight. So many years. It's hard to remember." He pauses. "Your mother and father wanted children very much. *That,* I remember. But no matter how hard they tried . . . Well, your father and mother were terribly discouraged. Then one afternoon, he came to my office, beaming. He told me to take the rest of the day off. We had something to celebrate. Your mother was pregnant."

Thinking of your parents and how much you miss them, you wince with grief. But restraining tears, you can't help saying, "That still doesn't explain why I was born in California."

"I'm coming to that." Your uncle rubs his wizened chin. "Yes, I'm starting to . . . Nineteen thirty-eight. The worst of the Depression was over, but times still weren't good. Your father said that with the baby coming, he needed to earn more money. He felt that California—Los

Angeles—offered better opportunities. I tried to talk him out of it. In another year, I said, Chicago will have turned the corner. Besides, he'd have to go through the trouble of being certified to practice law in California. But he insisted. And, of course, I was right. Chicago did soon turn the corner. What's more, as it happened, your father and mother didn't care for Los Angeles, so after six or seven months, they came back, right after you were born."

"That still doesn't . . ."

"What?"

"Los Angeles isn't Redwood Point," you say. "I never heard of the place. What were my parents doing there?"

"Oh, that." Your uncle raises his thin white eyebrows. "No mystery. Redwood Point was a resort up the coast. In August, L.A. was brutally hot. As your mother came close to giving birth, your father decided she ought to be someplace where she wouldn't feel the heat, close to the sea, where the breeze would make her comfortable. So they took a sort of vacation, and you were born there."

"Yes," you say. "Perfectly logical. Nothing mysterious. Except . . ." You gesture toward the coffee table. "Why did my father keep this woman's adoption agreement?"

Your uncle lifts his liver-spotted hands in exasperation. "*Oy vay.* For all we know, he found a chance to do some legal work while he was in Redwood Point. To help pay your mother's hospital and doctor bills. When he moved back to Chicago, it might be some business papers got mixed in with his personal ones. By accident, everything to do with Redwood Point got grouped together."

"And my father never noticed the mistake, no matter how many times he must have gone to his safe-deposit box? I have trouble believing . . ."

"Jacob, Jacob. Last month, I went to my safe-deposit box and found a treasury bond that I didn't remember even buying, let alone putting in the box. Oversights happen."

"My father was the most organized person I ever knew."

"God knows I love him, and God knows I miss him." Your uncle bites his pale lower lip, then breathes with effort, seized with emotion. "But he wasn't perfect, and life isn't tidy. We'll probably never know for sure how this document came to be with his private papers. But this much, I do know. You can count on it. You're Simon and Esther's natural child. You weren't adopted."

You stare at the floor and nod. "Thank you."

"No need to thank me. Just go home, get some rest, and stop thinking so much. What happened to Simon and Esther has been a shock to all of us. We'll be a long time missing them."

"Yes," you say, "a long time."

"Rebecca? How is . . ."

"The same as me. She still can't believe they're dead."

Your uncle's bony fingers clutch your hand. "I haven't seen either of you since the funeral. It's important for family to stick together. Why don't both of you come over for honey cake on Rosh Hashanah?"

"I'd like to, Uncle. But I'm sorry, I'll be out of town."

"Where are you going?"
"Redwood Point."

The biggest airport nearest your destination is in San
Jose. You rent a car and drive south down the coast, passing Carmel and Big Sur. Preoccupied, you barely notice
the dramatic scenery: the windblown pine trees, the
rugged cliffs, the whitecaps hitting the shore. You ask
yourself why you didn't merely phone the authorities at
Redwood Point, explain that you're a lawyer in Chicago,
and ask for information that you need to settle an estate.
Why do you feel compelled to come all this way to a
town so small that it isn't listed in your *Hammond Atlas*
and could only be located in the Chicago library on its
large map of California? For that matter, why do you feel
compelled at all? Both your wife and your uncle have
urged you to leave the matter alone. You're not adopted,
you've been assured, and even if you were, what difference would it make?

The answers trouble you. One, you might have a
brother or a sister, a twin, and now that you've lost your
parents, you feel an anxious need to fill the vacuum of
their loss by finding an unsuspected member of your family. Two, you suffer a form of midlife crisis, but not in the
common sense of the term. To have lived these many
years and possibly never have known your birth parents
makes you uncertain of your identity. Yes, you loved the
parents you knew, but your present limbo of insecure un-
certainty makes you desperate to discover the truth, one
way or the other, so you can dismiss the possibility of
your having been adopted or else adjust to the fact that

you were. But this way, not being certain, is maddening, given the stress of double grief. And three, the most insistent reason, an identity crisis of frantic concern, you want to learn if after a lifetime . . . of having been circumcised, of Hebrew lessons, of your bar mitzvah, of Friday nights at temple, of scrupulous observance of sacred holidays . . . of being a Jew . . . if after all that, you might have been born a Gentile. You tell yourself that being a Jew has nothing to do with race and genes, that it's a matter of culture and religion. But deep in your heart, you've always thought of yourself proudly as being *completely* a Jew, and your sense of self feels threatened. Who *am* I? you think.

You increase speed toward your destination and brood about your irrational, stubborn refusal to let Rebecca travel here with you. Why did you insist on coming alone?

Because, you decide with grim determination.

Because I don't want anybody holding me back.

The Pacific Coast Highway pivots above a rocky cliff. In crevasses, stunted, misshapen pine trees cling to shallow soil and fight for survival. A weather-beaten sign abruptly says REDWOOD POINT. With equal abruptness, you see a town below you on the right, its buildings dismal even from a distance, their unpainted, listing structures spread along a bay at the center of which a half-destroyed pier projects toward the ocean. The only beauty is the glint of the afternoon sun on the white-capped waves.

Your stomach sinks. Redwood Point. A resort? Or at

least that's what your uncle said. Maybe in 1938, you think. But not anymore. And as you steer off the highway, tapping your brakes, weaving down the bumpy, narrow road past shorter, more twisted pine trees toward the dingy town where your birth certificate says you entered the world, you feel hollow. You pass a ramshackle boarded-up hotel. On a ridge that looks over the town, you notice the charred, collapsed remnant of what seems to have been another hotel and decide, discouraged, that your wife and your uncle were right. This lengthy, fatiguing journey was needless. So many years. A ghost of a town that might have been famous once. You'll never find answers here.

The dusty road levels off and leads past dilapidated buildings toward the skeleton of the pier. You stop beside a shack, get out, and inhale the salty breezes from the ocean. An old man sits slumped on a chair on the few safe boards at the front of the pier. Obeying an impulse, you approach, your footsteps crunching on seashells and gravel.

"Excuse me," you say.

The old man has his back turned, staring toward the ocean.

The odor of decay—dead fish along the shore—pinches your nostrils.

"Excuse me," you repeat.

Slowly the old man turns. He cocks his shriveled head, either in curiosity or antagonism.

You ask the question that occurred to you driving

down the slope. "Why is this town called Redwood Point? This far south, there *aren't* any redwoods."

"You're looking at it."

"I'm not sure what . . ."

The old man gestures toward the ruin of the pier. "The planks are made of redwood. In its heyday"—he sips from a beer can—"used to be lovely. The way it stuck out toward the bay, so proud." He sighs, nostalgic. "Redwood Point."

"Is there a hospital?"

"You sick?"

"Just curious."

The old man squints. "The nearest hospital's forty miles up the coast."

"What about a doctor?"

"Used to be. Say, how come you ask so many questions?"

"I told you, I'm just curious. Is there a courthouse?"

"Does this look like a county seat? We used to be something. Now we're . . ." The old man tosses his beer can toward a trash container. He misses. "Shit."

"Well, what about . . . Have you got a police force?"

"Sure. Chief Kitrick." The old man coughs. "For all the good he does. Not that we need him. Nothing happens here. That's why he doesn't have deputies."

"So where can I find him?"

"Easy. This time of day, the Redwood Bar."

"Can you tell me where . . ."

"Behind you." The old man opens another beer. "Take a left. It's the only place that looks decent."

*   *   *

The Redwood Bar, on a cracked concrete road above the beach, has fresh redwood siding that makes the adjacent buildings look even more dingy. You pass through a door that has an anchor painted on it and feel as if you've entered a tackle shop or have boarded a trawler. Fishing poles stand in a corner. A net rimmed with buoys hangs on one wall. Various nautical instruments, a sextant, a compass, others you can't identify, all looking ancient despite their gleaming metal, sit on a shelf beside a weathered but polished navigation wheel that hangs behind the bar. The sturdy rectangular tables all have captain's chairs.

Voices in the far right corner attract your attention. Five men sit playing cards. A haze of cigarette smoke dims the light above their table. One of the men—in his fifties, broad-chested, with short sandy hair and a ruddy complexion—wears a policeman's uniform. He studies his cards.

A companion calls to the bartender, "Ray, another beer, huh? How about you, Hank?"

"It's only ten to five. I'm not off duty yet," the policeman says, then sets down his cards. "Full house."

"Damn. Beats me."

"It's sure as hell better than a straight."

The men throw in their cards.

The policeman scoops up quarters. "My deal. Seven-card stud." As he shuffles the cards, he squints in your direction.

The bartender sets a beer on the table and approaches you. "What'll it be?"

"Uh, club soda," you say. "What I . . . Actually, I want to talk to Chief Kitrick."

Overhearing, the policeman squints even harder. "Something urgent?"

"No. Not exactly." You shrug, self-conscious. "This happened many years ago. I guess it can wait a little longer."

The policeman frowns. "Then we'll finish this hand, if that's okay."

"Go right ahead."

At the bar, you pay for your drink and sip it. Turning toward the wall across from you, you notice photographs, dozens of them, the images yellowed, wrinkled, and faded. But even at a distance, you know what the photographs represent, and, compelled, repressing a shiver, you walk toward them.

Redwood Point. The photographs depict the resort in its prime, fifty, sixty years ago. Vintage automobiles gleam with newness on what was once a smoothly paved, busy street outside. The beach is crowded with vacationers in old-fashioned bathing suits. The impressive long pier is lined with fishermen. Boats dot the bay. Pedestrians stroll the sidewalks, glancing at shops or pointing toward the ocean. Some eat hot dogs and cotton candy. All are well dressed, and the buildings look clean, their windows shiny. The Depression, you think. But not everyone was out of work, and here the financially advantaged sought refuge from the summer heat and the city squalor. A splendid hotel—guests holding frosted glasses or fanning themselves on the spacious porch—is unmistakably the ramshackle ruin you saw as you drove in. Another building, expansive, with peaks and gables of Victorian design, sits on a ridge above the town, presumably the charred wreckage you noticed earlier. Ghosts. You shake your head. Most of the people in these photographs have long since died, and the buildings have died as well but just haven't fallen down. What a waste, you think. What *happened* here? How could time have been so cruel to this place?

"It sure was pretty once," a husky voice says from behind you.

You turn toward Chief Kitrick and notice he holds a glass of beer.

"After five. Off duty now," he says. "Thanks for letting me finish the game. What can I do for you? Something about years ago, you said?"

"Yes. About the time these photographs were taken."

The chief's eyes change focus. "Oh?"

"Can we find a place to talk? It's kind of personal."

Chief Kitrick gestures. "My office is just next door."

It smells musty. A cobweb dangles from a corner of the ceiling. You pass a bench in the waiting area, go through a squeaky gate, and face three desks, two of which are dusty and bare, in a spacious administration area. A phone, but no two-way radio. A file cabinet. A calendar on one wall. An office this size—obviously at one time, several policemen had worked here. You sense a vacuum, the absence of the bustle of former years. You can almost hear the echoes of decades-old conversations.

Chief Kitrick points toward a wooden chair. "Years ago?"

You sit. "Nineteen thirty-eight."

"That *is* years ago."

"I was born here." You hesitate. "My parents both died three weeks ago, and . . ."

"I lost my own dad just a year ago. You have my sympathy."

You nod, exhale, and try to order your thoughts. "When I went through my father's papers, I found . . . There's a possibility I may have been adopted."

As in the bar, the chief's eyes change focus.

"And then again, maybe not," you continue. "But if I *was* adopted, I think my mother's name was Mary Duncan. I came here because . . . Well, I thought there might be records I could check."

"What kind of records?"

"The birth certificate my father was sent lists the time and place where I was born, and my parents' names, Simon and Esther Weinberg."

"Jewish."

You tense. "Does that matter?"

"Just making a comment. Responding to what you said."

You debate, then resume. "But the type of birth certificate parents receive is a shortened version of the one that's filed at the county courthouse."

"Which in this case is forty miles north. Cape Verde."

"I didn't know that before I came here. But I did think there'd be a hospital. *It* would have a detailed record about my birth."

"No hospital. Never was," the chief says.

"So I learned. But a resort as popular as Redwood Point was in the thirties would have needed *some* kind of medical facility."

"A clinic," the chief says. "I once heard my father mention it. But it closed back in the forties."

"Do you know what happened to its records?"

Chief Kitrick raises his shoulders. "Packed up. Shipped somewhere. Put in storage. Not here, though. I know every speck of this town, and there aren't any medical records from the old days. I don't see how those records would help."

"My file would mention who my mother was. See, I'm a lawyer, and—"

The chief frowns.

"—the standard practice with adoptions is to amend the birth certificate at the courthouse so it lists the adopting parents as the birth parents. But the *original* birth certificate, naming the birth parents, isn't destroyed. It's sealed in a file and put in a separate section of the records."

"Then it seems to me you ought to go to the county courthouse and look for that file," Chief Kitrick says.

"The trouble is, even with whatever influence I have as a lawyer, it would take me months of petitions to get that sealed file opened—and maybe never. But hospital records are easier. All I need is a sympathetic doctor who . . ." A thought makes your heart beat faster. "Would you know the names of any doctors who used to practice here? Maybe *they'd* know how to help me."

"Nope, hasn't been a doctor here in quite a while.

When we get sick, we have to drive up the coast. I don't want to sound discouraging, Mr. . . ."

"Weinberg."

"Yeah. Weinberg. Nineteen thirty-eight. We're talking ancient history. I suspect you're wasting your time. Who remembers that far back? If they're even still alive, that is. And God knows where the clinic's records are."

"Then I guess I'll have to do this the hard way." You stand. "The county courthouse. Thanks for your help."

"I don't think I helped at all. But Mr. Weinberg . . ."

"Yes?" You pause at the gate.

"Sometimes it's best to leave the past alone."

"How I wish I could."

Cape Verde turns out to be a pleasant, attractive town of twenty thousand people, its architecture predominantly Spanish: red-tiled roofs, arched doorways, and adobe-colored walls. After the blight of Redwood Point, you feel less depressed, but only until you hear a baby crying in the hotel room next to yours. After a half-sleepless night, during which you phone Rebecca to assure her that you're all right but ignore her pleas for you to come home, you ask directions from the desk clerk and drive to the courthouse, which looks like a Spanish mission, arriving there shortly after nine o'clock.

The office of the county recorder is on the second floor at the rear, and the red-haired young man behind the counter doesn't think twice about your request. "Birth records? Nineteen thirty-eight? Sure." After all, those records are open to the public. You don't need to give a reason.

Ten minutes later, the clerk returns with a large dusty ledger. There isn't a desk, so you need to stand at the end of the counter. While the young man goes back to work, you flip the ledger's pages to August and study them.

The records are grouped according to districts in the county. When you get to the section for Redwood Point, you read carefully. What you're looking for is not just a record of *your* birth but also a reference to Mary Duncan. Twenty children were born that August. For a moment, that strikes you as unusual—so many for so small a community. But then you remember that in August the resort would have been at its busiest, and maybe other expecting parents had gone there to escape the summer's heat, to allow the mother a comfortable delivery, just as your own parents had, according to your uncle.

You note the names of various mothers and fathers. Miriam and David Meyer. Ruth and Henry Begelman. Gail and Jeffrey Markowitz. With a shock of recognition, you come upon your own birth record. *Parents: Esther and Simon Weinberg.* But that proves nothing, you remind yourself. You glance toward the bottom of the form. *Medical Facility: Redwood Point Clinic. Certifier: Jonathan Adams, M.D. Attendant: June Engle, R.N.* Adams was presumably the doctor who took care of your mother, you conclude. A quick glance through the other Redwood Point certificates shows that Adams and Engle signed every document.

But nowhere do you find a reference to Mary Duncan. You search ahead to September, in case Mary Duncan was late giving birth. No mention of her. Still, you think, maybe she signed the adoption consent forms *early* in her pregnancy, so you check the records for the remaining months of 1938. Nothing.

You ask the clerk for the 1939 birth certificates. Again he complies. But after you reach the April records and go so far as to check those in May and still find no mention of Mary Duncan, you frown. Even if she impossibly knew during her first month that she was pregnant and even if her pregnancy lasted ten months instead of nine, she still ought to be in these records. *What happened?* Did she change her mind and leave town to hide somewhere and deliver the two children she'd promised to let others adopt? Might be, you think, and a competent lawyer could have told her that her consent form, no matter how official and complex it looked, wasn't legally binding. Or did she—

"Death records, please," you ask the clerk, "for 1938 and 1939."

This time, the young man looks somewhat annoyed as he trudges off to find those records. But when he returns and you tensely inspect the ledgers, you find no indication that Mary Duncan died during childbirth.

"Thanks," you tell the clerk as you put away your notes. "You've been very helpful."

The young man, grateful not to bring more ledgers, grins.

"There's just one other thing."

The young man's shoulders sag.

"This birth certificate for Jacob Weinberg." You point toward an open ledger.

"What about it?"

"It lists Esther and Simon Weinberg as his parents.

But it may be that Jacob was adopted. If so, there'll be an alternate birth certificate that indicates the biological mother's name. I'd like to have a look at—"

"Original birth certificates in the case of adoptions aren't available to the public."

"But I'm an attorney, and—"

"They're not available to attorneys, either, and if you're a lawyer, you should know that."

"Well, yes, I do, but—"

"See a judge. Bring a court order. I'll be glad to oblige. Otherwise, man, the rule is strict. Those records are sealed. I'd lose my job."

"Sure." Your voice cracks. "I understand."

The county's Department of Human Services is also in the Cape Verde courthouse. On the third floor, you wait in a lobby until the official in charge of adoptions returns from an appointment. Her name, you learn, is Becky Hughes. She shakes your hand and escorts you into her office. She's in her thirties, blond, well dressed, but slightly overweight. Her intelligence and commitment to her work are evident.

"The clerk downstairs did exactly what he should have," Becky says.

Apparently, you don't look convinced.

"The sealed-file rule on original birth certificates in the case of adoptions is a good one, counselor."

"And when it's important, so is another rule: Nothing ventured, nothing gained."

"Important?" Becky taps her fingers on her desk. "In the case of adoptions, nothing's more important than preserving the anonymity of the biological mother." She glances toward a coffeepot on a counter. "You want some?"

You shake your head no. "My nerves are on edge already."

"Decaffeinated."

"All right, then, sure, why not? I take it black."

She pours two cups, sets yours on the desk, and sits across from you. "When a woman gives her baby up, she often feels so guilty about it . . . Maybe she isn't married and comes from a strict religious background that makes her feel ashamed, or maybe she's seventeen and realizes she doesn't have the resources to take proper care of the child, or maybe she's got too many children already, or . . . For whatever reason, if a woman chooses to have a child instead of abort it and gives it up for adoption, she usually has such strong emotions that her mental health demands an absolute break from the past. She trains herself to believe that the child is on another planet. She struggles to go on with her life. As far as I'm concerned, it's cruel for a lawyer or a son or a daughter to track her down many years later and remind her of . . ."

"I understand," you say. "But in *this* case, the mother is probably dead."

Becky's fingers stop tapping. "Keep talking, counselor."

"I don't have a client. Or to put it another way, I do, but the client is . . ." You point toward your chest.

"You?"

"I think I . . ." You explain about the drunk driver,

about the deaths of the man and woman that you lovingly thought of as your parents.

"And you want to know if they *were* your parents?" Becky asks.

"Yes, and if I've got a twin—a brother or a sister that I never knew about—and . . ." You almost add, "If I was born a Jew."

"Counselor, I apologize, but you're a fool."

"That's what my wife and uncle say, not to mention a cop in Redwood Point."

"Redwood Point?"

"A small town forty miles south of here."

"Forty or four thousand miles. What difference does any of this make? Did Esther and Simon love you?"

"They *worshiped* me." Your eyes sting with grief.

"Then they *are* your parents. Counselor, I was adopted. And the man and woman who adopted me *abused* me. That's why I'm in this office—to make sure other adopted children don't go into homes where they suffer what I did. At the same time, I don't want to see a *mother* abused. If a woman's wise enough to know she can't properly raise a child, if she gives it up for adoption, in *my* opinion, she deserves a medal. She *deserves* to be protected."

"I understand," you say. "But I don't want to meet my mother. She's probably dead. All I want is . . . I need to know if . . . The fact. *Was* I adopted?"

Becky studies you, nods, picks up the phone, and taps three numbers. "Records? Charley? How you doing, kid. Great. Listen, an attorney was down there awhile ago, wanted a sealed adoption file. Yeah, you did the right

thing. But here's what I want. It won't break the rules if
you check to see if there *is* a sealed file." Becky tells him
the date, place, and names that you gave her earlier. "I'll
hold." Minutes seem like hours. She keeps listening to
the phone, then straightens. "Yeah, Charley, what have
you got?" She listens again. "Thanks." She sets down the
phone. "Counselor, there's no sealed file. Relax. You're
not adopted. Go back to your wife."

"Unless," you say.

"Unless?"

"The adoption wasn't arranged through an agency
but instead was a private arrangement between the birth
mother and the couple who wanted to adopt. The gray
market."

"Yes, but even then, local officials have to sanction
the adoption. There has to be a legal record of the transfer. In your case, there isn't." Becky looks uncomfortable. "Let me explain. These days, babies available for
adoption are scarce. Because of birth control and legal-
ized abortions. But even today, the babies in demand are
WASPs. A black? A Hispanic? An Asian? Forget it. Very
few parents in those groups want to adopt, and even
fewer Anglos want children from those groups. Fifty
years ago, the situation was worse. There were so many
WASPs who got pregnant by mistake and wanted to sur-
render their babies . . . Counselor, this might offend you,
but I have to say it."

"I don't offend easily."

"Your last name is Weinberg," Becky says. "Jewish.
Back in the thirties, the same as now, the majority of parents wanting to adopt were Protestants, and they wanted

a child from a Protestant mother. If *you* were put up for adoption, even on the gray market, almost every couple looking to adopt would not have wanted a Jewish baby. The prospects would have been so slim that your mother's final option would have been . . ."

"The *black* market?" Your cheek muscles twitch.

"Baby selling. It's a violation of the antislavery law, paying money for a human being. But it happens, and lawyers and doctors who arrange for it to happen make a fortune from desperate couples who can't get a child any other way."

"But what if my mother was a *Scot*?"

Becky blinks. "You're suggesting . . ."

"Jewish couples." You frown, remembering the last names of the parents you read in the ledgers. "Meyer, Begelman. Markowitz. Weinberg. Jews."

"So desperate for a baby that after looking everywhere for a Jewish mother willing to give up her child, they adopted . . ."

"WASPs. And arranged it so none of their relatives would know."

All speculation, you strain to remind yourself. There's no way to link Mary Duncan with you, except that you were born in the town where she signed the agreement and the agreement is dated a week before your birthday. Tenuous evidence, to say the least. Your legal training warns you that you'd never allow it to be used in court. Even the uniform presence of Jewish names on the birth certificates from Redwood Point that August so long ago has a possible, benign, and logical explanation:

The resort might have catered to a Jewish clientele, providing kosher meals, for example. Perhaps there'd been a synagogue.

But logic is no match for your deepening unease. You can't account for the chill in the pit of your stomach, but you feel that something's terribly wrong. Back in your hotel room, you pace, struggling to decide what to do next. Go back to Redwood Point and ask Chief Kitrick more questions? *What* questions? He'd react the same as Becky Hughes had. Assumptions, Mr. Weinberg. Inconclusive.

Then it strikes you. The name you found in the records. Dr. Jonathan Adams. The physician who certified not only *your* birth but *all* the births in Redwood Point. Your excitement abruptly falters. So long ago. The doctor would probably be dead by now. At once your pulse quickens. Dead? Not necessarily. Simon and Esther were still alive until three weeks ago. Grief squeezing your throat, you concentrate. Dr. Adams might have been as young as Simon and Esther. There's a chance he . . .

But how to find him? The Redwood Point Clinic went out of business in the forties. Dr. Adams might have gone anywhere. You reach for the phone. A year ago, you were hired to litigate a malpractice suit against a drug-addicted ophthalmologist whose carelessness blinded a patient. You spent many hours talking to the American Medical Association. Opening the address book that you always keep in your briefcase, you call the AMA's national headquarters in Chicago. Dr. Jonathan Adams? The deep male voice on the end of the line sounds eager to show his efficiency. Even through the static of a long-distance line, you hear fingers tap a computer keyboard.

"Dr. Jonathan Adams? Sorry. There isn't a . . . Wait, there *is* a Jonathan Adams, *Jr.* An obstetrician. In San Francisco. His office number is . . ."

You hurriedly write it down and with equal speed press the numbers on your phone. Just as lawyers often want their sons and daughters to be lawyers, so doctors encourage their children to be doctors, and on occasion they give a son their first name. This doctor might not be the son of the man who signed your birth certificate, but you have to find out. *Obstetricians?* Another common denominator. Like father, like . . .

A secretary answers.

"Dr. Adams, please," you say.

"The doctor is with a patient at the moment. May he call you back?"

"By all means. This is my phone number." You give it. "But I think he'll want to talk to me now. Just tell him it's about his father. Tell him it's about the clinic at Redwood Point."

The secretary sounds confused. "But I can't interrupt when the doctor's with a patient."

"Do it," you say. "I guarantee he'll understand the emergency."

"Well, if you're—"

"Certain? Yes. Absolutely."

"Just a moment, please."

Thirty seconds later, a tense male voice says, "Dr. Adams here. What's this all about?"

"I told your secretary. I assumed she told *you.* It's

about your father. It's about 1938. It's about the Redwood Point Clinic."

"I had nothing to do with . . . Oh, dear Jesus."

You hear a forceful click, then static. You set down the phone. And nod.

Throughout the stressful afternoon, you investigate your only other lead, trying to discover what happened to June Engle, the nurse whose name appears on the Redwood Point birth certificates. If not dead, she'd certainly have retired by now. Even so, many ex-nurses maintain ties with their former profession, continuing to belong to professional organizations and subscribing to journals devoted to nursing. But no matter how many calls you make to various associations, you can't find a trace of June Engle.

By then, it's evening. Between calls, you've ordered room service, but the poached salmon goes untasted, the bile in your mouth having taken away your appetite. You get the home phone number for Dr. Adams from San Francisco information.

A woman answers, weary. "He's still at . . . No, just a minute. I think I hear him coming in the door."

Your fingers cramp on the phone.

The now-familiar taut male voice, slightly out of breath, says, "Yes, Dr. Adams speaking."

"It's me again. I called you at your office today. About the Redwood Point Clinic. About 1938."

"You son of a—"

"Don't hang up this time, Doctor. All you have to do is answer my questions, and I'll leave you alone."

"There are laws against harassment."

"Believe me, I know all about the law. I practice it in Chicago."

"Then you're not licensed in California. So you can't intimidate me by—"

"Doctor, why are you so defensive? Why would questions about that clinic make you nervous?"

"I don't have to talk to you."

"But you make it seem you're hiding something if you don't."

You hear the doctor swallow. "Why do you . . . I had nothing to do with that clinic. My father died ten years ago. Can't you leave the past alone?"

"Not *my* past, I can't," you insist. "Your father signed my birth certificate at Redwood Point in 1938. There are things I need to know."

The doctor hesitates. "All right. Such as?"

"Black-market adoptions." Hearing the doctor inhale, you continue. "I think your father put the wrong information on my birth certificate. I think he never recorded my biological mother's name and instead put down the names of the couple who adopted me. That's why there isn't a sealed birth certificate listing my actual mother's name. The adoption was never legally sanctioned, so there wasn't any need to amend the erroneous birth certificate on file at the courthouse."

"Jesus," the doctor says.

"Am I right?"

"How the hell would *I* know? I was just a kid when my father closed the clinic and left Redwood Point in the early forties. If you *were* illegally adopted, it wouldn't have anything to do with *me*."

"Exactly. And your father's dead, so he can't be prosecuted. Besides, the statute of limitations would have protected him, and anyway, it happened so long ago, who would care? Except *me*. But Doctor, you're nervous about my questions. That makes it obvious you know *something*. Certainly *you* can't be charged for something your father did. So what would it hurt if you tell me what you know?"

The doctor's throat sounds dry. "My father's memory."

"Ah," you say. "Yes, his reputation. Look, I'm not interested in spreading scandal and ruining anybody, dead or alive. All I want is the truth. About me. *Who* was my mother? *Do I have a brother or a sister somewhere? Was I adopted?*"

"So much money."

"What?" You clutch the phone harder.

"When my father closed the clinic and left Redwood Point, he had so much money. I was just a kid, but even *I* knew he couldn't have earned a small fortune merely delivering babies at a resort. And there were always *so* many babies. I remember him walking up to the nursery every morning. And then it burned down. And the next thing, he closed the clinic and bought a mansion in San Francisco and never worked again."

"The nursery?"

"The building on the ridge above town. Big, with all kinds of chimneys and gables."

"Victorian?"

"Yes. And that's where the pregnant women lived."

You shiver. Your chest feels encased with ice.

"My father always called it 'the nursery.' I remember him smiling when he said it. Why pick on him?" the doctor asks. "All he did was deliver babies. And he did it well. If someone paid him lots of money to put false information on birth certificates, which I don't even know if he did—"

"But you suspect."

"Yes. Goddamn it, that's what I suspect," Dr. Adams admits. "But I can't prove it, and I never asked. It's the Gunthers you should blame! *They* ran the nursery! Anyway, if the babies got loving parents, and if the adopting couples finally got the children they desperately wanted, what's the harm? Who got hurt? Leave the past alone!"

For a moment, you have trouble speaking. "Thank you, Doctor. I appreciate your honesty. I have only one more question."

"Get on with it. I want to finish this."

"The Gunthers. The people who ran the nursery."

"A husband and wife. I don't recall their first names."

"Have you any idea what happened to them?"

"After the nursery burned down? God only knows," Dr. Adams says.

"And what about June Engle, the nurse who assisted your father?"

"You said you had only *one* more question." The doctor breathes sharply. "Never mind, I'll answer if you promise to leave me alone. June Engle was born and raised in Redwood Point. When we moved away, she said she was staying behind. It could be she's still there."

"If she's still alive." Chilled again, you set down the phone.

The same as last night, a baby cries in the room next to yours. You pace and phone Rebecca. You're as good as can be expected, you say. You don't know when you'll be home, you say. You hang up the phone and try to sleep. Apprehension jerks you awake.

The morning is overcast, as gray as your thoughts. After checking out of the hotel, you follow the desk clerk's directions to Cape Verde's public library. A disturbing hour of research later, under a thickening, gloomy sky, you drive back to Redwood Point.

From the highway along the cliff, the town looks even bleaker. You steer down the bumpy road, reach the ramshackle boarded-up hotel, and park your rented car. Through weeds that cling to your pant legs, you walk beyond the hotel's once-splendid porch, find eroded stone steps that angle up a slope, and climb to the barren ridge above the town.

Barren with one exception: the charred timbers and flame-scorched, toppled walls of the peaked, gabled Victorian structure that Dr. Adams had called "the nursery." That word makes you feel as if an icy needle has pierced your heart. The clouds hang deeper, darker. A chill wind makes you hug your chest. The nursery. And in 1941, as you learned from old newspapers on microfilm at the Cape Verde library, thirteen women died here, burned to death, incinerated—their corpses grotesquely blackened and crisped—in a massive blaze, the cause of which the authorities were never able to determine.

Thirteen women. *Exclusively* women. You want to shout in outrage. And were they pregnant? *And were there also* . . . Sickened, imagining their screams of fright, their wails for help, their shrieks of indescribable agony, you sense so repressive an atmosphere about this ruin that you stumble back as if shoved. With wavering legs that you barely control, you manage your way down the unsteady stone slabs. Lurching through the clinging weeds below the slope, you stumble past the repulsive ruins of the hotel to reach your car, where you lean against its hood and try not to vomit, sweating despite the increasingly bitter wind.

The nursery, you think.

Dear God.

The Redwood Bar is no different from the way it was when you left it. Chief Kitrick and his friends again play cards at the table in the far right corner. The haze of cigarette smoke again dims the light above them. The waiter stands behind the bar on your left, the antique nautical instruments gleaming on a shelf behind him. But your compulsion directs you toward the wrinkled, faded photographs on the wall to your right.

This time, you study them without innocence. You see a yellowed image of the peaked, gabled nursery. You narrow your gaze toward small details that you failed to give importance the first time you saw these photographs. Several women, diminished because the cameraman took a long shot of the large Victorian building, sit on a lawn that's bordered by flower gardens, their backs to a windowed brick wall of the—your mind balks—the nursery.

Each of the women—young! so young!—holds an infant in her lap. The women smile so sweetly. Are they acting? Were they forced to smile?

Was one of those women your mother? Is one of those infants you? Mary Duncan, what desperation made you smile like that?

Behind you, Chief Kitrick's husky voice says, "These days, not many tourists pay us a second visit."

"Yeah, I can't get enough of Redwood Point." Turning, you notice that Chief Kitrick—it isn't yet five o'clock—holds a glass of beer. "You might say it haunts me."

Chief Kitrick sips his beer. "I gather you didn't find what you wanted at the courthouse."

"Actually, I learned more than I expected." Your voice shakes. "Do you want to talk here or in your office?"

"It depends on what you want to talk about."

"The Gunthers."

You pass through the squeaky gate in the office.

Chief Kitrick sits behind his desk. His face looks more flushed than two days ago. "The Gunthers? My, my. I haven't heard that name in years. What about them?"

"That's the question, isn't it? What about them? Tell me."

Chief Kitrick shrugs. "There isn't much. I don't remember them. I was just a toddler when they . . . All I know is what I heard when I was growing up, and that's not a lot. A husband and wife—they ran a boarding-house."

"The nursery."

Chief Kitrick frowns. "I don't believe I ever heard it called the nursery. What's that supposed to mean?"

"The Gunthers took in young women. *Pregnant* women. And after the babies were born, the Gunthers arranged to sell them to desperate Jewish couples who couldn't have children of their own. Black-market adoptions."

Chief Kitrick slowly straightens. "Black-market. Where on earth did you get such a crazy . . ."

You press your hands on the desk and lean forward. "See, back then, adoption agencies didn't want to give babies to Jews instead of WASPs. So the Gunthers provided the service. They and the doctor who delivered the babies earned a fortune. But I don't think that's the whole story. I've got a terrible feeling there's something more, something worse, although I'm not sure what it is. All I do know is that thirteen women—they were probably pregnant—died in the fire that destroyed the nursery in 1941."

"Oh, sure, the fire," Chief Kitrick says. "I heard about that. Fact is, I even vaguely remember seeing the flames up there on the bluff that night, despite how little I was. The whole town was lit like day. A terrible thing, all those women dying like that."

"Yes." You swallow. "Terrible. And then the Gunthers left, and so did the doctor. *Why?*"

Chief Kitrick shrugs. "Your guess is as good as . . .

Maybe the Gunthers didn't want to rebuild. Maybe they thought it was time for a change."

"No, I think they left because the fire happened in November and the authorities started asking questions about why all those women, and *only* women, were in that boardinghouse after the tourist season was over. I think the Gunthers and the doctor became so afraid that they left town to make it hard for the authorities to question them. They wanted to discourage an investigation that might have led to charges being filed."

"Think all you want. There's no way to prove it. But I can tell you this. As I grew up, I'd sometimes hear people talking about the Gunthers, and everything the townsfolk said was always about how nice the Gunthers were, how generous. Sure, Redwood Point was once a popular resort, but that was just during the tourist season. The rest of the year, the thirties, the Depression, this town would have starved if not for that boardinghouse. That place was always busy year-round, and the Gunthers always spent plenty of money here. So many guests. They ate a lot of food, and the Gunthers bought it locally, and they always hired local help. Cooks. Maids. Ladies in town to do washing and ironing. Caretakers to manage the grounds and make sure everything was repaired and looked good. This town owed a lot to the Gunthers, and after they left . . . well, that's when things started going to hell. Redwood Point couldn't support itself on the tourists alone. The merchants couldn't afford to maintain their shops as nice as before. The town began looking dingy. Not as many tourists came. Fewer and . . . Well, you can see where we ended. At *one* time, though, this town depended on the Gunthers, and you won't find anyone speaking ill about them."

"Exactly. That's what bothers me."

"I don't understand."

"All those pregnant women coming to that boarding-house," you say. "Year-round. All through the thirties and into the early forties. Even if the Gunthers hadn't hired local servants, the town couldn't have helped but notice that something was wrong about that boardinghouse. The people here *knew* what was going on. Couples arriving childless but leaving with a baby. The whole town—even the chief of police—*had* to be aware that the Gunthers were selling babies."

"Now stop right there." Chief Kitrick stands, his eyes glinting with fury. "The chief of police back then was my father, and I won't let you talk about him like that."

You raise your hands in disgust. "The scheme couldn't have worked unless the chief of police turned his back. The Gunthers probably bribed him. But then the fire ruined everything. Because it attracted outsiders. Fire investigators. The county medical examiner. Maybe the state police. And when they started asking questions about the nursery, the Gunthers and the doctor got out of town."

"I told you I won't listen to you insult my father! Bribes? Why, my father never—"

"Sure," you say. "A pillar of the community. Just like everybody else."

"Get out!"

"Right. As soon as you tell me one more thing. June Engle. Is she still alive? Is she still here in town?"

"I never heard of her," Chief Kitrick growls. "Right."

Chief Kitrick glares from the open door to his office. You get in your car, drive up the bumpy street, make a U-turn, and pass him. The chief glares harder. In your rearview mirror, you see his diminishing angry profile. You reduce speed and steer toward the left, as if taking the jolting upward road out of town. But with a cautious glance toward the chief, you see him stride in nervous victory along the sidewalk. You see him open the door to the bar, and the moment you're out of sight around the corner, you stop.

The clouds are darker, thicker, lower. The wind increases, keening. Sporadic raindrops speckle your windshield. You step from the car, button your jacket, and squint through the biting wind toward the broken skeleton of the pier. The old man you met two days ago no longer slumps on his rickety chair, but just before you turned the corner, movement on your right—through a dusty window in a shack near the pier—attracted your attention. You approach the shack, the door to which faces the seething ocean, but you don't have a chance to knock before the wobbly door creaks open. The old man, wearing a frayed, rumpled sweater, cocks his head, frowning, a homemade cigarette dangling from his lips.

You reach for your wallet. "I spoke to you the other day, remember?"

"Yep."

You take a hundred-dollar bill from your wallet. The old man's bloodshot eyes widen. Beyond him, on a table in the shack, you notice half a dozen empty beer bottles. "Want to earn some quick, easy money?"

"Depends."

"June Engle."

"So?"

"Ever heard of her?"

"Yep."

"Is she still alive?"

"Yep."

"Here in town?"

"Yep."

"Where can I find her?"

"This time of day?"

What the old man tells you makes your hand shake when you hand him the money. Shivering, but not from the wind, you return to your car. You make sure to take an indirect route to where the old man sent you, lest the chief glance out the tavern window and see you driving past.

"At the synagogue," the old man told you. "Or what used to be the . . . Ain't that what they call it? A synagogue?"

The sporadic raindrops become a drizzle. A chilling dampness permeates the car, despite its blasting heater. At the far end of town, above the beach, you come to a dismal single-story, flat-roofed structure. The redwood walls are cracked and warped. The windows are covered with peeling plywood. Waist-high weeds surround it. Heart pounding, you step from the car, ignore the wind that whips drizzle against you, and frown at a narrow path through the weeds that takes you to the front door. A slab of plywood, the door hangs by one hinge and almost falls as you enter.

You face a small vestibule. Sand has drifted in. An animal has made a nest in a corner. Cobwebs hang from the ceiling. The pungent odor of mold attacks your nostrils. Hebraic letters on a wall are so faded that you can't read them. But mostly what you notice is the path through the sand and dust on the floor toward the entrance to the temple.

The peak of your skull feels naked. Instinctively, you look around in search of a yarmulke. But after so many years, there aren't any. Removing a handkerchief from your pocket, you place it on your head, open the door to the temple, and find yourself paralyzed, astonished by what you see.

The temple—or what used to be the temple—is barren of furniture. The back wall has an alcove where a curtain once concealed the Torah. Before the alcove, an old woman kneels, her withered hips thrusting down on her bony legs, a handkerchief tied around her head. She murmurs, hands fidgeting, as if she holds something before her.

At last you're able to move. Inching forward, pausing beside her, you see the surprisingly incongruous object she clutches: a rosary. Tears trickle down her cheeks. As close as you are, you still have to strain to distinguish what she murmurs.

". . . deliver us from evil. Amen."

"June Engle?"

She doesn't respond, just keeps fingering the beads

and praying. "Hail Mary . . . blessed is the fruit of thy womb . . ."

"June, my name is Jacob Weinberg."

"Pray for us sinners now and at the hour of our death. . . ."

"June, I want to talk to you about Dr. Adams. About the clinic."

The old woman's fingers tighten on the rosary. Slowly she turns and blinks up through tear-brimmed eyes. "The clinic?"

"Yes. And about the Gunthers. About the nursery."

"God help me. God help *them*." She wavers, her face pale.

"Come on, June, you'll faint if you kneel much longer. I'll help you up." You touch her appallingly flesh-less arms and gently raise her to her feet. She wobbles. You hold her husk of a body against you. "The nursery. Is that why you're here, June? You're doing penance?"

"Thirty pieces of silver."

"Yes." Your voice echoes eerily. "I think I under-stand. Dr. Adams and the Gunthers made a lot of money. Did *you* make a lot of money, June? Did they pay you well?"

"Thirty pieces of silver."

"Tell me about the nursery, June. I promise you'll feel better."

"Ivy, rose, heather, iris."

You cringe, suspecting that she's gone insane. She seems to think that "the nursery" refers to a *plant* nursery. But she knows better. She *knows* that the nursery had nothing to do with plants, but instead with babies from unmarried pregnant women. Or at least she *ought* to know, unless the consequence of age and what seems to be guilt has affected her mind and her memory. She appears to be free-associating.

"Violet, lily, daisy, fern," she babbles.

Your chest cramps as you realize that those words make perfect sense in the context of . . . They might be . . . "Are those names, June? You're telling me that the women in the nursery called themselves after plants and flowers?"

"Orval Gunther chose them. Anonymous." June weeps. "Nobody would know who they really were. They could hide their shame, protect their identities."

"But how did they learn about the nursery?"

"Advertisements." June's shriveled knuckles paw at her eyes. "In big-city newspapers. The personal columns."

"*Advertisements?* But that was taking an awful risk. The police might have suspected."

"No. Not Orval. He never took risks. He was clever. So clever. All he promised was a rest home for unmarried pregnant women. 'Feel alone?' the ad read. 'Need a caring, trained staff to help you give birth in strictest privacy? No questions asked. We guarantee to relieve your insecurity. Let us help you with your burden.' Sweet Lord, those women understood what the ad was really about. They came here by the *hundreds*."

June trembles against you. Her tears soak through your jacket, as chilling as the wind-driven rain that trickles through the roof.

"Did those women get any money for the babies they gave to strangers?"

"*Get?* The opposite. They paid!" June stiffens, her feeble arms gaining amazing strength as she pushes from your grasp. "Orval, that son of a . . . He charged them room and board! Five hundred dollars!"

Her knees sag.

You grasp her. "*Five hundred?* And the couples who took the babies? How much did the Gunthers get from *them?*"

"Sometimes as high as ten thousand dollars."

The arms with which you hold her shake. Ten thousand dollars? During the Depression? Hundreds of pregnant women? Dr. Jonathan Adams, Jr., hadn't exaggerated. The Gunthers had earned a fortune.

"And Orval's wife was worse than he was. Eve! She was a monster! All she cared about was . . . *Pregnant women* didn't matter! *Babies* didn't matter. *Money* mattered."

"But if you thought they were monsters . . . June, why did you help them?"

She clutches her rosary. "Thirty pieces of silver. Holy Mary, mother of . . . Ivy, Rose, Heather, Iris. Violet, Lily, Daisy, Fern."

You force her to look at you. "I told you my name was Jacob Weinberg. But I might not be . . . I think my mother's name was Mary Duncan. I think I was born here. In 1938. Did you ever know a woman who . . ."

June sobs. "Mary Duncan? If she stayed with the Gunthers, she wouldn't have used her real name. So many women! She might have been Orchid or Pansy. There's no way to tell."

"She was pregnant with twins. She promised to give up both children. Do you remember a woman who . . ."

"Twins? *Several* women had twins. The Gunthers, damn them, were ecstatic. Twenty thousand instead of ten."

"But my parents"—the word sticks in your mouth—"took only *me*. Was that common for childless parents to separate twins?"

"Money!" June cringes. "It all depended on how much *money* the couples could afford. Sometimes twins were separated. There's no way to tell where the other child went."

"But weren't there records?"

"The Gunthers were smart. They *never* kept records. In case the police . . . And then the fire . . . Even if there *had* been records, *secret* records, the fire would have . . ."

Your stomach plummets. Despite your urgent need for answers, you realize you've reached a dead end.

Then June murmurs something that you barely hear, but the little you do hear chokes you. "What? I didn't . . . June, please say that again."

"Thirty pieces of silver. For that, I . . . How I paid. Seven stillborn children."

"Yours?"

"I thought that with the money the Gunthers paid me, my husband and I could raise our children in luxury, give them every advantage, send them to medical school or . . . God help me, what I did for the Gunthers cursed my womb. It made me worse than barren. It doomed me to carry lifeless children. My penance. It forced me to suffer. Just like—"

"The mothers who gave up their children and possibly later regretted it?"

"No! Like the . . ."

What you hear next makes you retch. "Black-market adoptions," you told Chief Kitrick. "But I don't think that's the whole story. I've got a terrible feeling there's something more, something worse, although I'm not sure what it is."

Now you're sure what that something worse is, and the revelation makes you weep in outrage. "Show me, June," you manage to say. "Take me. I promise it'll be your salvation." You try to remember what you know about Catholicism. "You need to confess, and after that, your conscience will be at peace."

"I'll *never* be at peace."

"You're wrong, June. You *will*. You've kept your secret too long. It festers inside you. You have to let out the poison. After all these years, your prayers here in the synagogue have been sufficient. You've suffered enough. What you need now is absolution."

"You think if I go there . . ." June shudders.

"And pray one last time. *Yes*. I beg you. Show me. Your torment will finally end."

"So long! I haven't been there since . . ."

"Nineteen forty-one? That's what I mean, June. It's time. It's finally time."

Through biting wind and chilling rain, you escort June from the ghost of the synagogue into the sheltering warmth of your car. You're so angry that you don't bother taking an indirect route. You don't care if Chief Kitrick sees you driving past the tavern. In fact, you almost *want* him to. You steer left up the bumpy road out of town, its jolts diminished by the storm-soaked earth. When you reach the coastal highway, you assure June yet again and prompt her for further directions.

"It's been so long. I don't . . . Yes. Turn to the right," she says. A half mile later, she trembles, adding, "Now left here. Up that muddy road. Do you think you can?"

"Force this car through the mud to the top? If I have to, I'll get out and push. And if *that* doesn't work, we'll walk. God help me, I'll carry you. I'll sink to my knees and *crawl*."

But the car's front-wheel drive defeats the mud. At once you gain traction, thrust over a hill, swivel to a stop, and frown through the rain toward an unexpected meadow. Even in early October, the grass is lush. Amazingly, horribly so. Knowing its secret, you suddenly recall—from your innocent youth—lines from a poem you studied in college. Walt Whitman's *Song of Myself*.

A child said What is the grass? *fetching it to me with*
        full hands;
How could I answer the child? . . . I do not know
        what it is any more than he.

I guess it must be the flag of my disposition . . .

You force your way out of the car. You struggle around its hood, ignore the mud, confront the stinging wind and rain, and help June waver from the passenger seat. The bullet-dark clouds roil above the meadow.

"Was it here?" you demand. "Tell me! Is *this* the place?"

"Yes! Can't you hear them wail? Can't you hear them *suffer*?"

> . . . *the flag of my disposition, out of hopeful green stuff woven.*

> *Or I guess it is the handkerchief of the Lord . . .*

> *Or I guess the grass is itself a child . . . the produced babe of the vegetation.*

"June! In the name of God"—rain stings your face— "tell me!"

> . . . *a uniform hieroglyphic,*
> . . . *Sprouting alike in broad zones and narrow zones,*
> *Growing among black folks as among white . . .*

"Tell me, June!"

"Can't you *sense*? Can't you feel the horror?"

"Yes, June." You sink to your knees. You caress the grass. "I can."

> *And now it seems to me the beautiful uncut hair of graves.*

"How many, June?" You lean forward, your face almost touching the grass.

"Two hundred. Maybe more. All those years. So

many babies." June weeps behind you. "I finally couldn't count anymore."

"But *why*?" You raise your head toward the angry rain. "Why did they have to die?"

"Some were sickly. Some were deformed. If the Gunthers decided they couldn't sell them . . ."

"They murdered them? Smothered them? Strangled them?"

"Let them starve to death. The wails." June cringes. "Those poor, hungry, suffering babies. Some took as long as three days to die. In my nightmares, I heard them wailing. I *still* hear them wailing." June hobbles toward you. "At first, the Gunthers took the bodies in a boat and dumped them at sea. But one of the corpses washed up on the beach, and if it hadn't been for the chief of police they bribed . . ." June's voice breaks. "So the Gunthers decided they needed a safer way to dispose of the bodies. They brought them here and buried them in paper bags or potato sacks or butter boxes."

"Butter boxes?"

"Some of the babies were born prematurely." June sinks beside you, weeping. "They were small, so terribly small."

"*Two hundred?*" The frenzied wind thrusts your words down your throat. With a shudder you realize that if your mother was Mary Duncan, a *Scot*, the Gunthers might have decided that you looked too obviously Gentile. They might have buried you here with . . .

Your brother or your sister? Your twin? Is your counterpart under the grass you clutch?

You shriek, "Two hundred!"

Despite the howl of the storm, you hear a car, its engine roaring, its tires spinning, fighting for traction in the mud. You see a police car crest the rain-shrouded hill and skid to a stop.

Chief Kitrick shoves his door open, stalking toward you through the raging gloom. "Goddamn it, I told you to leave the past alone."

You rise from the grass, draw back a fist, and strike his mouth so hard that he drops to the mushy ground. "You knew! You son of a bitch, you knew all along!"

The chief wipes blood from his mangled lips. In a fury, he fumbles to draw his gun.

"That's right! Go ahead, kill me!" You spread out your arms, lashed by the rain. "But June'll be a witness, and you'll have to kill her, as well! So what, though, huh? Two murders won't matter, will they? Not compared to a couple of hundred children!"

"I had nothing to do with—"

"Killing these babies? No, but your *father* did!"

"He wasn't involved!"

"He let it happen! He took the Gunthers' money and turned his back! That *makes* him involved! He's as much to blame as the Gunthers! The whole fucking town was involved!" You pivot toward the ridge, buffeted by the full strength of the storm. In the blinding gale, you can't see the town, but you scream at it nonetheless. "You sons of bitches! You knew! You all let it happen! You did nothing to stop it! That's why your town fell apart! God cursed you! Bastards!"

Abruptly you realize the terrible irony of your words. Bastards? *All* of these murdered children were bastards.

You spin toward the grass, "the beautiful uncut hair of graves." Falling, you hug the rain-soaked earth, the drenched lush leaves of grass. "Poor babies!"

"You can't prove a thing," Chief Kitrick growls. "All you've got are suppositions. After fifty years, there won't be anything left of those babies. They've long since rotted and turned into—"

"Grass," you moan, tears scalding your face. "The beautiful grass."

"The doctor who delivered the babies is dead. The Gunthers—my father kept track of them—died, as well. In agony, if that satisfies your need for justice. Orval got stomach cancer. Eve died from alcoholism."

"And now they burn in hell," June murmurs.

"I was raised to be . . . I'm a *Jew*," you moan, suddenly understanding the significance of your pronouncement. No matter the circumstances of your birth, you *are* a Jew, totally, completely. "I don't believe in hell. But I wish . . . Oh, God, how I wish . . ."

"The only proof you have," Chief Kitrick says, "is this old woman, a Catholic who goes every afternoon to pray in a ruined synagogue. She's nuts. You're a lawyer. You know her testimony wouldn't be accepted in court. It's over, Weinberg. It ended fifty years ago."

"No! It never ended! The grass keeps growing!" You feel the chill wet earth. You try to embrace your brother or your sister and quiver with the understanding that *all* of these children are your brothers and sisters. "God have mercy on them!"

*What do you think has become of the women and
     children?*
They are alive and well somewhere,
The smallest sprout shows there is really no death,
*And if ever there was it led forward life, and does
     not wait at the end to arrest it . . .*

All goes onward and outward, nothing collapses,
*And to die is different from what any one supposed,
     and luckier.*

"Luckier?" You embrace the grass. *"Luckier?"*

Through the rain-soaked earth, you think you hear
babies crying and raise your face toward the furious
storm. Swallowing rain, tasting the salt of your tears, you
recite the kaddish prayers. You mourn Mary Duncan,
Simon and Esther Weinberg, your brother or your sister,
all these children.

And yourself.

"Deliver us from evil," June Engle murmurs. "Pray
for us sinners now and at the hour of our death."

The Shrine

*I*t's amazing how long images can stay in the imagination until they're ready to be used in a story. Back in 1970, just after I finished graduate school at Penn State, I took a weekend off and drove with a close friend to his home near Pittsburgh. On an August afternoon, we went to a compound that some friends of his father had built in the mountains. It had a swimming hole, a barbecue pit, a bunkhouse, and—I still see it vividly—a shrine. Its contents haunted me until finally, twenty-two years later, I had to write about it. Again the theme is grief, a subject I returned to often after Matt's death. "The Shrine" was nominated by the Horror Writers Association as the best novella of 1992.

GRADY WAS IN THE MAUSOLEUM WHEN THE BEEP FROM his pager disrupted his sobbing.

The mausoleum was spacious and bright, with shiny

marble slabs that concealed the niches into which coffins had been placed. In an alcove near the high, wide windows that flanked the main entrance, glinting squares of glass permitted mourners to stare within much smaller niches and view the bronze urns that contained the ashes of their loved ones. Bronze-colored plastic letters and numbers that formed the names of the deceased as well as their birth and death dates were glued upon the squares of glass, and it was toward two of those panes, toward the urns behind them, that Grady directed his attention, although his vision was blurred by tears.

He'd chosen cremation for his wife and ten-year-old son, partly because they'd already been burned—in a fiery car crash with a drunken driver—but more because he couldn't bear the thought of his cherished wife and child decomposing in a coffin in a niche in the mausoleum or, worse, outside in the cemetery, beneath the ground, where rain or the deep cold of winter would make him cringe because of their discomfort, even though the remaining rational part of Grady's mind acknowledged that it didn't matter to his fiercely missed family, who now felt nothing because they were dead.

But it mattered to *him,* just as it mattered that each Monday afternoon he made a ritual of driving out here to the mausoleum, of sitting on a padded bench across from the wall of glassed-in urns, and of talking to Helen and John about what had happened to him since the previous Monday, about how he prayed that they were happy, and, most of all, about how much he missed them.

They'd been dead for a year now, and a year was supposed to be a long time, but he couldn't believe the speed with which it had gone. His pain remained as great as the day he'd been told they were dead, his emptiness as extreme. Friends at first had been understanding, but after three months, and especially after six, most of those friends had begun to show polite impatience, making well-intentioned speeches about the need for Grady to put the past behind him, to adjust to his loss, to rebuild his life. So Grady had hidden his emotions and pretended to take their advice, his burden made greater by social necessity. The fact was, he came to realize, that no one who hadn't suffered what he had could possibly understand that three months or six months or a year meant nothing.

Grady's weekly visits to the mausoleum became a secret, their half hour concealed within his Monday routine. Sometimes he brought his wife and son flowers and sometimes an emblem of the season: a pumpkin at Halloween, a Styrofoam snowball in winter, or a fresh maple leaf in the spring. But on this occasion, just after the Fourth of July weekend, he'd brought a miniature flag, and unable to control the strangled sound of his voice, he explained to Helen and John about the splendor of the fireworks that he'd witnessed and that they'd used to enjoy while eating hot dogs at the city's annual picnic in the sloped, wooded park near the river on Independence Day.

"If only you could have seen the skyrockets," Grady murmured. "I don't know how to describe . . . Their colors were so—"

The beep from the pager on his gun belt interrupted his halting monologue. He frowned.

The pager was one of many innovations that he'd introduced to the police force he commanded. After all, his officers frequently had to leave their squad cars, responding to an assignment or merely sitting in a restaurant on a coffee break, but while away from their radios, they needed to know whether headquarters was desperate to contact them.

Its persistent beep made Grady stiffen. He wiped his tears, braced his shoulders, said good-bye to his wife and son, and stood with effort, reluctantly leaving the mausoleum, locking its door behind him. That was important. Helen and John, their remains, needed to be protected, and the cemetery's caretaker had been as inventive as Grady had been about the pager, arranging for every mourner to have a key, so that only those who had a right could enter.

Outside, the July afternoon was bright, hot, humid, and horribly reminiscent of the sultry afternoon a year ago when Grady had come here, accompanied by friends and a priest, to inter the precious urns. He shook his head to clear his mind and stifle his tortured emotions, then approached the black-and-white cruiser, where he leaned inside to grab the two-way radio microphone.

"Grady here, Dinah. What's the problem?" He released the transmit button on the microphone.

Dinah's staccato response surprised him. "Public-service dispatch."

Grady frowned. "On my way. Five minutes."

Uneasy, he drove from the cemetery. "Public-service dispatch" meant that whatever Dinah needed to tell him was so sensitive that she didn't want a civilian with a police-band radio to overhear the conversation. Grady would have to use a telephone to get in touch with her. After parking at a gas station across from the cemetery, he entered a booth beside an ice machine, thrust coins in the telephone's slot, and jabbed numbers.

"Bosworth Police," Dinah said.

"Dinah, it's me. What's so important that—"

"You're not going to like this," the deep-voiced female dispatcher said.

"It's never good news when you page me. Public-service dispatch? *Why?*"

"We've got a combination one eighty-seven and ten fifty-six."

Grady winced. Those numbers meant a murder-suicide. "You're right." His voice dropped. "I don't like it."

"It gets worse. It's not in our jurisdiction. The state police are handling it, but they want you on the scene."

"I don't understand. Why would that be worse if it isn't in our jurisdiction?"

"Chief, I . . ."

"Say it."

"I don't want to."

"Say it, Dinah."

". . . You know the victims."

For a moment, Grady had trouble breathing. He clutched the microphone harder. "Who?"

"Brian and Betsy Roth."

Shit, Grady thought. Shit. Shit. Shit. Brian and Betsy had been the friends he'd depended upon after all his other friends had distanced themselves when his grief persisted.

Now one of *them* had killed the other?

And after that, the executioner had committed *suicide*?

Grady's pulse sped, making his mind swirl. "Who did what to—"

The husky-throated female dispatcher said, "Brian did. A forty-five semiautomatic."

Christ. Oh, Jesus Christ, Grady thought.

The puzzling directions Grady received took him not to Brian and Betsy's home, where he'd assumed the killings would have occurred, but instead through and past the outskirts of Bosworth, into the mountains west of town. Pennsylvania mountains: low, thickly wooded, rounded at their peaks. Among them, primitive roads led into hidden hollows. In a turmoil, confused, Grady wouldn't have known which lane to take if it hadn't been for the state police car blocking one entrance. A square-jawed trooper dropped his cigarette, crushed it into the gravel with his shoe, and narrowed his eyes when Grady stopped his cruiser.

"I'm looking for Lieutenant Clauson," Grady said.

When the trooper heard Grady's name, he straightened. "And the lieutenant's waiting for *you*." With remarkable efficiency for so large a man, the trooper backed his car from the entrance to the lane, allowing Grady to drive his own car up the narrow draw.

Leaves brushed against Grady's side window. Just before the first sharp curve, Grady glanced toward his rearview mirror and saw the state police car again block the entrance. At once, he jerked the steering wheel, veering left. Then, behind as well as ahead, he saw only forest.

The lane tilted ever more upward. It kept forcing Grady to zigzag and increased his anxiety as branches scraped the top of his car in addition to his windows. The dense shadows of the forest made him feel trapped.

Brian shot Betsy?

And then shot *himself*?

No!

Why?

I needed them.

I depended on . . .

I loved them!

What on earth had made them come out here? Why had they been in the woods?

The lane became level, straightened, and suddenly brought Grady from the forest to a sun-bathed plateau between two mountains, where an open gate in a chain-link fence revealed a spacious compound: several cinder-block buildings of various sizes on the left, a barbecue pit adjacent to them, and a swimming pool on the right.

Grady parked behind three state police cars, an ambulance, a blue station wagon marked MEDICAL EXAMINER, and a red Jeep Cherokee that Grady recognized as belonging to Brian and Betsy. Several state troopers, along with two ambulance attendants and an overweight man in a gray suit, formed a cluster at the near rim of the swimming pool, their backs to Grady. But as Grady opened his door, one of the troopers turned, studied him, glanced back toward the rim of the pool, again studied Grady, and, with a somber expression, approached him.

Lieutenant Clauson. Middle forties. Tall. Pronounced nose and cheekbones. Trim—Clauson's doctor had ordered him to lose weight, Grady remembered. Short, receding brown hair. On occasion, Clauson and Grady had worked together when a crime was committed in one jurisdiction and a suspect was apprehended in the other.

"Ben."

"Jeff."

"Did your dispatcher explain?" Clauson looked uneasy.

Grady nodded, grim. "Brian shot Betsy and then himself. Why the hell would he—"

"That's what we were hoping you could tell us."

Grady shivered despite the afternoon heat. "How would *I* know?"

"You and the Roths were friends. I hate to ask you to do this. Do you think you can . . . Would you . . ."

"Look at the bodies?"

"Yes." Clauson furrowed his brow, more uneasy. "If you wouldn't mind."

"Jeff, just because my wife and son died, I can still do my job. Even though Brian and Betsy were friends of mine, I can do whatever's necessary. I'm ready to help."

"I figured."

"Then why did you have to ask?"

"Because you're involved."

"*What?*"

"First things first," Clauson said. "You look at the bodies. I show you what your friend Brian had in his hand, clutched around the grip of the forty-five. And then we talk."

* * *

The stench of decay pinched Grady's nostrils. A waist-high wooden fence enclosed the swimming pool. Grady followed Clauson through an opening onto a concrete strip that bordered the pool. One of the policemen was taking photographs of something on the concrete while the overweight man in the gray suit suggested various angles. When the other policemen saw Clauson and Grady arrive, they parted to give them room, and Grady saw the bodies.

The shock made him sick. His friends lay facedown on the concrete, redwood deck chairs behind them, their heads toward the pool. Or what was left of their heads. The .45-caliber bullets had done massive damage. Behind Betsy's right ear and Brian's, the impact wound was a thick black clot of blood. On the opposite side, at the top of each brow near the temple, the exit wound was a gaping hole from which blood, brain, bone, and hair had spattered the concrete. A repugnant swarm of flies buzzed over the gore. The .45 was next to Brian's right hand.

"Are you all right?" Clauson touched Grady's arm.

Grady swallowed. "I'll manage." Although he'd been the police chief of Bosworth for almost ten years, he'd seen few gunshot victims. After all, Bosworth was a modest-sized town. There wasn't much violent crime. Mostly, the corpses he'd viewed had been due to car accidents. That thought suddenly reminded him of the accident in which his wife and son had died, and he felt grief upon grief: for his friends, for his family.

Determined to keep control, Grady sought refuge in

forcing himself to muster professional habits, to try to be objective.

"These corpses"—Grady struggled to order his troubled thoughts—"have started to bloat. Even as hot as it's been, they wouldn't be this swollen . . . unless . . . This didn't happen today."

Clauson nodded. "As close as we can tell, it was early yesterday."

The overweight man in the gray suit interrupted. "I'll know for sure when I do the autopsy."

The man was the county's medical examiner. He gestured for the trooper to stop taking photographs. "I think that's enough." He turned to the ambulance attendants. "You can move them now." He pivoted toward Clauson. "Provided you don't object."

Clauson thought about it and shrugged. "We've done as much as we can for now. Go ahead."

Feeling colder, Grady heard the zip of body bags being opened. To distract himself, he stared toward the glistening blue water of the swimming pool while the attendants put on rubber gloves. He was grateful when Clauson spoke, further distracting him.

"Brian and Betsy were expected home yesterday evening," Clauson said. "When Brian's sister phoned and didn't get an answer, she figured they must have changed their plans and spent the night here. But when she called again in the morning and still didn't get an answer, and when it turned out that Brian hadn't opened the restaurant this morning, his sister got worried. This place doesn't have a phone, so she drove out here. . . ."

"And found the bodies," Grady said, "and then phoned you."

Clauson nodded. In the background, the attendants strained to lift a bulging body bag onto a gurney, then rolled it toward the ambulance.

Grady forced himself to continue. "It looks as if they were both sitting in these deck chairs, facing the pool. The impact of the bullets knocked them out of the chairs."

"That's how we figure it," Clauson said.

"Which tends to suggest they weren't arguing, at least not so bad that it made Brian angry enough to shoot Betsy and then shoot himself when he realized what he'd done." Grady's throat tightened. "People are usually on their feet when they're shouting at each other. But it's almost as if the two of them were just sitting here, enjoying the view. Then Brian goes to get the pistol, or else he's already got it on him. But why? *Why would he decide to shoot her?* And why would Betsy just sit there, assuming she knew Brian had the gun?"

"He planned it," Clauson said.

"Obviously, or else he wouldn't have had the gun."

"That's not the only reason I know Brian planned it." Clauson pointed downward. "Look at the gun."

Grady lowered his gaze toward the concrete, avoiding the black clots at the rim of the pool and the contrasting white chalk silhouettes of where the bodies had been. He concentrated on the weapon.

"Yes." He sighed. "I get the point." The slide on the .45 was all the way back, projecting behind the hammer. The only time a .45 did that, Grady knew, was when the magazine in the pistol's handle was empty. "Brian didn't load the magazine completely. He put in only two rounds."

"One for Betsy, one for himself," Clauson said. "So what does that tell you?"

"Brian thought about this carefully." Grady felt appalled. "He respected guns. He didn't load the magazine completely because he knew that otherwise the gun would self-cock after he fired the second shot, after he killed himself and the pistol dropped from his hand as he fell. He didn't want whoever found him to pick up a loaded gun and accidentally fire it, maybe killing the person who held it. He tried to do this as cleanly as possible."

Grady forcefully shook his head from side to side. *Cleanly?* What a poor choice of word. But that was the way Brian had thought. Brian had always worried that an animal he shot might be only wounded, might escape to the forest and suffer for hours, maybe days, before it finally died. In that sense, the way Brian had arranged to kill his wife and then himself was definitely clean. Two shots placed efficiently at the soft spot behind each victim's ear. A direct route to the brain. Instantaneous, nonpainful death. At least in theory. Only the victims knew if their deaths had been truly painless, and they couldn't very well talk about it.

Grady frowned so severely that his head ached. Massaging his temples, thinking of the bullets that had plowed through Betsy's skull and then Brian's, he studied Clauson. "Usually someone does this because of marriage problems. Jealousy. One of the partners having an affair. But as far as I know, Brian and Betsy had a faithful relationship."

"You can bet I'll make sure," Clauson said.

"So will I. The only other reason I can think of is that Betsy might have had a fatal illness, something they kept hidden because they didn't want to worry their friends. When the disease got worse, when Betsy couldn't bear the pain, Brian—with Betsy's permission—*stopped* the pain, and then, because Brian couldn't stand the agony of living without Betsy, he . . ."

"That's something else I'll check for when I do the autopsy," the medical examiner said.

"And I'll talk to her doctor," Clauson said, determined.

Grady's sadness fought with his confusion. "So how does this involve me? You told me it was something about his hand. Something he clutched."

Clauson looked reluctant. "I'm afraid there's no good way to do this. I'm sorry. I'll just have to show you. Brian left a note."

"I was going to ask if he had. I need answers."

Clauson pulled a plastic bag from a pocket in his shirt. The bag contained a piece of paper.

Grady murmured, "If Brian left a note, there's no question. Combined with the way he loaded the forty-five, there's no doubt he made careful plans. Perhaps along with . . ." Grady shuddered. "I've got the terrible feeling Betsy agreed."

"That thought occurred to me," Clauson said. "But there's no way we'll ever know. He had this piece of paper clutched around the grip of the pistol. When the forty-five dropped from his hand, the note stuck to his fingers."

Grady studied it and shivered.

The note was printed boldly in black ink.

TELL BEN GRADY. BRING HIM HERE.

That was all.

And it was too much.

"Bring me here? Why?"

"That's why I said we had to talk." Clauson bit his lip. "Come on, let's get away from where this happened. I think it's time for a stroll."

They emerged from the swimming pool area and crossed a stretch of gravel, their footsteps crunching as they passed the barbecue pit as well as two redwood picnic tables and approached the largest of the cinder-block buildings. It was thirty feet long and half as wide. A metal chimney projected from the nearest wall and angled above the roof. There were three dusty windows.

"Bring you here." Clauson echoed Brian's note. "That can mean different things. To see the bodies, or to see the compound. I didn't know Brian well, but my impression is that he wasn't cruel. I can't imagine why he'd have wanted you to see what he'd done. It makes me wonder if . . ."

Grady anticipated the rest of the question. "I've never been here. In fact, I didn't know this place existed. Even with the directions you relayed through my office, I had trouble finding the lane."

"And yet you and the Roths were close."

"Only recently—within the last year. I met them at a meeting of the Compassionate Friends."

"What's—"

"An organization for parents who've lost a child. The theory is that only a parent in grief can understand what another parent in grief is going through. So the grieving parents have a meeting once a month. They begin the meeting by explaining how each child died. There's usually a speaker, a psychiatrist or some other type of specialist who recommends various ways of coping. Then the meeting becomes a discussion. The parents who've suffered the longest try to help those who still can't believe what has happened. You're given phone numbers of people to call if you don't think you can stand the pain any longer. The people you talk to try their best to encourage you not to give in to despair. They remind you to take care of your health, not to rely on alcohol or stay in bed all day, but instead to eat, to maintain your strength, to get out of the house, to walk, to find positive ways to fill your time, community service, that sort of thing."

Clauson rubbed the back of his neck. "You make me feel embarrassed."

"Oh?"

"When your wife and son were killed, I went to the funeral. I came around to your house once. But after that . . . Well, I didn't know what to say, or I told myself I didn't want to bother you. I suppose I figured you'd prefer to be left alone."

Grady shrugged, hollow. "That's a common reaction. There's no need to apologize. Unless you've lost a wife and child of your own, it's impossible to understand the pain."

"I pray to God I never have to go through it."

"Believe me, my prayers go with you."

They reached the largest cinder-block building.

"The lab crew already dusted for prints." Clauson opened the door, and Grady peered in. There were sleeping bags on cots along each wall, two long pine tables, benches, some cupboards, and a wood-burning stove.

"Obviously, more people than Brian and Betsy used this place," Clauson said. "Have you any idea who?"

"I told you that I've never been here."

Clauson closed the door and proceeded toward a smaller cinder-block building next to it.

This time, when Clauson unlatched and opened the door, Grady saw a wood-burning cookstove with cans and boxes of food, as well as pots, pans, bowls, plates, and eating utensils on shelves along the walls.

"I assume," Clauson said, "that the barbecue pit was for summer, and this was for rainy days, or fall, or maybe winter."

Grady nodded. "There were twelve cots in the other building. I noticed rain slickers and winter coats on pegs. Whoever they were, they came here often. Year-round. So what? It's a beautiful location. A summer getaway. A hunting camp in the fall. A place for Brian, Betsy, and their friends to have weekend parties, even in winter, as long as the snow didn't block the lane."

"Yeah, a beautiful location." Clauson shut the door to the kitchen, directing Grady toward the final and smallest structure. "This was the only building that was locked.

Brian had the key on a ring along with his car keys. I found the key in his pants pocket."

When Clauson opened the door, Grady frowned.

The floors in the other buildings had been made from wooden planks, except for firebricks beneath the stoves. But this floor was smooth gray slate. In place of the cinder-block walls in the other buildings, the walls in here had oak paneling. Instead of a stove, a handsome stone fireplace had a shielded slab of wood for a mantel, an American flag on each side, and glistening framed photographs of eight smiling youngsters—male and female—positioned in a straight line above the flags. The age of the youngsters ranged, Grady estimated, from six to nineteen, and one image of a boy—blond, with braces on his teeth, with spectacles that made him look uncomfortable despite his determined smile—reminded Grady distressingly of his own, so longed-for son.

He took in more details: a church pew in front of the photographs above the fireplace, ceramic candleholders on the mantel, and . . . He stepped closer, troubled when he realized that two of the smiling faces in the photographs—lovely, freckled, redheaded girls, early teens—were almost identical. Twins. Another pattern he noticed, his brow furrowing, was that the oldest males in the photographs, two of them, late teens, had extremely short haircuts and wore military uniforms.

"So what do you make of it?" Clauson asked.

"It's almost like . . ." Grady felt pressure in his chest. "Like a chapel. No religious objects, but it feels like a chapel all the same. Some kind of shrine. Those twin girls. I've seen them before. The photographs, I mean.

Brian and Betsy had copies in their wallets and showed them to me a couple of times when they invited me over for dinner. They also had larger, framed copies on a wall in their living room. These are Brian and Betsy's daughters." Grady's stomach hardened. "They died ten years ago when a roller coaster jumped its tracks at a midway near Pittsburgh. Brian and Betsy never forgave themselves for letting their daughters go on that ride. Guilt. That's something else grieving parents suffer. A lot of guilt."

Grady stepped even closer to the photographs, concentrating on the vibrant ten-year-old blond boy with glasses and braces who reminded him so painfully of his son. The likeness wasn't exactly the same, but it was poignantly evocative.

Guilt, he thought. Yes, guilt. What if I hadn't been working late that night? What if I'd been home and Helen and John hadn't decided to go out for pizza and a movie? That drunk driver wouldn't have hit their car. They'd still be alive, and it's all my fault, because I decided to catch up on a stack of reports that could just as easily have waited until the morning. But no, I had to be conscientious, and because of that, I indirectly killed my wife and son. Not showing it, Grady cringed. From a deep black torture chamber of his mind, he wailed silently in unbearable torment.

Behind him, Clauson said something, but Grady didn't register what it was.

Clauson spoke louder. "Ben?"

Without removing his intense gaze from the photograph of the young blond boy, Grady murmured, "What?"

"Do you recognize any of the other faces?"

"No."

"This is just a hunch, but maybe there's a pattern."

"Pattern?"

"Well, since those two girls are dead, do you suppose . . . Could it be that *all* the kids in these photographs are dead?"

Grady's heart lurched. Abruptly he whirled toward the sound of a splash.

"What's the matter?" Clauson asked.

"That splash." Grady moved toward the door. "Someone fell into the pool."

"Splash? I didn't hear anything."

Grady's eyes felt stabbed by sunlight as he left the shadows of the tiny building. He stared toward the state policemen at the concrete rim of the swimming pool. The medical examiner was getting into his station wagon. The ambulance was pulling away.

But the pool looked undisturbed, and if anyone had fallen in, the troopers didn't seem to care. They merely kept talking among themselves and didn't pay attention.

"What do you mean?" Clauson asked. "There wasn't any splash. You can see for yourself. No one fell into the pool."

Grady shook his head in bewilderment. "But I would have sworn . . ."

Disoriented, he did his best to answer more questions, then finally left the compound an hour later, shortly after five, just as Clauson and his men were preparing to lock the buildings and the gate to the area, then secure a yellow NO ADMITTANCE—POLICE CRIME SCENE tape across the fence and the gate.

Troubled, numb with shock, aching with sorrow, he trembled. He used his two-way radio to contact his office while he drove along the winding road through the looming mountains back to Bosworth. He had a duty to perform, but he couldn't let that duty interfere with his other duties. The office had to know where he'd be.

With Brian Roth's sister. The deaths of his wife and son—the rules he'd learned from attending the grief meetings of the Compassionate Friends—had taught him that you had to do your best to offer consolation. Compassion was the greatest virtue.

But when he finally stopped at Ida Roth's home, a modest trailer in a row of other trailers on the outskirts of Bosworth, he didn't get an answer after he knocked on her flimsy metal door. Of course, Grady thought. The undertaker. The cemetery. The double funeral. Ida has terrible arrangements to make. She'll be in a daze. I wish I'd been able to get here in time to help her.

To Grady's surprise, the woman next door came over and told him where Ida had gone. But his surprise wasn't caused by the gossipy woman's knowledge of Ida's schedule. What surprised him was Ida's destination. He thanked the neighbor, avoided her questions, and drove to where he'd been directed.

Five minutes later, at the restaurant-tavern that Brian and Betsy had owned, Grady found Ida Roth sternly directing waitresses while she guarded the cash register behind the bar.

The customers, mostly factory workers who regularly stopped by for a couple of beers after their shift was over, eyed Grady's uniform as he sat at the counter. Whenever he came in to say hello, he was usually off duty and in civilian clothes. For him to be wearing his uniform made this visit official, the narrowed eyes that studied him seemed to say, and the somberness of those narrowed eyes suggested as well that word had gotten around about what had happened to Brian and Betsy.

Grady took off his policeman's cap, wishing that the jukebox playing Roy Orbison's "Only the Lonely" wasn't so loud.

And who the hell had been morbid enough to choose *that* tune?

Then he studied Ida's gaunt, determined features.

Brian's only and older sibling, she was in her early fifties, but she looked sixty, partly because her hair was completely gray and she combed it back severely into a bun, thus emphasizing the wrinkles in her forehead and around her eyes, and partly because her persistent nervousness made her so thin that her cheeks looked hollow, but mostly because her pursed lips made her expression constantly dour.

"Ida," Grady said, "when some people tell you this, you've got every right to feel bitter. The automatic reaction is to think, Bullshit, get out of here, leave me alone. But you know that I've been where you are now, a year ago when my wife and son were killed. You know that I'm an expert in what I'm talking about, that these aren't empty words. I understand what you're feeling. With all my heart, I'm sorry about Brian and Betsy."

Ida glowered, jerked her face toward a waitress, blurted, "Table five's still waiting for that pitcher of beer," and scowled at Grady while pressing her hand on the cash register. "Sorry? Let me tell you something. Brian shut me out after his children died. We visited. We spent time together. But things between us were never the same. For the past ten years, it's been like we weren't blood kin. Like"—Ida's facial expression became skeletal—"like there was some kind of barrier between us. I *resented* that, being made to feel like a stranger. I tried all I could to be friendly to him. As far as *I'm* concerned, a part of Brian died a long time ago. What he did to Betsy and himself was wrong. But it might be the best thing that could have happened."

"I don't understand." Grady leaned closer, trying hard to ignore Roy Orbison's mournful song and the stares from the silent, intense factory workers.

"It's no secret," Ida said. "*You* know. The whole *town* knows. My husband divorced me eight years ago. After we were married, I kept having miscarriages, so we never had children. It *aged* me. How I hate that young secretary he ran off with. All I got from the settlement, from the greedy lawyers, from the goddamned divorce judge, is the rickety trailer I'm forced to shiver in when the weather gets cold. You're sorry? Well, let me tell you, right now, as much as I hurt, *I'm* not sorry. Brian had it all, and I had nothing! When he shut me out . . . The best thing he ever did for me was to shoot himself. Now this tavern's mine. Finally I've got something."

Grady felt shocked. "Ida, you don't mean that."

"The hell I don't! Brian treated me like an outcast. I *earned* this tavern. I deserve it. When they open the will"—Ida's stern expression became calculating—"if there's any justice . . . Brian promised me. In spite of the distance he kept from me, he said he'd take care of me. This tavern's mine. And I bet you could use a drink." She stiffened her hand on the cash register.

"Thanks, Ida. I'd like to, but I can't. I'm on duty." Grady lowered his gaze and dejectedly studied his hat. "Maybe another time."

"No time's better than now. This is happy hour. If you can't be happy, at least drown your sorrow. Call this a wake. It's two drinks for the price of one."

"Not while I'm in uniform. But please remember, I do share your grief."

Ida didn't listen, again barking orders toward a waitress.

Disturbed, Grady picked up his cap and stood from the stool at the bar. A professional instinct made him pause. "Ida."

"Can't you see I'm busy?"

"I apologize, but I need information. Where Brian . . . Where Betsy was . . . What do you know about where it happened?"

"Not a hell of a lot."

"But you must know *something*. You knew enough to go out there."

"There?" Ida thickened her voice. "*There?* I was *there* only once. But I felt so shut out . . . so unwelcome

. . . so bitter . . . Believe me, I made a point of remembering how to get there."

"Go over that again. Why do you think he made you feel unwelcome?"

"That place was . . ." Ida furrowed her already severely pinched forehead. "His *retreat*. His wall against the world." Her scowl increased. "I remember when he bought that hollow. His children had been dead five months. The summer had turned to fall. It was hunting season. Brian's friends made an effort to try to distract him. 'Come on, let's hunt some rabbits, some grouse,' they told him. 'You can't just sit around all day.' He was practically dragged from his bedroom." While Ida continued to keep her left hand rigidly on the cash register, she pointed her right hand toward the ceiling above the tavern, indicating where Brian and Betsy had lived. "So Brian—he had no energy; if it weren't for me, the tavern would have gone to hell—he shuffled his feet and went along. And the next day, when he came back, I couldn't believe the change in him. He was *filled* with energy. He'd found some land he wanted to buy, he said. He was . . . Frantic? That doesn't describe it. He kept jabbering about a hollow in the mountains. He'd wandered into it. He absolutely had to own it."

Ida gave more commands to her waitresses and swung her dour gaze toward Grady. "I figured Brian must have had a nervous breakdown. I told him he couldn't afford a second property. But he wouldn't listen. He insisted he had to buy it. So despite my warning, he used this tavern as—what do they call it?—collateral. He convinced the bank to loan him money, found whoever owned that hollow, and bought the damned thing. That's the beginning of when he shut me out.

"The next thing I heard—it didn't come from him; it was gossip from customers in the tavern—was he'd arranged with a contractor to put in a swimming pool out there, some buildings, a barbecue pit, and . . . The next year when construction was finished, he invited me out there to see the grand opening.

"I admit the place looked impressive. I figured Brian was getting over his loss, adjusting to the deaths of his children. But after he, Betsy, and I and their friends—and my fucking soon-to-be ex-husband—had a barbecue, Brian took me aside. He pointed toward the woods, toward the pool, toward the buildings, and he asked me . . . I remember his voice was low, hushed, the way people talk in church.

"He asked me if I felt anything different, anything special, anything that reminded me of . . . anything that made me feel *close* to his dead children. I thought about it. I looked around. I tried to understand what he meant. Finally I said no. The camp looked fine, I said. He was taking a risk with the bank. All the same, if he needed a place where he could get away and heal his sorrow, despite the financial risk, he'd probably done the right thing. 'Nothing about the swimming pool?' he asked. I told him I didn't understand what he meant, except that his children liked to swim. And with that, he ended the conversation. That was the last time he invited me out there. That was the real beginning of the distance between us. The barrier he put up. No matter that I saved his ass by taking care of the tavern back then, just as I'm taking care of it now."

Grady knew that he'd exceeded the limit of Ida's patience. He searched his troubled mind for a final question that might settle his confusion. "Do you know who owned that hollow, or why Brian suddenly felt compelled to buy it?"

"You might as well ask me who's going to win the lottery. He told me nothing. And *I* told *you*, I don't have time for this. *Please*. I'm trying my best not to be rude, but I've got customers. This is the busiest time of the day. Happy hour makes all these people hungry. I've got to make sure the kitchen's ready."

"Sure," Grady said. "I apologize for distracting you. I just wanted . . . I'm sorry, Ida. That's why I came here. To tell you how much I sympathize."

Ida glared toward a waitress. "Table eight still needs those onion rings."

Grady stepped back, ignored the stares of the factory workers, and left the tavern. As the screen door squeaked shut, as he trudged past pickup trucks toward his cruiser, he heard the customers break their silence and murmur almost loudly enough to obscure another mournful tune, this one by Buddy Holly: "I Guess It Doesn't Matter Anymore."

He radioed his office and told the dispatcher he was going home. Then he solemnly drove along sunset-crimsoned, wooded streets to the single-story house he'd shared with his wife and son.

The house.

It haunted him. Often he'd thought about selling it to get away from the memories that it evoked. But just as he hadn't disposed of Helen's and John's possessions, their clothes, the souvenir mugs that Helen had liked to collect, the video games that John had been addicted to playing, so Grady hadn't been able to convince himself to dispose of the house. The memories tormented him, yes, but he couldn't bear living without them.

At the same time, the house troubled him because it felt empty, because he hadn't maintained it since Helen and John had died, because he hadn't planted flowers this spring as Helen always had, because its interior was drab and dusty.

When he entered the kitchen, there wasn't any question what he'd do next. The same thing he always did when he got home, what he'd done every evening since the death of his family. He walked directly to a cupboard and pulled out a bottle of Jim Beam, poured two inches into a glass, added ice and water, and drank most of it in three swallows.

He closed his eyes and exhaled. There. The Compassionate Friends was emphatic in its advice that people in grief shouldn't seek refuge in alcohol. Brian and Betsy had emphasized that advice, as well. There'd been no liquor bottles or beer cans at the camp, Grady had noticed. Whatever the cause of the murder-suicide, anger caused by drunkenness had not been related.

He'd pretended to follow the advice of the Compassionate Friends. But at night, in the depths of his sorrow, he more and more had relied on bourbon to give him amnesia. Except that it didn't really dispel his memories. All it did was blur them, make them more bearable, stupify him enough that he could sleep. As soon as the bourbon impaired him enough to slur his speech, he would put on his answering machine, and if the phone rang, if the message was something important from his office, he would muster sufficient control to pick up the phone and say a few careful words that managed to hide how disabled he was. If necessary, he would mutter that he felt ill and order one of his men to take care of the emergency. Those were the only times Grady violated his code of professionalism. But just as he'd failed to maintain this house, so he knew and feared that one night he would make a mistake and inadvertently let outsiders know that he'd failed in other ways, too.

At the moment, however, that fear didn't matter. Sorrow did, and Grady hurriedly poured another glass, this time adding less ice and water. He drank that refill almost as quickly. Brian and Betsy. Helen and John. No.

Grady slumped against the counter and wept, deep outbursts that squeezed his throat and made his shoulders convulse.

Abruptly the phone rang. Startled, he swung toward where it hung on the wall beside the back door.

It rang again.

Grady hadn't put on the answering machine yet. The way he felt, he didn't know whether to let the phone keep ringing. Brian and Betsy. Helen and John. All Grady wanted was to be left alone so he could mourn. But the call might be from his office. It might be important.

Wiping his cheeks, he straightened, brooded, and decided. The bourbon hadn't begun to take effect. He would still be able to talk without slurring his words. Whatever this call was about, he might as well take care of it while he was still able.

His hand trembled as he picked up the phone. "Hello?"

"Ben? It's Jeff Clauson. I'm sorry to bother you at home, but this is important. When I phoned your office, one of your men told me where you'd be."

"Something important? What is it?"

"I've got some names. Tell me if they're familiar. Jennings. Matson. Randall. Langley. Beck."

Grady concentrated. "I can't put any faces to them. No one I've met. At least they didn't impress me enough to make me remember them."

"I'm not surprised. They don't . . . they didn't . . . live in Bosworth. They all came from nearby towns, to the west, between here and Pittsburgh."

"So why are they important? I don't get the point."

"They all died last Thursday."

"What?"

"After we finished at Brian's camp, we drove back to headquarters. We kept talking about what had happened. One of my men who wasn't on our assignment jerked to attention at the mention of Brian and Betsy Roth. He'd heard those names before, he told me. Last Thursday. One of the worst traffic accidents he'd ever investigated. Ten people killed. All in one van. A driver of a semitrailer had a tire blow, lost control, and rammed into them. The investigation revealed that the victims in the van had all been headed toward a Fourth of July celebration in the mountains. To a camp. And that's why I wanted to talk to you. The camp was owned by Brian and Betsy Roth."

Grady clutched the phone so hard that his hand cramped. "All ten of them were killed?"

"They met at one place, left their cars, and went in the van," Clauson said.

Another goddamned traffic accident! Grady thought. Just like Helen and John!

"So on a hunch, I made some calls," Clauson said. "To the relatives of the victims. What I learned was that Brian and Betsy got around. They didn't go to grief meetings just in Bosworth. They went to towns all around here. Remember, back at the camp, when I wondered about the photographs on the wall of the smallest building? You called it a shrine? Well, I had the notion that because two of the photographs showed Brian and Betsy's dead children, it could be there was a pattern and maybe the other photographs showed dead children, too."

"I remember."

"Well, I was right. Every one of the couples who were killed in that accident had lost children several years ago. Your description of that building was correct. That building *was* a shrine. According to relatives, the parents put up those photographs above the fireplace. They lit candles. They prayed. They—"

"What a nightmare," Grady said.

"You know about that nightmare more than I can ever imagine. All twelve of them. A private club devoted to sympathy. Maybe *that's* why Brian lost control. Maybe he murdered Betsy and then shot himself because he couldn't stand more grief."

"Maybe." Grady shuddered.

"The pictures of the older children, the two in military uniforms, those young men were killed in Vietnam. That's how far back it goes."

I have a feeling it lasts forever, Grady thought.

"The main thing is, now we've got an explanation," Clauson said. "Brian and Betsy were prepared for a weekend get-together. But it didn't work out that way. It turned out to be a weekend of brooding and depression and . . . With the two of them alone out there, Brian decided he couldn't go on. Too much sorrow. Too damned much. So he shot his wife. For all we know, he had her permission. And then he . . ."

"Shot himself." Grady exhaled.

"Does that make sense?"

"As much as we'll probably ever find out. God help them," Grady said.

"I realize this is hard for you to talk about," Clauson said.

"I can handle it. You did good, Jeff. I can't say I'm happy, but your theory holds together enough to set my mind to rest. I appreciate your call." Grady wanted to scream.

"I just thought you'd like to know."

"Sure."

"If there's anything more I hear, I'll call you back."

"Great. Fine. Do that."

"Ben?"

"What?"

"I don't want to make a mistake a second time. If you need someone to talk to, call me."

"Sure, Jeff. If I need to. Count on it."

"I mean what I said."

"Of course. And *I* mean what *I* said. If I need to talk to you, I will."

"That's all I wanted to hear."

Grady hung up the phone, pushed away from the wall, and crossed the kitchen.

Toward the bourbon.

The next morning, early, at four o'clock, Grady coughed and struggled from his bed. The alcohol had allowed him to sleep, but as its effects dwindled, he regained consciousness prematurely, long before he wanted to confront his existence. His head throbbed. His knees wavered. Stumbling into the bathroom, he swallowed several aspirins, palmed water into his mouth, and realized that he still wore his uniform, that he hadn't removed his clothes before he fell across his bed.

Tell Ben Grady. Bring him here. The dismaying note remained as vivid in Grady's memory as when he'd jerked his anguished gaze from the corpses and read the words on the plastic-enclosed piece of paper that Clauson had handed to him.

Why? Grady thought. Everything Jeff told me last night—the ten people killed in the van, the motive for Brian's depression—made sense. Brian had reached the end of his endurance. What *doesn't* make sense is Brian's insistence that I be contacted, that I drive to the camp, that I see the bullet holes.

Grady's mind revolted. Chest heaving, he leaned over the sink, turned on the cold water, and repeatedly splashed his clammy face. He staggered to the kitchen and slumped at the table, where the light he'd switched on hurt his eyes. Alka-Seltzer, he thought. I need—

But his impulse was canceled by the pile of envelopes and mail-order catalogs on the table. When he'd returned home last evening, he'd automatically grabbed his mail from the box outside while he'd fumbled for his key. He'd thrown the mail on the kitchen table, impatient to open the cupboard where he kept his bourbon. Now, having propped his elbows on the table, spreading the envelopes and catalogs, he found himself staring at a letter addressed to him, one of the few letters he'd received since Helen and John had died and Helen's relatives had stopped sending mail.

The address on the envelope: Benjamin Grady, 112 Cypress Street, Bosworth, Pennsylvania, then the zip code—had been scrawled in black ink. No return address.

But Grady recognized the scrawl. He'd seen it often enough on compassionate cards that he'd received, not only in the days and weeks after Helen and John had died but also month after month as the painful year progressed. Encouraging messages. Continuing sympathy.

From Brian. The envelope had been postmarked four days ago. On Friday.

Grady grabbed the letter and tore it open.

Dear Ben, it began, and on top of the nightmare that had fractured Grady's drunken sleep, a further nightmare awaited him. Grady shuddered as he read the message from his wonderful, generous, stubbornly supportive friend, who no longer existed.

Dear Ben,

When you receive this, Betsy and I will be dead. I deeply regret the sorrow and shock my actions will cause you. I don't know which will be worse, the shock initially, the sorrow persistently. Both are terrible burdens, and I apologize.

If our bodies are found before you read this letter . . . if the note I plan to write and place in my hand when I pull the trigger doesn't achieve my intention . . . if something goes wrong and you're not asked to come here . . . I *want* you to come here. Not to see the husks that contained our souls. Not to torment you with our undignified remains. But to make sure you see this place. It's special, Ben. It consoles.

I can't tell you how. What I mean is, I won't. You have to find out for yourself. If I raised your expectations and they weren't fulfilled, you'd feel guilty, convinced that you weren't worthy, and the last thing I want is to cause you more guilt.

Nonetheless, that possibility has to be considered. It may be you won't be receptive to this place. I can't predict. For certain, my sister wasn't receptive. Others weren't receptive, either. So I chose carefully. My friends who died on Thursday were the few who understood the comfort that this place provided.

But now they're dead, and Betsy and I don't want to be alone again. Too much. Too awful much. I've been watching you carefully, Ben. I've been more and more worried about you. I have a suspicion that you drink yourself to sleep every night. I know that you hurt as much as Betsy and I do. But we've been lucky enough to find consolation, and I'm afraid for you.

I had planned to bring you out here soon. I think you're ready. I think you'd be receptive. I think that this place would give you joy. So I will leave the note instructing the state police to bring you here. And now that—I presume—you've seen it, I need to tell you that after I drive into town to mail this letter, I'll make a side trip to visit my lawyer.

I intend to amend my will. My final compassionate act on your behalf is to give you this compound. I hope that it will ease your suffering and provide you with peace. You'll know what I mean if you're truly receptive, if you're as sensitive as I believe you are.

Forgive me for the pain that our deaths will cause you. But our deaths are necessary. You have to accept my word on that. We anticipate. We're eager. What I'm about to do is not the result of despair.

I love you, Ben. I know that sounds strange. But it's true. I love you because we're partners in misfortune. Because you're decent and good. And in pain. Perhaps my gift to you will ease your pain. When you read this, Betsy and I will

no longer be in pain. But in our final hours, we
pray for you. We wish you consolation. God
bless you, my friend. Be well.

Brian

Beneath Brian's signature, Betsy had added her own.

Grady moaned, his tears dripping onto the page, dissolving the ink on the final words, blurring the signatures of his sorely missed friends.

Jeff Clauson's frown deepened as he read the letter. He read it again, then again. At last, he leaned back from his desk and exhaled.

Grady sat across from him, brooding.

"Lord," Clauson said.

"I'm sorry for waking you," Grady said. "I waited as long as I could force myself, till after dawn, before phoning your home. Really, I thought you'd be up by then. I wanted to make sure you were going straight to your office instead of on an assignment. I assumed you'd want to see that letter right away."

Clauson looked puzzled. "See it right away? Of course. That isn't what I meant by 'a terrible way to start the morning.' I wasn't referring to me. *You*, Ben. I was sympathizing with *you*. Dear God, I'm surprised you waited till after dawn. In your place, I'd have called my friend—and that's what I hope you think I am—at once."

Grady shuddered.

"You don't look so good." Clauson stood and

reached toward a beaker of coffee. "You'd better have another jolt of this." He refilled Grady's cup.

"Thanks." Grady's hands trembled as he raised the steaming cup. "The letter, Jeff. What do you make of it?"

Clauson debated with himself. "The most obvious thing is that Betsy's signature proves she agreed to Brian's plan. This wasn't a murder-suicide, but a double suicide. Betsy just needed a little help is all."

Grady stared down at his cup.

"The other obvious thing is that the letter has gaps. Brian insists it was necessary to leave the note at the compound, sending for you, but he doesn't explain why. Sure, he says he wants you to see the place. But after you found out he'd given it to you in his will, you'd have gone up to see it anyhow. There wasn't any need for you to be forced to look at the bodies."

"Unless . . ." Grady had trouble speaking. "Suppose I was so repelled that the last thing I wanted was to see where Brian shot Betsy and himself. What if I decided to sell the compound without ever going up there? The truth is, I *don't* want the compound. Brian might have been afraid of that, so he left the note to make sure I *did* go up there."

Clauson shrugged. "Could be. He tells you he wants you to see the compound because it's"—Clauson traced a finger down the letter—"'special. It consoles.' But he refuses to tell you how. He says he's afraid he might give you expectations that won't be fulfilled."

"I thought about that all the time I was driving here." Grady's throat tightened. "Obviously, Brian, Betsy, and those ten people who died in the traffic accident consid-

ered the compound a refuge. A private club away from
the world. A beautiful setting where they could support
one another. Brian might have felt that if, in his letter, he
praised the compound too much, I'd be disappointed because the place didn't matter as much as the company
did. At the same time, the compound *is* special. It truly is
beautiful. So he gave it to me. Maybe Brian felt guilty because he'd never included me in the group. Maybe he
hoped that I'd start a group of my own. Who knows? He
was under stress. He wasn't totally coherent."

"So what are you going to do about it?"

"About . . ."

"The compound. You said you don't want it. Are you
really so repelled that you don't intend to go back, that
you'll sell the place?"

Grady glanced down. He didn't speak for several
moments. "I don't know. If he'd given me something
else—let's say a watch—would I throw it away because I
didn't want to be reminded? Or would I cherish it?"

Two days later, Ida Roth helped Grady choose. Not
that she intended to. At the cemetery.

Grady had hoped to be one of the pallbearers, but Ida
had failed to ask him. Grady had tried to get in touch with
her at her home and at the tavern, but he'd never been
able to succeed. Sweating from the morning's heat and
humidity, he was reminded of the heat and humidity a
year ago when he'd arrived at this same cemetery, carrying the urns of his wife and son into the mausoleum.
About to turn from the coffins and walk back to his car,
he felt a presence behind him, an *angry* presence, al-

though how he sensed the presence, he didn't know. But the anger was eerily palpable, and he froze when Ida growled from behind him, "You won't get away with this."

Grady pivoted. The glare in Ida's wrinkle-rimmed eyes was perplexing. He'd tried to get close to her before and after the funeral, but she'd avoided him. At the graves, he'd done his best to make eye contact, frustrated at the stubbornness with which she'd looked away.

Now, though, her gaze was disturbingly direct. "Bastard." Her gaunt face, framed by her tugged-back hair, looked even more skeletal.

Grady winced. "Why are you calling me that, Ida? I haven't done anything against you. I miss them. I'm here to mourn them. Why are you—"

"Don't play games with me!"

"What are you *talking* about?"

"The compound! Brian's attorney told me about the will! It wasn't enough that my brother had so much self-pity that he let the tavern go to hell. It wasn't enough that since he shot himself I've been scrambling to balance the tavern's accounts so his creditors don't take over the place. No, I have to find out that while he mortgaged the tavern, which *I* inherited, the camp in the woods, which *you* inherited, is paid off, free and clear! I don't know how you tricked him. I can't imagine how you used your dead wife and kid to fool him into giving you the compound. But you can bet on this. If it takes my last breath, I'll fight you in court. Brian swore he'd take care of me! By God, I intend to make sure he keeps his word. You don't deserve anything! *You* weren't there when his twins died. *You* weren't there to hold his hand. You came *later.* So count on this. If it's the last thing I do, I'll own that camp. I'm tempted to have the buildings crushed, the swimming pool filled in, and everything covered with salt. But damn it, I need the money. So instead, I'll have the will revoked and sell the place! I'll get the money I deserve! And you won't get *anything!*"

Grady felt heat shoot through his body. Ida's unforgivable accusation that he'd used his grief for his dead wife and son to manipulate Brian into willing him the compound made him so furious that he trembled. "Fine, Ida. Whatever you want to do." He shook more fiercely. "Or try to do. But listen carefully. Because there's something you don't realize. Until this minute, I intended to give up the compound and transfer my title to you. I believed you deserved it. But you made a mistake. You shouldn't have mentioned . . . Jesus, no, I've suddenly changed my mind. That compound's mine. I didn't want it. But now I do. To spite you, Ida. For the insult to my wife and son, you'll rot in hell. And *I'll* rot in hell before you ever set foot on that camp again."

Grady tore the yellow NO ADMITTANCE—POLICE CRIME SCENE tape from the chain-link fence at the compound's entrance. Using the key Clauson had given him, he unlocked the gate, thrust it open, and bitterly entered the camp.

The hollow between the mountains was oppressively silent as he flicked sweat from his brow and strode with furious determination toward the swimming pool, through the wooden gate, to the concrete border and the white chalk outlines of where the corpses had lain. A few flies still buzzed over the vestiges of blood, bone, and brain. Watching them, Grady swallowed bile, then straightened with indignant resolve.

Fine, he thought. I can clean this up. I can deal with the memories. The main thing is, I intend to keep what Brian gave me.

Ida won't have it.

In outrage, Grady spun from the chalk outlines, left the pool area, ignored the barbecue pit, and approached the cinder-block bunkhouse. Despite his preoccupation, he was vaguely aware that he was repeating the sequence in which Lieutenant Clauson had taken him from building to building. He glanced inside the bunkhouse, gave even less attention to the cookstove in the separate kitchen, and approached the smallest building, the one that he'd described to Clauson as a shrine.

Inside, the gloom and silence were oppressive. The slate floor should have made his footsteps echo. Instead, it seemed to muffle them, just as the oak-paneled walls seemed to absorb the intruding sounds of his entrance. He uneasily studied the church pew before the fireplace. He raised his intense gaze toward the photographs of the eight smiling children between the candleholders and the American flags above the mantel. Knees wavering, he approached the photographs. With reverence, he touched the images of Brian and Betsy's dead teenage twin daughters.

So beautiful.

So full of life.

So soon destroyed.

God help them.

At last, Grady shifted his mournful eyes toward the poignant photograph of the bespectacled ten-year-old boy who looked embarrassed to smile because of the braces on his teeth. He reminded Grady so much of his own son.

And again Grady heard the startling sound of a splash. He swung toward the open door. With a frown, he couldn't help recalling that the last time he'd been in here, he'd also heard a splash.

From the swimming pool. Or so Grady had been absolutely certain until he'd hurried outside and studied the policemen next to the swimming pool and realized that he'd been mistaken, that no one had fallen in; and yet the splash had been so vivid.

Just as now. With the difference that this time, as Grady hurried from the shadowy shrine into the stark glare of the summer sun, he flinched at the sight of a young man—late teens, muscular, with short brown hair, wearing swimming goggles and a tiny hip-hugging nylon suit—stroking powerfully from the near end of the swimming pool, water rippling, muscles flexing, toward the opposite rim. The young man's speed was stunning, his surge amazing.

Grady faltered. How the hell? He hadn't heard a car approach. He couldn't imagine the young man hiking up the lane to the compound, taking off his clothes, putting on his swimming suit, and diving in unless the young man felt he belonged here, or unless the teenager assumed that no one would be here.

But the kid must have seen my cruiser outside the

gate, Grady thought. Why didn't he yell to get my attention if he belongs here? Or go back down the lane if he *doesn't* belong? There weren't any clothes by the pool. Where had the kid undressed? What in God's name was going on?

Scowling, Grady overcame his surprise and ran toward the swimming pool. "Hey!" he shouted. "What do you think you're doing? You don't have any right to be here! This place is mine! Get out of the pool! Get away from—"

Grady's voice broke as he rushed through the gate to the swimming pool. The young man kept thrusting his arms, kicking his legs, surging across the swimming pool, rebounding off the opposite end, reversing his impulse, stroking with determination.

Grady shouted more insistently. "Answer me! Stop, damn it! I'm a policeman! You're trespassing! Get out of the pool before I—"

But the swimmer kept stroking, rebounded off the near rim, and surged yet again toward the opposite edge. Grady was reminded of an Olympic athlete straining to achieve a gold medal.

"I'm telling you one last time! Get out of the pool!" Grady yelled, his voice breaking. "You've got thirty seconds! After that, I radio for backup! We'll drag you out and—"

The swimmer ignored him, churning, flexing, stroking.

Grady had shouted so rapidly that he'd hyperventilated. He groped behind him, clutched a redwood chair, and leaned against it. His chest heaved. As his heart raced and his vision swirled, he struggled to keep his balance and focus on the magnificent swimmer.

Seconds passed. Minutes. Time lengthened. Paradoxically, it also seemed suspended. At last, the swimmer's strength began to falter. After a final weary lap, the young man gripped the far end of the swimming pool, breathed deeply, fumbled to prop his arms along the side, and squirmed onto the concrete deck. He stood with determination, dripped water, and plodded around the pool toward Grady.

"So you're finally ready to pay attention?" Grady heaved himself away from the redwood chair. "Are you ready to explain what the hell you're doing here?"

The swimmer approached him, ignoring him.

Grady unclenched his fists and shoved his anger-hardened palms toward the swimmer's shoulders.

But Grady's palms—he shivered—passed through the swimmer.

At the same time, the swimmer passed through *him.* Like a subtle shift of air. Of *cold* air. And as Grady twisted, unnerved, watching the swimmer emerge from his side, then his swiveling chest, he felt as if he'd been possessed, consumed, then abandoned.

"Hey!" Grady managed to shout.

Abruptly the young man, his sinewy body dripping water, his cropped hair clinging to his drooping head, his taut frame sagging, vanished. The hot, humid air seemed to ripple. With equal abruptness, the air became still again. The swimmer was gone.

Grady's lungs felt empty. He fought to breathe. He fumbled toward the redwood chair. But the moment he touched its reassuring firmness, his sanity collapsed, as did his body.

Impossible! a remnant of his logic screamed.

And as that inward scream echoed, he stared toward the concrete.

The wet footprints of the swimmer were no longer visible.

Grady sat in the chair for quite a while. At last, he mustered the strength to raise himself.

The young man had been a stranger.

And yet the young man had somehow looked unnervingly familiar.

No.

Grady wavered. Sweat streaming down his face, he obeyed an irresistible impulse and made his way toward the smallest building.

He entered the shrine's brooding confines, passed the church pew, clasped the mantel above the fireplace, raised his disbelieving gaze above the candles, and concentrated on a photograph to his right.

A young man in a military uniform.

A handsome youngster whom Clauson had said had been killed in Vietnam.

The *same* young man who'd been swimming with powerful strokes in the pool, who had passed coldly through Grady's body and had suddenly disappeared.

The bottle in the kitchen cupboard beckoned. With unsteady hands, Grady poured, gulped, grimaced, and shivered. He didn't recall his drive from the compound through the mountains into Bosworth.

I'm losing my mind, he thought, and tilted the bourbon over the glass.

But his anesthetic wasn't allowed to do its work.

The phone rang.

He grabbed it.

"Hello." His voice seemed to come from miles away.

"So you're finally home, you bastard," Ida said. "I just thought you'd like to know my lawyer agrees with me. My brother was obviously out of his mind. That will's invalid."

"Ida, I'm not in the mood to argue." Grady's head throbbed. "We'll let a judge decide."

"You goddamned bet. I'll see you in court!"

"You're wasting your time. I intend to fight you on this."

"But I'll fight *harder*," Ida said. "You won't have a chance!"

Grady's ear throbbed when she slammed down the phone.

It rang again.

Of all the . . .

He jerked it to his ear. "Ida, I've had enough! Don't call me again! From now on, have your lawyer talk to mine!"

"Ben?" A man's voice sounded puzzled.

"*Jeff?* My God, I'm sorry! I didn't mean to shout. I thought it was . . ."

"You don't sound so good."

Grady trembled.

"It must have been a rough day," Clauson said.

"You have no idea."

"The reason I'm calling . . . Do you need company? Is there any way I can help?"

Grady slumped against the wall. "No. But I appreciate your concern. It's good to know someone cares. I think I can manage. On second thought, wait, there *is* something."

"Tell me."

"When you phoned me the other night, when you told me about the traffic accident, about the friends of Brian and Betsy who'd been killed . . ."

Clauson exhaled. "I remember."

"The names of the victims. I was too upset to write them down. Who were they?"

"Why on earth would you want to know that?"

"I can't explain right now."

Clauson hesitated. "Just a minute." He made fumbling noises, as if sorting through a file. "Jennings. Matson. Randall. Langley. Beck."

"I need their addresses and phone numbers," Grady said.

Clauson supplied them, adding, mystified, "I don't understand why you want this information."

"Which parents lost their sons in Vietnam?"

"Langley and Beck. But why do you—"

"Thanks. I really appreciate this. I'll talk to you later."

"I'm worried about you, Ben."

Grady hung up the phone.

*   *   *

Langley and Beck.

Grady studied the phone numbers. Both sets of parents had lived in towns between Bosworth and Pittsburgh. He pressed the numbers for the Langley residence.

No one answered.

That wasn't surprising. Since the Langleys had been old enough to have lost a son in Vietnam, their other children—if they had any—would be in their thirties or forties, with homes of their own. No one would be living there now.

Grady urgently pressed the other number. He heard a buzz, then another buzz.

He rubbed his forehead.

A man's tired voice said, "Yes?"

"My name is Benjamin Grady. I'm the police chief of Bosworth. That's about forty miles east of—"

"I know where Bosworth is. What do you want? If this is about the accident, I don't feel up to talking about it again. You picked an inconvenient time. My wife and I have been trying to sort through my parents' effects, to settle their estate."

"This isn't about the accident."

"Then what *is* it about?"

"Your brother."

"Jesus, don't tell me something's happened to Bob!"

"No. I didn't mean . . . I'm referring to your brother who died in Vietnam."

"Jerry? I don't get it. Why after all this time would you want to know about him?"

"Was your brother a swimmer? A *serious* swimmer?"

"I haven't thought about that in years." The man

swallowed thickly. "The coach in high school said Jerry could have been a champion. My brother used to train every day. Three hours minimum. He could have made the Olympics."

Grady felt as cold as when the swimmer had walked along the side of the pool and passed through him.

"What did you say your name was?" the voice demanded. "Grady? And you claim you're the police chief over in— What the hell is this? A sick joke?"

"No. If there'd been another way to . . . I'm sorry for intruding. What you've told me is important. Thank you."

Despite the rising sun, Grady needed his headlights to drive up the bumpy, zigzagging lane through the shadowy trees to the compound. Finally at the top, he stared toward an eerie mist that rose off the swimming pool, spreading around it. Faint sunlight revealed the pines and maples on the dusky ridges that flanked the compound, but the compound itself was completely enshrouded. Grady's headlights glinted off the thick, almost crystalline haze.

He got out of his police car and nearly bumped into the chain-link fence before he saw it. After fumbling to unlock the gate, he swung it open. The silence around him remained as oppressive as the day before, so much so that when he stepped onto gravel, the crunch startled him. The cold mist dampened his clothes and beaded on his hackled skin.

I ought to turn around and drive back to town, he thought. This is crazy. *What am I doing here?*

He wished that he'd brought a flashlight. As he

moved through it, the mist became denser. It seemed un-natural. Too thick. Too . . .

Be careful, he warned himself. You're letting your imagination get control of you. Mist often rises from swimming pools at dawn. It's something to do with the change in temperature. There's nothing unusual happening.

Grady faltered, suddenly realizing that without a visible object to aim toward, he might lose his bearings and wander in a circle. He felt disoriented. He braved another step and flinched as he bumped against the waist-high wooden fence that bordered the swimming pool.

At the same time, he flinched for another reason. Because something passed from left to right before him, beyond the fence: the shadow of what seemed to be a man. The shadow's motion caused the mist to swirl. Then the shadow disappeared. The mist became still again.

When Grady heard a splash from the pool, he stepped back. The splash was followed by the echoing strokes of a powerful swimmer. Grady froze, paralyzed by conflicting impulses.

To charge through the gate and confront the swimmer.

But he'd done that yesterday, and he was terrified that the swimmer would again pass through him.

To stay where he was and shout to demand an explanation.

But he'd done that yesterday as well, with no effect, and anyway, if Grady tried to shout, he was certain that the noise from his mouth would be a shriek.

To pivot and scramble desperately from the pool,

frantic to find his way back through the gloom to the cruiser.

He heard a further splash. *Someone else diving into the water.* With increasing dismay, he saw *another* shadow—no, two!—pass through the haze beyond the fence. A woman, it seemed. And a child.

Grady screamed, swung, and recoiled as a *further* shadow appeared in the mist, this one approaching from the direction of the bunkhouse.

"No!" He saw three more shadows—two women and a girl—approach from the haze-obscured kitchen. He lurched sideways to avoid them and found himself confronted by still *another* shadow, this one coming from the direction of the shrine. His impetus was so forceful that he couldn't stop. He and the shadow converged. He lunged *through* the shadow, unbearably chilled, and despite the density of the mist, he managed to see the shadow's face. It was Brian Roth.

Grady's eyes fluttered. Something small inched across his brow, making his skin itch. A fly, he realized. He pawed it away, then opened his eyes completely. The stark sun was directly above him. He was on his back, sprawled on the gravel near the swimming pool.

As his consciousness focused, he managed to sit, peering around him, tense, expecting to be confronted by ghosts.

But all he saw was the silence-smothered compound.

He glanced at his watch. *Almost noon?* Dear Lord, I've been lying here for . . .

Brian!

No! I *couldn't* have seen him!

Terrified, he squirmed to his feet. His vision blurred, then focused again. In place of the dampness from the mist, his skin was now clammy from sweat, his stained uniform clinging to him. He managed to straighten, then scanned the otherwise-deserted compound.

I've lost my mind.

I'm having a nervous breakdown.

He stared at his police car. His staff would be wondering where he was. They'd have tried to get in touch with him. He had to let them know that he was all right. More important, he had to think of an acceptable reason for not having gone to the office, for not having responded to their calls. He couldn't let them know how out of control he was.

But as he reached the cruiser, about to lean in and grab the two-way radio microphone, he stiffened, hearing the jolt of a vehicle as it struggled up the bumpy lane. Pivoting, he saw that the vehicle belonged to the state police, that it veered from the trees to stop beside his car, and that Jeff Clauson got out, glanced solemnly around, then proceeded somberly toward him.

"Ben."

"Jeff."

The exchange was awkward.

"You've got a lot of people worried about you," Clauson said.

"I'm afraid the situation's difficult. I was just about to—"

"Your uniform. What have you been doing, sleeping in a ditch?"

"It's hard to explain."

"I bet. All the same, why not give it a try?"

"How'd you know I'd be here?"

Clauson studied him. "Process of elimination. After a while, the more I thought about it, the more this seemed the most logical place."

"Why *you*? How come *you're* out looking for me?"

"When your dispatcher kept failing to reach you, when she became concerned enough, she contacted all your friends. I'll say it again. You've got a lot of people worried about you, Ben. Why didn't you check in?"

"The truth is—"

"Sure. Why not? The truth would be refreshing."

"I . . ."

"Yes? Go on, Ben. The truth."

"I passed out."

"The note Brian left suggested you've been drinking a lot. But he's not the only one who noticed. When I phoned you at night, your voice was—"

"This morning had nothing to do with alcohol. I came up here before I was due at work so I could look around and decide if I was going to keep this place. Then everything caught up to me. I passed out. Over there by the pool."

Grady turned and pointed.

What he saw demanded that he use every remnant of his remaining willpower not to react. The area around the pool was crowded with people: six children, including Brian's twins; the two young men who'd been killed in

Vietnam; twelve adults, ten of whom Grady didn't recognize, although two were Brian and Betsy.

I'll bet the five couples I don't recognize are the people who died in that traffic accident last Thursday, Grady thought with a chill.

The group was having a barbecue, eating, talking, laughing, although the scene was weirdly silent, no sounds escaping from their mouths.

Grady's cheeks felt numb. His body shook. He managed not to whimper.

I really ought to be congratulated, he thought. I'm seeing ghosts, and I'm not gibbering.

Clauson looked toward the pool but showed no reaction.

Grady tensed with understanding. "Jeff, do you notice anything unusual?"

"What do you mean?"

Grady was amazed that he was repeating almost exactly what Ida Roth had said that *Brian* had said when he'd brought her to the camp. "Do you feel anything different, anything special, anything that reminds you of . . . that makes you feel close to Brian and Betsy?"

"Not particularly." Clauson frowned. "Except, of course, the memory of finding their bodies here."

"Nothing at the swimming pool?"

"That's where the bodies were, of course." Clauson drew his fingers through his short sandy hair. "Otherwise, no. I don't notice anything unusual about the pool."

". . . I need help, Jeff."

"That's why I'm here. Haven't I been asking you repeatedly to let me help? Tell me what you need."

"A reason my staff will accept for my not checking in. An explanation that won't affect the way they look at me."

"You mean like saying there was something wrong with your radio? Or that you had to leave town for an appointment you thought you'd told them about?"

"Exactly."

"Sorry, Ben. I can't do it. The only explanation I'll help you with is the truth."

"And you keep saying you're my friend."

"That's right."

"So what kind of friend would—"

"A good one. Better than you realize. Ben, you've been fooling yourself. You claim your problems haven't interfered with your work. You're wrong. And I don't mean just the alcohol. Your nerves are on edge. You always look distracted. You have trouble concentrating. Everybody's noticed it. The best way I can help is to give you this advice. Take a month off. Get some counseling. Admit yourself to a substance-abuse clinic. Dry out. Accept reality. Your wife and son are dead. You have to adjust to that, to try harder to come to terms with your loss. You've got to find some peace."

"A month off? But my job is all I've got left!"

"I'm telling you this as a friend. Keep acting the way you've been, and you won't even have your job. I've been hearing rumors. You're close to being fired."

"What?" Grady couldn't believe what Clauson was saying. It seemed as impossible as the ghosts at the swimming pool, as the silent party that Clauson couldn't see but Grady did. "Jesus, no!"

"But if you go along with my recommendations . . . No, Ben. Don't keep looking at the swimming pool. Look at *me*. That's right. Good. If you go along with what I recommend, I'll do everything in my power to make sure your staff and the Bosworth town council understand what you've been going through. Face it. You're exhausted. Burned-out. What you need is a rest. There's nothing disgraceful about that. As long as you don't try to hide your condition, as long as you admit your problem and try to correct it, people will sympathize. I swear to you, I'll make sure they sympathize. You used to be a damned good cop, and you can be one again. If you do what I ask, I swear I'll use all the influence I've got to fix it so you keep your job."

"Thanks, Jeff. I really appreciate that. I'll try. I promise. I'll really try."

Grady sat in the mausoleum, blinking through his tears as he looked toward the niches that contained the urns of his beloved wife and son.

"I've got trouble," he told them, his voice so choked that he could barely speak. "I'm seeing things. I'm drinking too much. I'm about to lose my job. And as far as my mind goes . . . well, hey, I lost that quite awhile ago.

"If only you hadn't died. If only I hadn't decided to work late that night. If only you hadn't decided to go to that movie. If only that drunk hadn't hit you. If only . . .

"It's my fault. It's all my fault. I can't tell you how much I miss you. I'd give anything to have you back, to make our life perfect the way it used to be, a year ago, before . . ."

The pager on Grady's gun belt beeped. He ignored it.

"Helen, when I go home, the house feels so empty, I can't stand it. John, when I look in your room, when I touch the clothes in your closet, when I smell them, I feel as if my heart's going to split apart, that I'll die on the spot. I want both of you with me so much, I . . ."

The pager kept beeping. Grady pulled it from his gun belt, dropped it onto the floor, and stomped it with the heel of his shoe. He heard a crack.

The pager became silent.

Good.

Grady blinked upward through his tears, continuing to address the urns.

"Perfect. Our life was perfect. But without you . . . I love you. I want you so much. I'd give anything to have you back, for the three of us to be together again."

At last, he ran out of words. He just kept sitting, sobbing, staring at the niches, at the names of his wife and son, at their birth and death dates, imagining their ashes in the urns.

A thought came slowly. It rose as if from thick darkness, struggling to surface. It emerged from the turmoil of his subconscious and became an inward voice that repeated sentences from the puzzling letter that Brian had written.

. . . I'm afraid for you. I had planned to bring you out here soon. I think you're ready. I think you'd be receptive. I think that this place would give you joy.

My final compassionate act on your behalf is to give you this compound. I hope that it will ease your suffering and provide you with peace. You'll know what I mean if

*you're truly receptive, if you're as sensitive as I believe
you are.*

Grady nodded, stood, wiped his tears, kissed his fingers, placed them over the glass that enclosed the urns, and left the mausoleum, careful to lock its door behind him.

The compound was enshrouded again, this time by a cloud of dust that Grady's cruiser raised coming up the lane. He stopped the car, waited for the dust to clear, and wasn't at all surprised to see Brian and Betsy, their twin daughters, the other children, the young men who had died in Vietnam, and the five couples who'd been killed in the accident.

Indeed, he'd expected to see them, grateful that his hopes had not been disappointed. Some were in the pool. Others sat in redwood chairs beside the water. Others grilled steaks on the barbecue.

They were talking, laughing, and this time, even from inside the cruiser, Grady could hear them, not just the splashes but also their voices, their mirth, even the spatter of grease that dripped from the steaks onto the smoking coals in the barbecue.

That had puzzled him: why he'd been able to hear the strokes of the swimmer but not the conversations of the ghosts whom he—but not Clauson—had seen this morning.

Now, though, he understood. It took a while to make contact. You had to acquire sensitivity. You had to become—how had Brian put it in his letter?—receptive. Each time you encountered them, they became more real, until . . .

Grady reached for the paper bag beside him and got out of the cruiser. He unlocked the chain-link fence and approached the compound, smiling.

"Hi, Brian. Hello there, Betsy."

They didn't acknowledge him.

Well, that'll come, Grady thought. No problem. I just have to get more receptive.

He chose an empty chair by the swimming pool and settled into it, stretching out his legs, relaxing. It was evening. The sun was nearly down behind the mountains. The compound was bathed in a soothing crimson glow. The young man he'd first encountered, the potential champion swimmer who'd died in Vietnam, kept doing his laps. A delighted man and woman, gray-haired, in their sixties, kept blurting encouragement to him.

Grady turned again to Brian and Betsy over by the barbecue. "Hey, how have you been? It's good to see you."

This time, Brian and Betsy responded, looking in his direction.

Yeah, all it takes is receptivity, Grady thought.

"Hi, Ben. Glad you could make it," Brian said.

"Me, too." Grady reached inside his paper bag and pulled out a bottle of bourbon. Untwisting its cap, he looked around for a glass, didn't find one, shrugged, and raised the bottle to his lips. He tilted his head back, feeling the yearlong tension in his neck begin to dissipate. After the heat of the day, the evening was pleasantly cool. He tilted the bottle to his lips again and swallowed with satisfaction.

Receptivity, he thought. Yeah, that's the secret. All I have to do is be sensitive.

But as he drank and smiled and waited, the miracle that he'd come for didn't happen. He kept looking around, struggling to maintain his calm. Helen and John. Where were they? They were supposed to be here.

They *have* to be!

He swallowed more bourbon. "Hey, Brian?"

"What is it, Ben?"

"My wife and son. Where are they?"

"I'm afraid they can't be here yet," Brian said.

"Why not?" Grady frowned.

"There's something you have to do first."

"I don't understand."

"Think about it."

"I don't know what you mean. Help me, Brian."

"Think about the shrine."

And then everything was clear. "Thank you, Brian."

Grady set down the bottle, stood, and left the swimming pool, walking toward the shrine. Inside, candles were lit. He passed the church pew in the sanctuary and reverently studied the photographs above the mantel, the pictures that grief-destroyed parents had hung there, the heartbreaking images of the eight dead children.

Is that all it takes? Grady thought. Is that all I need to do?

He removed his wallet from his trousers, opened it, caressed the photographs of Helen and John that he always carried with him, and removed them from their protective transparent plastic sleeves. After kissing them, he set them on the mantel.

Now? he wondered, his heart pounding. *Now?*

But Brian and Betsy don't have their photographs up here, he thought. The couples who were killed in the accident, *their* photographs aren't here, either.

Maybe, though, Grady wondered, maybe if you've been here long enough, it isn't necessary to put up photographs.

On the other hand, the children. They never had the chance to come here. They died before Brian built the shrine. For them, the photographs were necessary, just as photographs were necessary for . . .

Heart pounding faster, Grady turned and left the shrine, hurrying back to the swimming pool. He felt terrified that his loneliness wouldn't be broken, but at once he saw Helen and John waiting for him, and his chest hurt unbearably. Helen was holding out her arms. John was jumping up and down with excitement.

Grady ran.

Reached them.

Embraced them.

And felt his arms go through them just as their arms and bodies went *through* him.

"No!" he wailed. "I need to touch you!"

Then he realized. He had to give them time. In a little while, he'd be able to hold them. He spun to face them.

"I love you, Ben," Helen said.

Tears streamed down Grady's face.

"Dad, I've missed you," John said.

"And I love both of you, and I've missed you so much that—" Grady's voice broke. He sobbed harder. "It's so good to—"

Grady reached for them again, and this time, as his

arms went through them, he felt as if he'd reached through a cloud. The sensation was subtle but unmistakably physical. It was happening. They'd soon be—

Grady's knees felt weak.

"Sweetheart, you'd better sit down," Helen said.

Grady nodded. "Yes. The strain's been . . . I think I could use a rest."

As he walked with his wife and son toward the swimming pool, Brian, Betsy, and the others nodded with approval.

"Dad, the kids in the pool are having so much fun. Can I take a swim?"

"Absolutely. Anything you want, son. Your mother and I will watch."

Grady sat in his chair by the pool. Helen sat close beside him, stroking his arm. The sensation was stronger. Soon. Soon he'd be able to hold her.

Betsy called to him, "Ben, would you like a steak?"

"Not right now, thanks. I'm not hungry. Maybe later."

"Anytime. All you have to do is ask."

"I appreciate that, Betsy."

"Maybe another drink would improve your appetite."

"I bet it would." Grady raised the bottle to his lips. Helen stroked his arm, and now her touch was almost solid. John dove into the pool.

"Together," Helen said.

"Yes," Grady said. "At last."

It became the most wonderful evening of his life. In a while, Helen's touch was totally firm. Grady was able to hold her, to hug her, to kiss her. And John.

When the sun disappeared, a full moon lit the darkness, illuminating the festive specters.

There was just one problem. Before Grady had driven to the compound from the mausoleum, he'd made several stops in town. One had been to the liquor store. Another had been to the courthouse, to find out who'd owned the land that Brian had purchased to build the compound. Grady had hoped to be able to question whoever had owned the land and to find out if there was anything unusual about this area, anything—even an old campfire story—that might provide a hint, the start of an explanation for this miracle.

But the former owner had long ago moved away.

Several other stops had been to Brian Roth's former hunting companions. Grady had hoped that one of them might be able to describe what had happened to Brian the day they'd taken him hunting in this area. He'd hoped that they might have an explanation for Brian's sudden determination to buy this land.

But none of them had even remembered that afternoon.

Grady's final stop had been to his attorney. Ida Roth's lawyer had already been in touch with him. Ida was determined to contest the will and make sure that Grady didn't inherit the property. Grady was shocked to hear his attorney say that Brian had clearly not been in his right mind if he'd amended his will while contemplating suicide. Brian's own attorney apparently agreed. The consensus was that Grady would lose his fight against Ida. The compound would be denied to him.

So as Grady sat beside his wife and son, watching his eerily moonlit companions near the pool, he kept drinking and brooding and telling himself that he couldn't bear to be separated from his family again.

But what was the alternative?

Grady hugged Helen and John. "You might want to take a walk."

"We'll stay," Helen said. "So you won't be afraid."

"You're sure?"

"Yes. I don't want you to feel alone."

Grady kissed her, drank more bourbon, then unholstered his revolver.

He understood now why Brian and Betsy had made this choice. How lonely they must have felt, seeing their dead children and eventually their dead companions. In their presence but not truly with them.

Grady cocked his revolver. The final speck of his sanity told him, Your wife and son aren't real, you know. The others aren't, either. This is all your imagination.

Maybe, Grady thought. Maybe not.

But even if it is my imagination, when Ida gets control of the compound, I'll never have the chance to see Helen and John again. Even if I only imagine them.

It was an agonizing dilemma.

It required more thought.

So with his wife and son beside him, Grady held his revolver in one hand while he drank from his bottle with the other. The alcohol made him sleepy. The specters were beginning to fade. He'd soon have to make a choice, and he wondered what it would be. As the stupor from the bourbon overwhelmed him, which would feel heavier? Would the bottle drop from his hand first? Or would the revolver?

Afterword

FROM "THE DRIPPING" IN 1972 TO "THE SHRINE" twenty years later, these stories represent a substantial portion of my life—and significant events along the way. The year the final story was published, I made a further significant choice by leaving Iowa City, where I had lived since 1970, and taking up residence in Santa Fe, New Mexico, in the summer of 1992.

My wife and I did it suddenly. Watching a segment of Public Broadcasting's *This Old House* that was devoted to Santa Fe's distinctive adobe-pueblo style of architecture, we found the city of holy faith and its surrounding mountains so picturesque that we decided to spend a long weekend visiting there. It was my forty-ninth birthday. I had just finished a long novel, *Assumed Identity*. A little time off sounded good. But we weren't prepared for the impact that the mystical mountains and the high desert would have on us. In three days, we were looking at houses. On the fourth day, we selected one and flew back to Iowa City to make preparations to move. Three months later, we were living in Santa Fe.

Our decision had nothing to do with a change in our positive feelings about Iowa City. I had wonderful years at the university there. I made lifelong friends there. My wife and I raised a daughter and a son there. It's a special place, and it brought us happiness. But we also *lost* a son there, and sometimes it's necessary to get away from streets and buildings that cause painful memories.

Sometimes, too, a writer has to redefine himself, or, as my wife put it, "to start act three." In our new home, at an altitude of seven thousand feet, with wildflowers in front of our adobe house and piñon-treed mountains stretching off in every direction in what the locals call the Land of Enchantment, the Land of the Dancing Sun, I began to look at things differently. For certain, the move affected my fiction, not just in the obvious way that I stopped writing about the Midwest and switched my attention to New Mexico, using Santa Fe as a setting in several pieces.

A deeper change involved theme. The hero of one of my post-1992 novels, *Extreme Denial,* is a former intelligence operative who goes to Santa Fe to shut out his past and find himself. Substitute "former professor" and it's obvious that I was writing about myself. From Matt's death in 1987 until our move to Sante Fe in 1992, I wrote many more pieces about grief than I have included here. But after settling in our new home, I wrote only one more on the subject, a novel called *Desperate Measures,* in which an obituary writer whose son has died from cancer finds himself trapped in a harrowing conspiracy. Surviving, he comes to terms with his loss. Again I was writing about myself.

Thus, while this collection doesn't include all my short fiction, it *is* complete inasmuch as it follows the progress of my imagination until the conclusion of act two, when, after twenty-two years, I left Iowa City. Further into act three, I'll prepare another collection and bring you up to date, sharing more memories with you. Meanwhile, I wasn't prepared for the emotional impact that grouping these stories together would have on me. Pieces written years apart acquired new vividness for me when read in sequence over a couple of days. In particular, I was struck by how many of these stories are about threats to the main character's family. Philip Klass taught me to think of fiction writing as a form of self-psychoanalysis. "Write about what you most fear," he said. One day, my fear came true.

But I haven't lost my urge to tell stories, and that tells me other fears need to be expressed. The ferret keeps gnawing at my psyche. I persist in going after it.

Let me tell you a story.

"The Hidden Laughter," *The Twilight Zone Magazine*, August 1981.

"The Typewriter," *The Dodd, Mead Gallery of Horror*, ed. Charles L. Grant (Dodd, Mead, 1983).

"A Trap for the Unwary" (author's note to "But at My Back I Always Hear"), *Masters of Darkness III*, ed. Dennis Etchison (Tor, 1991).

"But at My Back I Always Hear," *Shadows 6*, ed. Charles L. Grant (Doubleday, 1983).

"The Storm," *Shadows 7*, ed. Charles L. Grant (Doubleday, 1984).

"For These and All My Sins," *Whispers 5*, ed. Stuart L. Schiff (Doubleday, 1985).

"Black and White and Red All Over," "Mumbo Jumbo," and "Dead Image," *Night Visions II*, ed. Charles L. Grant (Dark Harvest Press, 1985).

"Orange Is for Anguish, Blue for Insanity," *Prime Evil*, ed. Douglas L. Winter (New American Library, 1989).

"The Beautiful Uncut Hair of Graves," *Final Shadows*, ed. Charles L. Grant (Doubleday, 1991).

"The Shrine," *Dark At Heart*, ed. Joe and Karen Lansdale (Dark Harvest Press, 1992).

More
David Morrell!

Please turn this page
for a
bonus excerpt
from his new novel,

Burnt Sienna

available in hardcover
March 2000.

A little after ten in the morning, Bellasar's jet approached Nice's airport. The blue of the Mediterranean reminded Malone of the Caribbean. The palm trees too reminded him of home. But the overbuilt coastline and the exhaust haze were nothing like the clear solitary splendor he had enjoyed on Cozumel. Bitter, he looked away from the view. Some Chablis he had drunk with dinner, much of which he hadn't eaten, had helped to relax him enough to sleep, although his dreams had been fitful, interspersed with images of children being blown up by land mines and a beautiful woman's face rotting in a coffin.

He never got into Nice's airport. Officers from customs and immigration came out to the jet, where they stood on the tarmac and spoke to Potter, who apparently had an understanding with them, for they looked briefly into the aircraft, nodded to its occupants, then stamped the passports Potter handed them. Presumably, their expeditious attitude would be rewarded under less public circumstances. Letting Potter handle the details, Bellasar had gone to a cabin in the rear before the authorities arrived; he hadn't given Potter his passport; there was no proof that he had entered the country. Or that *I* did, either, Malone thought. When Potter had gone along the aisle collecting passports, he had taken Malone's, but instead of showing it to the authorities, Potter had kept it in his pocket. Malone was reminded of how easy it was to disappear from the face of the earth.

The group got off the plane and broke into two groups, most of them remaining to transfer luggage to a waiting helicopter while Bellasar, Potter, three bodyguards, and Malone walked to a second helicopter. The familiar *whump-whump-whump* of the rotors wasn't reassuring. Feeling the weight of liftoff, seeing the airport get smaller beneath him, Malone pretended that it was ten years earlier, that he was on a military mission. Put yourself in that mind-set. Start thinking like a soldier again. More important, start *feeling* like one.

He glanced toward the front of the chopper, comparing its levers, pedals, and other controls with those he had been familiar with. There were several advances in design, particularly a group of switches that the pilot didn't use and whose purpose Malone didn't understand, but at heart, the principle of flying this craft was the same, and he was able to detach his mind from the tension around him, to imagine that he was behind the controls, guiding the chopper.

Bellasar said something.

"What?" Malone turned. "I can't hear you. The noise of the rotors."

Bellasar spoke louder. "I said I've purchased the con-

2

tents of the best art-supply shop in Nice. The materials are at my villa, at your disposal."

"You were that certain I'd eventually agree?"

"The point is, *this* way you won't have any delay in getting started."

"I won't be able to start right away anyhow."

"What do you mean?"

"I can't just jump in. I have to study the subject first."

Bellasar didn't reply for a moment. "Of course."

Potter kept concentrating on Malone's eyes.

"But don't study too long," Bellasar said.

"You didn't mention there was a time limit. You told me I could do this the way I needed to. If I'd known there were conditions, I wouldn't have—"

"No conditions. But my wife and I might soon have to travel on business. If you can get your preparations concluded before then, perhaps you can work without her. From a sketch perhaps."

"That's not how I do things. You wanted an honest portrait. Working from a sketch is bullshit. If I can't do this right, I won't do it at all. You're buying more than just my autograph on a canvas."

"You didn't want to accept the commission, but now you're determined to take the time to do it properly." Belassar turned toward Potter. "Impressive."

"Very." Potter kept his eyes on Malone.

"There." Bellasar pointed through the Plexiglas.

Malone followed his gesture. Ahead, to the right, nestled among rocky, wooded hills, a three-story chateau made of huge stone blocks glinted in the morning sun. If Malone had been painting it, he would have made it impressionistic, its numerous balconies, gables, and chimneys blending, framed by a swirl of elaborate flower gardens, sculpted shrubs, and sheltering cypresses.

The pilot spoke French into a small micophone attached to his helmet, presumably identifying himself to his security controller on the ground. As the helicopter descended, Malone saw stables, tennis courts, a swimming pool, and another large stone building that had a bell tower and reminded Malone of a monastery. Beyond high walls, farmland spread out, vineyards, cattle. Small figures of people were working, and as the helicopter settled lower toward a landing pad near the chateau, the figures became large enough for Malone to see that many were guards carrying weapons.

"Can you tolerate it here?" Bélassar sounded ironic.

"It's beautiful," Malone acknowledged, "if you ignore the guards."

"It belonged to my father and grandfather and great-grandfather, all the way back to the Napoleonic Wars."

Thanks to arms sales, Malone thought.

The chopper set down, the roar of the motors diminishing to a whine.

"These men will show you to your room," Bellasar said. "I'll expect you for cocktails in the library at seven. I'm sure you're looking forward to meeting my wife."

"Yes," Malone said. "For seven-hundred-thousand dollars, I'm curious what my subject looks like."

4

The spacious bedroom had oak paneling and a four-poster bed. After showering, Malone found a plush white robe laid out for him. He also found that his bag had been unpacked and was on the floor next to the armoire. Opening the armoire, he saw that his socks and underwear had been placed in a drawer, his turtle-necks and a pair of chino slacks in another. He had used a packaged toothbrush and razor he had found on a ledge above the marble sink. Now he carried his toilet kit into the bathroom and arranged its various items on that shelf, throwing out the designer sham-poo and shaving soap Bellasar had provided. The small gesture of rebellion gratified him. He put on the chinos and a forest green turtleneck. Looking for the tan loafers that had been in his bag, he found them in the walk-in closet along with the sneakers he'd been wearing, and paused in surprise at the unfamiliar sport coats, dress slacks, and tuxedo hanging next to his leather jacket. Before he tried on one of the sport coats, he already knew it would fit him perfectly. Yes, there was little about him Bellasar didn't know, Mal-one realized warily. Except the most important thing: Bellasar didn't know about his deal with Jeb. Malone took that for granted, because if Bellasar *had* known, Malone would have been dead by now.

From his years in the military, Malone had learned that no matter how tired he was after a long flight, it was a mistake to take a nap. The nap would only confuse his already confused internal clock. The thing to do was push through the day and go to sleep when everybody else normally went to sleep. The next morning, he'd be back on schedule.

Opening the bedroom door, he found a man in the hallway. The man wore a Beretta 9 mm pistol and carried a two-way radio. With a slight French accent and perfect English, the man said, "Mr. Bellasar asked me to be at your disposal in case you wanted a tour of the grounds."

"He certainly pays attention to his guests."

Proceeding along the corridor, Malone listened to his escort point out the various paintings, tables, and vases on display, all from the French Regency period. Other corridors had their own themes, he learned, and every piece was museum quality.

They went down a curving stairway to a foyer topped by the most intricate crystal chandelier Malone had ever seen. "It's five hundred years old," the escort explained. "From a doge palace in Venice. The marble on this floor came from the same palace."

Malone nodded. Yes, Bellasar was definitely a collector.

Outside, the sun felt pleasant, but Malone ignored it, concentrating only on his surroundings as he strolled with his escort through gardens, past topiaries and ponds, toward the swimming pool.

Abruptly he whirled. Gunfire crackled.

"From the testing range," the escort explained, gesturing toward an area beyond an orchard. Several assault rifles made it sound as if a small war was taking place over there. The escort avoided going in that direction, just as he avoided going toward the large stone building whose belltower had made Malone think of a monastery and which was in the same direction.

"It's called the Cloister," the escort said. "Before the French Revolution, monks lived there, but after the Church's lands were confiscated, one of Mr. Bellasar's ancestors acquired the property. Not before a mob destroyed all the religious symbols, though. There's still a room that you could tell was a chapel—if you were allowed over there. Which you're not."

Malone shrugged, pretending to be interested only in what the escort showed him and in nothing that the escort avoided. For now, what he was mainly interested in were the high stone walls that enclosed the grounds and were topped by security cameras. The entrances at the back and front had sturdy metal barriers and were watched by guards with automatic weapons. Getting out wouldn't be easy.

When something blew up past the orchard, the explosion rumbling, none of the guards reacted. Malone's escort didn't even bother looking in that direction. "I'll show you where your painting supplies are. Mr. Bellasar suggests that you work in a sunroom off the terrace. It has the best light."

When Malone returned to his room, a thick pamphlet lay on his bedside table. Its paper was brown with age. Carefully, he picked it up and turned the stiff brittle pages. The text was in English, the author Thomas Malthus, the title *An Essay on the Principle of Population*. A handwritten note accompanied it. *I thought you'd enjoy some leisure reading.* Leisure? Malone thought. With a title like that? On an inside page, he read that the pamphlet had been published and printed in London in 1798. A priceless first edition. The note concluded, *Cocktails and dinner are formal.* To reinforce the point, the tuxedo that Malone had noticed in the closet was now laid out on the bed, along with a pleated white shirt, black pearl cuff-links and studs, a black silk cummerbund, and a black bow tie.

The last time Malone had worn formal clothes had been eight years earlier at his art dealer's wedding. He hadn't enjoyed it, had felt constricted. But he was damned if he was going to let Bellasar sense his discomfort. When he entered the library two hours later, he looked as if he wore a tuxedo every day of his life.

The large two-story area had shelves from floor to ceiling on all four sides, every space filled with books except where there were doors and windows. Ladders on rollers allowed access to the highest shelves on the main level. Similar ladders on rollers were on a walkway on the second level. The glow from colored-glass lamps reflected off leather reading chairs and well-oiled side tables.

Next to a larger table in the middle, Bellasar—commanding in his tuxedo, his dark hair and Italian features made more dramatic by his formal clothes—raised a glass of red liquid to his lips. A male servant stood discreetly in the background.

"Feeling rested?" Bellasar asked.

"Fine." Malone held up the pamphlet. "I'm returning this. I hate to think something might happen to it in my room."

"Just because it's a first edition?"

"It's awfully expensive bedside reading."

"All of these are rare first editions. I wouldn't read the texts in any other form. What's the point of collecting things if you don't use them?"

"What's the point of collecting things in the first place?"

"Pride of ownership."

Malone set the pamphlet on a table. "Perhaps a paperback is more my style."

"Did you get a chance to look through it?"

"It's a classic discussion of the causes of overpopulation and of ways to control it. I'd heard of Malthus before. I'd just never looked at his actual words."

Bellasar sipped more of the red liquid. "What would you like to drink? I'm told you like tequila."

"You don't miss much."

"I was raised to believe it's a sin to be uninformed. May I recommend a brand from a private estate in Mexico's Jalisco region? The agave juice is distilled

9

three times and aged twenty years. The family makes only limited quantities that it sells to preferred customers. This particular lot had a quantity of only two hundred bottles. I purchased them all."

"It'll be interesting to find out what the rest of the world is missing."

In the background, the servant poured the drink.

"And make me another of these," Bellasar said.

The servant nodded.

"Since you're a connoisseur, what special vodka do you prefer in your Bloody Mary?" Malone asked.

"Vodka? Good heavens, no. This isn't a Bloody Mary. It's a blend of fresh vegetable juices. I never drink alcohol. It damages brain and liver cells."

"But you're not bothered if the rest of us drink it?"

"As Malthus might have said, alcohol is a way of reducing the population." It wasn't clear if Bellasar was joking.

To the left, a door opened, and the most beautiful woman Malone had ever seen stepped into the room.

Malone had to remind himself to breathe.

It was obvious now why Bellasar had insisted that cocktails and dinner be formal. Bellasar wanted a stage in which to present another of his possessions.

The woman's evening dress was black but caught

the lampglow around her in a way that made it shimmer. It was strapless, leaving the elegant line of her tan shoulders unbroken. It was low cut, revealing the smooth tops of her breasts. Its waist left no doubt how firm her stomach was. Its sensuous line flowed over her hips and down to her ankles, emphasizing how long and statuesque her legs were.

But the ultimate effect was to focus attention on her face. The magazine cover hadn't done justice to the burnt-sienna color of her skin. Her features were in perfect proportion. The curve of her chin paralleled the opposite curve of her eyebrows, which further paralleled the way she had twisted her long lush fiery brunette hair into a swirl. But the grace of symmetry was only a partial explanation for her beauty. Her eyes were the key—and the captivating spirit behind them.

Captivating even though she was troubled. "The others are late?" Her voice made Malone think of grapes and hot summer afternoons.

"There won't be any others," Bellasar said.

"But when you told me the evening was formal, I thought . . ."

"It'll be just the three of us. I want you to meet Chase Malone. He's an artist. Perhaps you've heard of him."

Malone felt his cheeks turn warm with self-consciousness as she looked at him.

"I recognize the name." Her accent was American. She sounded hesitant.

"There's no reason you should know my work,"

Malone said. "The art world's too preoccupied with it-self."

"But you *will* know his work," Bellasar said.

She looked puzzled.

"He's going to paint you. Mr. Malone, allow me to introduce my wife: Sienna."

"You never mentioned anything about this," Sienna said.

"It's an idea I've been considering. When I had the good fortune to cross paths with Mr. Malone, I offered a commission. He graciously accepted."

"But why would—"

"To immortalize you, my dear."

Throughout the afternoon, Malone had begun to wonder if Jeb had been telling the truth about the danger Sienna was in. After all, Jeb might have been willing to say anything to get Malone to accept the assignment. But a darkness in Bellasar's tone now convinced him. For her part, Sienna seemed to have no idea how close she was to dying.

"Can you start tomorrow morning?" Bellasar asked her.

"If that's what you want." She sounded confused.

"If *you* want. You're not being forced," Bellasar said.

But that was exactly how Sienna looked—forced—when she turned toward Malone. "What time?"

"Is nine o'clock too early?"

"No, I'm usually up by six."

"Sienna's an avid horsewoman," Bellasar explained. "Early every morning, she rides."

Bellasar's pride in Sienna's riding seemed artificial, Malone thought. He sensed another dark undertone and couldn't help recalling that Bellasar's three previous wives had died in accidents. Was that how Bellasar planned for Sienna to be killed—in a faked riding accident? He nodded. "I used to ride when I was a kid. Nine o'clock, then. In the sun room off the terrace."

"Good." As Bellasar leaned close to kiss Sienna's right cheek, he was distracted by something at the edge of her eye.

"What's the matter?" she asked.

"Nothing." He turned toward Malone. "You haven't tasted your tequila."

The dining room had logs blazing in a huge fireplace. The table was long enough to seat forty and looked even longer with just the three of them. Bellasar took the end while Malone and Sienna sat on each side of him, facing each other. As candlelight flickered, the movements of servants echoed in the cavernous space.

"Food and sex," Bellasar said.

Malone shook his head in puzzlement. He noticed that Sienna kept her eyes down, concentrating on her meal. Or was she trying to avoid attracting Bellasar's attention?

"Food and sex?" Malone asked.

"Two of the four foundations of Malthus's argument." Bellasar looked at a plate of poached trout being set before him. "Humans need food. Their sexual attraction is powerful."

"And the other two?"

"Population grows at a geometric rate: one, two, four, eight, sixteen, thirty-two. In contrast, food production grows at a mathematical rate: one, two, three, four, five, six. Our ability to reproduce always outreaches our ability to feed the population. As a consequence, a considerable part of society is doomed to live in misery."

Bellasar paused to savor the trout. "Of course, we can try to check the growth of population by contraception, chastity, and limiting the number of children a woman may have. Some societies recommend abortion. But the power of the sex drive being what it is, the population continues to grow. This year alone, the world's population has swelled with the equivalent of everyone living in Scandinavia and the United Kingdom. We're approaching the six billion mark, with ten billion estimated by the middle of the twenty-first century. There won't—there can't—be enough food to sustain them all. But other factors come into play, for God's merciful plan arranges that, whenever there's a drastic imbalance between population and food supply, pestilence and war reduce it."

" 'God's merciful plan?' " Malone asked in disbelief.

"According to Malthus. But I agree with him. He was an Anglican minister, by the way. He believed that God allowed misery to be part of His plan in order to test us, to make us try to rise to the occasion and strengthen our characters by overcoming adversity. When those who have been sufficiently challenged and bettered die, they go on to their eternal reward."

"In the meantime, because of starvation, pestilence, and war, they've endured Hell on earth," Sienna said.

"Obviously, you haven't been listening closely, my dear. Otherwise, you wouldn't have missed the point."

Sienna concentrated on her plate.

"So war's a good thing," Malone said acidly. "And so are weapons merchants."

"It's easy to condemn what you don't understand. Incidentally, my great-great-great-grandfather had a friendship with Malthus."

"What?"

"After the first edition of his essay was published, Malthus traveled from England to the Continent. My ancestor had the good fortune to meet him at a dinner party in Rome. They spent many evenings together, exchanging ideas. That pamphlet I lent to you was given to my ancestor by Malthus himself."

"You're telling me that because of Malthus's ideas, your ancestor became an arms dealer?"

"He considered it a vocation." Bellasar looked with concern toward Sienna. "My dear, you don't seem to be enjoying the trout. Perhaps the rabbit in the next course will be more to your liking."

* * * * *

Malone lay in his dark bedroom, staring troubled at the ceiling. The evening had been one of the strangest he had ever experienced, the conversation on such a surreal level that he felt disoriented, his mind swirling worse than when he'd been tranquillized.

Getting out of bed, he approached the large windows opposite him. Peering out, he saw the shadows of trees across gardens and moonlight reflecting off ponds. Floodlights illuminated courtyards and lanes. A guard stepped into view, throwing away a cigarette, shifting his rifle from his left shoulder to his right. Far off, the angry voices of two men were so muffled that Malone couldn't tell what they shouted at each other. The guard paid them no attention. The argument stopped. As silence drifted over the compound, Malone wiped a hand across his weary face and returned to bed, about to sink back into sleep when he heard a distant gunshot. He was willing to bet that the guard didn't pay attention to that, either.